THE
LONG
EARTH

BOOKS BY TERRY PRATCHETT

The Dark Side of the Sun
Strata
The Unadulterated Cat
    (illustrated by Gray
    Jolliffe)
Good Omens (with
    Neil Gaiman)

FOR YOUNG ADULTS
The Carpet People
Nation

The Bromilead Trilogy
Truckers
Diggers
Wings

The Johnny Maxwell Trilogy
Only You Can Save Mankind
Johnny and the Dead
Johnny and the Bomb

THE DISCWORLD® BOOKS
The Color of Magic
The Light Fantastic
Equal Rites
Mort
Sourcery
Wyrd Sisters
Pyramids
Guards! Guards!
Eric (illustrated
    by Josh Kirby)

Moving Pictures
Reaper Man
Witches Abroad
Small Gods
Lords and Ladies
Men at Arms
Soul Music
Feet of Clay
Interesting Times
Maskerade
Hogfather
Jingo
The Last Continent
Carpe Jugulum
The Fifth Elephant
The Truth
Thief of Time
Night Watch
Monstrous Regiment
Going Postal
Thud
Where's My Cow?
    (illustrated by
    Melvyn Grant)
Making Money
Unseen Academicals
Snuff
The Last Hero
    (illustrated by
    Paul Kidby)
The Art of Discworld
    (with Paul Kidby)

TERRY PRATCHETT

THE LONG EARTH

DISCARD

STEPHEN BAXTER

HARPER

An Imprint of HarperCollins*Publishers*

www.harpercollins.com

THE LONG EARTH. Copyright © 2012 by Terry and Lyn Pratchett and Stephen Baxter. All rights reserved. Printed in the United States of America. No part of this book may be used or reproduced in any manner whatsoever without written permission except in the case of brief quotations embodied in critical articles and reviews. For information, address HarperCollins Publishers, 10 East 53rd Street, New York, NY 10022.

HarperCollins books may be purchased for educational, business, or sales promotional use. For information, please write: Special Markets Department, HarperCollins Publishers, 10 East 53rd Street, New York, NY 10022.

Terry Prattchett® and Discworld® are registered trademarks.

This book is a work of fiction. The characters, incidents, and dialogue are drawn from the authors' imaginations and are not to be construed as real. Any resemblance to actual events or persons, living or dead, is entirely coincidental.

The extract on page 283 from "Keep Right On to the End of the Road" by Harry Lauder (Sir Henry Lauder) is reproduced with the kind permission of Gregory Lauder-Frost (Sir Harry's great-nephew).

Published simultaneously in Great Britain by Doubleday, an imprint of Transworld Publishers, a division of Random House Group, Ltd.

FIRST U.S. EDITION

Diagram of the Stepper on page ix by Richard Shailer.

Library of Congress Cataloging-in-Publication Data has been applied for.

ISBN 978-0-06-206775-3

12 13 14 15 16   DIX/RRD   10 9 8 7 6 5 4 3 2 1

For Lyn and Rhianna, as always
—*T.P.*

For Sandra
—*S.B.*

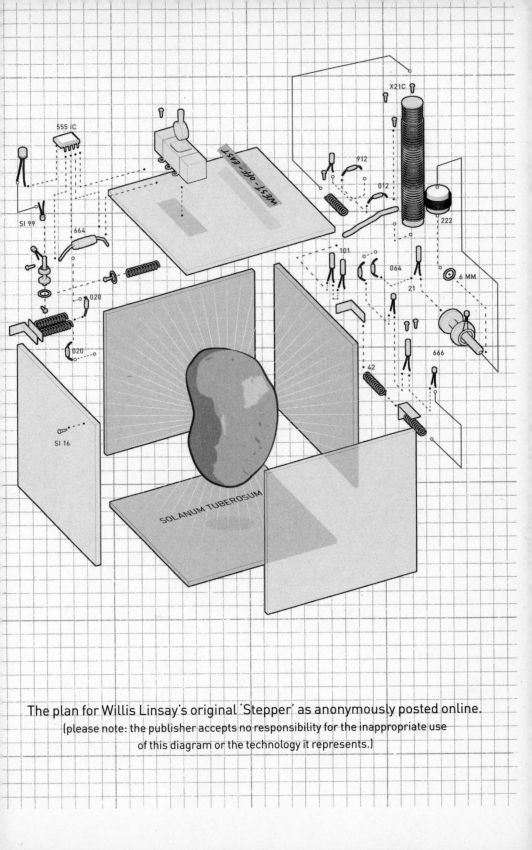

The plan for Willis Linsay's original 'Stepper' as anonymously posted online.
(please note: the publisher accepts no responsibility for the inappropriate use
of this diagram or the technology it represents.)

THE
LONG
EARTH

1

IN A FOREST GLADE:
Private Percy woke up to birdsong. It was a long time since he had heard birdsong, the guns saw to that. For a while he was content to lie there in the blissful quiet.

Although he was slightly worried, in a concussed kind of way, why he was lying in damp though fragrant grass and not on his bedroll. Ah yes, fragrant grass, there hadn't been much fragrance where he'd just been! Cordite, hot oil, burned flesh and the stink of unwashed men, that was what he was used to.

He wondered if he was dead. After all, it had been a fearsome bombardment.

Well, if he was dead then this would do for a heaven, after the hell of noise and screams and mud. And if it wasn't heaven, then his sergeant would be giving him a kicking, pulling him up, looking him over and sending him down to the mess for a cup of tea and a wad. But there was no sergeant, and no noise except the birdsong in the trees.

And, as dawn light seeped into the sky, he wondered, '*What trees?*'

When had he last seen a tree that was even vaguely in the shape of a tree, let alone a tree with all its leaves, a tree not smashed to splinters by the shelling? And yet here were trees, lots of trees, a forest of trees.

Private Percy was a practical and methodical young man, and

therefore decided, in this dream, not to worry about trees, trees had never tried to kill him. He lay back, and must've dozed off for a while. Because when he opened his eyes again it was full daylight, and he was thirsty.

Daylight, but where? Well, France. It had to be France. Percy couldn't have been blown very far by the shell that had knocked him out; this must still be France, but here he was in woods where woods shouldn't be. And without the traditional sounds of France, such as the thunder of the guns and the screams of the men.

It was all a conundrum. And Percy was dying for a drink of water.

So he packed up his troubles in what remained of his old kit bag, in this ethereal bird-haunted silence, and reflected that there was some truth in the song: what *was* the use of worrying? It *was* really not worthwhile, not when you have just seen men evaporate like the dew of the morning.

But as he stood up he felt that familiar ache in his left leg, deep in the bone, the relic of a wound that hadn't been enough to send him home but had got him a cushier posting with the camouflage boys, and a battered paint box in his kit bag. No dream this if his leg still hurt! But he wasn't where he had been, that was for sure.

And as he picked his way between the trees in the direction that appeared to have fewer trees in it than any other, a shimmering steely thought filled his mind: Why did we sing? Were we mad? What the hell did we think we were doing? Arms and legs all over the place, men just turning into a mist of flesh and bone! And we sang!

What bloody, bloody fools we were!

Half an hour later Private Percy walked down a slope, to a stream in a shallow valley. The water was somewhat brackish, but right now he would have been ready to drink out of a horse trough, right alongside the horse.

He followed the stream until it joined a river, not a very wide river as yet, but Private Percy was a country boy and knew there would be crayfish under the river bank. And in half an hour said crayfish were cooking merrily, and never had he seen such big ones! And so many! And so juicy! He ate until it hurt, twirling his catch on a green stick over his hastily built fire and tearing them apart with his hands. He thought now: Perhaps I really am dead and have gone to heaven. And that is good enough for me, because, O Lord, I believe I have seen enough of hell.

. That night he lay in a glade by the river, with his kit bag for a pillow. And as the stars came out in the sky, more brilliant than he had ever seen, Percy began to sing 'Pack Up Your Troubles in Your Old Kit Bag'. He fell silent before finishing the song, and slept the sleep of the just.

When the sunshine touched his face again, Percy woke, refreshed, sat up – and froze, motionless as a statue, before the calm gazes that inspected him. There were a dozen of the fellows in a row, watching him.

Who were they? What were they? They looked a bit like bears, but not with bear faces, or a bit like monkeys, only fatter. And they were just watching him placidly. Surely they couldn't be French?

He tried French anyway. 'Parley buffon say?'

They stared at him blankly.

In the silence, and feeling that something more was expected of him, Percy cleared his throat and plunged into 'Pack Up Your Troubles.'

The fellows listened with rapt attention until he had finished. Then they looked at one another. Eventually, as if some agreement had been reached, one of them stepped forward and sang the song back at Percy, pitch perfect.

Private Percy listened with blank astonishment.

And, a century later:

The prairie was flat, green, rich, with scattered stands of oaks. The sky above was blue as generally advertised. On the horizon there was movement, like the shadow of a cloud: a vast herd of animals on the move.

There was a kind of sigh, a breathing-out. An observer standing close enough might have felt a whisper of breeze on the skin.

And a woman was lying on the grass.

Her name was Maria Valienté. She wore her favourite pink angora sweater. She was only fifteen, but she was pregnant, and the baby was coming. The pain of the contractions pulsed through her skinny body. A moment ago she hadn't known if she was more afraid of the birth, or the anger of Sister Stephanie who had taken away her monkey bracelet, all that Maria had from her mother, saying it was a sinful token.

And now, this. Open sky where there should have been a nicotine-stained plaster ceiling. Grass and trees, where there should have been worn carpet. Everything was wrong. Where *was* here? Was this even Madison? How could she *be* here?

But that didn't matter. The pain washed through her again, and she felt the baby coming. There was nobody to help, not even Sister Stephanie. She closed her eyes, and screamed, and pushed.

The baby spilled on to the grass. Maria knew enough to wait for the afterbirth. When it was done there was a warm mess between her legs, and a baby, covered in sticky, bloody stuff. It, he, opened his mouth, and let out a thin wail.

There was a sound like thunder, from far away. A roar like you'd hear in a zoo. Like a lion.

A lion? Maria screamed again, this time in fear—

The scream was cut off, as if by a switch. Maria was gone. The baby was alone.

Alone, except for the universe. Which poured in, and spoke to him with an infinity of voices. And behind it all, a vast Silence.

His crying settled to a gurgle. The Silence was comforting.

There was a kind of sigh, a breathing-out. Maria was back in the green, under the blue sky. She sat up, and looked around in panic. Her face was grey; she was losing a lot of blood. But her baby was here.

She scooped up the baby and the afterbirth – she hadn't even tied off the cord – wrapped him up in her angora sweater, and cradled him in her arms. His little face was oddly calm. She thought she'd lost him. 'Joshua,' she said. 'Your name is Joshua Valienté.'

A soft pop, and they were gone.

On the plain, nothing remained but a drying mess of blood and bodily fluids, and the grass, and the sky. Soon, though, the scent of blood would attract attention.

And, long ago, on a world as close as a shadow:

A very different version of North America cradled a huge, land-locked, saline sea. This sea teemed with microbial life. All this life served a single tremendous organism.

And on this world, under a cloudy sky, the entirety of the turbid sea crackled with a single thought.

I . . .

This thought was followed by another.

To what purpose?

2

THE BENCH, BESIDE a modern-looking drinks machine, was exceedingly comfortable. Joshua Valienté was not used to softness these days. Not used to the fluffy feeling of being inside a building, where the furnishings and the carpets impose a kind of quiet on the world. Beside the luxurious bench was a pile of glossy magazines, but Joshua was not particularly good at shiny paper either. Books? Books were fine. Joshua liked books, particularly paperback books: light and easy to carry, and if you didn't want to read them again, well, there was always a use for reasonably thin soft paper.

Normally, when there was nothing to do, he listened to the Silence.

The Silence was very faint here. Almost drowned out by the sounds of the mundane world. Did people in this polished building understand how noisy it was? The roar of air conditioners and computer fans, the susurration of many voices heard but not decipherable, the muffled sound of telephones followed by the sounds of people explaining that they were not in fact there but would like you to leave your name after the beep, this being subsequently followed by the beep. This was the office of the transEarth Institute, an arm of the Black Corporation. The faceless office, all plasterboard and chrome, was dominated by a huge logo, a chesspiece knight. This wasn't Joshua's world. None of it was *his* world. In fact, when you got right down to it, he didn't have a world; he had *all* of them.

All of the Long Earth.

*

Earths, untold Earths. More Earths than could be counted, some said. And all you had to do was walk sideways into them, one after the next, an unending chain.

This was a source of immense irritation for experts such as Professor Wotan Ulm of Oxford University. 'All these parallel Earths,' he told the BBC, 'are identical on all but the detailed level. Oh, save that they are empty. Well, actually they are full, mainly of forests and swamps. Big, dark, silent forests, deep, clinging, lethal swamps. But empty of people. The Earth is crowded, but the Long Earth is empty. This is tough luck on Adolf Hitler, who hasn't been allowed to win his war anywhere!

'It is hard for scientists even to talk about the Long Earth without babbling about m-brane manifolds and quantum multiverses. Look: perhaps the universe bifurcates every time a leaf falls, a billion new branches every instant. That's what quantum physics seems to tell us. Oh, it is not a question of a billion realities to be experienced; the quantum states superpose, like harmonics on a single violin string. But perhaps there are times – when a volcano stirs, a comet kisses, a true love is betrayed – when you *can* get a separate experiential reality, a braid of quantum threads. And perhaps these braids are then drawn together through some higher dimension by similarity, and a chain of worlds self-organizes. Or something! Maybe it is all a dream, a collective imagining of mankind.

'The truth is that we are as baffled by the phenomenon as Dante would have been if he'd suddenly been given a glimpse of Hubble's expanding universe. Even the language we use to describe it is probably no more correct than the pack-of-cards analogy that most people feel at home with: the Long Earth as a large pack of three-dimensional sheets, stacked up in a higher-dimensional space, each card an Earth entire unto itself.

'And, most significantly, to most people, the Long Earth is open. Almost anybody can travel up and down the pack, drilling, as it were, through the cards themselves. People are expanding into all that room. Of course they are! This is a primal instinct. We plains apes still fear the leopard in the dark; if we spread out he cannot take all of us.

'It is all profoundly annoying. None of it fits! And why has this tremendous pack of cards been dealt to mankind just *now*, when we have never been more in need of *room*? But then science is nothing but a series of questions that lead to more questions, which is just as well, or it wouldn't be much of a career path, would it? Well – whatever the answers to such questions, believe you me, everything is changing for mankind . . . Is that enough, Jocasta? Some idiot clicked a pen while I was doing the bit about Dante.'

Of course, Joshua understood, transEarth existed to profit from all these changes. Which, presumably, was why Joshua had been brought here, more or less against his will, from a world a long way away.

At last the door opened. A young woman came in, nursing a laptop as thin as a sheet of gold leaf. Joshua kept such a machine in the Home, a fatter, antiquated model, mostly to look up wild-food recipes. 'Mr Valienté? It's so kind of you to come. My name is Selena Jones. Welcome to the transEarth Institute.'

She was certainly attractive, he thought. Joshua liked women; he remembered his few, brief relationships with pleasure. But he hadn't spent much *time* with women, and was awkward with them. 'Welcome? You didn't give me a choice. You found my mailbox. That means you're government.'

'As a matter of fact, you're wrong. We sometimes work for the government, but we're certainly not the government.'

'Legal?'

She smiled deprecatingly. 'Lobsang found your mailbox code.'

'And who is Lobsang?'

'Me,' said the drinks machine.

'You're a drinks machine,' said Joshua.

'You are wrong in your surmise, although I could produce the drink of your choice within seconds.'

'But you've got Coca-Cola written on you!'

'Do forgive me my sense of humour. Incidentally, if you had hazarded a dollar in the hope of soda-based refreshment I would definitely have returned it. Or provided the soda.'

Joshua struggled to make sense of this encounter. 'Lobsang *who*?'

'I have no surname. In old Tibet, only aristocrats and Living Buddhas had surnames, Joshua. I have no such pretensions.'

'Are you a computer?'

'Why do you ask?'

'Because I'm damn sure there isn't a human being in there, and besides, you talk funny.'

'Mr Valienté, I am more articulate and better spoken than anybody you know, and indeed *I* am not inside the drinks machine. Well, not wholly, that is.'

'Stop teasing the man, Lobsang,' said Selena, turning to Joshua. 'Mr Valienté, I know you were . . . *elsewhere*, when the world first heard about Lobsang. He is unique. He is a computer, physically, but he used to be – how can I put this? – a Tibetan motorcycle repairman.'

'So how did he get from Tibet to the inside of a drinks machine?'

'That *is* a long story, Mr Valienté . . .'

If Joshua hadn't been away so long he'd have known all about Lobsang. He was the first machine to successfully convince a court that he was a human being.

'Of course,' Selena said, 'other sixth-generation machines had tried it before. Provided they stay in the next room and talk to you via a speaker they can sound at least as human as some of the lunkheads you see around, but that proves nothing in the eyes of the law. But Lobsang doesn't claim to be a thinking machine. He didn't claim rights on that basis. He said he was a dead Tibetan.

'Well, Joshua, he had them by the shorts. Reincarnation is still a cornerstone of world faith; and Lobsang simply said that he had reincarnated as a computer program. As was deposited in evidence in court – I'll show you the transcripts if you like – the relevant software initiated at precisely the microsecond a Lhasan motorcycle repairman with a frankly unpronounceable name died. To a discarnate soul, twenty thousand teraflops-worth of technological wizardry on a gel substrate apparently looks identical to a few pounds of soggy brain tissue. A number of expert witnesses testified to the astonishing accuracy of Lobsang's flashes of recall of his previous life. And I myself witnessed a small, wiry old man with a face like a dried peach, a distant cousin of the repairman, conversing with Lobsang happily for several hours, reminiscing about the good old days in Lhasa. A charming afternoon!'

'Why?' Joshua asked. 'What could he gain out of it?'

'I'm right here,' said Lobsang. '*He*'s not made of wood, you know.'

'Sorry.'

'What did I gain? Civil rights. Security. The right to own property.'

'And switching you off would be murder?'

'It would. Also physically impossible, incidentally, but let's not go into that.'

'So the court's agreed you're human?'

'There's never actually been a legal definition of human, you know.'

'And now you work for transEarth.'

'I part-own it. Douglas Black, the founder, had no hesitation in offering me a partnership. Not only for my notoriety, though he's drawn to that sort of thing. For my transhuman intellect.'

'Really.'

Selena said, 'Let's get back to business. You took a lot of finding, Mr Valienté.'

Joshua looked at her and made a mental note to make it a lot *more* finding next time.

'Your visits to Earth are infrequent these days.'

'I'm *always* on Earth.'

'You know what I mean. This one,' said Selena. 'Datum Earth, or even one of the Low Earths.'

'I'm not for hire,' Joshua said quickly, trying to keep a trace of anxiety out of his voice. 'I like to work alone.'

'Well, that's rather an understatement, isn't it?'

Joshua preferred life in his stockades, on Earths far from the Datum, too far away for most to travel. Even then he was wary of company. They said that Daniel Boone would pull up sticks and move on if he could as much as see the smoke from another man's fire. Compared with Joshua, Boone was pathologically gregarious.

'But that's what makes you useful. We know you don't need people.' Selena held up a hand. 'Oh, you're not antisocial. But consider this. Before the Long Earth, no one in the whole history of mankind had ever been alone; I mean really *alone*. The hardiest sailor has always known that there's someone out there somewhere. Even the old moonwalker astronauts could *see* the Earth. Everyone knew that other people were just a matter of distance away.'

'Yeah, but with the Steppers they're only a knight's-move away.'

'Our instincts don't understand that, though. Do you know how many people pioneer solo?'

'No.'

'None. Well, hardly any. To be alone on an entire planet, possibly the only mind in a universe? Ninety-nine out of a hundred people can't take it.'

But Joshua never was alone, he thought. Not with the Silence always there, behind the sky.

'As Selena said, that's what makes you useful,' Lobsang said. 'That and certain other qualities we can discuss later. Oh, and the fact that we have leverage over you.'

Light dawned, for Joshua. 'You want me to make some kind of journey. Into the Long Earth.'

'That's what you're uniquely good at,' Selena said sweetly. 'We want you to go into the High Meggers, Joshua.'

The High Meggers: the term used by some of the pioneers for the worlds, most of them still little more than legend, more than a million steps from Earth.

'Why?'

'For the most innocent of all reasons,' said Lobsang. 'To see what's out there.'

Selena smiled. 'Information on the Long Earth is the stock in trade of transEarth, Mr Valienté.'

Lobsang was more expansive. 'Consider, Joshua. Until fifteen years ago mankind had one world and dreamed of a few more, the worlds of the solar system, all barren and horribly expensive to get to. Now we have the key to more worlds than we can count! And we have barely explored even the nearest of them. Now's our chance to do just that.'

'*Our* chance?' Joshua said. 'I'm taking you with me? Is that the gig? A computer is paying me to chauffeur it?'

'Yes, that's the size of it,' Selena said.

Joshua frowned. 'And the reason I'll do this – you said something about leverage?'

Selena said smoothly, 'We'll come to that. We've studied you, Joshua. In fact the earliest trace you leave in the files is a report by Madison PD Officer Monica Jansson, filed just after Step Day itself. About the mysterious boy who *came back*, bringing the other children with him. Quite the little pied piper, weren't you? Once upon a time you would have been called a celebrity.'

'And,' Lobsang put in, 'once upon another time you'd have been called a witch.'

Joshua sighed. Was he ever going to live that day down? He had never wanted to be a hero; he didn't like people looking at him in that funny way. Or, indeed, in any way. 'It was a mess, that's all,' he said. 'How did you find out?'

'The police reports, like Jansson's,' said the drinks machine. 'The thing about the police is that they keep everything on file. And I just love files. Files tell me things. They tell me who your mother was, for instance, Joshua. Maria was her name, was it not?'

'My mother's none of your business.'

'Joshua, everybody is my business, and everybody is on file. And the files have told me all about you. That you may be very special. That you were there on Step Day.'

'*Everybody* was there on Step Day.'

'Yes, but *you* felt at home, didn't you, Joshua? You felt as if you'd *come* home. For once in your life you knew you were in the right place . . .'

3

STEP DAY. FIFTEEN years ago. Joshua had been just thirteen.
Later, everybody remembered where they were on Step Day.
Mostly they were in the shit.

At the time, nobody knew who had uploaded the circuit
diagram for the Stepper on to the web. But as evening swept like a
scythe around the world, kids everywhere started putting Steppers
together, dozens in the neighbourhood of the Home in Madison
alone. There had been a real run on Radio Shack. The electronics
seemed laughably simple. The potato you were supposed to install
at the heart of it seemed laughable too, but it was important,
because it was your power supply. And then there was the switch.
The switch was vital. Some kids thought you didn't need a switch.
Just twist wires together. And they were the ones who ended up
screaming.

Joshua had put his first Stepper together *carefully*. He always did
things meticulously. He was the kind of boy who always, but
always, paints before assembly, and then assembles the pieces in
the right order, with every single component laid out with care
before commencing. Joshua always *commenced* things. It sounded
more deliberate than starting. In the Home, when he worked on
one of the old and worn and incomplete jigsaw puzzles, he would
always sort out the pieces first, separating sky and sea and edge,
before putting even two pieces together. Sometimes afterwards, if
the puzzle was incomplete, he would go into his little workshop
and very carefully shape the missing pieces out of hoarded scrap

wood and then paint them to fit. If you didn't know, you wouldn't believe that the puzzle had ever had holes. And sometimes he would cook, under the supervision of Sister Serendipity. He would collect all the ingredients, prepare them all in advance meticulously, and then work through the recipe. He even cleaned up as he went. He liked cooking, and liked the approval it won him in the Home.

That was Joshua. That was how he did things. And that was why he wasn't the first kid to step out of the world, because he'd not only varnished his Stepper box, he'd waited for the varnish to dry. And that was why he was certainly the first kid to get back without wetting his pants, or worse.

Step Day. Kids were disappearing. Parents scoured the neighbourhoods. One minute the kids were there, playing with this latest crazy toy, and the next moment they weren't. When frantic parent meets frantic parent, frantic becomes terrified. The police were called, but to do what? Arrest who? To look where?

And Joshua himself stepped, for the first time.

A heartbeat earlier, he had been in his workshop, in the Home. Now he stood in a wood, heavy, thick, the moonlight hardly managing to reach the ground. He could hear other kids everywhere, throwing up, crying for their parents, a few screaming as if they were hurt. He wondered why all the distress. *He* wasn't throwing up. It was creepy, yes. But it was a warm night. He could hear the whine of mosquitoes. The only question was, a warm night *where*?

All the crying distracted him. There was one kid close at hand, calling for her mother. It sounded like Sarah, another resident of the Home. He called out her name.

She stopped crying, and he heard her voice, quite close: 'Joshua?'

He thought it over. It was late evening. Sarah would have been in the girls' dormitory, which was about twenty yards away from his workshop. He had not *moved*, but he was clearly in a different place. This wasn't Madison. Madison had noises, cars, airplanes, lights, while now he was standing in a forest, like something out of a book, with not a trace of a streetlight anywhere he looked. But Sarah was here too, wherever this was. The thought constructed itself a piece at a time, like an incomplete jigsaw. Think, don't panic. In relation to where you are, or were, she will be where she is, or was. You just have to go down the passage to her room. Even though, here and now, there is no passage, no room. Problem solved.

Except that to get to her would mean walking through the tree right in front of him. An extremely big tree.

He worked his way around the tree, pushing through the tangled undergrowth, the briars, the fallen branches of this very wild wood. 'Keep talking,' he said. 'Don't move. I'm coming.'

'Joshua?'

'Look, I'll tell you what. Sing. Keep singing. That way I'll be able to find you in the dark.' Joshua switched on his flashlight. It was a tiny one that fitted into a pocket. He always carried a flashlight at night. Of course he did. He was Joshua.

She didn't sing. She started to pray. 'Our Father, who art in heaven . . .'

He wished people would do what he told them, just sometimes.

From around the forest, from the dark, other voices joined in. 'Hallowed be thy name . . .'

He clapped his hands and yelled, 'Everybody shut up! I'll get you out of here. Trust me.' He didn't know why they should trust him, but the tone of authority worked, and the other voices died away. He took a breath and called, 'Sarah. You first. OK? Everybody else, go towards the prayer. Don't say anything. Just head towards the prayer.'

Sarah began again: 'Our Father, who art in heaven . . .'

As he worked his way forward, hands outstretched, pushing through briars and climbing over roots, testing every step, he heard the sounds of people moving all around him, more voices calling. Some were complaining about being lost. Others were complaining about a lack of cellphone signal. Sometimes he glimpsed their phones, little screens glowing like fireflies. And then there was the desolate weeping, even moans of pain.

The prayer ended with an amen, which was echoed around the forest, and Sarah said, 'Joshua? I've finished.'

And I thought she was clever, thought Joshua. 'Then start again.'

It took him minutes to get to her, even though she was only half the length of the Home away. But he could see this forest clump was actually quite small. Beyond, in the moonlight, he saw what looked like prairie flowers, like in the Arboretum. No sign of the Home, though, or Allied Drive.

At last Sarah stumbled towards him and clamped herself on him. 'Where are we?'

'Somewhere else, I guess. You know. Like Narnia.'

The moonlight showed him the tears pouring down her face and the snot under her nose, and he could smell the vomit on her nightdress. 'I never stepped into no wardrobe.'

He burst out laughing. She stared at him. But because he was laughing, she laughed. And the laughter started to fill this little clearing, for other kids were drifting this way, towards the flashlight glow, and for a moment that held back the terror. It was one thing to be lost and alone, quite another to be lost in a crowd, and laughing.

Somebody else grabbed his arm. 'Josh?'

'Freddie?'

'It was terrible. I was in the dark and I *fell down*, down to the ground.'

Freddie had a tummy bug, Josh remembered. He'd been in the sanatorium, on the Home's first floor. He must have just fallen, through the vanished building. 'Are you hurt?'

'No . . . Josh? How do we get home?'

Joshua took Sarah's hand. 'Sarah, you made a Stepper?'

'Yes.'

He glanced at the mess of components in her hand. It wasn't

even in a box, not even a shoebox or something, let alone a box that had been carefully made for the purpose, like his. 'What did you use for a switch?'

'What switch? I just twisted the wires together.'

'Look. It definitely said to put in a centre-off switch.' He very carefully took her Stepper in his hands. You always had to be very careful around Sarah. She wasn't a Problem, but problems had happened to her.

At least there were three wires. He traced back the circuitry by touch. He'd spent hours staring at the circuit diagram; he knew it by heart. He separated the wires and put the ragged tangle back in her hands. 'Listen. When I say go, press that wire and that one together. If you find yourself back in your room, drop the whole thing on the floor and go to bed. OK?'

Sniffing, she asked, 'What if it doesn't work?'

'Well, you'll still be here, and so will I. And that won't be so bad, will it? Are you ready? Come on. Let's do a countdown from ten. Nine, eight . . .'

On zero she disappeared, and there was a pop, like a soap bubble bursting.

The other kids stared at where she'd been, and then at Joshua. Some were strangers: as much as he could see any faces at all, there were plenty he couldn't recognize. He'd no idea how far they'd walked in the dark.

Right now he was king of the world. These helpless kids would do anything he told them. It wasn't a feeling he liked. It was a chore.

He turned to Freddie. 'OK, Freddie. You next. You know Sarah. Tell her not to worry. Tell her a lot of kids are coming home via her bedroom. Tell her Joshua says it's the only way to get them home, and please don't get angry. Now show me your Stepper.'

One by one, pop after pop, the lost boys and girls disappeared.

When the last of those near by had gone, there were still voices further away in the forest, maybe beyond. There was nothing

Joshua could do for them. He wasn't even sure he'd done the right thing now. He stood alone in the stillness, and listened. Aside from the distant voices there was no sound but the skinny drone of mosquitoes. People told you that mosquitoes could kill a horse, in time.

He held his own carefully constructed Stepper, and moved the switch.

He was instantly back in the Home, by Sarah's bed, in her tiny cluttered room, just in time to see the back of the last girl he'd led home, still quite hysterical, disappearing into the hallway. And he heard the shrill sound of the Sisters' voices calling his name.

He hastily moved the switch again, to stand alone in the solitude of the forest. *His* forest.

There were more voices now, closer by. Sobbing. Screaming. One kid saying very politely, 'Excuse me. Can anybody help me?' And then a retch. Vomiting.

More new arrivals. He thought, why are they all sick? That was the smell of Step Day, when he remembered it later. Everyone had thrown up. He hadn't.

He set off into the dark, looking for the latest calling kid.

And after that kid there was another. And another, who had broken her arm, it looked like, falling from some upper storey. And then another. There was always another kid.

The first hint of dawn filled the forest clump with birdsong and light. Was it dawn back home too?

There were absolutely no sounds of humanity now, except for the sobbing of the latest lost boy, who had speared his leg on a jagged length of wood. There was no way the kid would be able to operate his own Stepper, which was a shame, because in the sallow light Joshua admired the craftsmanship. The kid had evidently spent some time in Radio Shack. A sensible kid, but not sensible enough to bring a flashlight, or mosquito repellent.

Carefully, Joshua bent, picked up the kid in his arms, and stood straight. The boy moaned. One-handed, Joshua groped for the switch on his own Stepper, glad once more he'd followed the instructions exactly.

This time, when they stepped over, there were lights glaring in his face, and within seconds a City of Madison police car screeched to a halt before him. He stood stock still.

Two cops got out of the car. One, a younger man in a fluorescent jacket, gently took the injured boy from Joshua, and laid him on the grass. The other officer stood before him. A woman, smiling, hands open. This made him nervous. It was the way a Sister smiled at a Problem. Arms outstretched in welcome could quickly become arms that grabbed. Behind the officers, there were lights everywhere, like a movie set.

'Hello, Joshua,' the woman officer said. 'My name is Monica Jansson.'

4

FOR MPD OFFICER JANSSON it had all started even earlier, the day before: the third time in the last few months she'd come out to the burned-out Linsay house, just off Mifflin Street.

She wasn't sure why she had come back here. There hadn't been a call-out this time. Yet here she was poking once more through the heaps of ash and charcoal that used to be furniture. Crouching over the smashed remains of an elderly flatscreen TV. Stepping gingerly over a carpet scorched and soaked and stained with foam, marked by the heavy footprints of firemen and cops. Leafing again through the charred relics of what must once have been an extensive set of notes, handwritten mathematical equations, an indecipherable scrawl.

She thought of her partner, Clancy, drinking the day's fifth Starbucks out in the cruiser, thinking she was an idiot. What could be left to find, after the detectives had crawled over everything and forensics had done their stuff? Even the daughter, that oddball college student Sally, had taken it all in without surprise or concern, calmly nodding when told that her father was wanted for questioning over suspected arson, incitement to terrorism, and animal cruelty, not necessarily in that order. Just nodding, as if all that was an everyday occurrence in the Linsay household.

Nobody else cared. Soon the place would be released as a crime scene, and the landlord could start the clean-up and the arguments with his insurance company. It wasn't as if anybody had got hurt, not even Willis Linsay himself, for there was no sign he'd died in

21

the pretty feeble fire. It was all just a puzzle that would likely never be resolved, the kind experienced cops came across all the time, said Clancy, and you had to know when to let it go. Maybe at twenty-nine Jansson was still too green.

Or maybe it was because of what she'd seen when they'd responded to that first call a few months back. Because the first call had come from a neighbour who had reported seeing a man carrying a goat into this single-storey house, here in the middle of Madison.

A *goat*? Cue predictable banter between Clancy and the dispatcher. Maybe goats gave this guy the horn – et cetera, et cetera, ha ha. But the same neighbour, an excitable woman, said she'd also seen the man on other occasions push calves in through his front door, and even a foal. Not to mention a cage of chickens. Yet there was no report of noise, no barnyard stinks. No evidence of live animals in there. What was the guy doing, screwing them or cooking them?

Willis Linsay turned out to have been living alone since the death of his wife in a road accident some years before. There was one daughter, called Sally, eighteen years old, a student at the University of Wisconsin-Madison, living with an aunt. Linsay had been some kind of scientist, and had even once held a theoretical physics post at Princeton. Now he earned his money as a peripatetic tutor at UW, and with the rest of his time – well, nobody quite knew what he did with the rest of his time. Though Jansson had found traces in the records that he'd done some work for Douglas Black, the industrialist, under another name. That was no great surprise. These days almost everybody ended up working for Black one way or another.

Whatever Linsay was up to, he wasn't keeping goats in his living room. Maybe it had been malicious all along, some busybody neighbour trying to make trouble for the oddball guy next door. You got that sometimes.

But the next call had been different.

Somebody posted online a plan for a gadget he or she called a 'Stepper'. You could customize the design, but it would be a portable gadget with a big three-position switch on top, and with various electronic components within, and with a power lead plugged into . . . a potato?

The authorities noted this, and became alarmed. It *looked* like the kind of thing a suicide bomber would strap to his chest, before taking a stroll down State Street. It also looked like the kind of thing that would appeal to every kid in the world who could knock one up from spare parts in his or her bedroom. Everybody thought the word 'potato' must be a cover word for something else, like a slab of Semtex.

But by the time a car had been dispatched to the Linsay place, due to rendezvous with Homeland officers at the scene, a third call had come in, entirely separate: the house was on fire. Jansson had been part of the response to that. And Willis Linsay was nowhere to be found.

It was arson. Forensics had found the oily rag, the cheap cigarette lighter, the heap of papers and smashed-up furniture that had started it. The purpose of the fire seemed to have been to destroy Linsay's heaps of notes and other materials. The perp could have been Linsay, or else somebody out to get him.

Jansson had the feeling it had been Linsay himself. She'd never met the man, never so much as seen a photograph. But her tangential contact with him had left impressions in her mind. He was clearly ferociously intelligent. You didn't get to do physics at Princeton otherwise. But there was something missing. His home had been a disorderly jumble. The neither-one-thing-nor-the-other fire attempt fitted too.

But what she didn't understand was what it was all *for*. What had he been up to?

Now Jansson found Linsay's own Stepper, the prototype, pre-sumably. It was in the living room, sitting on the mantelpiece above a fire that hadn't been lit in decades. Maybe he'd purpose-fully left it behind to be found. The forensics guys had seen it and abandoned it, heavily dusted for prints. It would probably be taken into store once the crime scene was broken down.

Jansson bent to inspect it. It was just a clear plastic box, a cube, about four inches on a side. Forensics thought the box might once have contained antique three-and-a-half-inch floppy discs. Linsay was evidently the kind of man who kept junk like that. Through the clear walls you could see electrical components, capacitors and resistors and relays and coils, connected with twisted and soldered copper wire. There was a big three-way switch on the lid, the positions labelled by hand with a black marker pen:

WEST – OFF – EAST

Right now the switch was set to OFF.

The rest of the box's volume was occupied by . . . a potato. Just a potato, no Semtex or acid vial or nails or any other element of the modern terror arsenal. One of the forensics boys had suggested it might be used as a power source, like the classic potato-run clock. Mostly people thought it was just a symptom of lunacy, or maybe some bizarre practical joke. Whatever it was, this was what kids all around the planet were racing to assemble right now.

The Stepper had been found holding down a bit of paper on which had been scrawled, in the same marker pen, the same hand, TRY ME. Very Alice in Wonderland. Linsay's parting shot. It occurred to Jansson that none of her colleagues had actually followed the instruction on the paper scrap: TRY ME.

She took the box, held it; it weighed nothing. She opened the lid. Another scrap of paper, headed FINISH ME, had simple instructions, what looked like a draft of the circuit diagram that had finished up on the net. You were supposed to use no iron parts, she read; that was underlined. She had to finish winding a couple of coils of copper wire, and then set contacts to tune the coils, somehow.

She got to work. Winding the coils was an oddly pleasant activity, though she couldn't have explained why. Just her and the bits of kit, like a kid assembling a crystal radio. Finding the tuning was easy too; she kind of felt it when she got the sliding contact set right – though again she couldn't have explained this, and didn't look forward to trying to write this up in her report.

When she was done she closed the lid and took hold of the switch, tossed a coin in her head, and turned the switch WEST.

The house vanished in a rush of fresh air.

Prairie flowers, all around, waist deep, like a nature reserve.

And it was like she had been punched in the stomach. She doubled over, grunting, dropping the box. Earth under her feet, her polished shoes on grass. The air in her nostrils fresh, sharp, the stink of ash and foam gone.

Had some perp jumped her? She grabbed for her gun. It was in its holster, but it felt odd; the Glock's polymer frame and magazine body looked OK, but the thing *rattled*.

Cautiously she straightened up. Her stomach was still bad, but she felt nauseous rather than bruised. She glanced around. There was nobody here, threatening or otherwise.

Nor were there four walls around her, no house just off Mifflin Street. Just prairie flowers, and a stand of hundred-foot-tall trees, and a blue sky clear of contrails and smog. It was like the Arboretum, the Herculean prairie reconstruction inside Madison's city limits. An Arboretum that had swallowed the city itself. Suddenly here she was, in the middle of all this.

She opined, 'Oh.' This response seemed inadequate in itself. After some consideration, she added, 'My.' And she concluded, although in the process she was denying a lifelong belief system of agnosticism shading to outright atheism, 'God.'

She put away her gun and tried to think like a cop. To *see* like a cop. She noticed litter on the ground at her feet, beside the Stepper she'd dropped. Cigarette butts. What looked like a cowpat. So was this where Willis Linsay had gone? If so, there was no sign of him, or of his animals . . .

The very air was different. Rich. Heady. She felt like she was getting high on it. It was all magnificent. It was impossible. Where *was* she? She laughed out loud, for the sheer wonder of it all.

Then she realized that every kid in Madison was soon going to have one of these boxes. Every kid everywhere else, come to that. And they were all going to start turning the switches. All around the world.

And *then* it occurred to her that getting home might be a good plan.

She grabbed the Stepper box from the ground, where she'd dropped it. It still had fingerprint dust on it. The switch had snapped back to OFF. With trepidation, she grabbed the switch, closed her eyes, counted down from three, and turned it EAST.

And she was back in the Linsay house, with what looked like metallic components of her gun on the ruined carpet at her feet. There was her badge, and name tag, even her tie clip, lying on the carpet. More bits of metal she hadn't noticed she was missing.

Clancy was waiting out in the car. She started figuring how she was going to explain all this to him.

When she got back to base, station manager Dodd's tracking board showed missing person calls coming in, one or two per neighbourhood. Slowly the whole board was lighting up.

Then the alerts came in from across the country.

'And all around the world,' Dodd said, wondering, after he'd flicked on CNN. 'A missing persons plague. Even China. Look at that.'

Then the night got more complicated, for all of them. There was a rash of burglaries, even one from a strongroom in the Capitol building. The MPD had trouble just fielding the call-outs. That was before the directives started coming in from Homeland Security and the FBI.

Jansson managed to collar the sergeant in charge. 'What's going on, sarge?'

Harris turned to her, his face grey. 'You're asking me? I don't know. Terrorists? Homeland are jumping up and down about that possibility. Space aliens? That's what some guy in a tinfoil hat out in the lobby insists is causing it all.'

'So what should I do, sarge?'

'Do the job in front of you.' And he hurried on.

She thought that over. If she were a citizen out there, what would she most care about? The missing kids, that's what. She left the station and got to work.

And she found the kids, and spoke to them, some of them in the hospital, and every other kid talked about one particular kid who was calm, a hero, leading them to safety, like Moses – only he was called Joshua, not Moses.

Joshua backed away from the cop.

'You are Joshua, aren't you? I can tell. You're the one kid that isn't dribbling vomit.'

He said nothing.

'They tell me Joshua saved them. They tell me he picked them up and carried them back home. You're a regular catcher in the rye. You ever read that book? You should. Although maybe it's banned in the Home. Yes, I know about the Home. But how did you do it, Joshua?'

'I didn't do anything wrong. I'm not a Problem,' he said, backing further away.

'I know you're not a Problem. But you did something different. I just want to know what you did. Tell me, Joshua.'

Joshua hated it when people kept repeating his name. It was what they did to calm you down when they thought you were a Problem. 'I followed the instructions. That's all. People don't understand. You just follow the instructions.'

'I want to understand,' she said. 'Just tell me. You don't have to be afraid of me.'

'Look,' said Joshua, 'even if you make a simple wooden box you have to varnish it, otherwise it gets damp and everything swells and that can pull things apart. Whatever you do you have to do it right. You have to follow the instructions. That's what they're there for.' He was saying too much, too fast. He shut up. Shutting up nearly always worked. Anyway what could he say?

Joshua baffled Jansson. Everybody had been panicking in the dark, evidently, the kids screaming and throwing up and tripping over and crapping their pants and being eaten by mosquitoes and walking into trees. But not Joshua. Joshua was calm. She looked at him now. He was slim, tall for his age, his face pale but his hair Mediterranean black. He was a calm enigma.

Out loud she said, 'You know, Joshua, I would have said that, given the stories they're telling, some of these kids must have been playing with drugs. Except that they were all covered in leaves and scratches. As if they really had been taking a walk in a forest right here in the middle of the city.'

She took another slight step forward, and he took another slight step back.

She stopped moving and lowered her hands. 'Look, Joshua, I know you're telling the truth. *Because I've been there myself.* No more games. Talk to me. The box you're holding looks pretty neat compared with the others. Can I have a look? I mean just put it down and step back, I'm not trying to trick you. I'm just trying to work out why kids all over town are getting stuck in some mysterious forest, frightened they're going to be eaten by orcs!'

Oddly enough that impressed Joshua. He did put the box down, and did step back. 'I'd like that back, I haven't got enough money to go to Radio Shack again.' He hesitated for a moment. 'You really think orcs?'

'No. I don't think orcs. But I don't know what to think. Look, Joshua, you put your box down for me, so I'm putting my card down here where you can pick it up, OK? My personal number. I have a feeling we should stay in touch, you and I.' She took a couple of steps back, holding the box. 'Good workmanship!'

But now another car was coming up, lights blazing. Officer Jansson looked around. 'Just other policemen checking up,' she said, 'don't worry—'

There was a faint *pop*.

She looked at the box in her hand, and at the empty pavement. 'Joshua?'

Joshua realized immediately that he'd left his box behind.

He'd stepped without the box! And, worse, that cop had *seen* him step without the box. Now he was in trouble.

So he got away. He just kept stepping, away from where he'd been, whatever *away* meant. He didn't stop, or slow down. He just kept going, one step after the next, each step like a soft jolt in his gut. One world after another, as if it was a series of rooms. One step after the next away from Officer Jansson. Deeper into this corridor of forest.

As he pressed on there was no more city, no buildings, no lights, no people. Just this forest, but a forest that changed with every step. Trees came out of nowhere with one step and disappeared with the next, like bits of scenery in the plays the kids had to put on in the Home, yet all the trees seemed real, all hard and solid and deep-rooted in the earth. Sometimes it was warmer, sometimes a little colder. But there was always the forest, around him. And it was always dawn. Some things didn't change, then: the ground, solid under his feet, the dawn sky. That pleased him, to detect order in this new world.

The instructions on the internet had said nothing about stepping without a box, but he was doing it anyhow. The thought gave him a lurching sensation, as if he were standing over a drop. But it was a thrill too, a rule-breaking thrill. Like the time he and

Billy Chambers had borrowed a bottle of Bud from the builders who had come to fix the busted window, and had drunk it in a corner of the boiler room, and then smashed the bottle and put it in the recycling bin. He grinned at the memory.

He just kept going, moving aside for the trees when he needed to. But the trees changed, gradually. Now he was surrounded by rougher bark, low branches with narrow prickly leaves. A forest of pine trees. Colder, too. But it was still a forest, and still he pushed on.

And he came to a Wall. A place where he couldn't step on, no matter how he walked sideways. He even took a few paces back and kind of ran at it, trying to force his way onward. It didn't hurt, it was like running into a huge upraised palm. But he couldn't go forward.

If he couldn't push through this thick forest maybe he could climb above it. He found a tall tree, the tallest around. He pulled himself up to the lowest branches, and scrambled up higher. Pine needles prickled his hands. Every six feet or so he would try stepping sideways, just to see if he could, but the Wall was still there.

And then it worked, suddenly.

He fell forward on to a flat floor, like uneven, smoothed-over concrete, hard and dry and grey. There was no tree, no forest. Just the air, the sky, and this floor. And it was *cold*, cold through the thin fabric of his jeans over his knees, cold under his bare hands. Ice!

He stood up. His breath steamed around his face. The cold was like daggers probing through his clothes to his flesh. The whole world was covered in ice. He was in a kind of broad gully, carved in the ice, which rose up in hard grey mounds around him. Old ice, dirty ice. The sky was clear, the empty blue-grey of an early dawn. Nothing moved, not a bird, not a plane, and on the ground he didn't see a building, or a single living thing, not so much as a blade of grass.

He grinned.

Then he stepped back to the pine forest, disappearing with a soap-bubble pop.

5

L OBSANG SAID, 'Jansson, that police officer, kept an eye on you. You know that, don't you, Joshua?'

Joshua was jolted back to the present. 'You know, you're smart for a vending machine.'

'You would be amazed. Selena, please take Joshua downstairs, will you?'

The woman looked startled. 'But Lobsang, we haven't put Joshua through the security screening yet.'

There was a clank from the drinks machine and a can of Dr Pepper thumped into the hopper. 'What's the worst that could happen? I would like our new friend to meet me properly. By the way, Joshua, the can is for you. On the house.'

Joshua stood. 'No thanks, I lost my taste for soda years ago.' And if I hadn't, he thought to himself, I would have done just now, having seen you excrete it.

As they headed towards the stairs Selena said, 'Good of you to shave, by the way. Seriously, chins are going out of style in these pioneering times. People are so faddy.' She smiled. 'I think we were expecting some kind of mountain man.'

'I used to be like that, I guess.'

This bland deflection evidently annoyed her; she seemed to want more from him.

They reached a landing that consisted of nothing but unmarked metal doors. One of these slid open as she approached, and slid noiselessly shut seconds after he had followed her through and on to another stairway, heading down.

'Joshua, I have to tell you,' she said with a kind of brittle humour, 'I would like to *push* you down these stairs! And you know why? Because you just walk in and suddenly you have a security rating of zero, a great big oh, which means technically you can be told everything that's going on here. I on the other hand have a security clearance of five. You outrank me and I have been working for transEarth and its affiliates since the start! Who exactly are you, who can just walk in and be told every secret?'

'Well, sorry about that. I am just Joshua, I guess. Anyway, what do you mean "since the start"? I was the start! That's why I'm here, isn't it?'

'Yes. Of course. But I suppose every person's first step is the start, for them . . .'

6

JIM RUSSO HAD taken his own first step out into what the excited online chatterers were soon calling the Long Earth for ambition. And because, at thirty-eight years old, after a lifetime of bad breaks and betrayals, he figured he was ahead of the pack.

Very soon after Step Day he'd come up with his plan, and worked out what he had to do. He headed straight for this corner of California. He brought maps and photographs and such, to locate the exact spot where Marshall had made his find, all those years ago. He was well aware that GPS didn't work in the stepwise worlds, so everything had to be on paper. But of course you didn't need a map to find Sutter's Mill, here on the bank of the South Fork American River, not in Datum Earth anyhow. It was in a State Historic Park. The place was a California Historical Landmark. They'd built a monument to show the site of the original mill, and you could see where James Marshall had first seen gold flakes glittering in the mill's tailrace. You could stand there, right on the very spot. Jim Russo did so now, the cogs whirring in his head.

And then he stepped, into West 1, and the reconstruction was gone. The landscape was just as wild as Marshall and Sutter and his buddies had found it when they came to build their sawmill. Or maybe wilder, because there hadn't even been Indians here before the stepping started. Of course there were other people here today, tourists from Datum Earth looking around the site. There were even a couple of little information plaques. Sutter West and East 1 had already been co-opted into the landmark, as an adjunct to what they had in Datum Earth. Jim smiled at the goggle-eyed foolishness of the few tourists here, their lack of imagination.

As soon as he felt able, when the nausea faded after ten or fifteen minutes, he stepped on further. And again. And again.

He paused in West 5, which he figured was far enough away. Nobody around. He laughed out loud, and whooped. No reply. There was an echo, and a bird called somewhere. He was alone.

He didn't wait for the nausea to pass. He crouched down by the stream, and dug out his sieve from his pack, breathing deep to settle his stomach. Right here, on January 24, 1848, James Marshall had noticed odd rock formations in the water. Within a day Marshall had been washing gold flakes out of the stream, and the California Gold Rush was on. Jim had dreams of finding the *exact same first flake* as Marshall had found, which was held by the Smithsonian Institution. What a stunt that would be! But there was no mill here, of course, and so no tailrace, and the river bed hadn't been disturbed as it had been in Marshall's day back in Datum Earth, and it seemed unlikely he'd find the identical flake. Well, he'd settle for getting rich.

This was his grand plan. He knew exactly where the Sutter's Mill gold was, for it had all been discovered and extracted by the miners who had followed Marshall. He had maps of the seams that still lay undisturbed, right here! For in this world, there had been no Sutter, no Marshall, no mill – and no Gold Rush. All that wealth, or a copy of it, still slept in the ground. Just waiting for Jim to take it for himself.

And there was laughter, from right behind him.

He whirled around, tried to stand, and stumbled and splashed back into the stream, getting his feet wet.

A man faced him, wearing rough denim clothes and a broad-brimmed hat. He carried a heavy orange backpack, and some kind of pick. He was laughing at Jim, showing white teeth in a grimy face. Others popped into existence around him: men and women, similarly dressed, grubby and tired-looking. They grinned when they saw Jim, despite the stepping nausea.

'Not another one?' said one woman.

She looked attractive under the dirt. An attractive woman, mocking him. Jim looked away, his face hot.

'Looks like it,' said the first man. 'What's the deal, buddy? You here to make your fortune with the Sutter gold?'

'What's it to you?'

The man shook his head. 'What is it with people like you? You kind of think one move ahead, but not the next, or the next.' He sounded like a college boy to Jim, smug, sneering. 'You figured out there's unmined gold on this spot. Sure there is, you're right. But what about the same site on West 6 and 7 and 8, and as far out as you can go? What about all the other guys just like you, out there panning the streams on all those stepwise worlds? You didn't think of that, did you?' He dug a nugget of gold the size of a pigeon's egg from his pocket. 'My friend, everybody else has had the same idea!'

The woman said, 'Oh, don't be too hard on him, Mac. He'll make some money, if he moves fast. Gold hasn't been totally devalued yet; there hasn't been much brought back. And he can always sell it as a commodity. It's just, well, gold isn't worth its weight in gold any more!'

More laughter.

Mac nodded. 'Another example of the surprisingly low economic value of all these stepwise worlds. A real paradox.'

That college-boy smugness maddened Jim. 'If it's worth nothing, smart ass, what are you guys doing here?'

'Oh, we've been mining too,' Mac said. 'We've been retracing the steps of Marshall and the rest, just like you. We went further out. We even built a copy of the mill, and a forge to make iron tools, so we could find the gold and extract it the way the pioneers did. It's history, a reconstruction. It'll be on Discovery next year; check it out. But we were *not* there for the gold itself. Here.' And he threw the egg of gold at Jim. It landed at his feet, and lay in the damp gravel.

'You assholes.'

Mac's smile faded, as if in disappointment at his manners. 'I don't think our new friend is a very good sport, gents and ladies. Oh, well—'

Jim lumbered at the group, swinging his fists. They kept laughing at him as they disappeared, one by one. He didn't land a single punch.

7

F OR SALLY LINSAY, her departure from Datum Earth, a year after Step Day, hadn't been first step at all. She left the world because her father had gone before her. And before him, most of her family. She was nineteen years old.

She had taken her time about it. Time to get her kit together, to resolve her affairs. After all, she wasn't planning to come back.

Then, early one morning, she slipped on her sleeveless fisherman's jacket with all the pockets, and picked up her pack, and left her room in her aunt's home for the last time. Aunt Tiffany was away, and that suited Sally; she didn't like goodbyes. She worked her way over to Park Street and strolled through the campus. Nobody around, not even a cleaner; UW was asleep. At that, the early morning was quieter than it used to be, she was sure. Maybe more people had stepped away than she'd thought. At the lake shore she cut past the library, headed west along the Lakeshore Path, and kept walking towards Picnic Point. There were a couple of sailboats out on Lake Mendota, and a hardy windsurfer in a lurid orange wetsuit, and a couple of boats of the UW Rowing Club, their coaches' bullhorn barks carrying across the water. The horizon was bounded by green.

To some all this was idyllic, the leafy university by the lake. Not to her. Sally liked nature, the real thing. To her the Long Earth wasn't some new-fangled novelty, a theme park that had opened up on Step Day. She had *grown up* out there. Now, looking at the rowboats and the surfer, all she could see was disturbance, idiots scaring away the birds. Just as was starting to happen in the other worlds as more idiots stumbled stepwise, slack-jawed. Even this limpid lakewater was just dilute waste to her. At least she had picked a fine day to say goodbye to this place, this city by the lake, where she hadn't always been entirely unhappy, and the air was fresh. But where she was going it would be fresher.

She found a quiet spot, and walked off the path into the shade of the trees. She checked over her kit, one last time. She carried weapons, up to and including a lightweight crossbow. Her Stepper was in a plastic box of the kind her father had used. As well as the basic apparatus itself it was crowded with spares, fine optician's tools, a length of solder, printouts of the circuit diagrams. There was the potato, of course, in the middle of the tangle of beat-up electronics. What a smart idea that was, a battery you could eat, if lunch became the priority. It was a professional traveller's piece of kit. She was nostalgic enough to have plastered the box with a UW sticker.

But the box was a cover. Sally didn't need a Stepper to step.

She knew the Long Earth, and how to travel across it. Now she was going out there to find her father. And, something that had puzzled her endlessly since she was a little girl playing outside her father's shed in a stepwise Wyoming, to figure out what it was all *for*.

She'd never been indecisive. She made a random choice of direction, grinned, and stepped. Around her, the lake, the clumps of trees persisted. But the footpath, the rowboats, the idiot on the windsurfer had gone.

8

PEOPLE HAD GONE OFF every which way in those early days, with a purpose or just for the hell of it. But nobody had gone further than Joshua.

In those first months, still aged only thirteen, fourteen, he'd built himself refuges in the higher Earths. Stockades, he called them. And the best of them *were* stockades, like Robinson Crusoe's. People had the wrong idea about Robinson Crusoe. The popular image was of a determined, cheerful man heavily into goatskin underwear. But at the Home had been an old, battered copy of the book itself, and Joshua, being Joshua, had read it from cover to cover. Robinson Crusoe had been on his island for over twenty-six years, and had spent most of the time building stockades. Joshua approved of this; the man obviously had his head screwed on right.

It had been harder when he'd first started. In Madison, Wisconsin, what you found on the other side of the reality walls, to East and West, was mostly prairie. Joshua knew now that the first time he'd stepped through he'd been lucky it hadn't been winter, which could have plunged him unprepared into temperatures of forty below. And that he hadn't landed in some marsh, in some place that on Datum Earth had been drained by people and turned into farmland long before he'd been born.

The first time he'd gone out alone into the wild worlds and tried to spend a night had been kind of rough. Blackberries had been the only food he'd recognized, but he got water from rainfall in cup plants. He'd taken a blanket, and it had been too warm for that, but he'd needed it as a mosquito net. He'd slept up a tree for security. It was only later that he'd learned that cougars could climb trees . . .

After that he'd taken over a few books from the Home and the city library to help him recognize stuff, and he asked Sister Serendipity, who knew about cookery through the ages, and he'd begun to see you'd have to be pretty stupid to starve out there. There were berries, mushrooms, acorns, walnuts, and cat-tails, big green reeds with roots rich in carbs. There were plants to use if you were ill – even wild quinine. The lakes were rich in fish, and traps were easy to make. He'd tried his hand at hunting, once or twice. Rabbits were OK, but the bigger game, the white-tailed deer and elk and moose, would have to wait until he was older. Even turkeys took some running down. But why bother, when there were passenger pigeons that were so dumb that they'd sit and wait for you to walk up to them and knock them over? The animals, even the fish, seemed so innocent. Trusting. Joshua had developed a habit of thanking his catch for its gift of its life, only to learn later that that was how Indian hunters treated their prey.

You had to prepare. You took over matches or a Fresnel lens for fire; he'd taught himself how to make a fire bow in an emergency, but the effort sucked for everyday use. He'd got mosquito repellent free from Clean Sweep, a government exchange for household chemicals on Badger Road. And household bleach, for purifying the water.

Of course you didn't want to become prey of anything yourself – but prey of what? There were animals that could take you down, certainly. Lynxes, dog-sized cats that stared at you and ran off in search of easier targets. Cougars, animals the size of German shepherds with faces that were the essence of cat. Once he saw a cougar bring down a deer, jumping on its back and biting into the carotid. Further out he'd glimpsed wolves, and more exotic animals – a thing like a huge beaver, and a sloth, heavy and stupid, that made him laugh. All these animals, he supposed, had existed in Datum Madison before humans came along, and now were mostly extinct. None of these creatures of the stepwise worlds had ever seen a human before, and even ferocious hunters tended to be wary of the unknown. Mosquitoes were more trouble than wolves, in fact.

In those early days Joshua had never stayed long, only a few nights at a time. Sometimes he perversely wished his stepping ability would switch off, so he'd be stuck out there, and see how he survived. When he came home Sister Agnes would ask him, 'Don't you find it lonely and frightening out there?' But it hadn't been lonely enough. And what was there to be frightened of? You might as well have said somebody who had stuck their toe into the water on a Pacific beach should be frightened of all that ocean.

Besides, pretty soon, in the Low Earths you couldn't move for trippers, coming to see what it was all about. Steely-eyed folk, some of them, with serious shorts and determined knees, striding across this new territory, or at least getting tangled in the underbrush. Folk with questions like, 'Whose land is this? Are we still in Wisconsin? Is this even the United States?'

Worst of all were the ones fleeing from the wrath of God, or maybe looking for it. There was an awful lot of that. Was the Long Earth a sign of the End of Days? Of the destruction of the old world, and a new world made ready for the chosen people? Too many people wanted to be among the chosen, and too many people thought that God would provide, in these paradisiacal worlds. God provided in abundance, it was true, vast amounts of food that you could see running around. But God also helped those who helped themselves, and presumably expected the chosen to bring warm clothing, water purification tablets, basic medication, a weapon such as the bronze knives that were selling so well these days, possibly a tent – in short, to bring some common sense to the party. And if you didn't, and if you were lucky, it would only be the mosquitoes that got you. *Only.* In Joshua's opinion, if you wanted to extend the biblical metaphor, then this apocalypse had four horsemen of its own, their names being Greed, Failing to Follow the Rules, Confusion and Miscellaneous Abrasions. Joshua had got sick of having to save the Saved.

He was soon sick of them all, actually. How did these people have the right to trample all over *his* secret places?

Worse yet, they got in the way of the Silence. He was already calling it that. They drowned out the calmness. Drowned out that distant, deep presence behind the clutter of the worlds, a presence he seemed to have been aware of all his life, and had recognized as soon as he was far enough away from the Datum to be able to hear it. He started resenting every tanned hiker, every nosy kid, and the racket they made.

Yet he felt compelled to help all these people he despised, and he got confused about that. He also got confused about having to spend so much time alone, and the fact that he *liked* it. Which was why he broached the subject with Sister Agnes.

Sister Agnes was definitely religious, in a weird kind of way. At the Home, Sister Agnes had two pictures on the walls of her cramped room: one of them was of the Sacred Heart, the other was of Meat Loaf. And she played old Jim Steinman records far too loudly for the other Sisters. Joshua didn't know much about bikes, but Sister Agnes's Harley looked so old that St Paul had probably once ridden in the sidecar. Sometimes extremely hairy bikers made interstate pilgrimages to her garage at the Home on Allied Drive. She gave them coffee, and made sure they kept their hands *off* the paintwork.

All the kids liked her, and she liked them, but especially Joshua, and especially after he had done a dream of a paint job on her Harley, including the slogan 'Bat Into Heaven' painstakingly delineated on the gas tank in a wonderful italic script that he had found in a book from the library. After that, in her eyes, Joshua could do no wrong, and she allowed him to use her tools any time he liked.

If there was anyone he could trust, it was Sister Agnes. And with her, if he'd been away too long, his usual taciturn reserve sometimes turned into a flood of words, like a dam breaking, and everything that needed saying got said, all in a rush.

So he'd told her about what it was like to have to keep on saving the lost and the silly and the unpleasant, and the way they stared, and the way they said, 'You are him, aren't you? The kid who can step without having to spend fifteen minutes feeling like dog shit.' He never knew *how* they knew, but the news got out somehow, for all Officer Jansson's assurances. And that made him different, and being different made him a Problem. Which was a bad thing, and you couldn't forget that, even here in Sister Agnes's study. Because just above those two pictures of the Sacred Heart and Meat Loaf, there was a little statue of a man who'd been nailed to a cross because He'd been a Problem.

She had said that it seemed to her that he might be trapped in a vocation, not unlike her own. She knew how difficult it was to make people understand what they didn't want to understand, for instance when she insisted that 'For Crying Out Loud' was one of the holiest songs that had ever been recorded. She told him to follow his heart, and also to come and go whenever he liked, because the Home *was* his home.

And she said that he could trust Officer Jansson, a good policewoman and a good Steinman fan (inserting 'Steinman fan' into the conversation at the point where another nun might have used the word 'Catholic'), who had been to see Sister Agnes, and had asked if she could meet Joshua, and ask for his help.

9

MEANWHILE, SIX MONTHS after Step Day, Monica Jansson's own career path had taken a decisive knight's-move sideways.

She had stood outside the Madison PD South District building, braced, slid the switch on her Stepper, and received the usual punch in the gut, as the station vanished to be replaced by tall trees, green shade. In a clearing cut into this scrap of primeval forest was a small wooden shack with the MPD crest on the door, and a low bench outside, and a Stars and Stripes hanging from a stripped sapling. Jansson sat on the bench, folded over, nursing the nausea. The bench was put here precisely to allow you to recover from the stepping before you had to face your fellow officers.

Since Step Day, things had moved on quickly. The techs had come up with a police-issue Stepper, robust components in a sleek black plastic case, resistant even to a close-range gunshot. Of course, as with all Steppers – just as she'd found at the start with Linsay's prototype – to make it work for you, you had to finish the assembly of the working components yourself. It was a nice piece of kit, although you had to ignore the jokes about the potatoes needed to run it. 'Do you want fries with that, Officer?' Ha ha.

But nobody had been able to do anything about the nausea that incapacitated most people for ten or fifteen minutes after a step. There was a drug that was supposed to help, but Jansson always tried to avoid becoming dependent on drugs, and besides it turned your piss blue.

When the dizziness and nausea started to subside, she stood up.

The day, in Madison West 1 anyhow, was still and cold, sunless but rainless. This stepwise world was still much as it had been the first time she'd stepped here, from out of the ruin of Willis Linsay's house: the rustle of leaves, the clean air, the birdsong. But it was changing, bit by bit, as clearings were nibbled into the forest and the prairie flowers were cut back: householders 'extending' their properties, entrepreneurs trying to figure out how to exploit a world of high-quality lumber and exotic wildlife, official presences like the MPD establishing a foothold in world-next-door annexes to their principal buildings. Already, it was said, there was smoky smog on very still days. Jansson wondered how long it would be before she would see airplane contrails in that empty sky.

She wondered where Joshua Valienté was, right now. Joshua, her own guilty secret.

She was almost late for her appointment with Clichy.

Inside the shack, the smell of long-brewed coffee was strong.

There were two officers here, Lieutenant Clichy behind his desk staring into a laptop – customized and non-ferrous – and a junior patrol officer called Mike Christopher who was painstakingly handwriting some kind of report in a big ledger of lined yellow paper. Still largely without electronic support, all over the country cops were having to learn to write legibly again, or as legibly as they ever had.

Clichy waved at her, without taking his eyes from the laptop. 'Coffee, seat.'

She fetched a mug of coffee so thick she thought it would dissolve the bronze spoon she used to stir it, and sat on a rough-hewn handmade chair across the desk. Jack Clichy was a squat, stout man with a face like a piece of worn-out luggage. She had to smile at him. 'You look right at home, Lieutenant.'

He eyed her. 'Don't shit me, Jansson. What am I, Davy Crockett? Listen, I grew up in Brooklyn. To me, downtown Madison is the wild west. *This* is a freaking theme park.'

'Why do you want to see me, sir?'

'Strategy, Jansson. We're being asked to contribute to a state-wide report on how we're intending to deal with this contingency of the extra Earths. Our plans in the short, medium and long term. A version will go up to federal level too. And the chief is bearing down on me because, as he points out, we don't *have* any plans, either short, medium or long term. So far we've just been reacting to events.'

'And that's why I'm here?'

'Let me find the files . . .' He tapped at the keyboard.

Christopher's radio crackled, and he murmured in response. Cellphones wouldn't work over here, of course. Conventional radio transmitters and receivers were OK so long as they were customized to exclude iron components, so they could be carried over intact. There was talk of laying down some kind of network of old-fashioned phone lines, copper wire.

'Here we go.' Clichy swivelled the laptop so that Jansson could see the screen. 'I got case logs here, snippets of video. I'm trying to make sense of it all. Your name kept on coming up, Jansson, which is why I called you in.'

She saw links to her reports on the fire at the Linsay residence, the first-night panic over the missing teenagers.

'So we had a tough first few days. Those missing kids, and the ones that came back with broken bones from falling through high-rise buildings, or with chunks bitten out of them by some critter or other. Prison escapes. A wave of absenteeism, from the schools, businesses, the public services. The economy took an immediate hit, nationwide, even globally. Did you know that? I'm told it was like an extra Thanksgiving break, before the assholes drifted back to work, or most of them . . .'

Jansson nodded. Most of those first-day Steppers had come quickly back. Some had not. The poor tended to be more likely to stay away; rich people had more to give up back in Datum. So, out of cities like Mumbai and Lagos, even a few American cities, flocks of street kids had stepped, bewildered, unequipped, into wild worlds, but worlds that didn't already belong to somebody else, so why shouldn't they belong to you? The American Red Cross and other agencies had sent care teams after them, to sort out the *Lord of the Flies* chaos that followed.

That was the main thing about the Long Earth, in Jansson's mind. Joshua Valienté's behaviour had shown it right from the beginning. It offered *room*. It offered you a place to escape – a place to run, endlessly as far as anybody knew. All over the world there was a trickle of people just walking away, with no plan, no preparation, just walking off into the green. And back home there were already reports of problems with the desolate, resentful minority who found they couldn't step at all, no matter how fancy their Steppers.

Lieutenant Clichy's priority, of course, was the way the new worlds were being used against Datum Earth.

'Look at the log,' he said. 'After a few days people start to figure out this shit, and we get more calculated crimes. Elaborate burglaries. A rash of suicide bombers in the big cities. And the Brewer assassination, or the attempt. Which is where your name started to get flagged up, Officer Jansson.'

Jansson remembered. Mel Brewer was the estranged wife of a drug baron, who had cut a deal with the DA to testify against her husband, and was headed for witness protection. She barely escaped the first attempt on her life by a stepping assassin. It had been Jansson who had come up with the idea of stashing her in a cellar. On the stepwise worlds West 1 and East 1, the space the cellar occupied was solid ground, so you couldn't step straight in. You'd either have to dig a parallel hole, or else come in at ground level and fight your way down. Either way, the element of surprise was lost. By the following morning the belowground facilities in all the police stations, even in the Capitol building, were being fitted out as refuges.

'You weren't the only one to figure that out, Jansson. But you were *among* the first, even nationally. I hear the President herself sleeps in some bunker under the White House now.'

'Glad to hear it, sir.'

'Yeah, yeah. Then it started getting more exotic.'

'Odd to hear you using that term without the word "dancer" attached to it, sir.'

'Don't push it, Jansson.' He showed her reports of various religious nuts. Apocalypse-minded types had gone flooding into the 'new Edens', believing their sudden 'appearance' was a sign of the End of Days. One Christian sect believed Christ must have survived the crucifixion and stepped out of the tomb by the time His disciples came looking for His body – and, it wasn't much of a leap to conclude, He was probably still out there in the Long Earth somewhere. All this presented public order challenges for the police.

Clichy pushed away the laptop and massaged the top of his fleshy nose. 'Who am I, Stephen Hawking? My brain is boiling. Whereas you, on the other hand, Officer Jansson, have taken to all this like a pig to shit.'

'I wouldn't say that, sir—'

'Just tell it to me the way you understand it. The most basic problem – I mean for Madison's finest – is that we can't carry through our pieces intact. Right?'

'Not even a Glock, no, because of the steel parts. No metallic iron can be carried over, sir. Or steel. You can take through whatever you can carry, save for that. I mean, there's iron ore in the other worlds, and you can dig it up and process it and manufacture iron over *there*, but you can't carry that stepwise either.'

'So you need to build a forge on every world you settle.'

'Yes, sir.'

'I'll tell you what puzzles even a doofus like me, Jansson. I thought we all got iron in our blood, or something. How come that doesn't get left behind?'

'In your blood, the iron's chemically bound up in organic

molecules. Inside your hemoglobin, one molecule at a time. Iron molecules can go over if they are in chemical compounds like that, just not in the form of metal. Why, rust can be carried over, because that's a compound of iron with water and oxygen. You can't take your piece over, sir, except for all the rust on the shaft.'

He eyed her. 'That isn't some kind of lewd remark, is it, Jansson?'

'Wouldn't dream of it, sir.'

'Anybody know why things are this way?'

'No, sir.' She had been following the discussions, as best she could. Some physicists had pointed out that iron nuclei were the most stable in nature; iron was the end result of the complicated fusion processes that went on at the heart of the sun. Maybe its reluctance to travel between the worlds was something to do with that. Maybe stepping between the worlds was something like quantum tunnelling, a low-probability passage between energy states. As iron had the most stable atomic nucleus, maybe it lacked the energy to escape from its energy well on Datum Earth . . . Or maybe it was magnetism. Or something. Nobody *knew*.

Clichy, a practical man, just nodded. 'At least we know the rules. Kind of a gut-wrench for most Americans to have gun control suddenly imposed on 'em, however. What else? There are no people in these other worlds, right? I mean, except for the ones who leaked over from ours.'

'That's right, sir. Well, as far as anybody knows. There has been no systematic exploration even of the nearby worlds, not yet. You can't know what's hiding over the next ridge. But they have sent up a few spy balloons and such, aerial cameras. No sign of people, anywhere we can see.'

'OK. So there's a whole chain of these worlds, right? In two directions, East and West.'

'Yes, sir. You just step from one into another, like passing down a corridor. You can go one way or another, East or West – though those are just arbitrary labels. They don't correspond to real directions, in our world.'

'No short cuts? I can't just beam over to world two million?'

'Not that anybody knows, sir.'

'How many of these worlds? One, two, many? A million, a billion?'

'Nobody knows that either, sir. We don't even know how far out people have walked. It's all –' She waved a hand. '– loose around the edges. Uncontrolled.'

'And every one of these worlds is a whole separate Earth, right?'

'As far as we know.'

'But the sun. Mars and Venus. The fucking moon. Are they the same as ours? I mean—'

'Every Earth comes with its own universe, sir. And the stars are the same. The date is the same, in all the worlds. Even the time of day. The astronomers have established that with star charts; they could tell if there were a slippage of a century, or whatever.'

'Star charts. Centuries. Jeez. You know, this afternoon I have to attend a conference chaired by the Governor about jurisdiction. If you commit a crime in Madison West fucking 14, do I even have the authority to arrest you?'

Jansson nodded. Not long after Step Day had come to pass, while some people had just drifted away into the wild, others had started staking claims. You settled down, hammered in your markers, and prepared to plant your crops and raise your kids, in what looked like virgin country. But who, in reality, owned what? You could stake your claim, but would the government endorse it? Were the parallel Americas even United States territory? Well, now the administration had decided to take a position on that.

Clichy said, 'Word is the President is going to declare that all the stepwise Americas *are* US sovereign territory, over which US laws apply. The stepwise territories are "under the aegis of the federal government", is the language. That will simplify things, I guess. If you can call having a beat suddenly become infinite "simple". We're all overstretched, all the agencies. You have the military being brought home from the war zones, Homeland dreaming up endless new ways the terrorists can get through, and meanwhile the corporations are quietly heading on out to see what there is to grab . . . Ah, shit. My momma told me I should have stayed in Brooklyn.

'OK, listen, Officer Jansson.' He leaned forward now, hands folded, intent. 'I'll tell you why I brought you in. Whatever the legal viewpoint, we're still charged with keeping the peace in Madison. And, how lucky for us, Madison is a kind of magnet for the nutjobs over this.'

'I know, sir . . .'

Madison had been the source of the Stepper technology in the first place, so it was a natural hub for that reason. And Jansson, studying reports about people coming here to begin long stepwise journeys, was also beginning to wonder if there was something else about the area that attracted them. Some way stepping was *easier* here. Maybe the Long Earth was about stability. Maybe the oldest, most stable parts of the continents were the easiest places to step – just as iron had the most stable nucleus. And Madison, sitting at the heart of North America, was one of the most stable places on the planet, geologically. If she saw Joshua again, she meant to ask him.

Clichy said, 'So we got a special challenge. Which is why I need you, Jansson.'

'I'm no kind of an expert, sir.'

'But you keep functioning, right through all the *Twilight Zone* shit. Even on that first night, you kept your head clear and your mind focused on the policing priorities, while some of your esteemed colleagues were busy pissing their pants or puking up their pretzels. I want you to be point man on this. You understand? I want you to take a lead, both on the individual incidents, and the patterns behind them. For sure those rascals out there are going to keep figuring out more ways to use this shit against us. I want you to be my Mulder, Officer Jansson.'

She smiled. 'Scully would be more appropriate.'

'Whatever. Look, I'm not promising you anything in return. It's an unconventional assignment. Your contribution will be hard to reflect in your record. I'll do my best, however. You might end up spending a lot of time away from home. A lot of time alone, even. Your personal life—'

She shrugged. 'I've a cat. She looks after herself.'

He tapped a key, and she knew he must be studying her personnel file. 'Twenty-eight years old.'

'Twenty-nine, sir.'

'Born in Minnesota. Parents still there. No siblings, no kids. A failed gay marriage?'

'I'm mostly celibate these days, sir.'

'Jansson, I sincerely do not want to know. OK, go back to Datum Earth, rework your assignments with your sergeant, figure out what you need to set up in this station and the one in East 1 – hell, just go look busy for the mayor, Officer.'

'Yes, sir.'

All in all Jansson had been pleased with the meeting, looking back on it, and her new assignment. It told her that guys like Clichy, and those in power above him, were handling this extraordinary phenomenon, the sudden opening up of the Long Earth, about as well as they could be expected to. Which wasn't true, she had learned from the news and other sources, in every country in the world.

10

'Surely, Prime Minister, we could just ban stepping? It is a manifest security risk!'

'Geoffrey, we might as well outlaw breathing. Even my own mother has stepped!'

'But the population is fleeing. The inner cities are ghost towns. The economy is collapsing. We must do *something*...'

Hermione made a tactful minute of the exchange.

Hermione Dawes was extremely good at taking minutes. She prided herself on the skill; it was an art to sift what people meant from what they said, and she had been practising this art quite satisfactorily for almost thirty years, for political masters of all hues. She had never married, and appeared to be quite comfortable with that fact, laughingly telling her fellow secretaries that her gold ring, which she wore all the time, was intended as a chastity belt. She was trustworthy, and trusted, and the only tiny flaw that her bosses had detected was that she owned every single track that Bob Dylan had ever cut.

Nobody she worked with knew her, she felt. Not even the gentlemen who, periodically, when she was known to be working, broke into her flat and searched it, always very carefully, no doubt sharing a little smile as they carefully replaced the tiny sliver of wood she pushed between the front door and its frame every day. Very similar to her own little smile when she noted that their big flat feet had once again crushed the scrap of meringue that she always dropped on the carpet just inside the living room door, a scrap they never ever noticed.

Since she never took off her gold ring, no one but she and God knew that inscribed, quite expensively, around the inner surface of the ring was a line from a Dylan song called 'It's Alright Ma (I'm Only Bleeding)' She wondered, these days, if any of the busy little bodies she worked with, including most of the ministers, would even recognize where the quote came from.

And now, a few years after Step Day, as the latest panicky discussion went on in the Cabinet Office, she wondered if she was too old to get a job with the masters, as opposed to the fools.

'Then they should be licensed. Stepper boxes. The Long Earth is a sink as far as the blessed economy is concerned, but penalizing the use of the boxes you need to access it would yield some tax revenue, at least!'

'Oh, don't be absurd, man.' The Prime Minister sat back in his chair. 'Come on. We can't just ban a thing because we can't control it.'

The minister responsible for health and safety looked startled. 'I don't see why not. It's never stopped us before.'

The Prime Minister tapped his pen on the table. 'The inner cities are emptying. The economy's imploding. Of course there is a bright side. Immigration is no longer a problem . . .' He laughed, but he seemed to crumple, and when he spoke again he sounded, to Hermione, almost in despair. 'God help us, gentlemen, the science chaps tell me that there might be more iterations of the planet Earth out there than there are people. What policy options can we possibly conceive in the face of *that*?'

Enough was enough: quite suddenly, that was how Hermione felt about all this.

As the picky, preposterous, pointless conversation continued, with a faint smile on her lips Hermione wrote a couple of lines of her immaculate Pitman shorthand, laid her pad on the desk in front of her, and after a nod of permission from the Prime

Minister she stood and left the room. Probably nobody else even noticed she was gone. She walked out into Downing Street, and stepped into the London next door, which swarmed with security guards, but she was such a familiar sight after all these years that they accepted her identity card and let her pass.

And then she stepped again. And again, and again . . .

Much later, when she was missed, one of the other secretaries was called in to translate the little note that she had written, the delicate strokes and swirling curves.

'It looks like a poem to me, sir. Or a song lyric. Something about people criticizing what they can't understand.' She looked up at the Prime Minister. 'Mean anything to you, sir? Sir? Are you all right, sir?'

'Have you got a husband, miss— sorry, I don't know your name?'

'It's Caroline, sir. I've got a boyfriend, a steady boy, good with his hands. I can get you a doctor if you want.'

'No, no. It's just we're all so bloody inadequate, Caroline. What a farce it is, this business of government. To imagine we were ever in control of our destinies. If I were you, Caroline, I would marry your steady boy right now, if you think he's any good, and *go*, go to another world. Anywhere but here.' He slumped in the chair and shut his eyes. 'And God help England, and God help us all.'

She wasn't sure if he was asleep or awake. At length she slipped out, taking Hermione's abandoned pad with her.

11

WITHIN A WEEK OF her meeting with Clichy, Jansson's colleagues had started calling her 'Spooky' Jansson.

And within a month, she had made an appointment at the Home, as Joshua called it. It was an orphanage, a run-down converted section-8 apartment complex on Allied Drive, in an area that was about as rough as it got in Madison. But you could see the place was well kept. And there she quietly met, once more, fourteen-year-old Joshua Valienté. She had sworn that if Joshua dealt through her she would guarantee that nobody would treat him as a Problem, but as somebody who might be able to help out, maybe, you know? Like Batman?

That was how, for several years after Step Day, Joshua's young life had been shaped.

'That must seem a long time ago to you now,' Selena said smoothly, leading Joshua deeper into the transEarth complex.

He didn't reply.

'So you became a hero. Did you wear a cape?' asked Selena.

Joshua didn't like sarcasm. 'I had an oilskin for rainy days.'

'Actually, that was a joke.'

'I know.'

Yet another forbidding door opened in front of them, another corridor was revealed.

'Makes Fort Knox look like a colander, this place, doesn't it?' Selena said nervously.

'Fort Knox *is* a colander nowadays,' said Joshua. 'It's just lucky that people can't carry out bars of gold by hand.'

She sniffed. 'I was merely making a comparison, Joshua.'

'Yes. I know.'

She halted. The way he'd paused in the middle of that reply was annoying, and even more annoying when what she'd really been trying to express was that, even now, all this business of stepwise worlds could be so frightening. Not to Joshua, it seemed. She forced a brief smile. 'This is where I leave you, at least for now. *I* am not allowed to get too close to Lobsang. Very few people are. I know Lobsang wants to discuss your difficulties with the congressional review that's been looking into the outcome of your earlier jaunt into the remote stepwise worlds.'

She was fishing, of course. Joshua suspected that this was, in fact, the leverage Lobsang hoped to use to recruit him.

He said nothing, and she couldn't gauge his reaction.

She guided him gently into the room beyond. 'Nice to have met you face to face, Joshua.'

He said, 'May I wish you the security rating you desire, Selena.'

She stared at the closing door. She was sure that impassive face had broken into a smile.

The room within this fortress-like inner sanctum was decorated like the study of an Edwardian gentleman, even down to the log fire blazing in the fireplace. The fire was a fake, however, and not entirely convincing, at least to Joshua, who lit a genuine log fire every night out in the wild. The leather on the chair standing invitingly beside the fire, however, was real.

'Good afternoon, Joshua,' said a voice from the air. 'I regret that you cannot see me, but in point of fact there is very little of me here to see. And what there is, I feel sure, would be quite dull to observe.'

Joshua settled down in the chair. For a time there was silence, almost companionable. Beside him, the fire crackled artificially.

You could tell, if you listened, because of certain sequences of crackle, that the soundtrack was repeated every forty-one seconds.

The voice of Lobsang said soothingly, 'I ought to have paid more attention to that. Yes – I mean the fire. Oh, don't worry, Joshua, I'm no mind-reader, not yet; you were glancing at the fire every few seconds and you have a tendency to move your lips soundlessly when you are counting. Interestingly enough, nobody else has noticed that little flaw, with the fire.

'But of course, Joshua, you *do* notice. You watch, and listen, and analyse, and inside that roomy cranium of yours you play yourself little videos of all the possible outcomes of the current situation that you can envisage. It was once said of an English politician that if you kicked him in the butt not a muscle would move on his face until he had decided what to do about it. It's one of the qualities that makes you so useful, that watchfulness.

'And you are not apprehensive, are you? I can detect no fear in you, none whatsoever. I believe this is because you are the only person who has been in this fortress of a room who knows that he could get out at any moment. Why? Because you can step without a Stepper box – oh, yes, I know about that. And without getting nauseous afterwards, too.'

Joshua did not rise to that. 'Selena said you had something to tell me, about the congressional review?'

'Yes, the expedition. You got into trouble with that one, didn't you, Joshua?'

'Look – there are only two of us in here, aren't there? So, if you give it some thought, there is no reason whatsoever why you should repeatedly *tell me what my name is.* I know why you're doing it. Dominance.' This was a lifelong bugbear for Joshua. 'I may not be too clever, Lobsang, but you don't have to be clever to work out what the rules are!'

For a while there was nothing but the repeated crackling of the false fire. Later, Joshua came to understand that if there was a pause in a conversation with Lobsang, it was for effect; at the clock speeds he worked at, Lobsang could answer any question a fraction of a second after you asked it, yet after the equivalent of a lifetime of contemplation.

'You know, we are like-minded, you and I, my friend,' said Lobsang.

'Let's stick to "acquaintance" for now.'

Lobsang laughed. 'Of course. I stand corrected. Or rather, float in a disembodied way corrected. But I would like to become your friend. Because, in the abstract, in any given situation, I believe that both of us are interested in finding out, above all, *what the rules are.*

'And I believe that you are a remarkably valuable individual. You are smart enough, Joshua – you couldn't have survived so much time out alone in the Long Earth otherwise. Oh, there are certainly others smarter than you, they are stacked high in the universities achieving little or nothing. But smart has to have a depth as well as a length. Some smart brushes over a problem. And some smart grinds exceeding slow, like the mills of God, and it grinds fine, and when it comes up with an answer, it has been tested. That's how it is with you, Joshua.' Lobsang laughed again. 'And by the way my laughter is not a recording. Each laugh is a unique product of the moment, demonstrably different from any other laugh I have ever emitted. That was a laugh just for you. I was human, you know. I still am.

'Joshua, let's get to know one another. I want to help you. And of course I want you to help me. I cannot think of a better person to go with me on the expedition I am planning, which will involve some very far stepping indeed. I think it might rather appeal to you. You like to be far from the maddening crowd, Joshua, don't you?'

'Thomas Hardy's title was about the madding crowd.'

'Oh, of course it was. But it's a good idea for me to make the odd little slip – not to appear all-knowing, every now and again.'

Joshua was growing impatient with this clumsy seduction. 'Lobsang, how are *you* going to help *me*?'

'I know that what happened to the congressional expedition was not your fault. I can prove it.'

Now they were getting down to brass tacks, Joshua thought. 'The assholes,' he said.

'Oh yes, assholes,' said Lobsang, 'and thusly you described them to the preliminary board of inquiry. An unknown species of primate resembling a particularly unpleasant carnivorous baboon. But I suspect the Linnaean Society will not approve your appellation. Assholes!'

'I didn't kill those men. Sure, I can get along without people. But I had no *reason* to kill anybody. Did you read the report? Those ass—'

'Can we stick to baboons, please, Joshua? It looks better on the transcript.'

It had been a paid jaunt for Joshua, a gig arranged by his old friend Officer Jansson. 'You've grown up while I've grown old, Joshua,' she'd said. 'And now I've got you some government work. You'll be a kind of bodyguard and guide . . .'

It was an official journey to the far West worlds with a party of scientists, lawyers and a Congressman, accompanied by a platoon of soldiers. It had ended in slaughter.

The scientists had been gathering data. The lawyers had been taking photographs of the Congressman setting foot on one world after another, making a kind of visual claim to the stepwise Americas, in order to establish symbolically the aegis of the Datum federal government. The soldiers complained about the food and the state of their feet. Joshua had been happy enough to help the party, for his fee, but sensible enough to make sure his ability to step without a box and without after-effects was concealed. So he carried a potion consisting of sour milk and diced vegetables that would pass muster as vomit, the product of stepping nausea. After all, who was going to look too closely?

It all worked fine. They had all bitched, squabbled and complained their way through two thousand Earths, and after every step Joshua faked nausea with splashes of ersatz vomit. And then the murderous attack had come.

They were apes, something like baboons, but smarter, more vicious. 'Superboons', some of the scientists had called them. 'Assholes', Joshua had decided, watching their pink butts go bobbing into the distance after he'd driven them off.

Or anyhow, that was his story of what had become of the party. The trouble was there had been no witnesses to back him up, and it had all happened too far out for an expedition to be sent to investigate, so far.

'The damn things could plan an attack! They never bothered *me* after I killed two of them, but the troops were overwhelmed, and the science guys never knew how to defend themselves worth a damn.'

'And you left the bodies for the baboons?'

'You know, it's hard to dig a grave with a wooden shovel in one hand while holding a plastic gun in the other. I burned the camp and got the hell out of there.'

'I thought the board of inquiry's tentative verdict was rather unfair on you. It left doubt. Now I want you to know that I can prove that what you said was true. I can *prove* that there is an outcrop of black rock about a kilometre from the campsite by the waterhole, just as you said, behind which still lies the remains of the corpse of the alpha animal, which you shot. Incidentally the rock was low-grade coal.'

'How can you know all this?'

'I retraced your steps. The records you returned were quite accurate. I went back, Joshua.'

'*You* went *back*? When?'

'Yesterday.'

'You got back yesterday?'

Lobsang said patiently, 'I went and returned yesterday.'

'You couldn't have done! It's impossible to step that fast.'

'So you say, Joshua. You'll find out in due course. You did make an attempt to cover the corpses with stones, and you left grave markers, just as you mentioned at the inquiry. I brought back photographic records. Proof of what you said, you see?

'In fact I reconstructed the whole thing. I used pheromone trails, checked angles of fire, the lie of the bodies. I found every bullet. And, of course, I took DNA samples. I even brought back the alpha's skull – and the bullet that killed it. It all fits with your testimony. None of the soldiers put up an effective defence when your asshole-baboons attacked, did they? The superboons are maniacs by the standards of the animal world. Appallingly aggressive. But I don't think they would have attacked if one of the grunts hadn't got nervy and fired first.'

Joshua squirmed with embarrassment. 'If you checked all this out, you know I crapped my pants in the course of the engagement.'

'Should I think less of you for that? Throughout the animal kingdom, it has always made good sense to jettison the cargo in a threatening situation. All battlefields attest to that, as does every soaring songbird. But then *you came back,* and stabbed one of the superboons in the brain, and drove off the rest, stopping only when you'd shot the leader dead. You came back, and that excuses a lot.'

Joshua thought for a moment. 'OK. That's leverage, all right. You can clear me. But why do you want to recruit me in the first place?'

'Well, we discussed that. It's the same reason Jansson suggested you for Congressman Popper's party in the first place. You have Daniel Boone syndrome, Joshua. Very rare. You don't need people. You quite like people, at least some people, but the absence of people does not worry you. That's going to be very useful where we're going. I don't expect to meet too many other human beings once the expedition is under way. Your assistance would be of great help to me because of that quality: you are able to focus, you're not distracted by the extraordinary isolation of the Long Earth. And, as Officer Jansson saw from the beginning, your unique stepping talent, your ability to step unaided and, more important, to recover quickly from each step, will be useful if trouble strikes – as it surely will.

'The rewards to you, should you agree to accompany me, will be excessively generous, and tailored to your particular preferences. Among them will be an authoritative account of the massacre of the congressional investigators, totally exonerating you, which will be received by the authorities on the day we depart.'

'Am I worth that much?'

Lobsang laughed again. 'Joshua, what is worth? What is value now, when gold is valued simply for its lustre, because every man can have a gold mine for himself? Property? The physics of the Long Earth means that every one of us can have a world entirely to himself, if he so wishes. This is the new age, Joshua, and there will be new values, new ideas of worth, including love, cooperation, truth – and above all, yes indeed, above all, the friendship of Lobsang. You should listen to me, Joshua Valienté. I intend to travel to the ends of the Earth – no, to the ends of the Long Earth. And I want you with me. Will you come?'

Joshua sat there, staring at nothing. 'Do you know, the crackling of your fire now sounds absolutely random?'

'Yes. Easy enough to fix. I thought it might put you a little more at your ease.'

'So if I come with you, you'll get that congressional review off my back?'

'Yes, certainly, I promise.'

'And if I don't choose to go with you, what then?'

'I'll deal with the review nonetheless. You did everything you could have done, I believe, and the loss of those people was definitely not your fault. Evidence of this will be presented to the panel.'

Joshua stood up. 'Right answer.'

*

That night Joshua sat in front of a screen in the Home and read up about Lobsang.

Apparently, so it was believed, Lobsang resided in extremely high-density, fast-access computer storage at MIT, and therefore not in the premises of transEarth at all. When Joshua read that, he felt a warm certainty that whatever was in a super-cooled box in MIT, it wasn't Lobsang, not the *whole* of Lobsang. If Lobsang were smart, and he was most surely smart, he would have got himself distributed *everywhere*. A hedge against an off switch. And he'd be in a position where nobody could command him, not even his super-powerful partner Douglas Black. *There* was somebody who knew the rules, Joshua thought.

Joshua switched off the screen. Another rule: Sister Agnes held it as a matter of faith that all left-on computer screens exploded sooner or later. He sat back in the silence, and thought.

Was Lobsang human, or an AI aping humanity? A smiley, he thought: one curve and two dots, and you see a human face. What was the minimum you needed to *see* a human being? What has to be said, what has to be laughed? After all, people are made of nothing but clay – well, metaphorically, although Joshua was not too good at metaphors, seeing them as a kind of trick. And you had to admit that Lobsang was pretty good at knowing what Joshua was thinking, just as a perceptive human would be. Maybe the only significant difference between a really smart simulation and a human being was the noise they made when you punched them.

But . . . the ends of the Long Earth?

Was there an end? People were saying there must be a whole circle of Earths, because the Stepper box took you either East or West, and everybody believed that East must meet West! But nobody *knew*. Nobody knew what all the other Earths were doing out there in the first place. Perhaps it was time somebody tried to find out.

Joshua looked down at the latest Stepper box he had just finished, using a double-pole, double-throw switch he had bought over the internet. Sitting on the desk beside him it was red and silver and looked very professional, unlike his first box, which had utilized a switch taken off Sister Regina's elderly stairlift. He had carried a Stepper ever since it had dawned on him that since he did not know how he stepped, the sensible thing would be to carry a Stepper box *anyway*; a talent that had come suddenly and inexplicably might just as easily disappear the same way. And besides, a box was cover. He didn't want to stand out from the stepping crowd.

Turning the box over in his hands, Joshua wondered if Lobsang realized what was the most interesting thing about Stepper-box construction. He'd noticed it on Step Day, and it was obvious when you thought about it; it was a strange little detail nobody seemed to think was important. Joshua always thought that details were important. Officer Jansson noticed details like this. It had to do with following the instructions. A Stepper would only work for you if you built it yourself, or at least finished its assembly.

He drummed his fingers on the box. He could go with Lobsang, or not. Joshua was twenty-eight years old; he didn't have to ask anybody's permission. But he did have the damn congressional review hanging over him.

And he always liked the idea of being out of reach.

Despite Jansson's promises all those years ago, the bad guys had got to him once or twice. There had been that trouble not long after Step Day, when men with badges had pushed their way into the Home and tried to send him to sleep so they could take him away, and Sister Agnes had laid one of them out with a tire iron, and pretty soon the cops were called, and that meant Officer Jansson showed up, and then the mayor had got involved, and it turned out that one of the kids who were helped by Joshua on Step Day had been his son, and that had been that, the three black anonymous cars had hightailed it out of town . . . That was when the rule was laid down that if anyone wanted to talk to Joshua then they had to talk to Officer Jansson first. Joshua was not the problem, the mayor had said. The problem was crime and escapes from jails and no security left in the world. Joshua, the city council was told, was perhaps a little strange, but also marvellously gifted and, as was testified by Officer Jansson, had already been of great help to the Madison police department. That was the official position.

But that wasn't always much comfort to Joshua himself, who hated being *looked at.* Who hated the fact that a growing number of people *knew he was different,* whether they thought he was a Problem or not.

In recent years Joshua had stepped alone, going further and further into the Long Earth, far beyond the Robinson Crusoe stockades he'd built as a teenager, out to worlds so remote he didn't have to worry about the crazies, even the crazies with badges and warrants. And when they did come he just stepped away again; by the time they had finished throwing up Joshua could be a hundred worlds away. Though sometimes he stepped back to tie their boot-laces together while they barfed. You had to have something to entertain yourself. Longer and longer jaunts, further and further away. He called these his sabbaticals. A way of getting away from the crowds – and from the odd pressure in his head when he was back on Datum Earth, or even the Low Earths nowadays. A pressure that got in the way of listening to the Silence.

So he was strange. But the Sisters said that the whole world was getting stranger. Sister Georgina had told him as much, in her polite English accent. 'Joshua, you may be just a little ahead of the rest of the human race. I imagine the first *Homo sapiens* felt the way you do when you look at the rest of us with our Stepper boxes and our vomiting. Like *H. sap.* wondering why the other chaps take such a long time to string two syllables together.' But Joshua wasn't sure if he liked the idea of being different, even if it was different in a superior sort of way.

Still, he liked Sister Georgina almost as much as Sister Agnes. Sister Georgina read Keats and Wordsworth and Ralph Waldo Emerson to him. Sister Georgina had studied at Cambridge or, as she put it, 'Not-the-one-in-Massachusetts-Cambridge-University-the-real-one-you-know-in-England.' Sometimes it occurred to Joshua that the nuns who ran the Home were not like the ones that he saw on television. When he asked Sister Georgina about that she laughed and said, 'Maybe it's because we are just like you, Joshua. We're here because we didn't quite fit anywhere else.' He was going to miss them all, he realized, when he went travelling with Lobsang.

Somehow the decision had made itself.

12

A WEEK AFTER HIS interview at transEarth Sister Agnes took Joshua to Dane County Regional Airport on the back of her Harley, a rare honour. He would always remember her saying as they arrived that God must have wanted him to catch that plane, because every stop light they encountered turned to green just before she needed to slow. (In so far as Sister Agnes ever did slow.) Joshua, however, suspected that the subroutines of Lobsang were responsible for this, rather than the hand of God.

Joshua had walked on countless Earths, but he had never actually flown before. Sister Agnes knew the routine, and she marched him to the check-in desk. Once the clerk had entered his booking reference he went very quiet, and picked up the phone, and Joshua began to realize what it meant to have a friend in Lobsang, as he was whisked away from the lines of passengers and led along corridors with the politeness you might observe when dealing with a politician belonging to a country that had nuclear weapons and a carefree approach to their deployment.

He was brought to a room with a bar the length of the burger counter in Disney World. Impressive though this was, Joshua didn't often drink, and would actually have preferred a burger. When he mentioned this jokily to the young man who was nervously dancing attendance on him, he received, after only minutes, a perfect burger so stuffed with trimmings that the patty could have fallen out and not been missed. Joshua was still digesting this when the young man reappeared and led him to the plane.

His seat was right behind the flight deck, and discreetly hidden from the other travellers by a velvet curtain. No one had asked to see his passport, which he didn't have in any case. No one bothered to check whether he was carrying explosives in his shoes. And nobody, once he was on the flight, spoke to him. He watched a news summary in peace.

At Chicago O'Hare he was taken to another plane some way from the main terminal, a surprisingly small craft. Within, what wasn't leather-upholstered was carpeted, and what wasn't leather-upholstered or carpeted seemed to consist of the dazzling teeth of a young woman who, as he sat down, provided him with a Coke and a telephone. He tucked his small personal pack under the seat before him, where he could see it. Then he turned on the phone.

Lobsang called immediately. 'Good to have you on board, Joshua! How are you enjoying the journey so far? The plane is all yours today. You will find a master bedroom behind you which I'm told is exceedingly comfortable, and don't hesitate to take advantage of the shower room.'

'It's going to be a long journey, is it?'

'I'll be meeting you in Siberia, Joshua. A Black Corporation skunk works. You know what that means?'

'A facility that's off the radar.' Where, he wondered, they were building *what*?

'Right. Oh, didn't I mention Siberia?'

There was a sound of engines starting.

'You've a human pilot, incidentally. People seem to like a warm uniformed body at the controls. But don't be alarmed. In a real sense *I* am the controls.'

Joshua sat back in the luxurious seat and put his thoughts in order. It occurred to him that Lobsang was full of himself, as the Sisters would have said. But maybe he had a lot of himself to be full of. Here was Joshua cocooned *in* Lobsang, in a sense. Joshua wasn't big on computers, and the marvellously interconnected electronic civilization of which they were part. Out in the stepwise worlds you never got a cellphone signal, after all, so the only thing that counted was *you*, and what you knew, and what you could do. With his prized knife of hardened glass he could keep himself alive, no matter what was thrown at him. He kind of liked that. Maybe there was going to be some tension with Lobsang over that – or with however much of Lobsang was ported along for the ride.

The plane took off, making about as much noise as would Sister Agnes's sewing machine in an adjacent room. During the flight Joshua watched the first episode of *Star Wars*, sipping gin and tonic, wallowing in boyhood nostalgia. Then he took a shower – he didn't need one but just for the hell of it – and tried the enormous bed, whereupon the young lady followed him in and asked him a couple of times if there was anything else he wanted, and seemed disappointed when he only asked for a glass of warm milk.

Some time later he awoke to find the attendant trying to strap him in. He pushed her away; he hated being restrained. She remonstrated with the sugar-coated steeliness bequeathed by her training, until a phone chimed. Then: 'I do apologize, sir. It would appear that the safety rules have been temporarily suspended.'

He had expected Siberia to be flat, windy, cold. But this was summer, and the plane descended towards a landscape where gentle hills were coated with dark shoots of grass, and wildflowers and butterflies were splashes of colour, red, yellow and blue. Siberia was unexpectedly beautiful.

The jet did not so much touch down as kiss the tarmac.

The phone rang. 'Welcome to No Such Place, Joshua. I do hope you'll fly with No Such Airlines in the future. You will find thermal underwear and appropriate outdoor clothing in the wardrobe just inside the door.'

Joshua refused, with a red face, the attendant's suggestion that she should help him on with the thermal underwear. However, he did accept the offer of her assistance with the bulky outer clothing, which he thought made him look like the Pillsbury Doughboy, but was surprisingly light.

He climbed down from the plane to join a group of men dressed as he was. Joshua immediately began to sweat in the mild air. One man grinned, called 'West!' to Joshua in a distinctly Bostonian accent, pressed a switch on the box strapped to his belt, and vanished. A moment later his companions began to follow.

Joshua stepped West, and arrived in an almost identical landscape – save that he emerged into a blizzard and realized why he needed the winter gear. There was a small shack nearby, with the Bostonian beckoning to him from a half-open door. It looked like a halfway house, a travellers' rest stop of the kind becoming common in the stepwise worlds. But it was utilitarian, just a place out of the wind where a man could upchuck in something like comfort before stepping on.

The Bostonian, looking queasy, shut the door behind Joshua. 'You really are him, aren't you? Feeling fine, are you? I don't suffer from it too bad myself, but . . .' He waved a hand.

Joshua looked towards the back of the shack where two men were lying face down over the edge of narrow beds, each with a bucket under his face; the smell told it all.

'Look, if you really feel OK, go on ahead. You're the VIP here. You don't have to wait for us. You need to take three more steps West. There are rest stations in each one – but I guess you won't need them . . . Are you for real? I mean, how do you do it?'

Joshua shrugged again. 'Don't know. Kind of a knack, I guess.'

The Bostonian opened the door. 'Hey, before you go, we like to say here: you're stepping, wait for it, on the steppe!' When Joshua tried but failed to summon up a laugh the Bostonian said apologetically, 'You can imagine we don't get too many visitors here. Best of luck, fella.'

*

The three further steps brought him out into rain. There was another shack near by, and another pair of workers, one of them a woman, who shook him by the hand. 'Good to see you, sir.' Her accent was richly Russian. 'Do you like our weather? Siberia's two degrees warmer in this world, and nobody knows why. I must wait a while for the rest of the gang, but you can just follow the yellow brick road.' She pointed to a line of orange markers on sticks. 'It's a short walk to the construction site.'

'Construction? Construction of what?'

'Believe me, you won't miss it.'

He didn't, because he couldn't. Acres of pine woodland had been cleared, and hovering over a circle of denuded land was what looked at first glance like a floating building. Floating, yes; through the rain he made out tethering wires. It was vast, an aerial whale. The partially inflated body was a bag of some toughened fibre plastered with transEarth logos, over a gondola like an Art Deco fantasy, several decks deep, all polished wood and portholes and plate glass.

An airship!

As he stared, yet another worker hurried towards him flourishing a phone. 'You are Joshua?' This man's accent was European, Belgian perhaps. 'Pleased to meet you, very pleased! Follow me. Can I help you with your bag?'

Joshua pulled his pack away so quickly that it would have burned the man's hand.

The worker stepped back. 'Sorry, sorry. By all means keep your bag; security is not an issue, not for you. Come with me.'

Joshua followed him across the soaking ground and under the formless envelope. The gondola, fashioned like a wooden ship's hull, appeared to be anchored to a metal gantry, presumably constructed of locally manufactured steel, at the bottom of which was a skeleton elevator cage. Cautiously, his guide climbed into the open cage and, when Joshua had joined him, pressed a button.

It was a short ride up to the underside of the gondola, and

through a hatch and out of the rain. Joshua found himself in a small compartment, suffused by a rich smell of polished wood. There were windows, or possibly portholes, but right now they showed nothing but the weather.

'Wish I was leaving with you, young man,' said the worker cheerfully. 'Going wherever this thing is going – none of *us* need to know, of course. If you get a chance, look around the engineering. Non-ferrous, of course, aluminium airframe . . . Well. We're all proud of her. Bon voyage, enjoy the journey!' He stepped back into the elevator, and as it descended out of sight a plate slid across to seal the polished floor.

The voice of Lobsang sounded in the air. 'Once again, welcome aboard, Joshua. Such dreadful weather, isn't it? Never mind, I will soon have us above it or, should I say, away from it.'

There was a jolt and the floor rocked. 'We've detached from the gantry. Are we airborne already?'

'Well, you wouldn't have been brought here if we weren't ready to go. Below us they will be breaking camp already, and then this site will suffer a minor version of the Tunguska event.'

'Security, I take it.'

'Of course. As for the workers, they are a mixed lot: Russians, Americans, Europeans, Chinese. None of them the kind of people who like to talk to the authorities. Clever folk who have worked for many masters, so very useful, and so commendably forgetful.'

'Who supplied the plane?'

'Ah. Did you enjoy your ride in the Lear? It is the property of a holding company who rent it out occasionally to a certain rock star, who tonight is fretting that the jet is unavailable because of an overhaul. But she will soon be distracted by learning that her latest album is two places higher in the charts than it was last night. The reach of Lobsang is great. Now that we are under way . . .'

An inner door opened smoothly, revealing a corridor of panelled wood and subtle lamps, leading to a blue door at the end.

'Welcome to the *Mark Twain*. Please make yourself at home. You will find on this corridor six staterooms, all identical; choose whichever one you like. You can shed your cold-weather gear. Notice also the blue door. That leads to a laboratory, workshop and fabrication plant, among other things. You will find a similar door on each deck. I would prefer if you do not go beyond unless invited. Any questions?'

Joshua changed in the room he'd chosen at random, and then explored the *Mark Twain*.

The tremendous envelope, rippling under partial pressurization, was evidently coated on the outside with solar-cell film for power, and there were propulsion units, big fragile-looking fans that could swivel and tilt. The gondola was as luxurious within as it had looked from the outside. There were several decks, with staterooms, a wheelhouse, an observation deck, and a saloon deck with a galley as well equipped as the kitchen of a high-class restaurant, and a spacious hall that could serve as a restaurant for fifty – or, incredibly, as a *cinema*. And on every deck there was that blue door, closed and locked.

As he thought it over, Joshua began to see the point of stepping in an airship – as long as you could get the thing to step in the first place, and how you'd do that he didn't yet understand. One problem with stepping rapidly was obstacles. He'd discovered on his very first night of exploration of the Long Earth that some obstacles simply couldn't be walked around, such as the ice cap, sometimes miles high, that typically blanketed much of North America during an Ice Age. The airship was an attempt to get around that: it would ride above such inconveniences as glaciers or floods, and a much smoother journey ought to be possible.

He asked the air, 'But did it have to be quite so grand, Lobsang?'

'Why not be grand? We can't hide, after all. I want my exploratory vessel to be like the Chinese treasure ships which struck awe into the natives of India and Arabia in the fifteenth century.'

'You'll strike awe, all right. And no iron in this thing, I take it?'

'I'm afraid not. The impermeability of the reality barrier to iron remains a mystery even to Black Corporation scientists. I get plenty of theorizing, but few practical results.'

'You know, when you talked about the journey, I thought I'd be carrying *you*, somehow.'

'Oh, no. *I* am wired into the airship's systems. The whole ship will be my body, in a sense. Joshua, *I* will be carrying *you*.'

'Only sentient creatures can step—'

'Yes. And I, like you, am sentient!'

And Joshua understood. The airship *was* Lobsang, or at least his body; when Lobsang stepped, the airship carcass came with him, just as Joshua 'carried' over his body, his clothes, whenever he stepped. And that was how an airship could step.

Lobsang was smug and boastful. 'Of course this would not work were I *not* sentient. This is further proof of my claims of person-hood, isn't it? I've already trialled the technology – well, you know that, I traced your earlier expedition as I told you. All rather thrilling, isn't it?'

Joshua reached the base of the gondola and entered the observation deck he'd spotted before, a blister of reinforced glass giving spectacular views of this Low Earth's Siberia. The construction site sprawled below, with ancillary workings cut into the forest, supply dumps, dormitories, an airstrip.

Joshua, thinking it over, began to realize just what an achievement Lobsang had pulled off here – *if* the airship stepped as advertised. Nobody before had found a way to make a *vehicle* capable of stepping between the worlds the way a human could, and that was throttling the expansion of any kind of trade across the Long Earth. In parts of the Near East, and even in Texas, they had human chains carrying over oil by the bucket-load. If Lobsang really had cracked this, essentially by becoming the vessel himself – well, he was like a modern rail pioneer; he was going to change the world, all the worlds. No wonder security was so tight. *If* it worked.

This was all experimental, evidently. And Joshua would be swimming across Long Earth in the belly of a silvery whale. 'You seriously expect me to risk my life in this thing?'

'More than that. If "this thing" fails I expect you to bring me home.'

'You're insane.'

'Quite possibly. But we have a contract.'

A blue door slid open, and, to Joshua's blank astonishment, Lobsang showed himself in person – or rather, in ambulatory unit. 'Welcome again! I thought I would dress for the occasion of our maiden voyage.' The automaton was male, slim and athletic, with movie star looks and a wig of thick black hair, and it wore a black lounge suit. It looked like a waxwork of James Bond, and when it moved, and worse when it smiled, it did nothing to dispel the artifice.

Joshua stared, struggling not to laugh.

'Joshua?'

'Sorry! Pleased to meet you in person . . .'

The deck vibrated as engines bit. Joshua felt oddly thrilled at the prospect of the voyage in a small-boy kind of way. 'What do you think we're going to find out there, Lobsang? I guess anything is possible if you go far enough. What about dragons?'

'I would suggest we might expect to find anything that *could* possibly exist in the conditions found on this planet, within the constraints of the laws of physics, and bearing in mind that the planet has not always been so peaceful as it is now. All creatures on Earth have been hammered on the anvil of its gravity, for example, which influences size and morphology. So I am sceptical about finding armoured reptiles who can fly and spout flames.'

'Sounds a little drab.'

'However, I would not be human if I did not acknowledge one important factor, which is that I might be totally wrong. And *that* would be very exciting.'

'Well, we'll find out – if this thing actually steps.'

Lobsang's synthetic face folded into a smile. 'Actually we've been stepping for the last minute or so.'

Joshua turned to a window and saw that it was true. The construction site had cleared away; they must have passed out of the sheaf of known worlds in the first few steps – although that word 'known' was something of a joke. Even the stepwise worlds right next to the Datum had barely been explored; humans were colonizing the Long Earth in thin lines stretched across the worlds. Anything could be living out back in the woods . . . And he, evidently, was going deeper into those woods than anybody before him.

'How fast will this thing go?'

'You'll be pleasantly surprised, Joshua.'

'You're going to change the world with this technology, Lobsang.'

'Oh, I know that. Up to now the Long Earth has been opened up on foot. It's been medieval. No, worse than that, we haven't even been able to use horses. Stone Age! But of course, even on foot humans have been moving out since Step Day. Dreaming of a new frontier, of the riches of the new worlds . . .'

13

MONICA JANSSON HAD always understood very well that it was the promise of the riches of the new worlds that drew the likes of Jim Russo out into the Long Earth to try their luck, over and over, with the law seeming at times no more than a minor obstacle in the face of their ambition.

On her first visit to Portage East 3, ten years after Step Day, it had taken Jansson a minute or two, even after she'd gotten over the step sickness, to figure out what was familiar about the place. This new Portage had big steam-driven sawmills with chimney stacks belching smoke, and foundries with a burned-metal smell. She heard the cries of the workers, the steam hooters, the steady clank of the smiths' hammers. It was like something out of a certain kind of fantasy novel that she'd read as a kid. Oh, in no novel she'd ever read would there have been teams of labourers hauling twelve-yard lengths of timber up on to their shoulders, and then vanishing. But she could testify that on this particular world, the modestly named Long Earth Trading Company was turning a corner of a stepwise Wisconsin into a steampunk theme park.

And here came the man who was driving it all.

'Sergeant Jansson? Thank you for stepping over to see my little enterprise.'

Jim Russo was shorter than she was. He wore a crumpled grey suit, and had well-tended hair of a suspiciously vivid brown hue, and a broad grin between cheeks that might or might not have had a little help to stay perky. She knew Russo was forty-five years old, had been declared bankrupt three times before but had always bounced back, and had now mortgaged his own home for seed-corn money for this new inter-world enterprise.

'No need to thank me, sir,' she said. 'You know we have a duty to investigate complaints.'

'Ah, yes, more anonymous whining from the hired hands. Well, it's par for the course.' He led her over the muddy ground, evidently hoping to impress her with the scale of his operation here. 'Although I think I would have expected a visit from the Portage PD. That's the local department.'

'Your registered office is in Madison.' And besides, 'Spooky' Jansson was often called into the more high-profile cases involving Long Earth issues around wider Wisconsin.

They paused to watch another team of handlers pick a tremendously long-looking log off a heap; a foreman called out a countdown – 'three, two, one' – and away they stepped, with a soft implosion.

'You can see this is a busy place, Sergeant Jansson,' Russo said. 'We started with nothing, of course. Nothing more than we could carry over, and no iron tools. In the early days the foundries were a high priority, after the sawmills. Now we have a flow of high-quality iron and steel, and soon we'll be building steam-driven harvesters and collectors, and then you'll see us rip through these forests like a hot knife through butter. And all this timber is stepped back to the Datum, to waiting fleets of flatbed trucks.' He brought her to an open-front log cabin that served as a kind of showroom. 'We're expanding into a lot of areas other than just raw materials. Look at this.' It was a kind of shotgun that gleamed like brass. 'No iron parts at all, meant for the new pioneer market.

'I know the opening up of the Long Earth has knocked us into an economic dip, but that's short term. The loss of a percentage of the low-grade workforce, a glut of some precious metals – that will pass. Back on Datum Earth the US went from colonial days to the moon in a few centuries. There's no reason we can't do the same again, on any number of other Earths. Personally I'm very excited. It's a new age, Sergeant Jansson, and with products and commodities like these I mean to be in on the ground floor . . .'

As did hundreds, thousands of other needy entrepreneur types, Jansson knew. And most of them were younger than Russo, smarter, not yet weighed down by previous failures, in Russo's case beginning with a comically naive attempt to go mine a stepwise copy of Sutter's Mill for gold, almost a cliché of a misunderstanding of the economic realities of the new age.

'It's a problem, isn't it, Mr Russo, to balance the profit you make against the pressure on your labour force?'

He smiled easily, prepared for the question. 'I'm not building pyramids here, Sergeant Jansson. I'm not whipping slaves.'

But neither was he running a philanthropic foundation, Jansson knew. The workers, mostly young and ill-educated, often had no real idea of what was going on out in the Long Earth before they came out here to work in places like this. As soon as they realized that they could be using their strength to build something for themselves, they tended to start agitating to join one of the new Companies and go trekking off into the deep crosswise to colonize – or else, as it dawned on them that there was an infinity of worlds out there none of which were owned by people like Jim Russo, they simply walked away, into the endless spaces. Some people just seemed to keep walking and walking, living off the land as best they could. Long Earth Syndrome, they called it. And that was where the complaints about Russo were coming from. He was said to be tying his workers up with punitive contracts to keep them from straying, and then going after them with hired muscle if they reneged.

She had the sudden instinct that this man was going to fail, as he had before. And when it all started going belly-up he was going to be cutting even more corners.

'Mr Russo, we need to get down to the specifics of the complaints against you. Is there somewhere we can talk privately?'

'Of course . . .'

All over the nearby Earths, Jansson knew, on worlds becoming sweatshops overnight, people were dreaming of escape, of freedom. As she waited for a coffee Jansson spotted a flyer in Russo's own in-tray, just a page crudely printed on pulpy paper, about the formation of yet another new Company to go trek up West. Dreams of the new frontier, even here in this minor businessman's office. Sometimes Jansson, nearing forty now, wondered if she should up sticks and go out herself, and leave the Datum and the increasingly murky Low Earths behind.

14

DREAMS OF THE Long Earth. Dreams of the frontier. Yes, ten years after Step Day, Jack Green had understood that. Because they had been his wife's dreams, and Jack had feared they were tearing his family apart.

> *January 1. Madison West 5. We came to stay at a lodge here for New Year after ~~Cristmas~~ Christmas at home but we will have to go ~~bak~~ back to the Datum for school. My name is Helen Green. I am ~~elven~~ eleven years old. My mother (Dr Tilda Lang Green) says I should keep a ~~jurnal jorunal~~ journal in this ~~bok~~ book which was a Christmas ~~presnt~~ present from Aunt Meryl because there ~~mite~~ might be no ~~electrics~~ electronics this thing have no spellchecker it drive me CRAYZEE!!! . . .*

Jack Green carefully turned the pages of his daughter's journal. It was like a fat paperback book, though with the pulpy graininess of much of the paper produced here in West 5. He was alone in Helen's room, on a bright Sunday afternoon. Helen was out playing softball in ParkZone Four. Katie was out too, he wasn't sure where. And Tilda was downstairs talking with a group of the friends and colleagues she had managed to snag into the idea of forming a Company to go West.

'. . . Empires rise and they fall. Look at Turkey. That was a great empire once and you wouldn't believe it now . . .'

'. . . If you're middle class you look to the left and see the activists undermining American values, and to the right and you see how free trade has exported our jobs . . .'

' . . . We believed in America. Now we seem to be mired in mediocrity, while the Chinese steam ahead . . .'

Tilda's voice: 'The notion of Manifest Destiny is historically suspect, of course. But you can't deny the importance of the frontier experience to the making of the American consciousness. Well, now the frontier is opening up again, for our generation and maybe for uncountable generations to follow . . .'

The group conversation broke up into a general susurrus of noise, and Jack smelled a rich aroma. Time for coffee and cookies.

He returned to the diary. At last he came to an entry that mentioned his son. He read on, skimming over the spelling errors and crossings-out.

March 23. We have moved to our new house in Madison West 5. It will be fun here in the summer. Dad and Mom take it in turns to go back, they have to work on the Datum for the money. And we had to leave Rod again with Auntie Meryl because he is a fobic [she meant phobic, a non-stepper – Jack tripped over that spelling] *and can't step it's sad I cried this time after we stepped away but Rod didn't cry unless he did after we had gone. I will write to him in the summer and will go back and see him IT IS SAD because it is fun here in the summer and Rod can't come . . .*

'Tut tut.' His wife's voice. 'That's private.'

He turned, guilty. 'I know, I know. But we're going through such changes. I feel the need to know what's going on in their heads. I think that trumps the privacy thing, just for now.'

She shrugged. 'That's your judgement.' She had brought him a coffee, a brimming mug. She turned and stood by the big picture window, the best in the house, the least flawed pane they could find of the locally manufactured sheet glass. They looked out over

Madison West 5, across which the afternoon shadows were just beginning to stretch. She wore her slightly greying strawberry blonde hair cut short, and the graceful curve of her neck was silhouetted against the window. 'Still a lovely day,' she said.

'Lovely place, too . . .'

'Yes. Nearly perfect.'

Nearly perfect. Under that phrase lurked a real bear trap.

Madison West 5 sprawled comfortably over essentially the same landscape dominated by its elder brother back on the Datum. But this was a place of grace and light and open spaces, with only a fraction of true Madison's population. That wasn't to deny that many of the buildings were massive. The architectural styles that had developed on the Low Easts and Wests were characterized by weight. Raw materials were dirt cheap on the virgin worlds, which meant that buildings and furnishings could often be variations on the theme of slab. Thus the town hall with its cathedral-thick walls, and roof beams laser-cut from whole trees. But there were a lot of electronics and other kinds of smartness around, lightweight and easily imported from the Datum. So you saw little pioneer log cabins with solar paint on the roofs.

But you could never forget you weren't on Earth, not on the Datum. At the perimeter of the city there was a wide system of fences and ditches, designed to keep out some of the more exotic wildlife. The migration of a herd of Columbian mammoths had once caused a rushed suburban evacuation.

In the first years after Step Day, a lot of couples like Jack and Tilda Green, with careers and kids and savings in the bank, had started looking at the new stepwise worlds with a view to buying a little extra property, a place for their kids to go play. They rapidly found that Madison West 1 was too much of a slave to the Datum, a jumble of hasty extensions to homes and office developments. At first the Greens had rented a small cabin on West 2. But the place soon came to feel like a theme park. Over-organized, too close to home. And the land already belonged to somebody else.

But then they'd discovered the project to develop Madison West 5, starting from a clean slate, high-tech, eco-friendly from the start, intended to be more than just another city. They'd both been enthused, and had invested a chunk of their savings to get in on the ground floor. Jack and Tilda had contributed a lot to the finalizing of the design, he as a software engineer working on details of the city's smarts, she as a lecturer in cultural history devising novel forms of local government and community forums. It was only unfortunate that they couldn't make enough of a living here, and they both had to cut back to the Datum to their regular jobs.

'This is our city. But it's only "nearly perfect"?' he said.

'Uh huh. We're living in a dream, but it's somebody else's dream. I want my *own* dream.'

'But our son the phobic—'

'Don't use that word.'

'Well, it's what people say, Tilda. *He* won't be able to share that dream.'

She sipped her coffee. 'We have to think about what's best for all of us. For Katie and Helen too, as well as Rod – we can't be tied down by that. It's a unique moment, Jack. Just now, under the aegis rules and the new Homestead Acts, the government is practically giving away the land in the stepwise Americas. That's a window that's not going to stay open for ever.'

Jack grunted. 'It's all ideology.' *The New Frontier*: that was the slogan, borrowed from an old John F. Kennedy election pitch. The federal government was encouraging emigration to the new worlds by Americans, and indeed by others, the sole understanding being that under the American aegis you would obey American laws, and pay American taxes: you would *be* an American. 'The federal government just wants to make sure all those stepwise versions of the US are colonized by us before somebody else moves in.'

'There's nothing wrong with that. The same sort of impulse drove the expansion west in the nineteenth century. Of course it's intellectually interesting that most Americans choose to go *West*, even though that's just an arbitrary label with no reference to geographical west. Similarly I heard that most Chinese emigrants are heading *East*...'

'Christ, the journey itself takes months. All for a chance to dump the kids in an uncivilized wilderness. And what use is a software engineer going to be out there? Or a lecturer in cultural history, come to that.'

She smiled fondly. It was infuriating; he could see she wasn't taking him remotely seriously. 'Whatever we need to know, we'll learn.' She put down her coffee and slipped her arms around him. 'I think we need to do this, Jack. It's our chance. Our generation. Our kids' chance.'

Our kids, he thought. All save poor Rod. Here was his wife, one of the most intelligent people he'd ever met, her head full of idealism about the future of America and mankind, and yet contemplating abandoning her own son. He rested his cheek on her greying hair, and wondered if he would ever understand her.

15

Dreams of the Long Earth, all across the old world. Some dreams were new, and at the same time very, very old . . .

The mates sat near the car, deep in the bush, drinking beer and pondering the changing world, and the stepping boxes they had all made that were resting on the red sand. Overhead, the central Australian sky was so full of stars that some had to wait their turn to twinkle.

After a while one of them said gloomily, 'Something clawed Jimbo's guts out, left him looking like a dugout canoe. You know that, don't you? It ain't no joke! A cop went in there too! *He* came out with his face off!'

Billy, who tended not to speak until he had thought for a while, like maybe a week, said, 'It's dreamtime stuff, mate, like it was before the ancestors came here. Don't you remember what that scientist bloke told us, one time? They dug up the bones of big, big animals all over the bloody place, as big as you like! Big, slow food, but with big, big teeth. All these new worlds under the same sky! And no people to be seen in any of them, right? Like this world before it was buggered up! Just think what we could do if we got out there!'

Somebody opposite the fire said, 'Yeah, mate, we could bugger it up all over again. And I like my head with a face on it!'

There was laughter. But Albert said, 'Know what happened? Our ancestors bloody well killed them all, ate them up. They wiped out everything except what we got now. But we don't have to do that, right? They say the world out there is just like here, except no men, no women, no policemen, no cities, no guns, just the land over and over again. The waterhole here is the waterhole there, all ready and waiting for us!'

'No, it isn't. The waterhole's half a mile over *there*.'

'Near enough, you know what I mean. Why don't we give it a go, boys?'

'Yeah, but this is *our* country. This one right here.'

Albert leaned forward, eyes sparkling. 'Yes, but you know what? *So are those others! All of them!* I heard the scientist guys talking. Every rock, every stone, all there. It's true!'

In the morning, the little group, slightly hungover, tossed coins to select the one who would give it a go.

Billy came back half an hour later, retching horribly, arriving out of nowhere. They picked him up and gave him water, and waited. He opened his eyes and said, 'It's true, but it's bloody raining over there, mates!'

They looked at one another.

Somebody said, 'Yeah, but what about all those creatures I've heard about, back in the old time? Roos with teeth! Bloody big ones! Big creatures with claws!'

There was silence. Then Albert said, 'Well, ain't we as good as our ancestors? They saw off these buggers. Why can't we?'

There was a shuffling of feet.

Finally Albert said, 'Look, tomorrow, *I'm* going over for good. Who's with me? It's all there, mates. It's all been left there waiting for us, since the beginning . . .'

By the end of the next day the songlines had begun to expand, as the never-never began to become the ever-ever. Although sometimes the blokes came back for a beer.

Later, there were towns, unfamiliar towns admittedly, and new ways of living, a mix of past and present, as old ways were seamlessly woven into new ones. The eating was good, too.

And later still, surveys showed that in the great post–Step Day migration a greater proportion of Australian Aborigines left Datum Earth for good than any other ethnic group on the planet.

16

Excerpts from the Journal of Helen Green, ~~resceptfully~~ respect-fully spellchecked by Dad, aka Mr J. Green:

> *Here is the story*
> *of how the Green family*
> *walked across the Long Earth*
> *to our new home.*

February 11, 2026. We rode on a helicopter, yay! We are going to start out from Richmond West 10, that's Richmond ~~Virgina~~ Virginia, because you have to trek from south of all the ice in the Ice Age worlds, and we went back to the Datum and we rode to Richmond on a helicopter!! But we had to say goodbye to Rod at Chicago airport and that was sad sad . . .

Jack Green had always had to do plenty of travelling in the course of his work in software, and in recent years travel had become a lot more interesting. Everybody made their long geographical trips on the Datum, with its elaborate transport networks. A Stepper would take you a thousand worlds stepwise but it wouldn't give you a foot of lateral movement. So transport had become one of the few boom elements in the Datum's slumping post-step economy. The Datum, in fact, was starting to look like the crossroads of the Long Earth.

And so you never knew who you might meet at the next rail station. Pioneer types, come back to buy a new set of bronze tools and to have their teeth fixed. High-tech hippies, trading goat cheese for mastitis cream. Once, a woman dressed like Pocahontas blissfully clutching a white wedding dress in a cellophane cover, and there was a whole short story just in her smile. People with new ways of living all jumbled up together in the Datum, at least for the duration of their journeys.

So for this last trip down to Richmond, Jack and Tilda had decided to treat the girls to a helicopter hop. In the future they would be riding in ox-drawn carts and dug-out canoes; why not let them enjoy a little high technology while they could?

Besides, it had distracted them from the distressing scene at the helipad where they had to say goodbye to Rod. Meryl, Tilda's sister, was willing to take the boy, but she didn't bother to hide her disapproval of how the family was being split up. And Rod, only thirteen years old, was blank. Jack suspected they had all been relieved when the chopper had finally lifted; he saw that small face upturned, the short-cut strawberry blond hair so like his mother's, and they were on their way, the girls shrieking with delight.

Richmond West 10 was making a living as the mustering point for treks heading for stepwise editions of the eastern United States, including Tilda's Company. Jack had had no idea what to expect.

He found himself standing in a bare earth street, in a grid pattern of houses built of heavy logs, clapboard, even lumps of sod. Hand-painted signs told him that the buildings on the main street included churches, banks, inns, hotels, stores offering food, clothing, and other essentials for the treks that began here. The Stars and Stripes fluttered from poles and rooftops, with a few Confederacy flags in amongst them. The place bustled with people, some of them clean-looking newcomers wearing bright artificial fabrics like the Greens, but most in worn-looking 'frontier' gear – much-patched jackets and trousers, even coats and cloaks of hand-cut leather. It all aped former times when Datum Richmond itself had been a trading post for furs, hides and tobacco, on the edge of an empty continent.

It was like a movie set for some old-fashioned western. Jack felt utterly out of place. He rubbed his stomach, willing away the stepping nausea.

The Prairie Marble Inn turned out to be named after what it was mostly built from – 'prairie marble', sod piled up around a wooden frame. It was gloomy, dank, but a big place, and heavily occupied. The woman behind the counter said the rest of their party was gathering in the 'ballroom', which was a barn with rough-hewn wooden furniture set out on a rag carpet. It was pretty full, with maybe a hundred people, mostly adults, a few children and infants. One man was speaking, a boisterous fellow with a spectacular mane of grey-blond hair. He was delivering some kind of lecture about the need for rotas. A few of the others turned to the new-comers, warily, some half-smiling.

Tilda smiled back. 'Most of these are people I dealt with online when we set all this up. Never met them in person before . . .'

These, Jack reflected, might be the people he would be spending the rest of his life with. Total strangers. Jack had left it all to Tilda, but he understood that it took some skill to assemble a viable Company for a trek. You had your professional captains to lead you, along with scouts, guides, porters; they were relatively easy to find and hire. But the core of the party were the people who would be settling together a hundred thousand worlds away. You needed complementary skill types: tailors, carpenters, coopers, smiths, wheelwrights, millwrights, weavers, furniture makers. Doctors, of course – a dentist if you could find one. Tilda, after being rejected by the first Companies she had approached, had retrained herself, packaging herself as a teacher and historian. Jack had gone for basic farming skills – he felt he was physically fit enough for that – and for backup medical competences.

It struck Jack, on this first glance at his new companions, that they were mostly like *him* and Tilda. A mix of ethnicities, but they all looked prosperous enough, earnest, a little anxious – middle-class types setting off into the unknown. That was the classic profile of the Long Earth pioneer, just as, according to Tilda, it had been in the Old West. The very rich wouldn't travel, for they were too comfortable back on the Datum to give it all up. And nor would the very poor, at least not in an organized party like this, for they didn't have the means to pay for the trek itself. No, it was the middle classes who were heading off into the far West, especially those distressed in difficult economic times.

The blowhard on his feet was called Reese Henry, Jack gathered, some kind of salesman, a survivalist in his spare time. He had moved on from latrine rotas. 'Once again young Americans are going out into the wild, to places where the streetlights do not shine, where there isn't a cop at the other end of a cellphone connection. Urbanized, online, civilized, pampered and preened – and now pitched back into nature in the raw.' He grinned. 'Ladies and gentlemen, welcome back to reality.'

17

RICHMOND WEST 10's only bookseller exulted with every sale he made to the would-be pioneers who passed through here. Books, printed on paper, every one of them! Dead tree technology! Information that, if carefully stored, would last for millennia! And no batteries required. It ought to be on a billboard, he thought.

If Humphrey Llewellyn III could have his way, every book ever written would be treasured, at least one copy bound in sheepskin and illuminated by monks (or specifically by naked nuns, his predilection being somewhat biased in that direction). So now, he hoped, here was a chance to bring mankind back into the book-loving fold. He gloated. There was still no electronics in the pioneer worlds, was there? Where was your internet? Hah! Where was Google? Where was your mother's old Kindle? Your iPad 25? Where was Wickedpedia? (Very primly, he always called it that, just to show his disdain; very few people noticed.) All gone, unbelievers! All those fancy toy-gadgets stuffed in drawers, screens blank as the eyes of corpses, left behind.

Books – oh yes, real books – were flying off his shelves. Out in the Long Earth humanity was starting again in the Stone Age. It needed to know the old ways. It needed to know what to eat and what not to eat. It needed to know how to build an outdoor privy, and how to manure fields with human and animal waste in safe proportions. It needed to know about wells. About shoemaking! Yes, it had to know how to find iron ore, but also how to work graphite, and how to make ink. And so Humphrey's presses ran hot, with geological maps and surveys and commonplace books and almanacs, reclaiming the knowledge that had been all but lost to the printed page.

He stroked a polished-leather volume. Oh, sooner or later all that knowledge once more would be precariously imprisoned by electricity. But for now the books had been patient long enough, and their time had come again.

In another part of Richmond West 10, meanwhile, there was a kind of labour market, where Companies tried to find recruits to fill the remaining gaps. Franklin Tallyman carefully pushed his way through the crowd, holding his sign above his head. It was a hot day and he wished he had drunk more water.

He was approached by a small party led by a middle-aged man. 'You are Mr Tallyman, the blacksmith? We saw your résumé at the Prairie Marble Inn.'

He nodded. 'Yes, sir, that's me.'

'We're looking to complete our Company.' The man stuck out a hand. 'The name's Green, Jack Green. This gentleman is Mr Batson, our Captain. Tallyman, isn't that a Caribbean name?'

'No, sir, it's a Caribbean job description, as far as I know. I could be wrong. I've never been there; I was born in Birmingham. In England, not in Alabama. The original and best.' He got back blank looks. 'So you have looked at my résumé?'

An anxious-looking woman asked, 'You really can do all you say? Make bronze? Does anyone do that these days?'

'Yes, ma'am. Back on West 1 I spent four years as apprentice to smiths who knew their stuff. As for iron, starting from scratch, all I need is the ore. I can make my own forge, I can make my own furnace, I can draw wires. By the way I'm a fair electrician; give me a waterwheel and I can fit up your colony with electricity. Oh, and weapons: I can knock up a decent musket – it couldn't compete with a modern design, but good enough for hunting.

'The engagement I'm looking for is three years.' He was warming to his pitch now. 'Under the aegis regulations I will have American citizenship by the end of the third year. You, ladies and gentlemen, will be way ahead of the curve.' He held out his notebook, opened at a page. 'And *this* is what you will pay me, please.'

There was a gasp from the would-be citizens of the New Frontier. Eventually Green said, 'Is this negotiable?'

'Only upwards, I'm afraid. You can make a deposit in Pioneer Support. Oh, if you want me to train up an apprentice then that will be extra, on account of they would be more of a hindrance than a help.'

He smiled before their doubtful faces. It wasn't the moment for a hard sell, he decided. They looked a decent bunch, just folk keen to step Westward with a group of like-minded individuals, looking for a place to spread out, a place where you could trust your neighbours, in a world where the air was clean and you could start over in search of a better future. It was the dream, it had *always* been the dream. Even their kids looked bright as buttons.

'Look, Mr Green, I've done my homework too. I've seen your Company's prospectus and I can see that a lot of thought has gone into your venture. You've got your medic, your carpenter, you've got a chemist. I like your style. Yours won't be the only offer I could get today, but you guys appear to be a solid bunch with your heads screwed on right. I'm with you if you want me. Do we have a deal?'

They had a deal.

That night Franklin packed his bags and his non-ferrous toolbox for the journey. Now all he had to do was to make sure he kept his secret for the duration of the trek, and *that* meant making sure he didn't try to step without a potato in his Stepper.

He had heard about natural steppers on the net. Then, back in West 1, just for the hell of it, one night he'd tried to step with the potato out of the box, a box without power. He was amazed when it worked. Oddly enough, he still needed the box, to throw the switch. He needed to hear the click to be able to step, it seemed; how weird was that?

Yes, he'd heard rumours about people like him. And other rumours, about beatings of such people. Like you were a freak, or unnatural. So he'd keep himself to himself on the trek, and replace the potato, and fake the nausea, and all the rest. It wasn't so hard when you got the habit.

Although you did start to wonder how many of those around you were similarly faking too.

He slept well that night, dreaming of hot forges and distant hills.

18

*D*AY THREE *(since Richmond West 10).*
    Three days already! But Captain Batson says it is going to take us a hundred days to cross the Ice Belt. And *then* we'll take months more to cross the Mine Belt, whatever *that* is. We have to get to where we're going before winter comes. And winter comes the same on all the worlds.

We're doing about a step a minute, for about six hours of every day. We take pills to stop from being sick all the time, but it's still an effort. They try to lead us to places where the ground level doesn't change much from world to world. It's a jolt if you drop down, and you can't step at all if your ankles would be five inches underground. But it's quite a sight to see two hundred people with all their packs and stuff twinkling out of sight, and then twinkling back in the next world, over and over.

I miss being online.

I miss my phone!!!

I miss school. Or some of the people in it, anyway. Not some others.

I MISS ROD. Even though he could be a weirdo.

I miss being a cheerleader.

Dad says I should say some of what I like too. Otherwise this journal won't be a fun read for his grandchildren. Grandchildren!? He should be so lucky.

Day Five.
    I like camping!

We used to do some of that in West 5, and we did it in pioneer studies, but it's a lot more fun out here.

After a couple of days we palled up with a family called the Doaks. They have four kids, two boys and two girls, and we arranged it so I'm in with the two girls, they are called Betty and Marge, and it's like a sleepover every night!

I can build a fire! I have a lens to start the flames, and I know about tinder and kindling and what wood burns best. I can find stuff to eat, weeds, roots, mushrooms. I know about hazelnuts and fruit and stuff too but it's not the season. I can make a fishing line out of old thread or even nettle stalks. I know where to look for the fish. Cool.

Today Mr Henry showed us how to make a trout trap in the river. You make a sort of walled pool, and they swim in, and get stuck. Mr Henry grins when he clubs the fish. I felt like crying. Mr Henry says The Youngsters Have To Learn.

Marge Doak used to be a cheerleader! We practise routines.

Day Eight.

Yesterday we hit an ice sheaf.

We're following a trail. There are markers and everything, and little cairns, and posts that tell you what number world you're on like highway signs, and sometimes caches of stuff. Even little boxes you can put post in to be carried East or West, depending who passes.

So we came to a sign that said ICE NEXT. We passed through a few Ice Age worlds in the first day or two, but just one at a time, and you could just rush quickly through them. Now we were coming to a band of them. We all had to stop, and the porters came and handed out the Arctic coats and trousers and ski masks and stuff. The next morning Captain Batson had us all tie up in groups of eight or ten with ropes, and made sure the babies were snug in their little papooses, with no fingers or toes sticking out.

We stepped, and it was dazzling, no clouds in a bright blue sky, and not much ice, but the ground was frozen hard as rock under my feet. And then the cold got to me, like little needles working into my cheeks.

And we stepped on, again and again. More winter worlds. Sometimes you'd come out into a white-out, or a blizzard. And other times you would come out and it would be a bit warmer, and then the ground was boggy so we left tracks if we walked, and there were these strange dwarf trees, all bent over. And midges! I saw a huge deer, with antlers like a chandelier (spelled out by Dad). Ben Doak says he saw a woolly mammoth, but nobody believes anything he says.

This is why we had to come so far south, to Richmond, to walk West. Because Datum Earth is in the middle of the Ice Belt, a bunch of worlds where they have Ice Ages, so you have to go south of the ice to where it's possible to step. But even away from the ice caps the whole world is affected by the cold.

Some people turned back after the first night in the cold. Said they hadn't been told about *that*, although they clearly had been, and should have listened.

Day Twenty-Five.

At night you have to cram into these little tents. It's a bit close. These are strangers after all. Marge Doak is OK, but Betty has this way of picking her teeth. And she snores.

Mom got in a fight with Mr Henry, who says the women should do all the cooking and cleaning! Captain Batson says Mr Henry's not in charge. He didn't say it to his face though, Dad says.

Trouble and strife, lah di dah!

Day Forty-Three.

I keep forgetting to write things down. I get too tired. Plus there's too much going on.

In the middle of the ice worlds you get milder types that are like home, 'interglacial' worlds (spelled by Dad). The interglacial worlds are just FULL of animals. I saw huge herds that turned out to be horses and funny-looking cows and antelopes and camels. Camels! Dad says these are like animals that were probably around in America before humans came along. Wolves. Coyotes. Elk. Curlews. Bears! Grizzlies in the forest clumps, Captain Batson says, so we keep out of there. Snakes everywhere, you have to watch out for them. Crows, ravens, turkey buzzards, owls. By day you hear the birds, and at night the frogs croaking and the mosquitoes whining, if you're anywhere near water. Sometimes the men hunt. Rabbit and duck and even antelope.

There are armadillos! Big ones, not like in zoos. Dad says they might have wandered up from South America where they evolved. Apparently people have seen apes, in America. Sometimes the continents join up and these animals cross over, and sometimes they don't. Nobody really knows. Nobody has a map of any of these worlds.

In some worlds we can't find any trees at all. Then we have to collect 'buffalo chips' for the fire. *Dung!!* It burns well, but you can imagine the smell, my dear.

And there are funny worlds, where everything is like ash, or like a desert, or something. Just one world thick. There are usually signposts if it's dangerous, and we have to put on hats or cover our mouths with filters. Captain Batson calls these worlds Jokers.

Sometimes you see where people have been before. Scruffy places, the ruins of shacks, burned-out tepees. Even crosses, stuck in the ground. In the Long Earth, hoping for the best isn't good enough, as Mr Batson puts it.

Day Sixty-Seven.

Ben Doak got sick. He drank from a waterhole that hadn't been checked out. They get polluted by buffalo piddle. He got pumped full of antibiotics. I hope he's OK. We've had a few people get sick, but nobody died.

More people have turned back. Captain Batson tries to talk them round, and Mr Henry laughs at them and calls them weak. I don't think it's weak to admit you made a mistake. That takes strength, if you ask me.

We must look very strange, to these animals who live here, and have never seen a human before, probably. What business have we got coming through here and messing everything up?

Day One Hundred and Two.

We're out of the Ice Belt! And only two days behind schedule!

Strange to think we've travelled across thirty-six thousand worlds, but the distance we've covered sideways has only been a few miles. Well, we're going to travel in earnest across this particular Earth, and go a few hundred miles north, to New York State. Then we'll step on across another sixty thousand worlds or so until we get to the place we're going to settle.

I thought we'd have to walk. No! There's a regular town here, well, a small one, a trading post. Here we can trade in our Ice Belt gear for stuff that's more suitable for the Mine Belt worlds.

And there's a wagon train waiting for us! With big covered wagons that Dad says are Conestogas. They look like boats on wheels, drawn by horses – funny-looking horses, but definitely horses. There's a foundry here to make the iron they need, and the wagons have got tires on their wheels, like car tires. When we saw the wagons we just whooped and hollered and ran! Conestogas! I wonder if it will be more fun than the chopper ride?

Day One Hundred and Ninety-Nine.

We are on Earth West Seventy Thousand Plus Change, as Dad would say. I'm writing in the early morning, before we break camp. Last night the adults stayed up late arguing about the chores. But when they're all gassing in their Group Meetings, we kids can slip away, just for a while.

Not that we do anything bad. Well, not mostly. Mostly, we

(Pause for thought. Search for word.)

watch. That's it. We watch. I know Dad frets that we're all turning into zombies because there's nothing to do out here but chores, and the schooling they try to force on us. But it's not like that. We just watch, with nothing to distract us. That's why we're quiet. Not because our brains are mush. Because we watch.

And we see things the adults don't see.

Some *very* odd animals and plants that don't fit any storybook of evolution I ever read.

The Joker Worlds, in the middle of these boring, arid Mine Belt worlds. The adults think they're mostly dead. They aren't. Believe me.

And the Greys.

We call them that, even though they're orange. They look like hairy little kids, but if you ever see one up close, and see the equipment in those orange crotches, believe me, they ain't kids. And big eyes, like cartoon aliens. They flicker around the camp. There, gone. Stepping, obviously.

Animals that step!

The Long Earth is stranger than anybody thinks. Even Dad. Even Captain Batson. Even Mr Henry.

Especially Mr Henry.

Day Two Hundred and Eighty-One.

Is it November? Dad will know.

We made it!

We made it to Earth West 100,000! – or, Good Old Hundred K, as us hardened pioneer types call it. The start of the Corn Belt.

Good Old Hundred K has a *gift shop*. You can buy T-shirts and mugs. 'I Stepped All The Way to Good Old Hundred K.' But the labels say Made in China!

The worlds had been changing for a bit. Greener. Damper. A different set of animals. And, most important, *trees*. Trees, wood, that's what you need above all else to build a colony and a town and all the rest of it. Which is why we've had to walk so far. Not enough trees in the Mine Belt. Here there is prairie and rainfall and trees: good farming country. Nobody knows how deep the Corn Belt is. Plenty of room out here, and it's hard to see how it could be filled up any time soon.

Anyhow, now we're here. And to prove the point they have a couple of fields out back of the shop where there's corn stubble and sheep grazing, just like home. Sheep! Dad said they were descended from little lambs that had to be carried out here from the Datum in the arms of stepping people, because there's no native sheep in North America, on any of the worlds that any-body's found.

At the shop they made a fuss of us kids. They had beer and lemonade, homemade stuff with pips in that was the most delicious drink I ever had. They asked us questions about what's going on back East on the Datum and the Low Earths. We yapped and bragged, and we told our own story, of our trek. Every year it's a little bit different, apparently.

An English woman who introduced herself as Hermione Dawes wrote down our story in a sort of big ledger, in a little library place full of records like that. Ms Dawes told Mom her place in life was writing things down, and she was happy to be out here, to have some real history to record. She'll probably be there for ever, writing stuff down as folk pass her by. People are strange, but if she's happy that's fine by me. Apparently she's married to a cowgirl.

We shopped! What a luxury.

And meanwhile the adults had to go register their claims. There is a US government official, rotated out once every few years, here to check and validate the land grants we bought back on the Datum before we set off. We all compared claim forms to work out where to go. In the event the adults picked a world at random: number West 101,753. A week's easy stroll. We formed up, the Doaks and Harry Bergreen and his fiddle, yay, and Melissa Harris, well, OK, and Reese Henry, the less said the better. A hundred in all.

And we set off. We stepped and camped with a discipline that would have made Captain Batson proud. Though Mrs Harris still didn't take her turns with the laundry.

A week later, when we got to 101,753, it was raining. So we all looked at each other, and held hands in our groups, and took another step into the sunshine.

And that was how we chose one whole world over another. Because it happened to be sunny when we got there! There might have been diamond mountains in Australia back in 753 and we'd never know. It didn't matter. Earth West 101,754: *our* Earth. We're there!

19

THAT FIRST AFTERNOON of flight, the *Mark Twain* stepped again and again, each transition causing a thrill to travel down Joshua's spine. The stepping rate was increasing, slowly, as Lobsang explored the capabilities of his ship. Joshua could count the passing worlds using little monitors Lobsang called earthometers, embedded in the walls of every cabin. They had enough digits, he saw, to allow them to count up to the millions.

And as it stepped, the airship was travelling laterally too, heading west across Eurasia. The monitors had a little map display so Joshua could follow its course; their position was derived from star sightings, but the layout of the landscapes they crossed on these unexplored worlds was based on guesswork.

On the observation deck, sitting opposite Joshua, Lobsang smiled his plastic smile. They both cradled coffees – Lobsang sipped his too, and Joshua imagined some tank in his belly filling up.

'How's the ride?' Lobsang asked.

'Fine so far.' In fact it was better than fine. As always when Joshua left the Datum behind, the oppressive sense of enclosure he invariably experienced there dissipated quickly: a pressure he'd not really been aware of when he was growing up, not until it wasn't there any more. The pressure of a world too full of other minds, he suspected, other human consciousnesses. It seemed to be a fine sensitivity; even on remote stepwise worlds he always registered it if somebody else showed up, anywhere near by, even a small party. But he'd discussed this strange quasi-telepathic facility, or disability, with nobody – bar Sister Agnes – not even Officer Jansson, and he didn't choose to talk it over with Lobsang now. Still, the sensation of freedom, of release, was there. That, and his peculiar awareness of the Silence, as of a mind far away, dimly sensed, like the toll of a huge and ancient bell in a far-off mountain range . . . Or rather he did sense this when Lobsang wasn't talking, as he was now.

'We will follow the line of latitude west, roughly. We can manage thirty miles an hour easily. A nice leisurely pace; we are out here to explore. That should bring us over the footprint of the continental US in a few weeks . . .'

Lobsang's face was not quite real, Joshua thought, like a slightly off CGI simulation. But here in this fantastic vessel, in this realization of Lobsang's astonishing dreams, Joshua was oddly warming to him.

'You know, Lobsang, I caught up with your story when I went back to the Home, after my interview at transEarth. People were saying that the smartest thing that any supercomputer could do the moment it was switched on would be to make certain that it couldn't be switched off again. And that the story about the reincarnated Tibetan was a front, precisely so you couldn't be switched off. We all talked about that, and Sister Agnes said, well, if a computer has a desire not to be switched off then it has to have a sense of self, and that means a soul. I know the Pope decreed otherwise later on, but I back Sister Agnes against the Vatican any time.'

Lobsang thought that over. 'I look forward to meeting Sister Agnes someday. I hear what you are saying. Thank you, Joshua.'

Joshua hesitated. 'While you're thanking me, maybe you could answer a question. Is this *you*, Lobsang? Or are *you* back on the Datum, in some store at MIT? Is that a meaningful question?'

'Oh, certainly it is meaningful. Joshua, back on the Datum I am distributed across many memory stores and processor banks.

That's partly for security, and partly for efficiency and effectiveness of data retrieval and processing. If I wished I could consider my *self* to be distributed among a number of centres, of foci of consciousness.

'But I am human, I am Lobsang. I remember how it was to look out of a cave of bone, from a single apparent locus of conscious- ness. And that is how I have maintained it. There is only one me, Joshua, only one Lobsang, though I have backup memory stores scattered over several worlds. And that "me" is with you on this journey. I am fully dedicated to the mission. And by the way, when I inhabit the ambulant unit, that too, for the duration, is "me", though there remains enough of "me" outside that shell to enable the airship to fly. If I were to fail or were lost then a backup copy on Datum Earth would be initiated, and synched with whatever you were able to retrieve of my memory stores on the ship. But that would be another Lobsang; he would remember me, but he would not *be* me . . . I hope that's clear.'

Joshua thought that over. 'I'm glad I'm just a standard-issue human.'

'Well, more or less, in your case,' Lobsang said dryly. 'Inciden- tally, now that we're under way, be sure that my report on the congressional expedition slaughter is already with the authorities. And, to be on the safe side, with such newspapers as I find trust- worthy. Including the *Fortean Times*, a boon to all researchers of the Long Earth phenomenon. You can access back issues on the screen in your stateroom . . . It's done. A deal's a deal.'

'Thank you, Lobsang.'

'So here we are – on our way! By the way, don't be alarmed if the coffee percolator talks to you; it's a beta-test AI from one of our associates. Oh, and do you have a thing about cats?'

'They make me sneeze.'

'Shi-mi won't.'

'Shi-mi?'

'Another first for transEarth. You've seen the size of this

gondola; it is lousy with hard-to-get-to spaces, and vermin may be a problem for us. It wouldn't be hard for them to scramble up our anchor cables when we land. The last thing we want is a rat nibbling on a wire. So, meet Shi-mi. Come, kitty kitty . . .'

A cat walked on to the deck. It was supple, silent, almost convincing. But there was an LED spark in each green eye.

'I can tell you that she—'

'She, Lobsang?'

'She can, on demand, make a pleasant purring noise designed to be optimally soothing to the human ear. She can track mice via infra red, and has excellent hearing. She will stun her prey with a low current, swallow it into a designated stomach with a small food and water dispenser, and then will carefully transfer the catch to a small holding vivarium, where the mouse can live happily until it can be relocated somewhere safe.'

'That's going to a lot of trouble for a mouse.'

'That is the Buddhist way. This prototype is clean and hygienic, will not harm her prey and, in general, will do most of the things you would expect of a domestic cat, except for shitting in your stereo headphones – a common complaint I'm told. Oh, in the default setting she will sleep on your bed.'

'A robot cat, on a robot ship?'

'There are advantages. She has a gel brain, just like my own ambulant, and is a whole lot smarter than the average cat. And synthetic hair. No sneezes, I promise—'

Suddenly the stepping stopped, and Joshua felt an odd lurch, like being thrown forward. The deck was flooded with light. Joshua glanced through the windows. They were evidently in a world that happened to be sunny. Sunny, but cloaked in ice.

'Why have we stopped?'

'Look down. There are binoculars in the lockers.'

A tiny multicoloured dot in the whiteness resolved into a Day Glo orange domed tent, and a couple of people moving stiffly around, made Doughboy-sexless by the thick Arctic gear they wore. A portable drilling rig had been set up on the ice, and a Stars and Stripes hung limply on a pole.

'Scientists?'

'A university party, from Rhode Island. Studying the biota, taking ice cores and such. I'm recording all traces of human presence I find, naturally. I was expecting these gentlemen, though they have travelled a few worlds further than the nominal target they logged.'

'But you found them even so.'

'My view is godlike, Joshua.'

Joshua, peering down, wasn't sure if the college guys had even noticed the airship, a whale suddenly hovering in the air above them. 'Are we going down?'

'That would serve no purpose. Though we could talk to them without landing. We carry a range of communications gear, from medium- and short-wave radios that ought to let us transmit to and receive from anywhere on an individual world, to – well, simpler means. A heliograph, Navy issue. Even a loudspeaker.'

'A loudspeaker! Lobsang, booming from above like Yahweh.'

'The equipment is merely practical, Joshua. Not every action carries symbolic freight.'

'Every human action does. And you are human, aren't you, Lobsang?'

Lobsang resumed the stepping without warning, another gentle lurch. The science camp winked into non-existence, and more worlds strobed past.

After his first night on the airship Joshua awoke feeling full of diamonds. The ship stepped steadily, the sound of its various mechanisms like the purring of a cat. In fact, he found the purring *was* the cat, curled up on his legs; when he stirred she elegantly rose, stretched, and loped away.

Prompted by the rumbling of his stomach, Joshua investigated the galley.

These days a decent meal out in the stepwise worlds was pretty easy to obtain, for him; the pioneering steppers kind of liked to see him around, they knew his name and reputation, and treated him as if he were a lucky mascot. And a meal was always his for the asking from any of the halfway houses, the travellers' lodges that were springing up across the nearer Earths. But it didn't pay to be a scrounger, Sister Agnes had always said, and so he always took a fresh-killed deer along, or some wild fowl. The greener pioneers liked their meat fresh but had as yet not come to terms with the idea of chopping up Bambi, so Joshua would spend a little time field-dressing his catch. He'd generally come away with maybe a couple of bags of flour and a basket of eggs, as long as he had a basket to carry them away in.

Well, the airship's galley was rather more luxuriously appointed than any halfway house. There was a freezer with a sufficiency of bacon and eggs, and a dry cabinet stacked with sacks of salt and pepper. Joshua was impressed with this: on many worlds a handful of salt would buy you dinner and a night's shelter, and the pepper was even more valuable. Joshua got to work on the bacon.

The voice of Lobsang startled him. 'Good morning, Joshua. I trust you slept well?'

Joshua flipped his bacon and said, 'I don't even remember dreaming. It's as if we weren't moving. Where are we now?'

'We are more than fifteen thousand steps from home. I have slowed the stepping for your comfort while you eat, and have steadied us at three thousand feet, occasionally going lower if the sensors find anything interesting. In many of the local worlds this morning it's a sunny day with a bit of dew on the grasses below, so I suggest you finish your breakfast and come down to the observation deck and enjoy the view. By the way, there are sacks of muesli in the larder; Sister Agnes would, I'm sure, want you to keep your bowel movements regular.'

Joshua glared at the empty air, given the lack of anyone to glare at, and said, 'Sister Agnes isn't here.' Even so, guiltily, bearing in mind that nuns somehow knew what you were up to wherever you were, he rummaged in the larder and munched his way through dried fruit and nuts, with a side order of watermelon.

Before he went back to his bacon.

And made himself a fried slice to mop up the bacon fat. After all, it was chilly up here; he needed the fuel.

Prompted by that thought, he went back to his stateroom. In its roomy closet, alongside the cold-weather gear he'd worn on arrival, he found a range of intermediate clothing, some of it in various camouflage patterns. Lobsang was thinking of everything, that was clear enough. He selected a parka and went down to the observation deck, and sat alone, watching Earths go by like a slideshow of the gods.

Without warning, the ship crossed a sheaf of ice worlds.

The light hit Joshua: dazzling, blinding sunlight reflecting from the ice and filling the air, as if the whole deck had suddenly turned into a flashbulb, with Joshua an insect trapped inside. The worlds below were plains of ice, gently folded, with only an occasional ridge of high ground showing as a dark bony stripe through the ice cover. And then into cloud, then hail, then sunlight again, depending on the local climate in each passing world. The flickering light was painful on the eye. From Earth to Earth the level of the ice cover rose and fell, he saw, like some tremendous tide. In each world the great ice sheet covering Eurasia must be pulsing, ice domes shifting, the southern edge rippling back and forth century by century; he was passing over snapshots of that tremendous continental flux.

And when the ice band had passed and they were sailing over interglacial worlds, mostly he saw tree tops. The Long Earth was big on tree tops, Earth after Earth, tree after tree.

Joshua seldom got bored. But as the morning wore on he was surprised to find himself growing bored now, so quickly. After all he was looking over thousands of landscapes no one, probably, had ever seen before. He remembered Sister Georgina, who liked her Keats:

> *Then felt I . . .*
> *. . . like stout Cortés when with eagle eyes*
> *He star'd at the Pacific – and all his men*
> *Look'd at each other with a wild surmise –*
> *Silent, upon a peak in Darien.*

At the time he'd thought a wild surmise was some kind of exotic bird. Well, he was now looking out over the new worlds with somewhat of a tame surmise.

There were footsteps behind him. Lobsang's ambulant unit appeared. He was dressed for the occasion in safari shirt and trousers. And how quickly, Joshua reflected, Lobsang had become a *he* and not an *it.*

'It can be disorienting, can't it? I recall my reactions to my own pioneer flight. The Long Earth goes on and on, Joshua. A surfeit of wonders will dull the mind.'

At random they paused at a world somewhere around twenty thousand. The sky here was overcast, threatening rain. Without the sunlight the rolling grassland below was a dull grey-green, with scattered clumps of darker forest. On this particular world Joshua could see no sign of mankind, not so much as a thread of smoke. Yet there was movement. To the north he saw a huge herd drifting over the landscape. Horses? Bison? Camels, even? Or something more exotic? And by the shore of a lake below he made out more groups of animals, a black fringe by the water.

Now they had stopped, the *Mark Twain*'s systems went to work. Hatches on the gondola and on top of the envelope opened to release balloons, and buoys which fluttered to the ground under parachutes, each marked with the transEarth logo and the Stars and Stripes. There were even small sounding-rockets that flew up with a hiss, creating streaky smoke columns in the air.

'This will be our regular routine when we stop to sample an Earth,' Lobsang said. 'A way for me to extend my study of any particular world beyond this single viewpoint. I will gather some data now, and data from ongoing observations will be downloaded from the probes when we return through this world, or when another craft passes this way in the future.'

Among the creatures by the lake below were some kind of rhino, giant beasts with oddly slender legs. They clustered at the water's edge, shoving each other aside as they tried to get a drink.

Lobsang said, 'You'll find binoculars and cameras throughout the observation deck. Those animals look something like an elasmotherium, perhaps. Or a much-evolved descendant.'

'That means nothing to me, Lobsang.'

'Of course not. You want a species of your own? Name them if you like; I'm recording everything we see, hear, say and do, and will lodge the claims when we get home.'

Joshua sat back. 'Let's go on. We're wasting time.'

'Time? We've all the time in the worlds. However—'

The stepping began again, and the rhino-like herd disappeared. Joshua felt the ride now as a gentle jolting, like a car with good suspension travelling over a rutted road.

He figured they were now crossing an Earth every couple of seconds, over forty thousand new worlds a day, if they kept this up around the clock (which they wouldn't). Joshua was impressed, but he wasn't about to say so. Landscapes swept beneath the prow of the ship, only their broadest features possible for him to discern, whole worlds passing to the beat of his own pulse. Animal herds and lone beasts were no sooner glimpsed than they were gone, whisked into the unreality of stepwise otherness. Even the tree clumps shifted in shape and size from world to world, shift, shift, shift. And there were flickers – plunges into brief darkness, occasional flares of light, washes of odd colours across the land-scape. Exceptional worlds of some kind, pulled from his sight before they could be comprehended. Otherwise there was only the chain of worlds, Earth after Earth smoothed to uniformity by the ship's motion.

'Joshua, do you ever wonder where you are?'

'I know where I am. I'm here.'

'Yes, but where is *here*? Every few seconds you enter a different stepwise world. So *where* is this world in relation to the Datum? And the next, and the next? How can there be room for them all?'

Actually Joshua had wondered about that. It was impossible to be a stepper without asking such questions. 'I know Willis Linsay left a note: "The next world is the thickness of a thought away."'

'Unfortunately that was about the only comprehensible thing he did write down. Apart from that we're floundering. So where is *this* world, this particular Earth? It's in exactly the same space and time as Datum Earth. It's like another mode of vibration of a single guitar string. The only difference is that now we can visit it; we couldn't even detect it before. That's pretty much the best answer transEarth's tame physicists can supply.'

'Is all this science stuff in Linsay's notes?'

'We don't know. He seems to have invented his own mathematics. We have Warwick University working on that. But he also compressed everything he wrote into a fantastically arcane code. IBM won't even quote on untangling *that*. Also his handwriting's appalling.'

He kept talking, but Joshua managed to tune him out. It was a skill, he suspected, he was going to have to develop.

Music filled the deck, the cold notes of a harpsichord.

'Would you mind shutting that off?'

'It's Bach,' Lobsang said. 'A fugue. A clichéd choice for an entity of mathematics such as myself, I know.'

'I prefer silence.'

'Of course you do.' The music died. 'It will not offend you if I continue to listen, in my head, as it were?'

'Do what you like.' Joshua stared at the latest landscape blankly. And the next, and the next.

He rolled off his couch and tried out the deck's can. It was a chemical toilet with a narrow bay for a shower, inside a plastic-walled compartment. Joshua wondered if Lobsang had eyes in here too. Well, of course he did.

Thus the day wore away. At last it grew dark on all the Earths, the myriad suns sinking to their respective horizons.

'Do I have to go up to my stateroom to sleep?'

'Your couch will fold out. Pull the lever to your right. There are blankets and pillows in the trunk.'

Joshua tried it out. The couch was like a first-class airliner seat. 'Wake me if anything interesting happens.'

'It's all interesting, Joshua. Sleep now.'

As he settled under a comfortingly heavy throw, Joshua listened to the thrum of the engines, and felt the slight, vertiginous tug of the stepping. For Joshua Valienté, to rock between worlds was almost soothing. He slept easily.

When he woke, the airship had stopped again.

20

THE SHIP HAD descended near a clump of heaped-up rock, into which Lobsang had thrown out an anchor. It was early in the day, the sky a deep blue littered with scattered cloud. But this was a typical Ice Belt world, and snowfields dazzled, though a little way away was a scrap of open water.

Joshua refused to even look out of the window until he had used the coffee spigot.

'Welcome to West 33157, Joshua. We've been stationary since before dawn. I've been waiting for you to wake up.'

'I take it you found something interesting.'

'Look down.'

On the outcrop to which they were anchored, black rock protruding through the snow, stood a natural monument: a lonesome pine, big, elderly and isolated. But the tree had been neatly cut down close to the root, the tangled branches and the upper trunk lying discarded on the ground, and a pale disc of core wood exposed to the air. An axe had evidently been used.

'I thought you might be drawn to that sign of humanity. And, Joshua, the second reason: it's time to try out my backup ambulatory unit.'

Joshua glanced around the gondola. 'Which is?'

'You.'

A trunk held the gear. On his chest he was to wear a lightweight pack which contained a facemask and an emergency oxygen supply, a first-aid kit, a flashlight, a gun of some non-ferric metal, a length of very fine rope, other items. On his back would go a canvas pack containing an enigmatic module in a hard, robust, sealed case. He would wear an old-fashioned-looking bluetooth-type earpiece to talk to Lobsang, but he suspected the gear contained other speakers and microphones.

He went back to his stateroom, returned in his bulky Pillsbury gear, and hauled on the backpack. 'This damn thing's heavy.'

'You'll wear it at all times outside the ship.'

'And inside the sealed module in the backpack is?'

'Me,' Lobsang said shortly. 'Or a remote unit. Call it a backup. As long as the airship survives, the pack will stay synched with the main processors aboard. If the airship is lost the pack will host my memory until you can get home.'

Joshua laughed. 'You've wasted your money, Lobsang. In what circumstances do you imagine this will be useful? Far enough out, if the airship is lost, neither of us is going home.'

'It never hurts to plan for all conceivable contingencies. You are my ultimate failsafe, Joshua. That's why you're here. Anyhow your kit isn't complete yet.'

Joshua looked into the trunk again, and pulled out another gadget. It was a framework bristling with lenses, microphones, other sensors, sitting atop a shoulder unit. 'You have got to be kidding me.'

'It's lighter than it looks. The sensor bus should strap securely on your shoulder, and there's a data feed that plugs into the backpack—'

'You're expecting me to explore Earth Million with this *parrot* on my shoulder?'

Lobsang sounded offended. 'Parrot it is, if you must . . . I didn't expect vanity from you, Joshua. Who's going to see you? Besides, it's very practical. I'll see what you see, hear what you hear; we'll be in constant touch. And if you have trouble—'

'What will it do, lay an egg?'

'Just wear it, please, Joshua.'

It fitted snugly on Joshua's right shoulder, and was as light-weight as Lobsang had promised. But Joshua knew he was never going to be able to forget the thing was there, that Lobsang was literally at his shoulder with every breath. The hell with it. He hadn't expected this trip to be a joyride anyhow, and the parrot hardly made it any worse. Besides, the thing would probably break down soon enough.

Without further conversation Joshua went down to an access deck, pulled the door open against the cabin's slight overpressure – the air pressure was kept high to ensure no external atmosphere could enter the ship until Lobsang had tested it for safety – and stepped into a small elevator cage. A winch lowered him smoothly to the ground, beside the rocky outcrop.

Once on the ground, knee deep in snow, he took a deep breath of the air of this cold Earth, and turned slowly around. The sky had clouded over now, and there was a translucent quality to the air: snow threatening. 'I take it you're seeing this. Standard-issue snowfield.'

Lobsang whispered in his ear. 'I see it. You know, the parrot has nose filters which would enable me to smell—'

'Forget it.' Joshua took a few paces, turned and surveyed the airship. 'Can you see this? Just giving you a chance to check for wear and tear.'

'Good thinking,' murmured the parrot.

Joshua knelt beside the tree. 'There are little flags, marking the trunk rings.' He plucked one, and picked out the lettering. 'University of Krakow. Scientists did this. What's the point?'

'For climate records from the tree rings, Joshua. Just like on the Datum. Interestingly, such records suggest the split between neighbouring worlds is usually around fifty years deep. Within the lifetime of your average pine tree. Of course that raises a lot of questions.'

Joshua heard a rumble, a splashing sound, a kind of shrill trumpet. He turned slowly; evidently he wasn't alone on this world. A short distance inland he glimpsed a scene of predator and prey: a cat-like creature with fangs so heavy it could barely lift its head, it seemed, was tracking a waddling beast with a hide like a tank. These were the first animals he had seen on this world.

Lobsang saw what he saw. 'The over-armed in pursuit of the over-armoured: the result of an evolutionary arms race. And one that has played out on Datum Earth many times, in various contexts, until both parties succumbed to extinction, all the way back to the dinosaur age and beyond. A universal, it seems. As on the Datum, so on the Long Earth. Joshua, go around the rocky outcrop. You'll come to the open water.'

Joshua turned and walked easily around the outcrop. The snow was deep, heavy to push through, but it felt good to stretch his legs after so many hours in the gondola.

The expanse of the lake opened up before him. On the lake itself ice lay in a sheet, but there was open water close to the shore, and here there was movement, massive, graceful: elephants, a family of them, furry adults with calves between their towering legs. Some of them were wading out into the shallow water. The adults had extraordinary shovel-shaped tusks that they used to scoop at the lake bed, muddying the water for yards around. In a crystalline sparkle of spray a mother played with a calf. Fresh snow started to fall now, big heavy flakes that settled on the fur of the oblivious elephantids.

'Gompotheres,' Lobsang murmured. 'Or relatives, or descendants. I'd keep away from the water. I suspect there are crocodiles.'

Joshua felt oddly moved by the scene; there was a sense of calm about these massive creatures. 'This is what you brought us down to see?'

'No. Although these worlds are full of elephant types. A plethora of pachyderms. I wouldn't normally have brought them to your attention. But they are a high-order prey species, and it appears that they are being tracked. And, interestingly, so are you.'

Joshua stood quite still. 'Thank you for sharing.' He looked around, peering through the thickening snow, but saw nothing else moving. 'Just tell me when to run, OK? I don't mind if you say *right now . . .*'

'Joshua, the creatures moving cautiously towards you are holding a conversation about you, though I doubt very much if you can hear it because it is very high pitched. Your fillings might tingle.'

'I have no fillings. I always brushed my teeth properly.'

'Of course you did. The communication is also quite complex, and becoming more rapid, as if some kind of conclusion is being reached as to what they're going to do. It comes and goes because they are constantly stepping. This is almost too fast to see – too fast for *you* to see. From this behaviour I can deduce that they have a very ingenious method of triangulating the point at which all of their major hunters will surround the victim, which is to say, *you—*'

'Hold on. Rewind. You said they are *stepping*? Stepping animals, stepping predators?' The world pivoted around Joshua. 'Well, that's new.'

'Indeed.'

'These creatures are the reason you stopped here, aren't they?'

'By the way, I see no need for you to be afraid.'

'*You* see no reason for *me* to be afraid?'

'Well, they appear to be inquisitive creatures. As opposed to hungry creatures. Possibly more frightened of you than you currently are of them.'

'How much do you want to bet? My life, for instance?'

'Let's see how this plays out. Joshua, wave your hands in the air, please. That's good. Let them see you. The snow is reducing visibility, obviously. Now shuffle round in a circle. That's right, just stand there until I say otherwise. Don't worry. I'm in control of the situation.'

This reassurance meant nothing to Joshua. He kept as still as he could. The snow was coming down hard now. If he panicked he might inadvertently step, and he would step into . . . what? Given the presence of stepping predatory animals he might land in some even worse situation.

Lobsang murmured in his ear, apparently aware of his tension, trying to calm him. 'Joshua, just remember that I built the *Mark Twain*. And it, which is to say of course *I*, watches over *you* at all times. Anything that I perceive is attempting to do harm to you will be dead before it knows it. I am of course a pacifist, but the *Mark Twain* carries weapons of many types, from the invisibly small to the invisibly large. I will not mention the word nuclear, of course.'

'No. Really don't mention nuclear.'

'Then we are of one accord. This being so, would you now please sing a song?'

'A song? What song?'

'*Any* song! Choose a song and sing. Something jaunty . . . *just sing the song!*'

Lobsang's command, while wholly insane, had the authority of Sister Agnes's voice at the extreme limit of her patience, when even the cockroaches knew to get out of town. So Joshua launched into the first song that came to mind: 'Hail to the Chief, he's the chief and we must hail him. *Hail to the Chief, he is the one we have to hail . . .*'

When he finished, there was silence on the snowfield.

Lobsang said, 'Interesting choice. Another legacy of those nuns of yours, no doubt. Spirited when it comes to political debate, are they? Well, that should do it. Now we wait. *Please do not move.*'

Joshua waited. And just as he opened his mouth to declare that enough was enough, there were dark figures all around him. They were jet black, holes in the snow, with wide chests, big heads and enormous paws, or rather hands, which thankfully did not seem to have claws; they were hands that looked more like boxing gloves, or maybe catcher's mitts.

And they were singing, with big pink mouths opening and shutting with every sign of enjoyment. But this wasn't the political silliness that Joshua had sung, and nor was it some animal howl. It was *human*, and he could understand all the words as they were repeated again and again, with the singers chiming in with different harmonies and repetitions, multi-part chords hanging in the air like Christmas decorations. It went on for minutes, the avenues and trajectories of this wild music, until it gradually converged into one great warm silence.

And the main refrain had gone like this: *'Wotcher!' all the neighbours cried, 'Oo yer gonna meet, Bill? 'Ave yer bought the street, Bill?' Laugh? – I fort I should've died. Knocked 'em in the Old Kent Road . . .*

Astonished, Joshua could barely breathe. 'Lobsang—'

'Interesting song choice. Written by one Albert Chevalier, a native of Notting Hill, London. Curiously enough it was later recorded by Shirley Temple.'

'Shirley Temple . . . Lobsang, I'm guessing there's a good reason why these Mighty Joes in the blizzard are singing old comedy songs from England.'

'Oh, certainly.'

'And I'm also guessing you know what that good reason is.'

'I've a fair idea, Joshua. All in good time.'

Now one of the creatures walked right up to him, with tennis-racket-sized hands cupped as if cradling something. Its mouth was open, and it was still panting with the energy of the singing; there were a lot of teeth in there, but the general expression was a smile.

'Fascinating,' Lobsang breathed. 'A primate, certainly, surely some species of ape. As convincingly upright as any hominid, but that doesn't necessarily imply a correlation with human evolution—'

'It's not the time for a lecture, Lobsang,' Joshua murmured.

'Of course you're right. We must play out the moment. Take the gift.'

Joshua cautiously took a step forward and held out his own hands. The creature seemed excited, like a child who'd been given an important job to do and wanted to make certain that it was done exactly right. It dropped something moderately heavy into Joshua's hands. Joshua looked down. He was holding what looked like a large salmon, beautiful and iridescent.

He heard the voice of Lobsang. 'Excellent! I can't say that this is what I expected, but it is most certainly what I had hoped for. By the way it would be appropriate if you gave them something of yours.'

The previous keeper of the magnificent fish was beaming encouragingly at Joshua.

'Well, I've got my glass knife, but somehow I don't think this guy ever needs a knife.' He hesitated, feeling awkward. 'And it *is* my knife, I knapped it myself from a bit of imported obsidian.' A gift from somebody whose life he had saved. 'Been with me a long time.'

Lobsang said impatiently, 'Consider the following. A little while ago you were expecting to be viciously attacked, yes? And now we have the obvious point that it was *his* fish and *he* gave it to *you*. I suspect the act of giving is more important than the gift here. Should you feel naked without a weapon, please do help yourself later to one of the laminated knives in the armoury, OK? But right now, *give him the knife.*'

Angry, mostly at himself, Joshua said, 'I didn't even know we had an armoury!'

'We live and we learn, my friend, and be grateful that you still have the chance to do both. A gift has a worth that has little to do with any currency. Hand it over with a cheerful smile for the cameras, Joshua, because you are making history: first contact with an alien species, albeit one which has had the decency to have evolved on Earth.'

Joshua presented his beloved knife to the creature. The knife was taken with extravagant care, held up to the light, admired, had its blade gingerly tested. Then there was a cacophony in his headset that sounded like bowling balls in a cement mixer.

After a few seconds this mercifully stopped, to be replaced by Lobsang's cheerful voice. 'Interesting! They sing to you using the frequencies that we think of as normal, while among themselves they appear to communicate in ultrasonics. What you heard was my attempt to translate the ultrasound conversation down to a range that a human could perceive, if not understand.'

And then, in an instant, they were gone. There was nothing to show that the creatures had been there, apart from very large footprints in the snow, already being filled in by the blizzard. And, of course, the salmon.

Back on the ship Joshua dutifully put the huge fish in the galley's refrigerator. Then, cradling a coffee, he sat in the lounge outside the galley, and said to the air: 'I want to speak to you, Lobsang. Not to a voice in the air. A face I can punch.'

'I can see you are annoyed. But I can assure you that you were never in any danger. And as you must have guessed you are not the first person to have met these creatures. I have a strong hypothesis that the first person who did meet them thought they were Russians . . .'

And Lobsang told Joshua the story of Private Percy Blakeney, as reconstructed from notes found in his diary, and comments he made to a very surprised nurse in the hospital in Datum France where he was taken after appearing there suddenly in the 1960s.

21

For Private Percy, faced by his row of impassive singing strangers in the green of his unsmashed forest, the penny had quickly dropped.

Of course! They had to be Russians! The Russians were in the war now, weren't they? And hadn't there been a copy of *Punch* magazine passed around in the trenches which showed Russians looking, yes, just like bears?

His granddad, who had been a Percy too, had once been taken prisoner in the Crimea, and he was always ready to talk about the Russians to an attentive boy. 'Stank, they did, lad, dirty sods to a man, savages to my mind, and some of them from God knows where in the wilds, well, I've never seen the like! So much fur, and beards a man could keep a goat in, except I would warrant the goat would leap out straight away being particular about the company it kept. But they could sing, lad, stinking though they was, they could sing, better than the Welsh, oh yes, *they* could sing! But if you hadn't been told, you would have thought they were animals.'

Now Percy looked at the row of hairy, emotionless, but not particularly hostile faces, and said boldly, 'Me English Tommy, yes? On your side! Long live the Czar!'

This won some polite attention, with the hairy men looking at one another.

Maybe they wanted another song. After all, hadn't his mother told him that music was the universal language? And at least they weren't imprisoning him, or shooting him, or suchlike. So he gave them a resounding chorus of 'Tipperary', and finished by saluting and crying, 'God save the King!'

Whereupon the Russians surprised him by waving their heavy great hands in the air and booming 'God save the King!' with considerable enthusiasm, their voices sounding like men shouting into a tunnel. Then they put their shaggy heads together as if reaching a conclusion, and once again broke into 'Pack Up Your Troubles'.

Only this wasn't the same kit bag and nor were they the same troubles. Private Percy tried hard to understand what he was listening to. Oh, yes, the song was there, but they sang it like a Sunday choir. Somehow the singers took his song apart so that it gained a strange life of its own, harmonies that broke and twisted into one another like mating eels and then came apart again in another bubble-rush of sound, and yet it was still good old 'Pack Up Your Troubles'. No, it was a better 'Pack Up Your Troubles', it was more, well, *there*, more real. Private Percy had never heard music like it, and clapped his hands, and so did the Russians with a sound like heavy artillery. They clapped as enthusiastically as they sang, possibly more so.

And now it occurred to Percy that last night's crayfish had been more of a snack than a meal. Well, if these Russians were his friends, then maybe they had some Russian rations to share? They looked bulky enough under those furry greatcoats. It had to be worth a try, so Percy rubbed his stomach, poked his finger suggestively in his mouth and looked hopeful.

After their singing, again they huddled amongst themselves, and the only sounds he could make out were whispers as faint as a gnat, that tiny annoying whine that keeps you awake at night. However, once they had reached some sort of accord, they burst into song again. This time it was whistles and trills, very much like im-pressions of birds, and good impressions at that, a touch of nightingale, a hint of starling, birdsong that flowed like the best dawn chorus he had ever heard. Still, somehow he got the impression that they were talking, or rather singing, about *him.*

Then one of them walked closer to him, watched carefully by the others, and sang, in the voice of Percy, 'Tipperary' perfectly all the way through, and it was *his own voice*, he was certain, his mother would have known it.

After that a couple of Russians disappeared into the woods, leaving the rest sitting around Percy placidly.

When Percy sat on the ground with the Russians, waves of tiredness suddenly washed over him. He'd had years of war and not even a day of this peaceful green, and maybe he deserved a little nap. So he drank a few scoops of water from the river and, despite the presence of the hairy Russians all around him, lay down on the grass and closed his eyes.

He surfaced only slowly from his nap.

Private Percy was a practical and methodical young man. And therefore, still lying in the grass, he decided, in this waking dream, not to worry about these Russians, as long as the Russians weren't trying to kill him. Save your worrying for your boots, boys, the veterans always said.

Boots! So his sleepy brain reminded him. They were the thing! Look after your boots and your boots would look after you! He had always spent a lot of time thinking about his boots.

At this point it occurred to Private Percy, waking slowly, still somewhat battered by his war and adrift in time and space, to wonder if he still had any legs on which to hang those boots. You could lose your legs and not know until the shock wore off, or so he had been told. It was like poor old Mac who never knew his feet had gone until he tried to stand up. He remembered walking around this forest, of course he did, but maybe *that* was all a dream as like as not, and maybe he was back in the mud and the blood after all.

And so he tried gingerly to pull himself upright, and was cheered by the realization that at least he appeared to have both hands. Shifting gently he moved his aching body until he could rise enough to see, yes, boots! Blessed boots! Apparently on legs that were probably his and, as a bonus, apparently still attached to him.

They could be treacherous, could boots, just like legs. Like the time when a forty-pounder hit a box of ammunition and he was part of the detail that had to go and sort things out. The sergeant had been a bit quiet, and uncharacteristically soothing when Percy was in distress because, even though he found a boot, lying in the churned-up mud, he couldn't find a man's leg to go with said boot. And the sergeant had said, patting Percy on the shoulder, 'Well lad, seeing as he has no head either, I reckon he won't notice, don't you? Just stick to doing what I told you, lad: pay-books, watches, letters, anything that can identify the poor sods. And then stick 'em looking up over the top of the trench. Yes, lad, stick those dead bodies up there! They might take a bullet but, as sure as salvation, they won't feel anything where they've gone, and there will be one bullet less for you or me. Good lad. Fancy a tot of rum? It's the medicine for what ails you.'

So the discovery of feet, his own feet, still attached as per, exhilarated Private Percy, known to his chums as Pimple because when your name is really and truly Percy Blakeney, pronounced 'Black-knee', *and* you still have bad acne in your twenties, you accept Pimple as a nickname and are grateful that it wasn't anything worse. He lay back again and must've dozed off for a while.

The next time he opened his eyes, it was still full daylight, and he was thirsty. He sat up. The Russians were still here, patiently watching. Looking at him almost kindly, through those furry faces, he thought.

Maybe his head was clearing, a bit. It occurred to him for the first time that he ought to have a good look at his kit.

He opened up his kit bag and emptied out the contents on the green ground. And he found that somebody had robbed him! His canteen had gone, his bayonet blade had gone, as had the blade of his entrenching tool. Come to that, his helmet was nowhere to be found; he didn't remember having that when he woke up, although he did find the strap around his neck. Blimey, they'd even taken the aglets off his boots and the nails out of the heels! All the bits of steel. And what was very odd was that even though his canteen had gone, what was actually missing was the steel flask – there was the stitched-leather container lying on the grass, intact. But his pay-book was untouched, and nobody had bothered about the few pennies in his kit bag, and even the glass bottle containing his rum ration was still here. It must have been a funny sort of thief! And he still had his paints – but the metal box that had contained the little tubes had vanished. Not only that, somebody had even taken the trouble to unwrap the metal bands around the bristles of his paint brushes, so that the little bits of stubble were left lying at the bottom of the canvas bag. Why?

And what about his weapons? He checked the pistol at his belt. All that was left of *that* was the wooden stock. Again, why? Steal a pistol, yes, but you would have a devil of a job to use it without the stock. It made no sense. But then, what did? Where, on the western front, had good sense ever played a part?

The Russians watched, silent, apparently baffled by his fiddling about with all this stuff.

Memory came trickling back from whatever foxhole it had been hiding in.

Private Percy had been seconded to the camouflage corps after his leg wound. This was because, amazingly enough, the Army had recognized that he had once been a draftsman, and sometimes this Army who needed men who could hold a gun, and even more men who could take a bullet, also needed men who could wield a pencil, and select from God's good rainbow just the right hue of paint to turn a Mark I tank into a harmless haystack, albeit with a wisp of smoke coming out of it if the lads were having a quick drag behind it. He'd been happy for the respite. And that was why he carried a paint box, for colour matching, and for bits of fine work after the usual application of daubs of camouflage green.

What else could he remember? The very last thing before the shelling? Oh yes, the sergeant roasting the new kid because he had one of those wretched Testaments that fitted into his breast pocket, the kind of thing mothers and sweethearts sent to the front in the hope that the holy words would keep their boys safe, and maybe, if words alone did not do the trick, then the gunmetal coating might achieve what mere faith could not. And Percy, packing up his gear to go on to the next job, remembered the sergeant was apoplectic, waving the offending article in front of the kid and screaming, 'You bloody, bloody idiot, ain't your bloody mother ever heard of shrapnel? There was a sapper once, a good lad, and a round hit his bloody iron Testament and it drove the living heart right out of his body, poor devil!'

And then he had been rudely interrupted by the shelling. Why had the red-faced kid and the sergeant disappeared into the incandescence of a bomb which hit only a little way away from Percy, who was now sitting here in this peaceful world, in the company of these friendly-looking Russians, and still managing to hear the wonderful birdsong? Deep inside, Percy knew he was never going to get answers to such questions.

Best not to ask, then.

The Russians, sitting there in the green, watched him patiently as he struggled to climb out of the black pit inside his head.

When the two Russian hunters returned, one of them was carrying a freshly killed deer, a big floppy animal, with apparent ease.

Having the carcass of a deer dropped right in front of him by a huge furry Russian might have perplexed a lesser man. But Private Percy's brief adolescence as a poacher, and years of near mal-nutrition on the front line, combined firmly around one purpose. The butchery was a messy job without steel, but the button rod in his small pack was thin brass and helped a little, and so did smashing the bottle that had contained the last of his rum ration to make a few more cutting edges.

He was disconcerted by the way the Russians ate with their bare hands, and carefully picked out the creature's guts and the lungs, what Percy had grown up calling the lights, and crammed them into their mouths, but he took the charitable view that the poor souls probably knew no better. He saw no steel, and certainly not any rifles, and that was odd. After all, the Russians had come to fight alongside the English, yes? Surely they would have had guns of some sort, because what was a soldier without a weapon?

Light dawned, for Private Percy. Of course, some might say that *he* was a deserter, although heaven only knew what had really happened to him. Maybe these Russians were deserters. They had surely flung their weapons away and kept only their enormous hairy greatcoats. And if that was so, why should Percy worry? That was their business, and the Czar's.

So he took a venison steak for himself, diplomatically walked away to avoid staring at the Russians' table manners, found some dry grass, pulled some dried twigs off some half-rotted branches of a fallen tree, and used one more precious lucifer to light another fire.

Five minutes later, as the steak cooked, they were sitting around him as if he had become King himself.

And later, when they walked away with him, singing as they went, he regaled them with every music-hall song he knew.

22

'How do you know all this, Lobsang?'

'About Private Percy? Mostly from that chronicle of the unexplained, the *Fortean Times*. The December 1970 issue recounted the story of an elderly man wearing antiquated British battledress being admitted to a French hospital some years before. He appeared to be trying to communicate by whistling. According to the British Army pay-book still in his blouse he was Private Percy Blakeney of a Kent regiment, recorded as missing in action after the battle of Vimy Ridge. Nevertheless, he appeared well nourished and in good, if somewhat puzzled spirits – although severely injured, having been run over by the tractor driven by the farmer who brought him into the hospital. The farmer protested to the police that the man had just stood there in the middle of the field, as if he'd never seen such a vehicle before, and the farmer had been unable to stop in time.

'Despite the efforts of the hospital staff, Percy died of wounds from the collision. An ironic end! But not before one of the nurses who spoke English heard him say something like, "In the end I told the Russians that I wanted to go back, to see how the war was getting on. They were good lads, found me a way home. Good lads, loved singing. Very kind . . ." And so forth.

'The fact that the man was wearing the remains of a British Army uniform and mentioned the word "Russians" raised sufficient security concerns to cause the gendarmerie to be called to investigate. Well, according to the British Legion, there was indeed a Percy Blakeney involved in the fighting on Vimy Ridge, who was reported missing after the opening bombardment. There appears to have been no attempt at an official explanation as to why his pay-book should show up decades later in the hands of a mysterious itinerant now buried in a graveyard in central France.'

'But you have an explanation, I take it.'

'I'm sure you can see it, Joshua.'

'He stepped there? Into the forest with his Russians?'

'Possibly,' said Lobsang, 'or perhaps one of the trolls found itself in the trenches by accident, and helped him away.'

'"Trolls"?'

'That seems the mythological term that best describes these creatures, extrapolating from legends that must derive from even older sightings: creatures glimpsed in our world only to vanish again, entirely misunderstood, the seeds of legend . . . a term that already has become current in some parts of the Long Earth, Joshua. Percy's wasn't the only sighting.'

'So you anticipated finding these – stepping humanoids, did you?'

'From logical extrapolation. And I anticipated the singing from Percy's own account. Consider: humans can step; chimps can't – there have been experiments to establish that. But perhaps our hominid relatives of the past, or rather their modern descendants, were, or *are*, able to step. Why not? To have encountered such beings so early in our journey is of course the achievement of a major goal. And we must expect, we must hope at least, to meet many more such groups as we continue. What an intellectual thrill this is, Joshua!'

'So they kept Percy alive, all those years?'

'It seems so. These "Russians" found Percy wandering in a France which had no Frenchmen living in it, and they were kind to him, for decades. Over several of their generations, perhaps. Remarkable. As far as I know, he never understood the truth about his friends. But Percy probably had never seen *anybody* from another country before being shipped to France, and, of course, being English and unlettered, was probably half prepared to believe that a foreigner could look like just about anything. Why shouldn't a Russian look like a big hairy ape?

'For much of the rest of his life Private Percy travelled with his "Russians" across a calm, well-wooded, well-watered world where they kept him fed with meat and vegetables, and were in all respects considerate in their treatment of him, right up until the day when he made it clear – and I must say that I don't know how he communicated this to them – that he wanted to go back to the place where he had come from.'

'Songs can be very expressive, Lobsang. You can sing your homesickness.'

'Perhaps. And, as we've experienced ourselves, they learned those songs well, and remember them. They must have been passed between generations of trolls, perhaps even from group to group . . . Intriguing. We must learn something of the social lives of these creatures. Well – in the end the trolls took him home, as good fairies should, back to France, but fortunately not in an era when man was disassembling man with high explosives.'

Now the ambulant unit strolled through the blue door at the rear of the deck, and seamlessly, and rather eerily, took up the conversation from its disembodied counterpart. 'You have further questions, Joshua?'

'I've read about that war. It didn't last all that long. Why didn't he go back earlier?'

The ambulant unit put a cold hand on Joshua's shoulder. 'Would you have done? It was a terrible, inhuman conflict, a war that had become a machine for killing young men as efficiently, if as horribly, as possible. How keen would he be to walk back into that? And don't forget he didn't really know he was a stepper. He *thought* that he had been blown into another part of France. Besides, his "Russians" were happy to know him. I suspect it was the songs that clinched it. He says they loved hearing him sing. He taught them all the songs that he knew – and you, Joshua Valienté, heard one of them today.

'So – our first field trip. Perhaps we need an operational debrief. You thought I'd put you in harm's way, didn't you? Please believe me, I would not do that. It would not be in my own interest, would it?'

'You know a hell of a lot about what we're encountering, even before we've encountered it. You might have warned me what was coming.'

'Yes. I accept that. We must work on our communication. Look – we have barely begun our epic journey; we barely know each other. What would you say to some quality time together?'

Sometimes, the only thing you can do is stare blankly. *Quality time*, said the artificial man! Joshua knew the term, of course, if only because Sister Agnes went into a rage every time she heard it. As rages went they were not volcanic: few bad words were said – apart from 'Republican', which was an extremely bad word to Sister Agnes – and certainly nothing was ever thrown, at least not very hard, and never anything that could hurt. But terms like 'me time' and 'quality time' lit her fuse. 'Terms cut out of fog! Watering down the currency of expression, causing anything to mean whatever you want it to mean, until nothing is *meant* and nothing is *precise!*' He remembered the day when someone on the television used the fatal term, 'Think outside the box.' Some of the kids went and hid in advance of the explosion.

Quality time, with Lobsang.

Joshua looked at the ambulant's simulated face. He looked oddly weary, or stressed, in as much as his expression could be reliably read at all. 'Do you ever sleep, Lobsang?'

Now that face assumed an affronted expression. 'All my components have a downtime cycle, with secondary systems taking the load as required. I assume this could be considered sleeping. I see you frowning. Is the answer not sufficient?'

Joshua was aware of all the subtle sounds of the ship, its organic creaking and groaning, its subsystems' humming – Lobsang, constantly at work. How must that level of continual consciousness feel? As if Joshua had to control each individual breath he took, or regulate every heartbeat. Lobsang certainly had to control the stepping, an artifact of consciousness. 'Is there anything specific bothering you, Lobsang?'

The visage broke into a smile. 'Of course there is. Everything bothers me, especially the things I don't *know*, and can't control. To *know* is after all my job, my task, my reason for existing. My mental health is optimal, however. I think this needs to be said. I don't know where I could even *find* a bicycle made for two, although I am certain that I could fabricate a reasonably speedy tandem within a couple of hours . . . You don't know what I'm talking about, do you? Tonight we will try out the cinema option, and *2001* will be the lead feature. We must complete your education, Joshua.'

'Accepting for the moment that you are in fact human, with human weaknesses, is it possible you get stressed out? If so it would do you some good to get out of yourself every so often. Sure, let's spend some "quality time" together. Just don't tell Sister Agnes I said so.' A bizarre thought occurred to him. 'Can you fight?'

'Joshua, I could lay waste to whole landscapes.'

'No, no. I meant hand to hand.'

'Explain.'

'A bit of sparring every now and again tones you up. Back home some of us lads would spar just to keep our hand in, you know, on the street. Even having a workout with a punch-bag seems to pull you back together. Might be fun, too. What do you say? It's a very human thing. And it would be a chance for you to explore the responses of this body of yours.'

There was no immediate reply.

'Come on, how about it?'

Lobsang smiled. 'Sorry. I was watching the Rumble in the Jungle.'

'You were what?'

'Yes, between George Foreman and Muhammad Ali. I always do my research, Joshua. I see Ali won with the use of guile, being the older and more experienced fighter. Excellent!'

'Are you telling me that you have every single televised boxing match in some portable memory?'

'Yes, of course. Why not? Anticipating and extrapolating, I have now begun the fabrication of two pairs of sparring gloves, the associated hand wraps, two pairs of shorts, two gum shields for the look of the thing, and one plastic protective for your genitals.'

Joshua could hear accelerated activity on the fabrication decks, and, with the protection of his genitals very much at the forefront of his mind, he said, 'The Rumble in the Jungle wasn't a sparring match, you understand, Lobsang. It was more like a small war. I've seen it a couple of times. Sister Simplicity watches the great bouts occasionally. We all think she has a thing about big sweaty men—'

'I have studied the rules of sparring for an adequate time,' said Lobsang, standing up. 'Two millionths of a second, to be precise. Sorry, did that sound smug?'

Joshua sighed. 'Actually, it sounded like exaggeration for humorous effect.'

'Good!' said Lobsang. 'That's exactly what I intended.'

'*That* sounds smug.'

'Well, it must be said that I have a lot to be smug about, don't you think? And if you'll excuse me . . .'

Lobsang walked away. When Joshua had first seen the ambulant unit move it was rather jerky, obviously artificial, and he couldn't help noticing that now it moved like an athlete. Lobsang clearly believed in self-improvement. He reappeared after a few minutes, dressed in a heavy white robe, and handed Joshua a kit. Joshua turned his back and began to get changed.

Lobsang recited, 'Sparring: a healthy way of getting exercise while at the same time honing those parts of the brain responsible for observation, deduction and anticipation, and, not least, developing the spirit of fair play. I suggest that we use the rules devised for a training session rather than an all-out fight, as laid down in 1891 by Brigadier General Houseman. Who, I notice, was shortly afterwards accidentally shot in the head by one of his own men in the Sudan, an incident from which no level of sparring expertise could have saved him. Ironic! Subsequent to this I have since picked up several thousand other allusions to the sport. Really, Joshua, I commend your modesty in turning your back on me when pulling on your shorts, although it is not really required.'

Joshua turned – and saw a new Lobsang. When he slipped off the robe, under boxing vest and shorts was a body that would scare Arnold Schwarzenegger.

'You do take things seriously, don't you, Lobsang?'

'What do you mean?'

'Never mind. OK,' he said. 'The idea is to touch gloves, step back, and we'll go for it . . .' He glanced out of the window at worlds scrolling past. 'But shouldn't you also be keeping an eye on the *Mark Twain*? I'm not sure I like the idea of the two of us exchanging blows while the ship steps on blindly.'

'Don't worry about that. I have autonomous sub-units that will take care of the ship for a while. And, by the way, Mark Twain himself would find this situation remarkably fitting! I will tell you about that after I have won. Shall we dance, Joshua?'

Joshua was not surprised to find that he could still spar pretty well. After all, out in the Long Earth, you either kept up good reflexes and stamina, or you died. So now he seemed to be laying more glove on Lobsang than Lobsang was laying on him. He said, as he blocked the next blow, 'Are you sure you are giving it all you've got, Lobsang?'

They moved apart and Lobsang grinned. 'I could kill you with a single blow; if necessary, these arms could serve as pile drivers.' He carefully stepped away from a tentative attack from Joshua. 'That's why I let you hit me first, so that I could calibrate a suitable response. I am fighting you at your own strength, but regrettably not with your speed, which I suspect is innately better than mine because of the phenomenon of muscle memory – embodied cognition, the muscles as part of one's overall intelligence, amazing! I am going to have to reflect that in my own anatomy, a more distributed processing design, in the next upgrade of this body. And, Joshua, you are also pretty good at deceit, even with your limited body language. I salute you for that.'

Which was true, because at that moment Joshua landed a blow in the middle of that enormous chest. Joshua said, 'I am not certain that it's Tibetan, but there is an old saying: "If you are fighting, don't talk, fight!"'

'Yes, of course you are right. One must fight with the whole mind.'

And suddenly there was a fist right between Joshua's eyes. It didn't actually connect; Lobsang had pulled the punch with astonishing precision, and Joshua could feel only a slight pressure on the tiny hairs of his nose.

Lobsang said, 'There *is* an apt old Tibetan saying: "Don't stand too close to a Tibetan chopping wood." You are much too slow in every respect, Joshua. Still, perhaps you can defeat me with guile for a while longer, until I pass your level of competence. I find this exercise therapeutic and invigorating and educational. Shall we continue?'

Joshua got back to work, breathing hard. 'You're actually enjoying this, aren't you? Although with your background I was half expecting you were going to try some kind of kung fu stuff.'

'You have been watching the wrong kind of movies, my friend. I was a motorcycle repairman, remember, better with all things mechanical and electrical than with my fists or feet. I once wired a magneto on to the door of my work room, so that the gentleman next door who regularly came in to steal from me got quite a large electric shock. A little bit of instant karma, and that was the only time I ever laid anyone low. No kick-boxing required.'

They broke again.

Lobsang said, 'And now you, my friend, have been instrumental in helping me emulate the original Mark Twain who, if we can believe his autobiographical *Life on the Mississippi*, fought with another pilot on a stern-wheeler in full steam, the man having been bullying a trainee pilot. Every now and again he had to leave the fight and make sure the vessel was still on course – rather as I am guiding our ship through the worlds, even as we spar. Given Twain's cheerful tendency to put a shine on any anecdote, I am not certain of the truth of this, but I admire the man, which is why I named this ship after him ... Actually he would have called his book *Stepping Westward*, but the title, alas, had already been claimed by William Wordsworth. The old sheep of the Lake District: very fine poet, but somehow "exploring on the *Wordsworth*" does not quite have the appropriate ring, does it?'

Joshua said, 'Wordsworth had his moments, according to Sister Georgina. *It is a beauteous evening, calm and free . . .*'

'I know it, of course. *The holy time is quiet as a nun breathless with adoration.* Very apt! Are we sparring with poetry too, Joshua?'

'Shut up and box, Lobsang.'

23

WHEN THEY WERE done the sun was setting on all the worlds. Joshua took a shower, musing on all the meanings and usages of the word 'strange'. Boxing like a nineteenth-century steamboat captain with an artificial man, while multiple worlds flickered by beneath. Could his life get any odder? Probably, he thought, resigned.

He was coming to like Lobsang, although he was not entirely certain why. Nor was he certain, even now, what exactly Lobsang was. Strange, that was for sure. But then of course plenty of people called *him* strange, and worse.

He dried himself off, got into a new pair of shorts, put on a fresh T-shirt which bore the slogan 'Don't worry! On another Earth it already happened', and headed back to the saloon deck. The empty staterooms he passed bothered him; it made the *Mark Twain* feel like a ghost ship, with himself as the first, and possibly the last, ghost.

He walked into the galley, and there was Lobsang, dressed in a bland coverall, standing patient as a statue. 'Dinner time, Joshua? According to a preliminary cladistic analysis your salmon is not, strictly speaking, salmon, but salmon enough for the grill. We have all the relevant condiments. We also have tracklements, and I bet you have never heard of *them* before.'

'Tracklements are those things which complement the main ingredient of a meal and, traditionally, at least, may be found in the vicinity of the said ingredient – for example, horseradish root in good beef country. I am impressed, Lobsang.'

Lobsang looked pleasantly shocked. 'Well, if it comes to that, so am I, given that I am a certifiable genius with access to every dictionary ever published. May I ask how you came across such an archaic word?'

'Sister Serendipity is a world expert on cookery through the ages. In particular she has a book by somebody called Dorothy Hartley, called *Food in England*. Serendipity knows all that stuff; she can make a good meal out of anything. You should see her roadkill hot pot, always a favourite. She taught me a lot about living off the land.'

'It is remarkable for a woman with such skills to devote her time to unfortunate young people. Such dedication.'

Joshua nodded. 'Well, yes. And maybe also because she is wanted by the FBI, which is why she doesn't go out much and sleeps in the basement. Sister Agnes said that it was all a big misunderstanding, and in any case the bullet missed the senator by a mile. They don't talk about it much.'

Lobsang began walking backwards and forwards along the deck, turning smartly when he reached a bulkhead and striding back again, like a sentry.

Joshua set about dressing the salmon, but the endless striding and the creaking of the floorboards began to get on his nerves. When Lobsang came past for the twelfth time he said, 'You know Captain Ahab used to do that? And look what happened to him, right? What's on your mind now, Lobsang?'

'On *my* mind! Practically everything. Although I have to say that gentle physical exercise, such as our sparring, does indeed do wonders for the cognitive processes. A very human observation, don't you think?' The pacing continued.

Finally the quasi-salmon was cooking, although Joshua had to keep an eye on it.

Lobsang stopped pacing at last. 'You are good at concentrating, aren't you, Joshua? You can ignore distractions, a very useful skill, and it makes for a certain tranquillity.'

Joshua didn't respond. Through the window, light flared: a distant volcano blossoming against the endless Eurasian green, to be snatched out of existence in a heartbeat, as they stepped on, and on.

Lobsang said, 'Listen, Joshua. Let's talk about natural steppers. Like you.'

'And Private Percy?'

'You asked me about my researches. Since Step Day I have endeavoured to explore all aspects of this remarkable new phenomenon. As one example I sent researchers off around the world, to study cave systems used by early man. They were tasked to inspect similar caves in the adjoining worlds, to investigate parallel habitations, if any. It was an expensive endeavour but it yielded fruit, because my researchers quickly found in a cave near Chauvet in a stepwise France, among other things, a painting. More accurately it was the badge of a certain Kent regiment at the time of the First World War, and rendered with great accuracy.'

'Private Percy?'

'Quite. Well, I already knew about him and his stepping exploits. But then, in a stepwise version of the caves at Cheddar Gorge in Somerset, England, my indefatigable investigators found the complete skeleton of a middle-aged man, in possession of a corked flagon of cider, a few coins, and one gold watch of mid-eighteenth-century manufacture with only the gold and brass remaining of the metal parts. This was a wet cave, but his boots had survived, slightly glistening like the poor man himself, thanks to a sheen of calcium carbonate deposited by drips from the roof. Interestingly, the hobnails and the aglets on his laces were not there.'

'Aglets?'

'The small steel caps once fitted to the end of a lace . . . I'm painting a picture for you here, Joshua.'

'It's kind of a dull picture, Lobsang.'

'Patience. The intriguing thing about this particular find is that the corpse was discovered only because he was lying with the fingers of one hand jammed into a very small space at the bottom of the cave. My operatives found the gentleman in fact as they were exploring a lower cave. They saw the bones protruding through the roof, as if the man had been trying fruitlessly to widen the little gap. All very Edgar Allan Poe, don't you think? Of course they broke their way through from the cave below, and you can work out the rest. The man was a notorious thief and ne'er-do-well known locally as Passover.'

'He was a stepper, wasn't he?' said Joshua, flatly. 'And I just bet that there was no other entrance to the cave.' For a moment he imagined the drip of icy water oozing over bleeding fingers in the darkness, a man trying to scrabble his way out of a cave like a coffin . . . 'So maybe he'd had a few drinks. Sister Serendipity once told me that Somerset cider was made of lead, apples and hand-saws. He lost his bearings, *stepped*, ended up in his small cave without even knowing that he'd stepped at all, which would of course make him even more disorientated. He tried to feel his way out, banged his head, knocked himself out. How am I doing?'

'Superbly. And the skull itself was, indeed, slightly damaged,' said Lobsang. 'Not a good death, and I wonder how many other individuals get themselves trapped in some corner before they know what is happening to them.

'*Natural steppers*, Joshua. The history of Datum Earth is full of them, if you know how to interrogate the record. Mysterious dis-appearances. Mysterious arrivals! Locked-room mysteries of all kinds. Thomas the Rhymer is a favourite example of mine, the Scots prophet who, it is said, kissed the queen of the elves and left this world . . . In more modern times there are plenty of cases documented in the black scientific and intelligence literature, of course.'

'Of course.'

'You are unusual, you see, Joshua, but not unique.'

'Why are you telling me all this now?'

'Because I don't want there to be secrets between us. And

because now I am going to tread on dangerous ground. And tell you about your mother.'

The *Mark Twain* stepped Westward, with little sound other than the pop of the air getting out of the way.

Carefully, Joshua turned down the heat on the cooking fish. He said, as casually as he could, 'What about my mother? Sister Agnes told me everything there is to know.'

'I don't think so, because *she* didn't know all of it. I do. And let me say that the whole truth is, on the whole, a good truth, and a truth that explains many things. I think it would be good for you to know. But I will put it out of my mind if you tell me to. That is, I will actually delete the subject from my memory for good. The choice is yours.'

Calmly, Joshua kept his attention on the fish. 'In what world can I say anything other than "Tell me about her"?'

'Very well. You know, surely, or at least you must have worked out, that Sister Agnes took over the Home in the first place as a result of the affair. I mean the scandalous business that surrounded your birth. It was a coup that made the throwing of the money-lenders out of the Temple look like a bachelor party. I've seen the files, believe me; I doubt whether a convocation of cardinals would try to take Agnes's office away from her now. She knows all the dirt. Moreover, she knows what's *under* the dirt . . .

'Your mother was young when she became pregnant with you, far too young. The Home failed her in that, clearly. And your father, by the way, is unknown, even to me.'

'I know that. Maria would say nothing about him.'

'Under the old regime, her world was one of daily penance. Relevant affidavits to demonstrate how this penance was administered exist in Sister Agnes's personal safe, as well, of course, as in my own files, awaiting the right time to be revealed. The regime was utterly inappropriate in the modern age – and would have been in any age, though it might once have been tolerated.'

Joshua faced Lobsang and said in a flat voice, 'I know that somebody took her monkey bracelet off her. It was a silly thing, but it was given to her by her own mother. It was sort of all she had. Sister Agnes told me. I suppose it was considered superstitious or something.'

'They did think that way, yes. Although there was a strong streak of petty cruelty in the mix. Maria was in the late stages of pregnancy at the time. Yes, it seems a trivial incident, but it tipped her over the edge, at the worst of times. And so that evening, when the labour pains first started, Maria tried to flee the home, and panicked, and *stepped*. At which point you entered the situation.

'She actually stepped *twice*. She gave birth to you, and stepped back to the Datum, emerging near the road outside the Home where Sister Agnes caught up with her. Agnes tried to calm her down; Maria was clearly in a dreadful state. But she realized what she had done, and stepped yet again. And when she returned she brought you back with her, wrapped in her pink angora sweater, and handed you over to an astonished Sister Agnes, who understood nothing of what had happened. It was not until Step Day, when stepping became common, that she began to grasp the truth.

'And Maria died, Joshua, of post-partum hemorrhaging. I'm very sorry. Sister Agnes, quick to react though she was, could not help her.

'All of which leaves you, my friend, as most unique, being, at the moment of birth, if only for a matter of a minute or two, the only person, almost certainly, *in a universe*. Totally solitary, utterly alone! I wonder what that must have done to your infant consciousness?'

And Joshua, aware all his life of the far-off, solemn presence of the Silence, wondered about that too. My miraculous birth, he thought.

Lobsang went on, 'Now – you weren't aware of any of these details, were you? Does that help you understand yourself a little better?'

Joshua stared blankly at Lobsang. 'I should serve the fish before it spoils.'

Silently, Lobsang watched Joshua eat a respectable part of the fish, cooked with finely chopped onions (there being no shallots on board), and green beans, and a dill sauce the composition of which even Lobsang's forensic nose could not entirely work out although undoubtedly there was a lot of fennel in it. He watched as Joshua methodically washed and dried every utensil until it sparkled, and stacked everything away in an order that could only be called shipshape.

And then he watched Joshua wake up, it seemed to Lobsang, as if reality flowed over him like a spring tide.

Lobsang said gently, 'I have something for you. Which I suspect your mother would have liked you to have.' He produced a small item wrapped in soft paper and laid it gently on the bench, downloading as he did so a number of recommended works on dealing with grief and the aftermath of loss, and all the while making background system checks of the ship.

Joshua opened the packet cautiously. It contained his mother's cheap, precious plastic bracelet.

Then Lobsang left Joshua alone.

Lobsang walked back along the length of the ship, surprised once more at how the process of walking helped thinking, just as Benjamin Franklin had once remarked. An aspect of embodiment, he supposed, embodied cognition, a phenomenon he must explore – or remember. Behind him, as he walked, lights dimmed as the ship went into night-running mode.

When he got to the wheelhouse he opened the screen, enjoying the freezing fresh air of world after world washing against the nanosensors embedded in his artificial skin, and he stared out at the Long Earth, as revealed by the light of many moons. The landscape itself seldom changed significantly: the basic shapes of the hills, the paths of the rivers – although occasionally there was sufficient volcanism to light up the sky, or a lightning-struck forest blazing in the dark. The moon, the sun, the basic geometry of the Earth itself, made a static stage for the shifting, swarming biologies on the fleeting worlds. But even the moonlight was not a constant across the worlds. Lobsang paid a lot of attention to the moons, and he saw how that familiar, ancient face shifted and flowed, subtly, as he crossed the worlds. While the ancient lava seas endured, in each reality a different selection of random cosmic rocks had battered the lunar surface, leaving a different pattern of craters and rays. Sooner or later, he knew, they were bound to come across a world with a *missing* moon, a negative moon. After all the moon was itself a contingency, an outcome of accidental collisions during the creation of the solar system. An absence of moon was an inevitability if you travelled far enough across the Long Earth; Lobsang only had to wait, as for many other contingencies he had anticipated.

He understood a great deal. But the further they travelled, the more the very mystery of the Long Earth worried Lobsang. Back home he employed tame professors who spoke of the Long Earth as some kind of quantum-physical construct, because that kind of scientific language seemed at least to paint the right picture. But he was coming to believe that on the contrary, his boffins might not just have the wrong picture, they might be in the wrong art gallery entirely. That the Long Earth might be something much stranger altogether. He didn't know, and he *hated* not knowing things. This evening, he knew he would worry and watch until the moons set, and then he would worry until it was daylight and it was time for the chores of the day, which in his case would include ... worrying.

24

THE NEXT DAY Joshua, almost shyly, asked Lobsang for more information about natural steppers. Others like himself, and his mother. 'Not legends from history: modern-day examples. I imagine you have plenty of material.'

So Lobsang told Joshua the story of Jared Orgill, one of the first natural steppers to come to the attention of the authorities.

It had been just another game of Jack in the Box: that was what they called it in Austin, Texas, although kids had independently invented variants of the game across the planet, with lots of different names. And this particular day it was the turn of Jared Orgill, ten years old, to be Jack.

They'd found an old fridge on the illegal garbage dump, Jared and his friends. A big slab of stainless steel, lying on its back amid the garbage. 'It looks like a robot's coffin,' remarked Debbie Bates. Once they'd pulled out the shelves and plastic boxes and stuff it was more than big enough to take one of them.

Jared wasn't bullied into going into the box, though his parents would later protest otherwise. In fact he would have fought the others for his turn. He handed his cellphone to Debbie – you never took in a phone, of course – climbed in and lay down. It wasn't comfortable, with the bumps and ridges of the fridge's inner fittings poking into him, and there was a stink of some chemical or other. The big heavy lid slammed down, shutting out the sky, the grinning faces. It didn't bother him, it would only be for a few minutes. For a while he heard bumps and bangs and scrapes, as the others followed the usual routine of heaping up garbage on top of the fridge to pin down the lid.

Then there was a moment of quiet, a few more scrapes – and the fridge started rocking. The other kids had thought of a better way of pinning him in there. It took them a minute to get organized, but soon the half-dozen of them were lined up, heaving at the heavy fridge, rocking it a little further with each pull. The fridge rolled over, and fell forward so its weight trapped the door closed. Jared, buffeted by the rolling in the dark, landed face down on the inside of the door . . . and he heard something crunch. His Stepper, at his waist, was just a plastic box full of a jumble of components, tied on to his belt with string. Kind of fragile.

The game was that he would wait five minutes, ten – maybe as long as an hour. Of course he couldn't tell the time. Then he would step out to West 1 or East 1, move aside from the fridge, and step back – ta-da! – there would be Jack, out of the box.

But he'd fallen on his Stepper.

It might still work. He didn't try it, not straight away. He didn't want to look chicken by coming out too soon. Also, he didn't want to *know* that the Stepper was broken, and that he was stuck.

He didn't know how long he waited. The air already felt hot, stuffy. Maybe it was ten minutes, maybe more.

He felt for the sliding switch on the Stepper, closed his eyes, pulled it over to East. Nothing. Only the stuffy dark. Fear stabbed again. He pulled the slider to West, with no result. He yanked the slider this way and that, until it broke off in his hand. He tried not to scream. He turned on his back and pummelled at the fridge carcass. 'Help! You guys! Get me out! Debbie! Mac! Help, get me out!'

He lay, listened, waited. Nothing.

He knew what they'd do, for he would do the same. They'd wait for minutes, a half-hour, an hour, maybe even more. Then they'd start to fret that something had gone wrong, so they'd split up and run home. They would blab in the end, and everybody would drive out to the dump, and Dad would scream at the others to tell him where the damn fridge was, and he'd pull off the garbage with his bare hands . . .

The trouble was, that could be hours away. The air was already starting to feel thick, it strained his chest to breathe. He panicked again. He pulled at the wreck of the Stepper until it started to come apart in his hands. He screamed, and banged the hull of the fridge, and pissed his pants. He started to cry.

Then, exhausted, he lay back down again, and felt over the wreck of his Stepper in the dark: the potato, the power lead, the bits of circuit board. He shouldn't have pulled it about like that. He should have tried to fix it. Maybe if he remembered how he'd made it in the first place he could put it back together now. He remembered the circuit diagram, as it had first come up glowing on the screen of his phone. He had a good memory for stuff like that. He *thought* his way around the diagram, the coils, the tuning, and he—

And he fell, a foot or so, and landed with a thump on soft ground. Suddenly there was sky above him, dazzling bright, and the air rushed into his lungs.

Out! He got to his feet, trembling. Bits of the Stepper fell to the ground. He was dizzy with the richness of the air. As if he'd been dead, and was alive again. His pants were damp, to his shame.

He looked around. He was in a thick forest clump, but he could see lights through the trees: Austin East 1 or West 1, whichever. He had to get home. How? The Stepper was even more of a mess than before. Still, he walked a couple of paces from where the fridge would be—

And he was standing on a heap of smashed-up, stinking debris, beside a big mound that had to be the fridge with its covering of junk. He'd stepped back, to the Datum. He didn't get it. This time he hadn't even touched the Stepper. He didn't even feel nauseous.

He didn't care. He was home! He ran off, away from the fridge.

Maybe his parents wouldn't have missed him yet. Elated, he started planning how he would get back his phone and brag to his friends.

Unfortunately for Jared, he had been missed. His parents had already called the cops, one of whom was bright enough to notice the smashed Stepper, and ask the crucial question: how had Jared managed to step between the worlds without a Stepper? To Jared's dismay he was kept off school for medical checks, and counselling by 'experts' in stepping and in the Long Earth, such as they were, a physicist and a psychologist and a neurologist.

The story made it into a local news site before it was pulled. After that the incident took some covering up, but the US government, an old hand at such assignments, was able to deny the whole thing, discredit the witnesses including Jared himself, and bury the whole thing in classified files.

Of course Lobsang was fully aware of the contents of those files.

Joshua asked, 'So why do people need Steppers at all?'

'Perhaps in a more indirect way than is imagined, Joshua. The brief notes Linsay left insist that the placing of every component is crucial and needs pin-sharp care, so that the builder's attention is totally wrapped up in the task. The need to align the two home-wound coils reminds me of the tuning of early metal detectors. As for the other components, they appear to be there for the *look* of the thing, and the look can be very important. The winding of the coils themselves is especially hypnotic. If I may be Tibetan for a moment, I believe that what we have here is a kind of technological mandala, designed to tilt the mind into a subtly different state, disguised as a bit of everyday western technology. It is the act of making a Stepper that enables one to step, you see, not the gadget itself. I myself went through the physical process of constructing a Stepper, via an ambulant unit. I might venture to suggest that it is unlocking a door within us that most of us don't know exists. But as Jared Orgill's story illustrates – or even your own – some people are finding they don't need the Steppers at all, when they step accidentally with a broken box, or step in a panic without a box at all.'

'We're all natural steppers,' Joshua said, wondering. 'It's just that most of us don't know it. Or we need this aid to make those muscles in the head work.'

'Something like that. But not *all*, you're wrong about that. Enough steppers have been studied now to draw up some rough statistics. Perhaps a fifth of mankind are thought to be natural steppers, to whom the Long Earth is as accessible as a city park – without any aids at all, perhaps with a little coaching, or mental disciplines of the kind Jared inadvertently came across when visualizing his circuit diagram. On the other hand, perhaps another fifth can never leave the Datum at all, unless humiliatingly carried by somebody else.'

Joshua pondered the implications. Suddenly humanity was fundamentally divided – even if it didn't know it yet.

25

JOSHUA WATCHED WORLDS pass like the turning pages of a picture book. And, heading steadily geographical west, they passed a boundary marker of their own: the Ural mountains, a north–south band of crumpled landscape that endured across most of the worlds.

But the worlds were different now. Both Ice Belt and Mine Belt were far behind them. Now the Earths below were Corn Belt worlds, as the American scouts and trek captains liked to call them: rich, warm worlds, and at least in North America covered with grassland and prairie littered with familiar-looking trees and scrub and dense with herds of healthy-looking animals. Worlds ripe for farming. The Earths below now numbered over a hundred thousand on Lobsang's earthometer. It took trekkers nine months to come out as far as this, on foot. The airship had made it in four days.

Whenever they stopped, Lobsang scanned for short-wave radio transmissions, which ought to carry around the curve of any Earth with an ionosphere. They paused at a couple of Corn-Belt-worlds to listen, one being West 101,754, where they got a long and chatty news update from a colony in a stepwise New England: some kid, originally from Madison as it happened, blogging by reading from her journal. One of a whole trail of such hopeful townships, Joshua imagined, scattered thin across the continents of the Long Earth. And each, he supposed, would have its own story to tell . . .

*

Hi, my loyal listeners, Helen Green here, your low-tech blogger clogging up the airwaves again. This bit's from three years ago. It was July 5 – which, as you will be aware, is the day after July 4. Here goes . . .

Is this what they call a hangover?

Oh! My! God!

Yesterday was Independence Day! Yay. We've been here eight months, and nobody's dead yet, yay! That's an excuse for a party if ever there was one. We're Americans, and this is officially America, and it was July 4, and that was that.

Though to look at us, this first summer, you'd imagine we were Indians. We're all living in lean-tos and tepees and benders and big square communal houses, and some folk are still using their trek tents. There are chickens and puppy dogs that people carried here on their backs, running around everywhere. We ain't farming. Next year will be the first harvest. We have a rota clearing the fields – burn, slash, haul away the rocks, all brute labour, nothing but human muscle available to do it. For the future we've brought seeds, corn and beans and flax and cotton, enough to survive years of failed crops if necessary. Oh, we've already planted pumpkins and squash and beans in the cleared ground near the houses, in our 'gardens'.

But for now we're hunter-gatherers! And it's a rich country to hunt and gather in. In the winter we got bass from the river. In the forest we took things that look like rabbits and things that look like deer and some of those funny little horses, though we were all a bit squeamish about that, it was like eating a pony. Now in the summer we're spending more time at the coast, where we're fishing and collecting clams.

You do feel like you're out in the wild. Back home on the Datum I was living on top of centuries of other people's efforts to *tame* everything. Here the forest has never been cleared, the swamps never drained, the river never dammed or leveed. It's strange. And dangerous.

I think my Dad thinks some of the people are dangerous too. We're all learning more about each other, but slowly, you can't always tell from the outside. Some folk have come out here, not to go somewhere, but to get away from something. An army veteran. A woman who my Mom thinks was abused, as a child. Another woman who lost a child. Well, that's fine by me.

But anyhow, we're here. And if you go tracking in the woods or up river you can see the little plumes of smoke rising up from the houses, and hear the voices of the workers in the fields. You can feel the difference if you step even just a world or two to either side. A world with humans in, versus a world without. Honestly, it's true, you can feel it in your head.

We had a big argument about what to call our new community. The adults had a meet about it, and it turned into the usual word fest. Melissa was determined it should be called some long uplifting name like 'New Independence' or 'Deliverance' or maybe just 'New Hope', but my Dad laughed at that one and made a joke about *Star Wars*.

I'm not sure if it was just my suggestion or Ben Doak's, but we found something that stuck. Or at least that nobody hated enough to veto loudly. When it was agreed, Dad and a few others made up a sign, on the trail up from the coast.

WELCOME TO REBOOT
FOUNDED 2026, A.D.
POP. 117

'Now all we need is a zip code,' said my Dad.

And now here's a bit from a year later than that, written by my Dad! Well, he has helped me out with this journal, including with the spelling, huh. Thanks, Dad! . . .

My name is Jack Green. I guess if you're reading this you'll know I'm Helen's father. I have special permission from Helen to add a few notes to this journal, which has become a rather precious thing itself. Just now Helen herself is otherwise engaged, but this is her birthday, and I wanted to be sure the day was marked properly.

So, where do I begin?

We have our houses built now, mostly. And fields we're slowly clearing. Usually I have my head down, working. We all do. But every so often I take a walk around the town, and I see how we're nibbling into the green.

The sawmill is working. That was the first big communal project. I can hear it now, as I write – we try to keep it going day and night, with that distinctive two-stroke sound as it slowly processes forest into town. We have a pottery kiln, and a lime kiln, and a soap kettle, and of course our forge thanks to our Brit boy wonder Franklin. The geological survey maps were spot on. In some ways it's incredible how fast we've been able to progress.

But we were able to rely on help from outside. A family of Amish came our way, following a lead from the Reverend Herrin, our itinerant preacher. Odd folk they are, but friendly enough, and very competent at what they do. Such as when they helped us set up our pottery kiln, which is a boxy oven with a chimney stack. Our pots are rough as hell, but you can't imagine the pride you get in setting a vase you made on a shelf you built, full of flowers you grew in the garden you dug out from the raw earth.

But that's nothing compared to the first iron tools from Franklin's forge. We couldn't function without our iron and steel tools, of course. But the iron has had an odd impact on our domestic economy. When we arrived the hundred of us actually spread out over a thin sheaf of nearby worlds, rather than in just one. Why not? There was room. But of course you can't carry iron across the worlds, even stuff manufactured locally. So people are slowly moving back into 754, the world with the forge in it, rather than start up the whole process over again somewhere else (although Franklin offered to do just that for multiples of his fee).

Strikes me that everything about the way humanity is opening up the Long Earth is shaped by one simple fact: that you can't step metallic iron across. As an example, we had the idea of opening up parallel fields on next-door Earths so no single crop could be lost to a blight or poor weather. Not worth it; better to use the iron tools we have already made here to extend our holdings on 754.

The way we pay visitors like the Amish for their services is interesting, by the way. Well, I find it so. Money! What has worth, out here in the Long Earth? What has value when every man can own his own goldmine? Interesting theoretical question when you think about it, isn't it?

Among ourselves we do use Datum currencies. Since the Long Earth recession cut in, the yen and the US dollar have held up, especially since they are unforgeable. The British pound collapsed earlier, when half the population fled from that crowded little island – including Franklin, our invaluable smith. Nevertheless, Britain, not for the first time, showed the way out of adversity. In their bad economic years the Brits evolved the 'favour', a currency of flexible worth. In short, it was a unit notional coin whose value was agreed by the buyer and seller at the point of transaction – which made it rather difficult to tax, and so it worked very badly back on the Datum. But it's the ideal currency in the new worlds, which is not surprising since the system was once used in the embryo United States of America, when there was no coin to be had and no effective government to validate its use even if there were.

In places like Reboot, you see, your life is full of small trades. You boil animal fats and make tallow, and since you made too much, maybe your neighbour could use some, and indeed she could, and offers a pound of iron ore in return. That isn't very useful to you, but it certainly is to Franklin the smith, and you hand it over to him in exchange for favour, to be repaid at some future time. So you are now *owed* a favour, which might be something solid, or even an offer to bring back store-bought goods next time he has to go to Hundred K or the Datum. Or whatever.

It's no system to run a civilization on, but a pretty good one for a colony of a hundred people every single one of whom you know personally, and they know you. No point in cheating; *that* will only work for a little while. After all you don't want to be the person who has the doors shut on you when you most desperately need help.

And so every day or so you total up your favours, positive and negative, and if you are ahead of the game then you might take a day off and go fishing. The nurses and midwives do particularly well. How many favours is a successful birth worth? What price an injured hand, treated so conscientiously that you can work again?

Common sense works well in a small community like this, where everybody ultimately depends on the goodwill and good humour of everybody else. It even applies to the way we treat the hobos, as we call them, who occasionally come trickling through our landscape. Drifters, working their way from world to world across the Long Earth, without any intention of settling down like us so far as I can see, just walking through the green and helping themselves to the low-hanging fruit. Well, why not? In the Long Earth there's plenty of room for people to live like that. They come to us drawn by the smoke of the fires; we make them welcome, we'll feed them and have our doctors treat them if they need it.

We make it clear we expect something in return, usually a little labour, maybe just interesting news from home. Most people accept that kind of deal easily enough. People, unfettered, know how to live, how to treat each other. I imagine Neanderthal man learned all this. I guess sometimes the lesson doesn't stick. Sometimes they seem kind of stunned, as if they've been staring at the horizon too long, and they find it difficult to sit still in any one Earth. Long Earth Syndrome, it's called, so I'm told.

We've had more formal contact from home. A postman does the rounds! A good man called Bill Lovell. From the mail we learned that some remote federal agency has validated our various land claims. The most important missive for me was a statement from

Pioneer Support, the government agency that was set up to handle the affairs of emigrants. My bank accounts and investment funds are still running. I'm providing for Rod, of course, our 'phobic' son, our 'homealone', as I'm told current Datum slang has it. Tilda feels this is somehow cheating. Not in the pioneer spirit. But my intention was never to have any of us suffer out here. Why should we? This is my solution, my compromise to ensure my family is protected.

There's been no letter from Rod, not one. We do write to him; he hasn't written back. For better or worse we don't discuss this. It breaks my heart slowly, however.

I want to finish this on a joyous note.

It's now twenty-four hours or more since Cindy Wells went into labour, the colony's first birth. Cindy called in her friends, and Helen went along, who's training up on midwifery. She's only just fifteen, my God. Well, the labour was long, but the birth came without complications. And as I write, it's not long past dawn, they're all still with Cindy.

I can't tell you how proud I am. On Helen's birthday too. (Thanks, Dad!)

So I have one extra chore to perform today. That town sign of ours needs modifying:

WELCOME TO REBOOT
FOUNDED 2026, A.D.
POP. ~~117~~ 118

And in a sky on the other side of the world a gaudy airship hovered in the dawn light, listening to such whispered stories, before it vanished into deeper stepwise realities.

26

Joshua woke up. The big woollen throw he preferred to sleep under was slightly musty, rather heavy, somehow very reassuring. Outside, he saw through his stateroom window, Earths flickered by. There was the endless Eurasian forest, sometimes burning, occasionally covered in snow. Another morning on the *Mark Twain*.

He carefully negotiated his way out of bed, had a shower, dried himself off and slipped the monkey bracelet on to his wrist. It was the only thing of his mother's that he had ever possessed. It was cheap plastic, marginally too tight round his wrist, but in his mind it was worth more than gold could ever be.

The *Mark Twain* gave that tiny little lurch he had learned to expect when the stepping stopped. In theory, he knew there was no reason why there should be a lurch, but every ship has its idiosyncrasies. He looked out of his window again.

Now, against expectation, the ship was hovering over an ocean that, as far as he could see, went on for ever. They had been crossing the vast landscapes of Eurasia for days. Joshua was a Madisonian who had grown up with the lakes near by. God, he thought, I could do with a swim. He stripped down to trunks.

Then, without consulting Lobsang, he ran to the gondola's elevator and let it down until the open cage was only a little way above the deep blue sea, an ocean as calm as a lake.

The ambulant unit appeared in the hatch above him. 'There you are. If you are thinking of a dip in this briny sea, I suggest you think twice. I've sent up my usual balloons and sounding-rockets, and I am pretty certain that if there is any dry land on this planet there is little of it. The sea level is very high: we hover over drowned continents, probably.'

'An ocean world, then.'

'I have no idea if there is anything so sophisticated as a fish swimming around in there. There *appears* to be nothing much more than floating seaweed, some of it extremely green. This is a fascinating world, and exploring it would be an excellent under-taking. However, while I cannot forbid you to go swimming, I urgently counsel you against doing so before I have checked for safety.'

The untroubled sea sparkled beguilingly. 'Oh, come on. It can't hurt, surely.' He heard the sound of mechanical activity up above in the ship.

Lobsang said, 'Can it not? But who knows how evolution might have proceeded on such a world? Joshua, until I check it out, for all we know something might just come up from the depths and you will depart this and all other worlds with a sound that might be accurately described as "clop", with everything that sound suggests.'

Now Joshua heard a hatch opening on the ship, followed by a splash as something dropped into the water.

Lobsang said, 'Such a singular person as you has no right to be the guinea pig when there are creatures more qualified – in this case, my underwater ambulant unit. Behold!'

Something like a mechanical dolphin barrelled out of the sea, stood in the air and dived back in again.

Joshua looked up at Lobsang. He continued to wonder whether the expressions on that engineered face were carefully crafted or whether they were reflexes in some way, true expressions of inner feelings. Either way, right now Lobsang was evidently awash with happiness as he watched his new creation. He did like his toys.

But the grin quickly faded. Lobsang said, 'Various fish noted, water specimens obtained, plankton identified, depth to ocean bed uncertain . . . something coming up . . . it might just be an idea to get back on board – hold on tight!'

The elevator suddenly rose, clanging when it hit the stops. Joshua looked down and saw the wonderful aquatic unit spin into the air one last time, before huge jaws closed on it with dreadful finality.

Shaken, he turned to Lobsang. 'Would you call that a clop?'

'In fact, I think it might be, actually, when all is considered, a CLOP!!'

'Consider me chastened. I'm sorry about your toy submarine. Was it expensive?'

'Astonishingly so, and heavily patented, but, alas, not heavily armoured. However, we have spares. Come on. I'll make the breakfast, for a change.'

When the meal was done, Lobsang waited for Joshua on the observation deck.

'I have labelled our hungry visitor a shark for now. Extremely large sharks have certainly existed on Earth, and I got a good picture of it; the ichthyologists can decide. Please enjoy, with my compliments, the continued use of your legs.'

'All right. I get it. Thank you . . .'

The *Mark Twain* was already stepping onwards. Joshua found himself looking down on forests again, the ocean world far behind: no more sea, no more brilliant sunshine. In a manner that was becoming a habit, Lobsang and Joshua sat together in silence. Though their relationship was reasonable now, hours could pass like this, with barely a word spoken between them.

And, as he turned his mind Westward once more, Joshua felt an odd pressure in the head. It was almost as if he were heading home to the Datum, not further outwards.

For the first time, for some reason, he found himself speculating about an end to this journey. 'Lobsang, how much further are you intending to go? I am with you for the long haul, that's the deal. But I do have responsibilities at home. Sister Agnes and the rest of them are not so spry as they were . . .'

'Interesting reaction from the great loner,' Lobsang said dryly. 'It occurs to me that you, Joshua, are very much like the old-time trackers and hunters of the Old West. Like Daniel Boone, to whom I have compared you before, you shun the company of other people, but not all the time. And remember that even Daniel Boone had a Mrs Boone and a lot of little Boones.'

Joshua said, 'Although some of the little Boones weren't *his* Boones, but the Boones of his brother, if I'm to believe what I once read.'

'I do understand you, Joshua. That's what I'm trying to tell you.'

Joshua bristled. 'I very much doubt that you understand anything about me, tin man.'

'Well, how about this for a deal? If we don't find anyone for you to talk to in the next two weeks, shall we say, I will turn the ship around and head back. We surely already have enough data to keep my friends at the universities as happy as a bucket of clams. You can get some R&R, and I will start work on plans for the *Mark Trine*, trusting that the shade of Mr Clemens will forgive me.' He looked at Joshua's puzzled expression, and relented. 'In the dialect that gives us "twain", meaning the number two, "trine" means three. Just my little joke.'

'I thought you trashed your airship workshop. A small Tunguska event, you said.'

'The Black Corporation has many skunk-work facilities, Joshua. Interesting, incidentally, that you've suggested turning back just as I'm learning that our singing friends from that frosty world some way back have had the same idea.'

'The trolls? What do you mean?'

'I've been observing scattered bands of them, travelling across the worlds. Trolls, and what appear to be other related species, of variant forms. It's difficult to tell in our brief glimpses; there is much to be studied. But simple demographic tracking suggests that on the whole they are heading *back* along the line of our journey, quite a number of them, too. Possibly some kind of migration.'

'Hmm,' Joshua said, feeling that faint pressure in his head. 'Or maybe they're fleeing something.'

'Either way, it's interesting, don't you think? Stepping humanoids! And I wonder what will happen when more of the migrant trolls reach the Datum itself.'

'*More* of them? What do you mean by that?'

'I've told you of fragmentary reports from old traditions – glimpses of transitory beings, tales from myth. I believe that trolls and other species have been visiting our Earth for millennia – perhaps simply to pass through, perhaps for other purposes. The frequency of such reports drops in recent centuries, because of the growth of scientific literacy perhaps.'

Or sheer mental pressure, Joshua thought, as the Earth's population grew, if the trolls and their cousins had the same reaction to crowds as he had.

'But in recent decades, and even since Step Day, such sightings have been on the increase again. The wavefront of the migration we are witnessing, perhaps. Let me give you an example, of a case that now makes a certain kind of sense . . .'

27

A CCORDING TO THE report filed by the two students later – filed and briskly covered up under Britain's Official Secrets Act – the night of the incident had been cloudy, the sky black. This was darkest Oxfordshire, the very centre of England. By the light of their battery-powered storm lantern Gareth unpacked his canvas rucksack and set out the instruments: a cricket bat and stump, a baseball bat, drumsticks filched from the college orchestra's percussion section, even a croquet mallet. Stuff to hit the standing stones with.

While Lol was thumping his forehead against an oak tree.

The oak, with its fellows, towered over the stones, which were like a ring of broken giants' teeth stuck in the ground. This was said to be one of the oldest monuments in the country – possibly it even pre-dated the age of the farmers who had produced most of the great stone monuments in Britain. But nobody knew for sure, because there'd been no decent archaeological investigation of the site. There was no nicely laid footpath, no information trail with boards of factoids to guide the visitors who never came. Just the stones, and the forest that had all but overwhelmed them – and a legend, that these stones would sing, to keep elves and other demons out of the world. A legend that had brought Gareth here in the first place.

Lol wrapped his arms around the tree's gnarly trunk. 'Trees! Trees root us, Gaz. They nurture us. There have been trees on this planet for three hundred million years. Did you know that? Great huge tree ferns back in the Carboniferous. A tree is defined by its form, not by its species. Once we *lived* in trees. Trees are at the centre of all our myths! There are stories from all over of world trees, like ladders to the sky.'

They were both science students, twenty-year-old under-graduates, Lol studying quantum physics, Gareth acoustics. Lol looked younger than his age, like a fifteen-year-old in biker fancy dress, and he did live at home with his parents. But for all the green mythology stuff he liked to spout, you had to remind yourself that Lol had a sharp mind. Gareth found the non-linear equations of fluid mechanics that underlay the acoustics he studied pretty chal-lenging, but Lol's quantum physics was *hard*...

Gareth heard a pop, like somebody stepping. He turned. He thought he glimpsed movement in the long shadows the stones cast in the lantern light. Some forest creature out foraging?

Lol said now, 'Give me a beer.'

Gareth stared at him. 'You were bringing the beers.'

'*You* were.'

'I brought the mallets. Christ. You never do buy your round.' He threw a kettledrum stick, narrowly missing Lol's head. 'If we've got no ale let's get this over with, and get back to the pub before we sober up.'

'Sorry, man.' Lol picked up the drumstick.

Gareth dug out his phone and set it to record the sounds they would make when they started to strike the stones.

He was doing this to make a girl notice him.

She was on an arts course, and Gareth sometimes saw her on the bus ride into town, but he had nothing to talk to her about. Certainly not his geeky engineering studies. He'd vaguely thought this archaeo-acoustics experiment of his might impress her.

For centuries archaeologists had been missing the element of *sound* in the monuments they studied. Gareth had once heard a barbershop quartet perform in a Neolithic chambered tomb. Awesome; the place had obviously been designed for its acoustics. Now he was trying to *play* these standing stones to see if they were laid out for their acoustic properties – an idea that came from the obvious lead offered by their traditional local name, the Singing Stones, and the attached legend that the stones would sing to keep out malevolent spirits. And to explore, vaguely, the way legends of ghosts and spirits and other transients had come to have a whole new interpretation in this age of the Long Earth, when reality had suddenly become porous.

Maybe it was all a bit too geeky. And he hadn't achieved his main objective: here he was with Lol, not *her*. But at least it was a more imaginative way of thinking about the new worlds than you mostly got in Britain. This was just a few years after Step Day. Gareth had spent a gap year summer in the US where they were talking about treks out to the remote worlds, of building an infinity of stepwise Americas. Whereas in England, it was all a kind of dull nothingness. The Long Earth just hadn't inspired John Bull. Of course it didn't help that the stepwise Englands were uniformly choked with forest, but basically, all you saw in England West or East was little rectangular plots cut into the forest, precisely mapping suburban back gardens where middle-class families popped over to grow beans or to catch the sunshine when it rained at home, or, just occasionally, to get savaged by a wild boar. And meanwhile the disadvantaged, young and old, drifted away from the dole and their dead-end jobs and just vanished into the green, and the cities were dying from their empty inner suburbs outward, and the economy slowly crumbled . . .

Lol had been silent for a long time. A long time for him, anyhow. Gareth looked up.

Lol was staring.

Something stood at the precise centre of the stone ring, a group of squat stumpy shapes, that hadn't been there before. At first glance the figures looked like more standing stones to Gareth, more monoliths in a rough circle. No, they weren't monoliths. They had chimp faces, and black, hairy bodies, and they stood upright. Like children in monkey suits. The light of the lantern was uncertain, the shadows deep black.

'They must have stepped in,' Lol breathed.

'Is this some kind of joke? Trick or treat? It's not Halloween, losers.' Gareth was nervous; he always was around unsupervised kids. 'Look, if you lot don't—'

And, as one, the little people opened their mouths and sang. They went straight into a chord, a multipart harmony. Then, after holding the chord for an unreasonable time, they launched into a kind of song. It was fast-moving, shapeless to Gareth's ears. But the harmonies were pitch-perfect, and beautiful, so much so they made Gareth's guts twist.

Lol, on the far side of the ring, looked terrified. He clamped his hands over his ears. 'Make them stop!'

Gareth had an inspiration. He grabbed his mallets. 'Hit the stones! Come on!' He whacked the nearest stone with the baseball bat. It *rang*.

He and Lol hammered the stones wildly. Dull tones rang out, ugly and discordant. Despite his fear of the ape-things, Gareth felt a stab of triumph, of vindication. He'd been right. These stones were lithophones, shaped for the sound they made, not for the way they looked. So he bashed and thumped the stones, and Lol did the same.

And the ape-things were disturbed. Their tight formation broke up, and those monkey-mask faces crumpled, teeth bared, and their song dissolved into hoots and chatters. One by one they began to wink away, disappearing stepwise. Was this what the Singing Stones were *for*? To make these ugly discords, to stop these singing ape-things stepping into the world – just as the legend said?

Soon the clearing between the stones was empty once more.

Gareth stared around at the stones, at the long shadows. The walls of the world seemed very thin.

All of which was how Lobsang and Joshua, on the *Mark Twain*, learned, on considering records of such incidents, that the pioneers of the trolls' enforced migration had already penetrated further than anybody had dreamed.

28

JOSHUA AND LOBSANG pressed deeper into the Long Earth, extending their tentative survey.

Embedded in the blandness of the Corn Belt were plenty of Jokers. Here was a locust world; the airship appeared right in the middle of a flying plague of big heavy insects that battered briefly against the gondola walls. They lingered in one world where, Lobsang suspected, the Tibetan plateau, an accident of tectonic collision, had never formed. His aerial drones revealed that without the Himalayas the climate of the whole of central and southern Asia, even Australia, was radically different.

And there were worlds they couldn't understand at all. A world immersed in a perpetual crimson-red dust storm, like a nightmare version of Mars. A world like a bowling ball, utterly smooth, under a cloudless deep blue sky.

The stepping halted again. There was that usual odd lurch, like falling off a swing. Joshua looked down. This was a world of yellowed grass and spindly trees. The airship drifted over a river that had shrivelled in its bed, exposing wide borders of cracked mud. Animals crowded thick around the water, eyeing each other nervously. Joshua glanced at the earthometer: 127,487. A meaningless string of digits.

'You can see this world is suffering a particularly dry season,' Lobsang said. 'Which has drawn an unusual concentration of animals to the water. It gives us an opportunity to observe efficiently. You may have noticed I am making a habit of pausing at such convenient locales.'

'There are a hell of a lot of horses.'

And so there were, small and large, ranging in size from a Shetland pony to a zebra, and of subtly different designs, some shaggier, some tubbier, some with two toes on each foot, or three or four . . . None of them looked quite like *real* horses, like Datum horses.

But in amongst the herds, jostling to get to the water, were other animals. One family of tall, spindly beasts were like camels rebuilt to the plan of a giraffe. Their young, with legs like drinking straws, looked heartbreakingly fragile. And there were elephants, with a variety of tusk types. And things like rhinos, things like hippos . . . These herbivores, temporarily forced together, were skittish, nervous, for there were carnivores too. There were always carnivores. Joshua spotted what looked like a pack of hyenas, and a cat not unlike a leopard. Waiting, watching the throngs of wary drinkers at the lake.

Now a creature looking very much like a beefy ostrich approached. A family of rhino-like beasts backed off nervously. But the bird stretched out its neck, opened its beak wide, and fired out a ball, like a cannonball. This slammed into the ribcage of a big male rhino, that went down bellowing. The family scattered, and the bird closed in to feed on the fallen male.

Lobsang used an anaesthetic rifle mounted on the gondola to bring down the bird, and sent down his ambulant unit to inspect it. The bird had a separate stomach sac which filled up with a mixture of faeces, bones, gravel, bits of wood, other indigestibles. All this was mortared together with guano to make a large ball as hard as teak. The Long Earth truly was full of wonders, and for Joshua the cannonball bird duly took its place in the gallery.

The world was logged, and the airship moved on. That night the movie was Lobsang's choice: *Galaxy Quest*. Joshua couldn't concentrate on the action, but, rocking with the stepping, mumbling 'Never give up! Never surrender!', he slowly fell asleep.

*

He woke to bright sunlight. The ship had stopped again, and sounding-rockets soared into an unsuspecting sky.

In this world, that bit warmer than those earlier – Lobsang observed a steadily warming trend as they ploughed ever further West – a string of lakes had been cut into the forest blanket. Lobsang speculated that they were the result of a multiple meteorite strike. Two of the lakes were separated by a narrow strip of land, a striking feature that reminded Joshua of the isthmus between Mendota and Monona at Madison.

Lobsang announced, 'This is Earth West 139,171. We're still in the Corn Belt.'

'Why have we stopped?'

'Look to the north.'

Joshua saw the smoke. It was a thin black column, a few miles away to the north-east.

'It's not a campfire,' said Lobsang. 'Or a forest fire. A burning township, perhaps.'

'Human, then.'

'Oh, yes. And I'm picking up a radio signal.' Lobsang played a scrap of it, a pleasant recorded female voice broadcasting her presence to a silent world, in English, Russian, French. 'Spindrift colonizers. The signal claims they are the First Heavenly Church of the Cosmic Confidence Trick Victims. We are far from home; there can be few substantial settlements much further out . . . That fire is from burning buildings. Evidently something has gone wrong here.'

'Let's go see.'

'The danger is unknowable. Unquantifiable.'

Joshua might be a loner, but there was an unwritten rule out in the reaches of the Long Earth that you helped the other, the wanderer, the community in trouble. 'We're going.'

The airship's big rotors started up, and they moved off towards the smoke.

'Shall I tell you about the Confidence Trick Victims?'

So Joshua learned that while the mainstream religions remained concentrated on the Low Earths because of access to the holy sites on the Datum – the Vatican, Mecca – many splinter religious communities had gone out deep into the Long Earth, each seeking freedom of expression, as similar communities had done for millennia on Earth. Such pilgrims would often choose places that (in Datum context) were geographically remote too, like this one: on this distant Earth they were still far to the east of the location of Moscow. And yet, even among these maverick groups, the Cosmic Confidence Trick Victims stood out as somewhat unusual.

'They consider their religion to reflect the truth about the universe, which is its essential absurdity. True Victims believe that there is one Born Again every minute. And they must be fruitful and multiply, to create more human minds to appreciate the Joke.'

Joshua murmured, 'I don't think this Joke has had a good punchline.'

They sailed over a few square miles of cleared forest around a central township, built around a hillock, the only high point on the isthmus. A relatively grand building sat atop the hillock. There were fields, marked by rows of stones. Lobsang pointed out a characteristic tint to some of the crops: marijuana plants, acres of them, which told you a lot about the nature of this community.

There were corpses everywhere.

Lobsang took the ship up to five hundred feet and hovered. Rooks, disturbed, flapped and rose, to descend again. The Victims of the Cosmic Confidence Trick apparently preferred to wear green robes, and so the central square and the dirt roads radiating away from it were littered with emerald splashes. Who would come all the way up here to wipe out several hundred peaceful souls, whose only eccentricity lay in believing life was a gold brick?

'I'm going down,' Joshua said.

Lobsang said, 'This happened recently. This crime, this attack. Observe that the bodies have not yet been scavenged. Something, or somebody, butchered three hundred people, Joshua. The attackers may still be down there.'

'And maybe the three-hundred-and-first is still alive.'

'The big building in the centre of the village, on that hillock.' The hill was the only high point on the isthmus. 'That's the source of the radio beacon.'

'Put me down a hundred yards away.' Joshua thought it over. 'And then jump a few worlds away, shift a little in space, and step back. Maybe if there is somebody still here you can lure them out.'

' "Lure them out." Hardly a reassuring idea.'

'Just do it, Lobsang.'

The airship descended.

There was a stink of grease, of burning meat.

Joshua, with parrot on his shoulder, walked down a straight-line dirt street. A few rooks, irritated, climbed into the air. It was a surprisingly well-developed community to find so far out. The buildings were wattle and daub on sturdy timber frames, set out in neat rectilinear rows. He supposed the pioneers who had laid out these plots and street had dreamed of the city to be built one day on this plan. Now many of the buildings were burned out; further away, a whole district smoked fitfully.

He came to his first body. She was a middle-aged woman who had had her throat ripped out. No human had done this, surely.

Joshua walked on. He found more people, in a ditch, in the doorways, inside the houses, men, women and children. Some of them looked as if they had been running when they were struck down. None of them seemed to be wearing Steppers, but that wasn't unusual. They had been at home here, in this world; they thought they were safe.

He reached the big central building on its hillock. If this place followed the pattern of most religion-based colonies, this was most likely the church, the holy building, the first permanent structure to be erected, and as such it would house a lot of the community's common property like the radio station and any power unit. It was also the place of refuge when disaster struck, as churches had been throughout western history. There were certainly a lot of bodies around the building. Maybe the enemy had struck just after morning prayers, or whatever equivalent ceremony the Victims had. Morning Stand-Up, perhaps.

The doors were closed. There could be anything inside. Black clouds of flies flew up as Joshua approached, and rooks watched resentfully from rooftops.

The airship reappeared, right above him.

'Lobsang, any movement?'

'No hot spots near you.'

'I'm going to try the church. Temple, whatever.'

'Be careful.'

He came to double doors set in a stout wall, of stone faced with some kind of plaster. Joshua tried a kick, and nearly broke his ankle. He braced for another try.

'Save your fragile endoskeleton,' Lobsang said dryly. 'There's an open door at the back.'

The back door was, in fact, smashed off its hinges and sagged outward into the street. Joshua walked through the broken frame into a little radio room where a transmitter was still sending its innocent message to the universe. Joshua respectfully shut it off. Another door led to a utility room, the kind of combined kitchen and junk store that every church or church hall would have; there was a tea urn, and playgroup toys of crudely carved wood. There were even children's finger paintings on the walls, and a cleaning rota, written in English. It would have been Sister Anita Dowsett's turn next week.

A further door led into the main hall. And this was where most of the bodies were. Blood filmed the floor and spattered the walls, and flies buzzed in a cloud over the slumped, still forms.

Moving into the room, Joshua had to step over the bodies, a handkerchief to his mouth. He turned some of them over, inspecting wounds. At first he thought they'd fled in here, seeking the safety of thick walls and heavy doors – even these far-flung pioneers would fall back on ancient instincts. But there was something odd about the pattern.

'Joshua?'

'I'm here, Lobsang.' He reached an altar. The centrepiece was a big silver hand thumbing a golden nose. 'These were comedy atheists. It must have been *fun* living here. They didn't deserve this. If it's a crime, if humans did this, we'll have to report it when we go back.'

'It wasn't people, Joshua. Look around. All the wounds are gouges. Bites. Crushed skulls. This was the work of animals, frightened animals. And that door behind you was broken outwards, not inwards. Whatever did this didn't come in through the door. It *stepped* in here, and pushed its way *out* through the door.'

Joshua nodded. 'So maybe the townsfolk didn't seek shelter in here. They were here already, at their morning service. And whatever it was erupted right in the middle of them. Stepping animals, that were fleeing – something.'

'The beasts panicked, evidently. But I do wonder what effect the weed fumes I detect in the air had on them . . .'

Joshua found himself staring down at one broken body. Naked, hair-covered – not human. A body of roughly human proportions, slim, obviously bipedal, of evident wiry strength, on which was set a small head, like a chimp's, with an ape's flat nose. Not a troll, but some other kind of humanoid. It had been killed by a knife wound to the throat; the chest was soaked with drying blood. Somebody had had the guts to fight back, then, against the fury of the terrified super-strong ape-men that had stepped into the middle of his or her family.

'You see this, Lobsang?'

Cameras on the parrot whirred and panned. 'I see it.'

Joshua stepped back from the corpse and stood, eyes closed, imagining. 'We're on a hilltop, the highest point for a good way around. A dense forest is a difficult place to step in a hurry. If you wanted to flee with your family across many worlds you'd be forced to congregate in an open place, a high point, because you'd otherwise be blocked by the trees. But in this particular world the townsfolk had built their church on the highest point. Right in the way.'

'Go on.'

'I think these creatures were stepping. Gathered on the hilltop, heading East, fleeing away from the worlds further West, like the trolls. Stampeding.'

Lobsang asked, 'Stampeding from *what*? That's a question we will have to answer before we can go home, Joshua.'

'Suddenly they found themselves *here*, in this enclosed space, with all these humans. They panicked. More and more of them piled in . . . They killed everybody in here, they broke out, they hunted down everybody else.'

'From what we know of them, Joshua, trolls wouldn't do that. Consider how they treated Private Percy. They could have killed him easily.'

'Perhaps not. But these weren't trolls.'

'I would like to suggest we label these creatures *elves*. I'm drawing on more mythology, partial records of more tentative, misunderstood encounters, with mysterious, slender, human-like creatures who passed through our world, ghost-like. The existence of a variety of stepping humanoids could justify a large body of mythology, Joshua.'

'And no doubt you're drawing on other encounters out in the Long Earth you haven't told me about,' Joshua said dryly.

'That too. By the way,' Lobsang said more urgently, 'I've spotted something else. Maybe a quarter-mile west of your position.'

'Humans? Trolls? What?'

'Go see.'

29

HE HURRIED OUT of the church, relieved to be in the open air, away from the stink of blood.

A quarter-mile west, Lobsang had said. Joshua glanced at the position of the sun, turned and ran that way. Before he had gone a couple of hundred yards he heard the moaning.

It was a humanoid, lying in the dirt, on her back. Not a troll, perhaps a variant of elf, given Lobsang's definition based on what he had found in the temple, but not identical to the one he'd inspected there – at any rate another species new to Joshua. Maybe five feet tall, skinny, coated with hair, she was a stretched, upright-posture chimp with a hauntingly human face, despite her flat, chimp-like nose. And, unlike the beast in the temple, her head seemed to bulge, the cranium outsized for her body to Joshua's eyes – the brain was evidently larger even than a human's. And she was in trouble. She was heavily pregnant. Barely conscious, she moaned and thrashed, and tore at the fur over her swollen belly, and watery blood leaked out between her legs.

As Joshua bent over her, her eyes opened. She had big slanting eyes, like a cartoon alien's, but ape-brown, lacking the whites of a human's. Eyes that widened in alarm, briefly, and looked at him imploringly.

He felt the creature's stomach. 'She's close to term. Something's wrong. The baby should have been born by now.'

Lobsang murmured, 'I would have hazarded that the big head of this creature's baby would make it impossible for her to deliver it.'

'What did you put in this pack?' Before Lobsang had a chance to reply he had the pack on his chest open and was rummaging inside it for the first-aid box. 'And, Lobsang? Get that ship down here. I'm going to need more supplies before we're done.'

'Done with what?'

'I'm going to get that baby out.' He stroked the cheek of the female. His own mother had once lain alone in a world, in the throes of labour. 'Too posh to push, are we? Let's do it the American way.'

'You're going to perform a caesarean?' Lobsang asked. 'You don't have the capacity to do that.'

'Maybe not, but I'm quite certain you do. And we're going to do this together, Lobsang.' He dumped out the contents of the med kit, trying to think. 'I'll need morphine. Sterilizing fluid. Scalpels. Needles, thread . . .'

'We're very far from home. You'll exhaust our medical supplies on this stunt. I have the facility to manufacture more, but—'

'I need to do this.' He could do nothing for the Victims, but he could do something for this elf female – or at least he could try. It was Joshua's way of fixing the world, just a little bit. 'Help me, Lobsang.'

An aeons-long pause. Then: 'I have of course full records of most major medical procedures. Even obstetrics, though I scarcely imagined it would be needed on this trip.'

Joshua fixed the parrot so Lobsang could see what he was doing, and spread out his tools. 'Lobsang. Speak to me. What's first?'

'We must consider whether to make a longitudinal incision or a lower uterine section . . .'

Joshua hastily shaved the beast's lower stomach. Then, trying to keep a steady hand, he held a bronze scalpel over the abdomen wall. And just as he was about to cut into the flesh, the baby vanished. He felt its absence, as the womb imploded.

He sat back in shock. 'It stepped! Damn it – the baby stepped!'

Then the adults came. Two females: a mother, a sister? They

moved in a blur of sprint paces and steps, flickering in and out of existence all around him. Joshua wouldn't have believed stepping at that speed was possible.

Lobsang murmured, 'Just stay still.'

The adults glared at Joshua, scooped up the mother and disappeared with soft pops.

Joshua slumped. 'I don't believe it. What just happened?'

Lobsang sounded exhilarated. 'Evolution, Joshua. Evolution just happened. All upright humanoids have trouble giving birth. You know that, and your mother learned it the hard way. As we evolved, the female pelvis shrank to allow for bipedalism, but at the same time the baby's brain grew bigger – which is why we're born so helpless. We emerge with a lot of growing to do before we're independent.

'But it appears that in this species the problem of the pelvis has been sidestepped. Literally.' He laughed gently. 'Here, the baby isn't born through the birth canal. It *steps* out of the womb, Joshua. Placenta, umbilical and all, I imagine. It makes sense. An ability to step must shape all aspects of a creature's life ways, if you give evolution time to exploit it. And if you don't have to go to all the trouble of being born, your brain can get as big as you like.'

Joshua felt empty. 'They care for their ill. If I'd have opened her up, the mother wouldn't have survived the wound I'd have inflicted.'

Lobsang murmured in his ear, 'You weren't to know. You tried your best. Now come home. You need a shower.'

30

FURTHER WEST YET, the Long Earth gradually became greener, arid worlds rarer. The forested worlds were blanketed thicker, with oak-like trees spreading out of the river valleys and lapping at the higher ground, like a rising tide of green. Out on the rarely glimpsed plains the animals still mostly looked familiar to Joshua – kinds of horses, kinds of deer, kinds of camels. Yet sometimes he glimpsed stranger beasts, blocky, low-slung predators that were neither cats nor dogs, herds of huge long-necked herbivores that looked like elephants crossed with rhinos.

On the nineteenth day, around Earth West 460,000, Lobsang somewhat arbitrarily declared they had reached the limit of the Corn Belt. The worlds here were surely too warm, the forests too thick, to make farming worthwhile.

And about the same time they crossed the Atlantic coast of Europe, somewhere around the latitude of Britain. A journey that had become a dull jaunt across a largely unbroken green blanket of forest became duller yet as they sailed out over the breast of the sea.

Joshua sat in the observation deck for hour upon hour. Lobsang rarely spoke, which was a mercy for Joshua. The gondola was almost soundless, save for the whisper of the air pumps, the whirring of suspended instrument pallets as they turned this way and that. Cooped up in this drifting sensory deprivation tank, Joshua fretted about the loss of muscle tone and fitness. Sometimes he performed stretching exercises, yoga postures, or jogged on the spot. One thing the airship lacked was a gym, and Joshua didn't feel like asking Lobsang to fabricate any equipment; he'd only end up in rowing-machine challenges with the ambulant unit.

Lobsang had increased their lateral speed over the ocean. On the twenty-fifth day they crossed the eastern coast of America, some-where around the latitude of New York, and found themselves coasting over another forest-blanketed landscape.

There was no more talk of stopping, or turning back. They both recognized the need to go on as long as they could, until they had made some inroads into the mystery of whatever was driving the humanoid migration. Joshua found himself shuddering when he imagined the panicky carnage he had witnessed in the town of the Cosmic Confidence Trick Victims unleashed in Madison, Wisconsin.

But, once over land again, they reached an arrangement. Lobsang travelled on during the night. This didn't trouble Joshua's sleep, and Lobsang's senses were infinitely finer even in the dark than Joshua's were by daylight. By day, however, Joshua negotiated a stay of at least a few hours each day in which he could stand on the good Earth, whichever good Earth it happened to be. Sometimes Lobsang, in the ambulant unit, came down in the elevator with him. To Joshua's surprise he handled even rugged terrain with ease, strolling, occasionally taking a swim in a lake, very realistically.

Generally speaking the lapping forest endured, in these remote worlds. During his daily descents Joshua observed differences of detail, different suites of herbivores and carnivores, and a gradual change of character in the grander frame: fewer flowering plants, more ferns, a drabber feel to the worlds. Joshua was covering twenty or thirty thousand new worlds in every day-night cycle. But, truth to tell, as thousands more worlds clicked by it was a case of see one and you've seen them all. In between stops, while Lobsang catalogued his observations and drafted his technical papers, Joshua sat in his couch and slept, or let his mind float in green, teeth-filled dreams so vivid he wasn't always sure if he was awake or asleep.

There were occasional novelties. Once, somewhere near where Tombstone would have been had anyone been there to name it, Joshua dutifully took samples from enormous man-high fungi that would have proved something of an obstacle to Wyatt Earp and Doc Holliday had they come riding down the street. The fungi had a creamy look, and not to put too fine a point on it smelled wonderful, a thought which had also occurred to the little mice-like creatures that had honeycombed them like Emmental cheese.

In the earpiece Lobsang said, 'Try some if you wish. And in any case, bring me back a reasonably large piece for testing.'

'You want me to eat some before you know if it's poisonous?'

'I think that is very unlikely. In fact, I intend to try it myself.'

'I shouldn't be surprised. I've seen you drink coffee. So you eat too?'

'Why, yes! A certain input of organic matter is essential. But as I digest the fungus I will break it down and analyse it. A mildly tedious process. Many humans with special dietary requirements must go through the same routine, but without using a mass spectrometer, which instrument is part of my anatomy. You would be surprised how many foodstuffs actually do contain nuts . . .'

Lobsang's verdict that evening was that a few pounds of the flesh of the giant mushrooms contained enough proteins, vitamins and minerals to keep a human alive for weeks, although in culinary terms totally bored. 'However,' he added, 'something that grows so quickly, contains all the nutrients a human being needs, and can flourish more or less anywhere, is undoubtedly something for the fast food industry to take an interest in.'

'Always glad to help transEarth make a quick buck, Lobsang.'

To break up the routine, that night Joshua sat up to witness the journey in the dark. Sometimes there were fires, scattered across the darkened landscapes. But there are always fires, wherever you've got trees and lightning and dry grass. Move on, folks, nothing to see here.

He complained about the drabness of the view.

'What did you expect?' said Lobsang. 'Generally speaking, I would expect many Earths to be, at least at a first glance – and remember, Joshua, a first glance is mostly all we get – rather dull. Remember when you were young, all those pictures of dinosaurs in the Jurassic? All those different species gathered in one snappy frame, with a tyrannosaur wrestling with a stegosaur in the foreground? Nature generally isn't like that, and nor were dinosaurs. Nature, by and large, is either reasonably silent, or earth-shakingly noisy. Predators and their prey spread out sparsely. Which is why I have maintained my habit of stopping in relatively drought-stricken worlds, where many specimens collect at waterholes, albeit in rather artificial conditions.'

'But how much are we missing, Lobsang? Even when we stop at a world we barely take a look at it before going on, despite your probes and rockets. If all we are getting is one first glance after another . . .' From his own experience on his sabbaticals, Joshua had a visceral feeling that you needed to live in a world to understand it, rather than scan it as you riffled the Long Earth pack. This was the thirty-third day of the journey. 'So where are we now?'

'I assume you mean in terms of Earth geography? Approximately around Northern California. Why?'

'Let's take a halt. I've been more than a month in this flying hotel. Let's spend at least one whole day in one place just, well, chilling out, OK? And *experiencing*. One whole day, and a night. You could fill up your water tanks. And frankly I am getting stir crazy.'

'Very well. I can hardly object. I will find a suitably intriguing world and cease stepping. As we are over California, would you like me to fabricate a surfboard for you?'

'Ha ha.'

'You have changed, Joshua, do you know that?'

'You mean because I'm arguing with you?'

'As a matter of fact, yes. I am intrigued; you are quicker, less hesitant, less like a person walking around in his own head. Of course, you're still you. Indeed I'm wondering if possibly you are more *you* than you have been for a very long time, now that you know how you were born.'

Joshua shrugged this off. 'Don't push it, Lobsang. Thanks for the bracelet. But you're no therapist. Maybe travel broadens the mind—'

'Joshua, if *your* mind was any broader it would start pouring out of your ears.'

Though it was midnight Joshua wasn't sleepy, and he began to fix a meal.

'How about a movie, Joshua?'

'I'd prefer to read. Any suggestions?'

The book screen lit up. 'I know of no more apposite a title!'

Joshua stared. '*Roughing It*?'

'In many respects, Twain's best work, I always think, although I will always have a soft spot for *Life on the Mississippi*. Read it. It is what it says, a journey into new territory, and often very funny in an acerbic way. Enjoy!'

And Joshua enjoyed it. He read, and dozed, and this time dreamed of Indian attacks.

The next day, around noon, the stepping stopped with that familiar lurch. Joshua found himself looking down at a lake, a shield of grey-blue that broke up the forest.

Lobsang announced, 'Surf's up, dude.'

'Oh, good grief.'

On the ground, the forest was a pleasant place to be. Squadrons of bats hurtled after flies in the green-lit air above, air that smelled of damp wood and leaf mould. The soft sounds around Joshua were, oddly, much *quieter* than mere silence would have been. Joshua had learned that absolute silence in nature was such an unusual state that it was not only noticeable but positively menacing. But the murmur of this deep forest was a natural white noise.

Lobsang said, 'Joshua, look to your left. Quietly now.'

They were like horses, shy-looking, furtive creatures, with oddly curving necks and padded feet, the size of puppies. And there was something like an elephant with a stubby trunk, but only a couple of feet tall at the shoulder.

'Cute,' said Joshua.

'The lake is straight ahead,' Lobsang said.

The lake was surrounded by a wall of tree trunks and a fringe of open ground. The still water was choked with reeds and rushes, and in the rare open sunlight, under a blue sky, exotic-looking birds descended in clouds of pink-white flapping. On the far shore Joshua glimpsed a dog-like animal, tremendously large – it had to be four, five yards long, with a massive head and enormous jaws that must themselves have protruded for another yard. Before he could raise his binoculars it had slipped into the forest shadows.

He said, 'That was surely a mammal. But it had jaws like a crocodile.'

'A mammal, yes. In fact I suspect it's a distant relative of the whale – our whale, I mean. And there are real crocodiles in the water, Joshua, as usual. A universal.'

'It's as if parts of animals have been jumbled up – as if somebody's been playing at evolution.'

'We are now many hundreds of thousands of steps from the Datum, Joshua. In this remote world we're seeing representatives of many of the animal orders we have on our branch of the probability tree, but as if reimagined. Evolution is evidently chaotic, like the weather—'

He heard a kind of grunting, like a pig, a big heavy-chested pig, coming from behind him.

'Joshua. Don't run. Behind you. Turn very slowly.'

He obeyed. He visualized the weapons he carried, the knife at his belt, the air gun in his chest pack. And up above was the airship, Lobsang with a flying arsenal at his command. He tried to feel reassured.

Huge hogs. That was his first impression. Half a dozen of them, each as tall as a man at the shoulder, with powerful-looking legs, and backs that rose in bristling humps, and tiny coal-black eyes, and jaws long and strong. And each of them carried a humanoid – not a troll, a skinny upright figure with a chimp face and rust-brown hair, sitting astride his hog as if riding a huge ugly horse.

Joshua was a long way from the cover of the trees.

'More elves,' Lobsang whispered.

'The same breed that wiped out the Victims?'

'Or their first cousins. The Long Earth is a big arena, Joshua; there must be many speciation events.'

'You sent me down here to encounter these creatures, didn't you? This is what you call a restful break?'

'You can't deny it's interesting, Joshua.'

One elf called out, a pant-hoot cry like a chimp's, and kicked his mount in the ribs. The six beasts trotted forward at Joshua, with guttural grunts.

'Lobsang, your advice?'

The hogs were speeding up.

'Lobsang—'

'Run!'

Joshua ran, but the pigs ran faster. He had barely closed any ground on the descending airship, or the forest, when a huge body came plummeting past him. Joshua smelled dirt and blood and shit and a kind of greasy musk, and a small fist slammed into his back and sent him sprawling.

The pigs capered around him, oddly playful despite their size and bulk. Their huge random violence was terrifying. He expected to be crushed, or gored on the canine teeth embedded in the tips of their snouts. But instead the pigs kept running by him, and the humanoids, the elves, whooping and hooting, leaned over to make passes at him. Blades flashed at him – blades of stone! He cowered and rolled.

At last they pulled back, into a loose circle around him. Shaking, he got to his feet, feeling for his own weapons. He wasn't cut, he realized, save for nicks on his face, and on his shoulder where a swipe had gone through the cloth of his coverall. But they had cut the supply pack from his chest, even pickpocketed the knife at his waist. He had been expertly stripped, leaving only the parrot on his shoulder, the processor pack on his back.

The elves were toying with him.

Now the elves stood up on the backs of their strange mounts. They weren't like the trolls, they were much skinnier, more graceful, lithe, strong, their hairy upright bodies like those of child gymnasts. They had long tree-climbing arms, very human legs, and small heads with wizened chimp-like faces. They all seemed to be male. Some of them were sporting skinny erections.

Joshua looked for positives. 'Well, they're smaller than me. Five feet, maybe?'

'Don't underestimate them,' Lobsang's whisper in his headset urged. 'They're stronger than you. And this is their world, remember.'

The pant-hooting cries began again, and seemed to reach a crescendo. Then one of the elves kicked his animal's ribs. The beast, its own eyes fixed on Joshua, began to stride steadily forward. The elf bared human-looking teeth and hissed.

This time they weren't playing.

There are moments when terror is like a treacle that slows down time. Once when Joshua was a kid he had slipped over an edge at a limestone quarry, just a ten-minute bike ride from the Home, and his friends couldn't haul him back, and he had had to hang on while they ran for help. His arms had hurt like hell. But what he remembered most of all was the tiny detail of the rock right in front of his eyes. There had been flecks of mica in it, and lichen, a miniature forest dried yellow by the sun. That little landscape had become his whole world, until somebody somewhere started yelling, and some other guy's hands grabbed his wrists, hauled on arms that felt like they were filled with hot lead . . .

The elf leapt in the air, and flickered out of existence. The hog trotted on, grunting, speeding up. The realization came to Joshua, with all the clarity of a mica fleck on a sun-warmed rock, that the elf was stalking him. And it had *stepped*.

The hog was still coming. Joshua stood his ground. At the last second it hesitated, stumbled, veered away from him.

And the elf returned, stretching, its feet braced on the hog's back, its hands clamped around Joshua's neck – hands in place to throttle Joshua, *even as it stepped back into the world*. Joshua was astonished at the precision of the manoeuvre.

But now the elf's strong ape hands were squeezing, and Joshua was driven to the ground, unable to breathe. He reached, but the elf's arms were longer than his; he flailed, unable to reach the creature's snarling face, and blackness rimmed his vision. He tried to think. His weapons, his pack, were stolen and scattered, but the parrot still sat on his shoulder. He grabbed the parrot's frame with both hands, and shoved it in the face of the elf. Bits of glass and plastic erupted, the elf fell back screaming, and mercifully that death grip at his throat was released.

But the other elves on their hogs screamed and closed.

'Joshua!' A loudspeaker, booming from the air. The airship was coming down, slowly, ponderously, dangling a rope ladder.

He got to his feet, gasping for breath through a crushed throat, but a bank of elves on hogs stood between him and the ladder, and the injured elf on the ground shrieked its fury. The only gap in the circle surrounding him was the way that lead elf had come.

So he ran that way, away from the airship, but out of the circle of elves. The wrecked parrot was still attached to his coverall by cables; it dragged through the dirt behind him. The yelling elves pursued him. If he could somehow double back, or maybe reach the forest—

'Joshua! No! Watch out for the—'

The ground suddenly gave way under him.

He fell a yard or so, and found himself in a hollow surrounded by dogs – no, like a mix of dogs and bears, he'd glimpsed this kind before, lithe canine bodies with powerful heads and muzzles like bears. Their black-furred bodies squirmed all around him, females, puppies. This was some kind of den, not a trap. But even the puppies were snapping, snarling packets of aggression. The smallest of them, it was almost cute, closed its bear-like jaws on Joshua's leg. He kicked, trying to loosen the little creature's grip. The other dog-bears barked and snarled, and Joshua expected them to fall on him in a moment.

But here came the elves on their swinish mounts. The adult dogs rose up out of their den in a pack, and hurled themselves at the hogs. The fight erupted in a cloud of yelps, barks, grunts, cries, pant-hoots, snapping teeth, screams of pain and sprays of blood, while the elves flashed in and out of existence, as if glimpsed under a strobe lamp.

Joshua climbed out of the den and ran away from the fight, or tried to. But that stubborn pup clung to his leg, and he was still dragging the absurd wreckage of the parrot. He glanced up. The airship was almost overhead. Joshua jumped for the rope ladder, grabbed it, and viciously kicked away the pup. The airship rose immediately.

Below, the dogs had now encircled the huge hogs, which fought back ferociously. Joshua saw one big dog-bear sink its teeth into the neck of a screaming hog, which crashed to the ground. But another hog scooped up a dog in its big tusked jaw and threw it through the air, squealing, its chest ripped open. Meanwhile the elves flickered through the carnage. Joshua saw one elf face a dog that leapt for his throat. The elf flicked away and reappeared beside the dog as it sailed through the air, spun with balletic grace, and swiped at the animal's torso with a thin stone blade, disembowelling the dog before it hit the ground. The elves were fighting for survival, but Joshua got the impression they were fighting individually, not for each other; it wasn't a battle so much as a series of private duels. It was every man for himself. Or would have been, if they had been men.

And the airship rose up, beyond the reach of the trees, and into the sunlight. The fight was reduced to a dusty, blood-splashed detail in a landscape across which the airship's shadow drifted serenely. Joshua, still barely able to breathe, climbed the ladder, and spilled into the gondola.

'You kicked a puppy,' Lobsang said accusingly.

'Add it to the charge sheet,' he gasped. 'Next time you pick a vacation site, Lobsang, think a bit more Disneyland.' Then the darkness around his vision that had been there ever since the close encounter with the elf folded over him.

31

HE WAS PRETTY badly hurt, he learned later. Lots of minor
injuries, many of which he hadn't noticed at the time. The
damage to his neck, his throat. Scratches, cuts, even a bite mark –
not from the puppy at his ankle, this was the imprint of human-
like teeth in his shoulder. Lobsang's ambulant treated the cuts,
dosed him with antibiotics, and fed him painkillers.

He drifted away. Sometimes he woke briefly, fuzzily, to see bone-
white stars above, or green carpets rolling beneath the airship. The
steady swinging rhythm of stepping was comforting. He slept away
days, in the end.

But the further they travelled, heading ever West, the more
Joshua became aware of that odd pressure in his head, even as he
dozed. The kind of stuffy feeling he always got when he had to go
back to the Datum: the pressure of all those crowding minds,
drowning the Silence. Could it be, as some said, that the Long
Earth was a kind of loop that closed back on itself, and he was
being brought back to the start, back to the Datum? That would be
strange enough. But if not, what lay ahead? And what was driving
the trolls across the arc of worlds?

When he finally awoke fully the stepping had stopped once
more. He sat up on his couch and looked around.

'Take it easy, Joshua,' came Lobsang's disembodied voice.

'We've stopped.' His voice was husky, but it worked.

'You've slept deeply. Joshua, I'm glad you're awake. We must
talk. You do realize you were never in any real danger, don't you?'

He rubbed his throat. 'It didn't feel that way at the time.'

'I could have taken out those elves individually at any time. I have advanced laser sighting on—'

'Why didn't you?'

'You'd asked for shore leave. I thought you were enjoying yourself!'

'As you said before, we need to work on our communication, Lobsang.'

Joshua pushed back the throw, stood up and stretched. He was wearing shorts and a T-shirt that he couldn't remember putting on. He didn't feel like running a marathon, but on the other hand he wasn't passing out. He went to the head, walking carefully, and briskly washed some of the sweat off his body. His small scars were healing, and his throat no more than twinged. He emerged, and took fresh clothing from the closet.

Through the stateroom window he saw that the airship was anchored over a thick reef of rainforest that stretched to a green-cloaked horizon. Mist banks hung over swathed valleys. The sun was low; Joshua guessed it was early morning. The airship was maybe a hundred feet up.

Lobsang said, 'We haven't been stopping every day, but it's difficult to observe much from up here.'

'Because of the thickness of the forest?'

'I've been sending down the ambulant unit. We're far from home, Joshua. We're over nine hundred thousand steps out. Think of that. You can see how it is here – this is typical, forest blanketing the landscape as far as we can see. Probably covering the whole continent. Difficult to make observations.'

'But there's evidently something here you're interested in, yes?'

'Look at the live feed,' Lobsang said.

The image in the wall screen was jittery, uncertain, taken from a camera far away. It showed an opening in the forest, a gash in the canopy evidently caused by the fall of a giant tree, whose trunk lay at the centre of the clearing, coated with lichen and exotic fungi.

The access of light had allowed saplings and under-storey shrubs to shoot up.

And the new growth attracted humanoids. Joshua spotted what looked like a pack of trolls. They were sitting in the open in a tight cluster, patiently grooming, each picking insects from the back of the one in front. They sang, all the time, snatches of melody like half-forgotten songs – scraps of harmony in two, three, four parts, improvised on the spot and then forgotten, dimly heard by distant microphones.

'Trolls?'

'Apparently,' Lobsang murmured. 'It would take musicologists a century to unravel the structure of that singing. Keep watching.'

As Joshua's eyes became accustomed to the shaky images, he began to see more groups of humanoids, across the clearing and in the forest shadows, some of kinds he didn't recognize, at play, working, grooming, maybe hunting. They were all humanoids, it seemed, rather than apes; any time one of them stood up you could see the neatness of its bipedal stance. He said, 'They don't seem to bother each other. The different kinds.'

'Evidently not. In fact quite the opposite.'

'Why have they congregated here? After all, they're different species.'

'I suspect, in this particular community, they have become co-dependent. They use each other. They probably have subtly different sensory ranges, so that one kind may detect a danger before the others: we know that trolls use ultrasonics, for example. Similarly, you get different species of dolphins swimming together. I'm following your advice, you see, Joshua. I've been taking more time to inspect Long Earth marvels like this aggregation of humanoids. Remarkable sight, isn't it? It's like a dream of humanity's evolutionary past, many hominid types together.'

'But what of the future, Lobsang? What happens when human colonists get out here in earnest? How can this survive?'

'Well, that's another question. And what happens if they are all driven East in the greater migration? Do you wish to go down?'

'No.'

Later, as the airship sailed on, they talked it over, the strange uniqueness of mankind in the Long Earth. And Lobsang described how, not long after Step Day, he had initiated searches for human cousins across a thousand Earths, and he told Joshua the story of a man called Nelson Azikiwe.

32

ACCORDING TO THE official family story he was christened Nelson after the famous admiral. However, in reality he was probably named after Nelson Mandela. According to his mother *that* Nelson now sat on God's right hand, and Nelson junior, growing up, took the view that this was a good thing, in that Mandela would be in a position to prevent the vengeful god of the Israelites loading yet more troubles on the backs of humanity.

His mother had raised him in Jesus, as she put it, and for her sake he persevered, and in the end, after a somewhat complicated career, and a still more complicated philosophical journey, he took holy orders. Eventually he was invited to Britain to bring the Good News to the heathen: proof positive that what goes around comes around. He quite liked the English. They tended to say sorry a lot, which was quite understandable given their heritage and the crimes of their ancestors. And for some reason the Archbishop of Canterbury sent him to a rural parish that was so white it glared. Perhaps the Archbishop had a sense of humour, or wanted to make a point, or possibly she just wanted to see what would happen.

This wasn't the United Kingdom that his mother had talked about when he was young, that was certain. Now, with her long dead, he walked through a London that contained a great multi-hued population. You hardly saw a news bulletin that wasn't delivered by a reader whose recent ancestors had walked under African stars. Hell, there were even black men and women to tell you when it was going to rain on the cradle of democracy. This despite the eeriness of an emptying country, a capital city being abandoned suburb by suburb.

He said as much to the retiring incumbent of St John on the Water, the Reverend David Blessed, a man who clearly supported the theory of nominative determinism. And who said, when he saw Nelson Azikiwe for the first time, 'My son, you won't be short of a dinner invitation for the next six months at least!' That turned out to be a successful prophecy on the part of the Reverend Blessed who, with the help of some family money, was retiring early to his own cottage, so that, in his own words, he could 'watch the fun when you take your first service.'

He left the occupancy of the rectory to Nelson, who had it to himself apart from an elderly woman who cooked him his lunch every day and tidied up around the place. She wasn't very talkative, and for his part he didn't know what to talk to her about. Besides he had enough on his plate due to the fact the presbytery had no draft-proofing whatsoever, and a plumbing system that the Lord Himself could surely barely understand; sometimes it flushed itself in the middle of the night for no apparent reason.

This was a part of England miraculously untouched by the Long Earth. Or even, as far as Nelson could see, the twenty-first century. The Middle English were the Zulus of the British, he concluded. It seemed to Nelson that every other man in the village had at some time been a warrior, quite often of high rank. Now retired, they looked after their gardens, drilling potatoes instead of men. But he was taken aback by their courtesy. Their wives baked him so many cakes that he had to share them with the Reverend Blessed (retired), who, Nelson suspected, had been told to hold on and report back on Nelson's progress to the authorities in Lambeth Palace.

They were talking in David's cottage while the Reverend Blessed's wife was at a meeting of the Women's Institute.

'Of course there will always be those who are perennially un-reconstructed,' said David. 'But you won't find very many of them around here, because the reflexes of the English class system take over, you see? You are tall, handsome, and speak English considerably better than their own children do. And when you quoted passages from W. H. Hudson's *A Shepherd's Life* at the funeral of old Humphrey, after the service – which incidentally you took magnificently – some of them sidled up to me and asked if I had put you up to that. Of course, I told them that I hadn't. And believe me when that news got around, well, you had passed. They realized that you are not only very fluent in English, but also fluent in *England*, which means a lot down here.

'And then, to cap it all, you took an allotment, and are seen digging and planting and in general tilling the soil of the Good Earth, and that got everybody on your side. You see, everybody was a little nervous when they heard about you coming. They were, and how can I put this, expecting you to be a little more ... earnest? You seem remarkably well prepared for your mission among us.'

Nelson said, 'In a way my whole life has prepared me for this, yes. You know, as a child I was lucky, very lucky for a *bongani* like me, running around in the South Africa of those days. But my parents could see a better future for those prepared to work for it. You might have thought them tough parents, and I suppose you might be right. But they kept me off the streets and made me go to school.

'And then of course the Black Corporation came up with its "Searching for the Future" programme, and my mother picked it up on her radar and made sure I got myself an interview, and after that it was as if I had been selected by fate. Apparently I hit the mark on every test they set. Suddenly the Corporation found it had got itself a poster boy, a poor African kid with an IQ of 210. They more or less told me to ask for the moon. But I didn't know what I wanted to do. Not until Step Day ... Where were you on Step Day, David?'

The elderly priest walked over to a large oak desk, produced a large day book, turned the pages, and said, 'I see that I was getting ready for evensong when I first heard what was going on. What did I think of it? Who had time to think coherently at all?

'It wasn't too bad around here. The countryside is different from the town, you see? People don't panic so easily, and I don't think many of the kids round here were very much interested in fiddling with electronic components. Well, the closest place with a ready supply would be Swindon. But everyone watched what was happening on television. Around here people were looking at the skies to see if they could *see* these other worlds – that was how little we understood. But the wind was still blowing in the trees, the cows got milked, and I think we just spent our time listening to the news bulletins, interspersed with *The Archers*.

'I don't really remember formulating any sort of position what-soever until it was definitively announced that there were indeed other Earths, millions of them, as close to us as a thought and, apparently, ours for the taking. Now *that* made ears prick up around here. It was about land! In the countryside land gets attention.' He looked into his brandy glass, saw that it was empty and shrugged. 'In short, I must say I found myself wondering "What hath God wrought?"'

'Book of Numbers,' said Nelson, instinctively.

'Well done, Nelson! And also, rather pleasingly, they were the first official words sent by Samuel Morse over the electric telegraph in 1838.' He topped up his brandy glass, and made a complex little sign to enquire of Nelson if he might like another.

But the younger man seemed distracted. 'What hath God wrought? Let me tell you what God wrought, David, oh, indeed. Step Day came, and we found out about the Long Earth, and suddenly the world was full of new questions. By this time I had read all about Louis Leakey, and the work he and his wife did in Olduvai Gorge. I was thrilled at the thought that everyone in the world was an African at the core. So I said to the Corporation that I wanted to know how man had become man. I wanted to learn *why*. Most of all, I wanted to know what it was that we were supposed to be doing here, in the new context of the Long Earth. In short, I wanted to know what we were *for*.

'Of course, my mother and her faith had lost me by then. I was too smart for my own God, so to speak. I had found time to read up about the affairs of the four centuries following the birth of the infant Jesus, and indeed to look at the erratic progress of Christianity since then. It seemed to me that whatever the truth of the universe was, it certainly wasn't something that could have been discerned by a quarrelsome bunch of antique ecclesiasticals.'

David barked a laugh.

'And I loved palaeontology. I was fascinated by the bones and what they could tell us. Especially now that we have tools that researchers even twenty years ago couldn't have dreamed of. *That* was the way to the truth. And I was good at it. Extremely good, it was as if the bones sang to me . . .'

The Reverend Blessed wisely stayed silent.

'So, it was not long after Step Day, I got a call from the people at the Black Corporation, who said they had fixed it for me to set up and lead expeditions to as many iterations of Olduvai Gorge as funds would allow. To the birthplace of mankind, on the new worlds.

'Now when you are dealing with the Black Corporation, funds are essentially without limit. The problem we had was a shortage of skilled people. It was a very good time to be a palaeontologist, and we trained up many youngsters. Anyone with a suitable degree and a trowel could have a gorge of his or her very own to work. Whatever else was happening, the bone-hunters had found their Eldorado.

'Well, something like the African Rift Valley persists across much of the Long Earth; geology is relatively fixed. And, as hoped, we did find on many occasions bones in the target area that were definitely hominid. I worked on the project for four years. We extended our fields of work, and it was always the same: oh yes, there were bones, there were always bones. I selected other likely sites around the world which might possibly have been the home of a different Lucy – a Chinese branch, for example, the result of an early diffusion out of Africa.

'But after more than two *thousand* excavations in contiguous Earths, by Black Corporation-funded expeditions and others, we never found any sign of the development of nascent humanity beyond those very early bones, some deformed, some mauled by animals, most of them very small. There was nothing past the australopithecines, the Lucies. The cradles of mankind were empty.

'There are still workers out there, still searching, and until last year I was still running the programme. But in the end the emptiness of the Long Earth – empty of humanity at least – disturbed me so much that I resigned. I took the generous amount that the Black Corporation gave me as a farewell present, although I know they hope that one day I will return to the fold.

'I'd had enough, you see, enough of those empty skulls. Enough of those little bones. You could see the striving, but not the arriving. And one day I suddenly found myself wondering where it had all gone wrong, in all those other worlds. Or maybe it went wrong *here*? Maybe the evolution of mankind is some ghastly cosmic mistake.'

'And so you returned to the Church? Quite a change of course.'

'I've been told that no one in recent history has been ordained as quickly as I was. I understand that in times past the Church of England was benign to people who, in those days, were considered natural philosophers. Many a vicar spent his Sunday afternoons cheerfully trapping new species of butterfly in jars. I always thought what a wonderful life that was: the Bible in one hand and a stout bottle of ether in the other.'

'Isn't that how Darwin got started?'

'Darwin didn't get as far as Holy Orders. He became rather distracted by beetles . . . And that is why you see me here. I needed a new framework, I suppose. I thought, why not get to grips with theology? Take it seriously. See what I am able to tease out of it. My tentative preliminary conclusion, by the way, is that there is no God. No offence.'

'Oh, none taken.'

'That means I must find out what there *is* instead. But right now, as for my own philosophy, there is a quotation that rather sums it up: "When you arise in the morning, think of what a precious privilege it is to be alive – to breathe, to think, to enjoy, to love."'

The Reverend Blessed smiled. 'Ah, good old Marcus Aurelius. But, Nelson, he was a pagan!'

'Which rather proves my point. May I help myself to another splash of brandy, David?'

'Nelson was essentially right,' Lobsang told Joshua. 'The hominid line, and the apes from which they came, clearly had great evolutionary potential. But if the ability to step first originated on the Datum, evidently the stepping humanoids quickly moved out far from Datum Earth, leaving scant traces in the fossil record; only on the Datum will you find bones to illustrate the slow plod towards mankind.'

'What does it mean, Lobsang? That was Nelson's question. What is the Long Earth *for*?'

'I suppose that's what we came out here to find out. Shall we proceed?'

33

O N THEY SAILED, leaving the intricate humanoid community far behind. They were travelling east for now, away from the Pacific coast and back into the interior of the continent.

And, almost unobserved, they passed another milestone: a million steps from Datum. There was no dramatic change, no new perception, only the silent turning-over of a new digit on the earthometers. But now they were in the worlds the wavefront pioneers called the High Meggers. Nobody, not even Lobsang, knew for sure if anybody had actually stepped this far before.

The jungle that clad North America gradually grew thicker, denser, steamier. From the air you saw little but a green blanket, punctured here and there by scraps of open water. Lobsang's aerial surveys suggested that in these worlds there might be forests all the way to the ice-free poles.

As before, every day Lobsang paused to allow Joshua down to explore, and stretch his legs. Joshua would find himself in a dense forest of ferns of all sizes, and trees both unfamiliar and familiar, strung with climbers like honeysuckle and grapevines. The flowers were always a riot of colour. Some days Joshua came back with bunches of grape-like fruit, small and hard compared with domesticated varieties of grape, but still sweet. The dense forest inhibited the growth of large animals, but there were strange hopping animals, a little like kangaroos but with long flexible snouts. Joshua learned to trust these creatures, whose trails, cleared through the undergrowth, led reliably to open water. And he saw aerial creatures in the canopy itself. Giant flapping wings. And, once, a flopping, squirming thing that looked for all the world like an octopus, spinning like a Frisbee through the canopy trees. How the hell had *that* got there?

He spent a couple of nights outside the ship, just for old time's sake. It was almost like his sabbaticals, especially if he stepped a world or two away from Lobsang, but his lord and master didn't approve of that. Still, when he got the chance he would sit by his fire, listening for the Silence. On a good night he thought he could feel the other Earths, vast empty spaces all around him, just beyond the reach of his tiny circle of firelight. Untold possibilities. And then he would climb back up to the airship, leaving behind a whole world with its own unique mysteries barely examined.

On they would travel, to another, and another yet.

And then, after fifty days, more than one and a third million worlds from home, the land and air seemed to shimmer, and the forest melted as the worlds cleared away, to reveal a sea that stretched to the horizon, foam-flecked and glimmering, at the heart of North America.

Still stepping, Lobsang turned the airship south, looking for dry land.

On world after world the sea persisted, teeming with life, the green of algal blooms, pale white shapes that might have been coral reefs, and creatures that jumped and swam that might have been dolphins. Cautious dips to the water level proved that the sea was saline. That didn't necessarily mean this American Sea was open to the wider world ocean; inland seas could become saline through evaporation. The water samples Lobsang retrieved were full of exotic seaweed strands and crustaceans – exotic to a specialist any-how. Lobsang stored specimens and images.

At last, heading south, they hit a coastline. Lobsang cut the stepping, and they inspected one particular world of this latest band, selected at random. They came to fog banks first, then huge bird-like forms swooping low over the sea, and then the land itself, where dense forest spilled almost all the way down to the shore. Lobsang thought that the higher land they were approaching might be some relative of the Ozark Plateau.

From here they sailed east until they came to a tremendous valley, perhaps carved by some distant cousin of the Mississippi or the Ohio. They followed this north to an estuary where the river spilled into the inland sea. The fresh water pushing into the saline ocean was visible from a muddy discoloration that persisted miles out from the coast.

And here, in the open, by the banks of the freshwater river, the animals came to drink. As they cruised on, once more stepping through the worlds, Joshua watched herds of tremendous beasts flick into existence and vanish, quadrupeds and bipeds, creatures that might almost have been elephants, others that might almost have been flightless birds, with lesser creatures running at their feet. A few seconds' glimpse, and then another extraordinary, unearthly scene, and then another.

'Like a Ray Harryhausen show reel,' Lobsang said.

Joshua asked, 'Who's Ray Harryhausen? And what's a show reel?'

'Tonight's movie will be the original version of *Jason and the Argonauts*, followed by an illustrated talk. Don't miss it. But – what a find, Joshua! This American Sea, I mean. All this coastline. What a place to come and colonize! *This* North America has a second Mediterranean, an enclosed sea, with all the riches and cultural connectivity that promises. As for the potential for colonization, it knocks the Corn Belt into a cocked hat. Why, this could be the seat of a new civilization altogether. Not to mention the opportunities for tourism. Just one of these worlds alone – and we've already sailed over hundreds of them.'

Joshua said dryly, 'Maybe they'll call it "the Lobsang Belt".'

If Lobsang got the joke he didn't reveal it.

*

Another night, another easy sleep for Joshua.

And when he awoke the next morning the monitor in his room showed what looked like a close-up of a campfire.

Joshua jumped out of bed. Lobsang came into his room when he was pulling on his pants, causing him to pull a little quicker. He would have to teach Lobsang the meaning of the word *knock*.

Lobsang smiled. 'Good morning, Joshua, on this auspicious day.'

'Yeah, yeah.' Joshua had no time for Lobsang's nonsense today. The idea of company, authentic, undeniably human company, was electrifying. Socks, sturdy boots . . . 'OK, I'm ready to go down. Lobsang – that fire, whoever built it. Are they human?'

'Apparently so. You might find her sunbathing among the dinosaurs.'

'Dinosaurs! Her! Sunbathing!'

'You'll have to see for yourself. But be careful, Joshua. The dinosaurs look amiable enough. Well, some of them. But *she* might bite . . .'

Apart from the elevator there was now a second means of getting to the ground, a highly technical business which consisted of an old car tire (scavenged from a store of random garbage in the airship's capacious hold), a length of rope and a simple panic button on Joshua's chest pack which could call the tire down, or, more importantly, get it moving quickly back up if he were being chased. Joshua felt better for having installed this escape mechanism as a backup after his encounter with the murderous elves, and these days always insisted on having the tire at ground level, ready to run directly towards in an emergency.

Now he was being lowered towards a new Earth, once again. And there was another human here . . . somewhere. He could *feel* it. He really could. People made a world feel different, to Joshua.

As was becoming customary for Lobsang, he had decided to land Joshua a little way from the target to allow for a cautious approach, as opposed to a drop from out of the open sky. So the airship floated over the edge of the estuary, a place of scattered trees, scrub, marshland and small lakes. The air was fresh but laden with the smells of salt, and a kind of wet-rot stink from the jungle's edge – and a subtler, drier scent, Joshua thought as he descended, that he couldn't quite place. The denser forest lapped to the edge of this muddy plain, tumbling down from the higher land to the south. And that thread of smoke rose up from somewhere inland.

Joshua came down a little way from the water's edge, in the forest. Once on the ground he walked forward, watchfully, heading for the smoke. 'I smell . . . dryness. Rust. It's like the reptile house in a zoo.'

'This world may be very different from the Datum, Joshua. We've come a long way across the contingency tree.'

The forest cleared away, revealing a stretch of beach, the slow-moving water. And on a bluff of rocks, close to the water, Joshua came upon a group of fat, big, seal-like creatures lazing in the sun, around a dozen including a few infants. Pale blond hair lay streamlined along their heavy bodies, and they had small, almost conical heads with black eyes, and small mouths, and flat nostrils like a chimp's. They were like seals with humanoid faces. The parrot on Joshua's shoulder, repaired since being used as a club, whirred as lenses panned and zoomed.

The seal-beasts noticed the visitor long before he got close. They looked up, ape heads swivelling, and with hoots of alarm they clambered off their rocks and slithered over the sand towards the water, the calves scuttling after the adults. Joshua saw that their limbs were a kind of compromise between ape-like arms and legs and true flippers, with stubby hands and feet that had webbing stretched between fingers and toes. They slid easily into the water, evidently much more graceful in the sea than on land.

But then there was a flurry of spray, and an upper jaw the size of a small boat came levering out of the water. The seal-beasts scattered in panic, squealing and thrashing.

'Crocodile,' Joshua muttered. 'Every damn place you go.' He picked up a flat stone and headed for the water's edge.

'Joshua, be careful—'

'Hey, you!' He hurled the stone as hard as he could, skipping it over the water. He was gratified to see it slam into the croc's right eye. The beast turned in the water, rumbling.

And it came bursting out of the sea, upright, on powerful-looking hind legs. The croc must have been twelve yards long; it was as if some amphibious craft had suddenly raced out of the water. He could feel the very ground shudder as the croc's footsteps slammed into the earth. And it was coming for him, enraged.

'*Shit.*' Joshua turned and ran.

He reached the cover of another forest clump, and pushed his way into the trees' damp shadow. Excluded by the trees the beast roared, turned its huge head, baffled – and then bounded away along the beach, after some other prey.

Joshua leaned on a tree, breathing hard. There were flowers on the trees around him, and on the ground; the place was full of colour, despite the shade. And there was noise everywhere, calls echoing around the forest: squeaking cries from the canopy, deeper grumbles from further away.

'You were lucky with that super-croc,' Lobsang said. 'Stupid, but lucky.'

'But if he's snacking on those humanoids right now, it's my fault. They *were* humanoids, weren't they, Lobsang?'

'I would say so. But they're only part-adapted – two million years isn't long enough to turn a bipedal ape into a seal. These humanoids are like Darwin's flightless cormorants . . .'

Shadows shifted, huge. Something passed across Joshua's sky, a tremendous mass, like a building on the move. A foot slammed down, round like an elephant's – a leg, thick as an oak trunk and taller than he was. He squinted, not daring to break out of the cover of the trees, and peered up at a body, the skin heavy and wrinkled and pocked with old scars, crater-like, as if inflicted by artillery shells.

Then a predator came running, out of nowhere, like a

tyrannosaur maybe, with massive hind legs, smaller clawed fore-arms, a head like an industrial crusher, a beast itself the size and speed of a steam locomotive. Joshua flinched back into deeper cover. The hunter leapt up at the giant beast, closed vast jaws and ripped away a chunk of flesh the size of Joshua's torso. The big beast bellowed, a distant noise like a supertanker's foghorn. But it kept moving, as oblivious to the huge wound as Joshua might have been to a flea bite.

'Lobsang.'

'I saw it. I *see* it. Jurassic dining.'

'More like snacking,' Joshua said. 'Have we found dinosaurs, Lobsang?'

'*Not* dinosaurs. Though I suspected you would use the name. In this case there has surely been too *much* evolution for that. Some of these are the much-evolved descendants, perhaps, of the Cretaceous-age reptiles, in a sheaf of worlds where the dinosaur-killer asteroid never fell. There was a dinosaur kisser here, perhaps, a gentle brush with death . . . But the picture is not simple, Joshua. The big herbivore that almost stepped on you is not reptilian at all, but a mammal.'

'Really?'

'It was a female – a kind of marsupial, I think. If you'd had the chance you would have seen an infant the size of a carthorse carried in her pouch. I will show you the images later. On the other hand, the morphology – really big herbivores preyed upon by really ferocious predators – *was* common in the dinosaur era and may be another universal.

'Joshua, always remember, you have not travelled back in time, or forward. You have travelled far across the contingency tree of the possible, on a planet where dramatic but quasi-random extinction events periodically obliterate much of the family of life, leaving room for evolutionary innovation. On each Earth, how-ever, the outcomes will differ, by a little or a lot . . . You are close to the campfire now. Head for the water.'

With a crunch of trampled undergrowth a new set of animals moved through the forest clump, heading for the estuary and the fresh water. Through the trees Joshua glimpsed low-slung bodies, horns, tremendous coloured crests. There were several of these animals, the adults taller than Joshua at the shoulder, the calves weaving through the moving pillars of the adults' legs. Immense beasts, but dwarfed by the big marsupial he'd glimpsed earlier. They were making for the water, so Joshua followed as best he could.

He came to the edge of the forest by a braid of fresh water. Across the estuary's marshy plain huge flocks of birds, or bird-like creatures, strutted, squabbled and fed. The marsh flowers were a mass of colour under a deep blue sky. Joshua thought he saw the ridged backs of more crocodilians sliding through the deeper water. By the water's edge, those big crested beasts crowded to drink.

And at the edge of a beach of white sand, upright, bipedal lizards were catching some rays, basking. Smaller specimens chased back and forth across the sand and occasionally dived into the surf, such as it was. They were remarkably human in their playfulness, like Californian teenagers. Then one of the bigger bipeds noticed Joshua and prodded its nearest neighbour. There was an exchange of hissing, after which the miniature dinosaur of the second part returned to snoozing, while the first one sat up and watched Joshua with bright-eyed interest.

'Fun, aren't they?' A woman's voice.

Joshua whirled around, his heart hammering.

The woman was short, sturdy, her blonde hair tied back in an efficient bun. She wore a useful-looking sleeveless jacket that was all pockets. She looked a little older than Joshua: early thirties, maybe. Her face was square, regular, strong rather than pretty, tanned deep by the weather. She eyed him, appraising.

'They're quite harmless unless attacked,' she said. 'Smart, too;

they have a division of labour and they make things that you might call tools. Digging sticks, at least, for the clams. On top of that, they make crude but serviceable boats, and fairly sophisticated fish traps. That means observation, deduction, cogitation and team-work, and the concept of mortgaging today for a better tomorrow . . .'

Joshua was staring.

She laughed. 'Don't you think it's time you closed your mouth?' She held out her hand.

Joshua looked at it as if it were a weapon of war.

'*I know you.* You're Joshua Valienté, aren't you? I knew I would run into you some day. Small worlds, don't you think?'

Joshua was frozen. 'Who are *you*?'

'Call me . . . Sally.'

In Joshua's ear the voice of Lobsang insisted, 'Invite her to the ship! Tempt her! We have superb cuisine, somewhat wasted on you, I must say. Offer her sex! Whatever you do, get her on this damn ship!'

Joshua whispered, 'Lobsang? You really don't know anything about human relationships.'

He sounded offended. 'I have read every treatise on human sexuality ever written. And I had a body once. How do you think that baby Tibetans are made? Look, it doesn't matter. *We must bring this young lady aboard.* Think about it! What is a nice girl like her doing in the High Meggers?'

Lobsang had a point. Whoever she was – how had she got here, more than a million steps out? Was she a natural stepper, someone who didn't get the nausea, like Joshua? Fine. But there were only so many times you could step in a day. *He* could manage a thousand steps a day unaided. Surely everybody needed to sleep and eat? You could step-hunt an unwary deer once you had the hang of it, but field dressing and cookery couldn't be hurried, and that slowed you down . . . It would take years to step out this far.

She was watching him suspiciously. 'What are you thinking? Who were you talking to?'

'Umm, the captain of my ship.' Not exactly a lie, and since the Sisters had always been rather down on lying, Joshua was relieved.

'Really? You mean that ridiculous floating gasbag, I suppose. And how big is the crew of that monster? Incidentally, Robur the Conqueror, I hope you have no designs on this world. I rather like these little guys.'

Joshua looked down. The miniature dinosaurs had formed a circle around the pair of them and were carefully balancing upright, like meerkats, with curiosity just outweighing caution.

'The captain would like you to come aboard,' Joshua managed.

She smiled. 'Aboard that thing? Not a chance in hell, mister, no offence meant . . . However,' she said more hesitantly, 'do you have any soap? I make my own lye soap, of course, but I wouldn't say no to something a little more easy on the skin.'

'I'm sure—'

'Maybe with rose scent.'

'Is that all?'

'And some chocolate.'

'Of course.'

'In exchange I offer . . . information. OK?'

The voice in Joshua's ear prompted, 'Ask her what information she can give us that we cannot find out for ourselves.'

When asked, Sally snorted. 'I don't know. What *can* you find out for yourselves? By the look of all those aerials and dishes up there you could probably hack God's email.'

Joshua said, 'Look, I'm going back up, and will grab some soap and chocolate, and will come right back down, OK? Just don't go away.'

To his embarrassment Sally burst out laughing. 'My-oh-my, a *real* gentleman. I bet you were a Boy Scout.'

As he rose up to the *Mark Twain* Lobsang whispered in his ear, 'If there is a more efficient way of stepping, it is vital that we find out what it is!'

'I know, Lobsang, I know! I'm working on it.' But right now a stepping mystery was the last thing on Joshua's mind.

They ate lunch on the beach: fresh-caught oysters on an open fire.

The encounter fazed Joshua more than somewhat. He wasn't used to the company of women, not women without wimples anyhow. Back in the Home all the girls were more or less like his sisters, and the nuns were all possessed of laser eyesight and over-the-horizon hearing: when it came to the opposite sex you were under constant surveillance. And if you spent a lot of time out on the new Earths, seldom seeing another person at all, anyone that you *did* meet was a nuisance, taking up *your* space.

And, right now, there was the added distraction of a circle of miniature dinosaurs, craning their necks this way and that so as not to miss the action. It was like being watched by a bunch of curious kids. He felt as if he should be offering them a few bucks to take themselves to the movies.

But he needed to talk to this enigmatic Sally. It was a tension within him, a huge unfulfilled need. And, looking at her, he thought she felt the same.

'Don't worry about the dinos,' she said. 'They're no threat, though they are pretty smart. And they're very bright when it comes to keeping clear of the larger dinos and the crocs. I make a point of coming back to see how they're doing every so often.'

'*How?* How did you get here, Sally?'

Sally poked the embers of her fire, and the little creatures jumped back, startled. 'Well, that's none of your business. That was the code of the Old West, and it's sure as shit the same here. These oysters roast up wonderfully, don't they?'

They did. Joshua had just eaten his fourth. 'I taste something like bacon, and I've seen plenty of pig-like animals, they look like a universal. But this tastes as if it's got Worcester sauce in it. Am I right?'

'More or less. I travel prepared.' Sally looked at him, with the juice of oysters Kilpatrick leaking from her lips. 'A deal, right? I will be frank with you, and you will be frank with me. Well, within limits. Let me tell you what I already think I know about you. First, that bloody great thing floating up there contains only one person, I'm guessing. Because when you found me, any crew would have been swarming all over me and my little world. And, plus you, that means a crew of two people. Big ship for two people, no? Second, it looks mighty expensive, and since the universities don't have that kind of money and governments don't have the imagination, that means some corporation or other. I guess it was Douglas Black?' She smiled. 'Don't blame yourself, you didn't give anything away. Black is smart, and this is just his style.'

There was silence from Joshua's earpiece.

She read Joshua's slight hesitation. 'No word from headquarters? Oh come on! Sooner or later anyone who has a talent that interests Douglas Black ends up working for him. My own father did. Although in fact the money isn't really the lure. Because if you're really good, your friend Douglas will give you a sack of toys to play with, like that airship up there. Isn't that right?'

'I'm not an employee of Black.'

'Just contracting, is that the fig leaf?' she said dismissively. 'You know, in their headquarters in New Jersey every employee of the Corporation wears a little earpiece just like yours, so that Douglas himself can talk to them individually whenever he likes. Even his silence is threatening, they say. But one day my father said, "I am not going to wear this thing any more." And right now, Joshua, you will do me the courtesy of taking yours off. I don't mind talking to *you*. I heard about you, how you saved all those kids on Step Day, you're obviously a decent human being. But take off that modern-day slave bracelet.'

Joshua did so, feeling guilty.

Sally gave a little nod of satisfaction. 'Now we can talk.'

'There's nothing sinister about us,' Joshua said tentatively –

although he wasn't entirely sure how true that was. 'We are out here to explore. To look and learn, to map the Long Earth. Well, that's the expedition's intention.' Or was, he thought, before it became focused on the issue of the humanoid migrations, the disturbance they perceived in the Long Earth.

'Not *your* intention. You aren't an explorer, Joshua Valienté, whatever else you are. Why are *you* here?'

He shrugged. 'I'm a failsafe, if you want the truth. Hired muscle.'

She grinned at that. 'Ha!'

He said, 'You say your father worked for Black.'

'Yes.'

'What did he do?'

'He invented the Stepper. Though that was on his own time.'

'Your father was *Willis Linsay*?' Joshua just stared, thinking of Step Day, and how his own life had been changed by what Linsay had done.

She smiled. 'All right. You want the full story? I'm from a family of steppers. Natural steppers . . . Oh, close your mouth, Joshua. My grandfather could step, my mother could step and I can step. My father *couldn't* step, however, and that's why he needed to invent something like the Stepper box. So he did. I first stepped when I was four. And I soon found out that Dad could step if he was holding my hand. They took a photograph of us. I never had any problem with it, the magic-door stuff, because of Mom. Mom was a reader, and she read to me Tolkien and Larry Niven and E. Nesbit and just about everything else. I was home-schooled, needless to say. And I grew up with my own Narnia! To tell the truth, since Step Day I've become pissed at having to share *my* secret place with the rest of the world. But back then Mom explained to me that I shouldn't ever tell anyone what I could do.'

Joshua listened, dumbfounded. He could barely imagine how it must have been to be part of a family of steppers, a family all like himself.

'It was pretty good in those days. I often hung out with Dad in his shed, because the shed was in another world – though, of course, I had to lead him in and out of that other Wyoming.

'But Dad was hardly ever there, because he was always jetting away, wherever the Black people wanted him, and that could be anywhere from MIT to some research lab in Scandinavia or South Africa. Sometimes, late at night, a helicopter might turn up, and he'd get in, and then maybe an hour later he'd be back home and the chopper was flying away. When I asked him what he'd been doing, it was always, "Just some stuff, that's all." But that was OK by me because my Dad knew best. He knew *everything*.

'I didn't know anything about his work projects. But I wasn't surprised when he succeeded in inventing the Stepper. He was an unusual mix of brilliant theoretician and hands-on engineer; I believe he's come closer than anybody else to figuring out the true nature of the Long Earth . . . But it did him no good when Mom died. That was one problem he couldn't untangle with technology. Things got weird after that.' Sally hesitated. 'I mean more weird than before.

'He kept working. But I got the impression that he stopped caring about what he was working on, and what it was for. He'd always been ethical, you know? A hippie from a long line of hippies. Now he didn't care.

'But he was living a double life. He kept stuff like the Stepper hidden away. Dad did like hiding things. He said he learned it in his hippie days when he hid his marijuana plantation in the cellar. He showed me once. It had a secret door that would only open if *one* loose nail was pushed just so far and *one* of the paint pots was turned ninety degrees, and then a panel would slide, and there was a large space that you couldn't believe was there, and you could still smell where the plants had been . . .

'So that's my story. I always stepped, I grew up with it; Step Day was just a bump in the road to my family. Whereas you had to discover stepping for yourself, didn't you, Joshua? I heard you were brought up by nuns. It's part of your legend.'

'I don't want a legend.'

'Nuns, eh? Did they beat you up, or try anything . . . funny?'

Joshua narrowed his eyes. 'There was none of that stuff. Well, apart from Sister Mary Joseph, and Sister Agnes had her out of there in an hour, boy, had she got the wrong number. But, yeah, it was a totally weird place, looking back. But the right kind of weird. Good weird. The nuns had a lot of freedom. We read Carl Sagan before the Old Testament.'

'Freedom. Well, I can sympathize with that. That's why my father walked out on Douglas Black. Douglas found out about the Stepper box one day, he somehow forced it out of my Dad. With Mom gone and everything I think Dad was beginning to hate people anyhow. But what Black did was the final straw. One day Dad just disappeared. He took a post at Princeton under phony credentials. But that was kind of high profile, so when he got a sniff of a pursuit by Black he went out to Madison, took a college post under another assumed name. He took the Stepper technology he was developing with him. I followed and went to college out there. Didn't see much of him. I guess I kept a watching eye on him, however. His real name isn't Willis Linsay, by the way.'

'I didn't think it was.'

'And that was when he decided, because he suspected the Black Corporation was on his tail *again*, that he would give stepping to the whole world, so no one could own it or put chains around it, or slap a tax on it. He really didn't like big industry, and he really didn't like governments. I think he hoped the world would be a much better place if everybody was able to step out of their grasp. As far as I know he is still alive out here somewhere.'

'And is that why you're out here? Looking for him?'

'One reason.'

There was a curious change in the air. The little dinosaurs stood, stretching, their gaze combing the sky. Joshua looked at Sally. She didn't react; she was carefully retrieving the last wayward oyster in the pan with a stick.

He asked, 'Do you think he was right to do what he did? With the Stepper?'

'Well, maybe. At least he gave people a new option. Although he said people were going to have to learn to *think*, out there in the Long Earth. He said once, "I am giving mankind the key to endless worlds. An end to scarcity and, may we hope, war. And perhaps a new meaning to life. I leave the exploration of all these worlds to your generation, my dear, though personally I think you will fuck it up royally." Why are you looking at me like that?'

'Your father said *that* to you?'

Sally shrugged. 'I told you. He was a hippie born of generations of hippies. He was always saying things like that.'

At that moment the loudspeaker voice of Lobsang boomed out over the beach, startling the small dinosaurs again. 'Joshua! Back to the ship right now! Emergency!'

There was a strange new smell in the air, like burning plastic. Joshua looked at the northern horizon; there was a grey cloud, and it was getting bigger.

'I call them suckers,' said Sally calmly. 'Rather like dragonflies. They pump a venom into anything organic, which breaks down cells remarkably fast, and you become a bag of soup that they suck up, as if through a straw. For some reason they don't bother the dinosaurs. Your electronic friend is right about the emergency, Joshua. Now run along, there's a good boy.'

And she disappeared.

34

A S SHE STEPPED AWAY, Joshua took a step back, to the East, away from the direction of travel of the airship. That was the instinctive way when you were in danger, to step back into the world you'd just arrived from, because the world downstream might be even worse. Now he was in a timber world, fairly standard stuff, nothing but endless trees as far as he could see – which was only a hundred yards or so, because of the aforesaid trees. No girl, no dinosaurs, no airship.

He could see a little more light than average to his right, so he got up and strolled that way. He emerged into a vast area of burned stumps and ash fields: not a recent fire, already new saplings were poking shoots through the stinking black mess, with green leaves apparent here and there. Just a forest fire, a dieback. It was all part of the great cycle of nature which, when you've seen it one point three million times, squarely pisses you off.

The airship was above him suddenly; its shadow sprawled across the clearing, an abrupt eclipse. Joshua clipped his earpiece back on.

Lobsang's voice was an irritating whine. 'We have lost her! Could you not have beguiled her into the ship? Clearly she has discovered a new way to step! And what's more—'

Joshua plucked out his earpiece again. He sat down on a stump, a crumbling mass of colourful fungus. He felt stunned by the encounter with Sally, the blizzard of words that had evidently been pent up inside her. And she was travelling alone, as he used to. It was a slightly electrifying thought. On his sabbaticals, he had survived in any number of worlds like this.

Suddenly it occurred to him that he didn't want or need a giant damn airship hovering over his head any more.

Joshua put the earpiece back on, and considered what to say. What was the phrase that Sister Agnes always used when some high-flying ecclesiastical or other tried to throw his weight around at the Home? 'Can you hear me, Lobsang? You ain't the boss of me, sir, you surely ain't. The only thing you could do right now is kill me, and you *still* wouldn't be the boss of me.'

There was no reply.

He got up and strolled downhill, in so far as there was a hill at all. But it was a definite slope, and that would mean a river, and *that* would mean open ground, cover and, almost certainly, game of some sort. All he'd need to survive here.

Lobsang replied at last. 'You are right, Joshua. I am not the boss of you and have no desire to be. On the other hand I can't believe you are serious in the hints you are giving that you might jump ship. We are travelling with a purpose, remember.'

'Whatever your purpose I'm not about to kidnap anybody, Lobsang.' He stopped. 'OK, I'll come aboard. But under certain conditions.'

The airship was right overhead now.

'The foremost of these is that I come and go to the ground any time I wish, OK?'

This time Lobsang replied by loudspeaker, a booming celestial voice. 'Are you trying to *negotiate* with me, Joshua?'

Joshua scratched his nose. 'Actually I'm trying to demand, I think. And as for Sally, I have a feeling we shall see her very shortly, regardless of you and your plans. *You'll* never be able to find a solitary human being in all these forest worlds, but she will find it very easy to see a damn great airship in the sky. *She* will find *us*.'

'But she travels alone, as you do. She's travelled much further in fact. Perhaps she doesn't need people, and will not be motivated to find us at all.'

Joshua walked across the damp ashes towards the lift-ring that was descending to the ground. 'She doesn't need people. But I believe she *wants* people.'

'How can you possibly know that?'

'Because of the way she talked to me. All those words pouring out, because they needed to be said. Because your precious mountain men were probably just the same at their rendezvous. Because *I'm* the same. Because this human called Joshua keeps going back home, just every now and then, to visit, to be with folk. To be fucking human, not to put too fine a point on it, and Daniel Boone can kiss my ass.'

'I've said it before, Joshua. Travel has most definitely broadened your mind, if not your vocabulary.'

'And besides, there's something else, Lobsang. Something you're missing. Do you imagine it's *chance* that she happened to show up under our keel, with her campfire blazing?'

'Well—'

'She knew we were coming, Lobsang. I'm certain of it. She wants something from us. The question is what?'

'Your point is well made. I'll consider it. Incidentally I have captured and dissected several of those flying creatures. They appear to be remarkably like wasps, although they act more like bees. A new order. Which is why one should be wary of arbitrarily applying labels like "dinosaurs".'

'Have you changed your voice?'

'Yes, indeed, it is warm and reflective, is it not?'

'It makes you sound like a rabbi!'

'Ah yes, close enough; actually, it is the voice of David Kossoff, a Jewish actor prominent in the 1950s and 60s. I believe the occasional hesitation and slight air of bemused amiability has a friendly and calming effect.'

'It does, but I'm sure you are not supposed to tell me that it does. It's like a conjuror telling you how the trick was done—' Damn it. Lobsang was making him laugh again. It was very hard to stay mad at him. 'OK, I'm coming aboard. Now do we have an arrangement?'

The ring ascended smoothly.

Aboard, ambulant Lobsang was waiting for Joshua in his stateroom. There had been more upgrades.

Joshua burst out laughing, despite everything. 'You look like a hotel doorman! What's that all about?'

Lobsang purred, 'I hoped to give the effect of a British butler circa 1935, sir, and rather spiffily, if you don't mind me saying so. I believe the effect is not so creepy as the *Blade Runner* killer-replicant chic I experimented with before, although I am open to suggestions.'

Spiffily. 'Well, at least it's a different kind of creepy. I guess it works. But knock it off with the sir, would you?'

The butler bowed. 'Thank you . . . Joshua. Let me say, Joshua, that I think that on this journey we are *both* learning. For now, I will step us at no more than an average human's daily pace until the young lady wishes to make her presence known.'

'Good plan.'

There was the usual, brief feeling of mild disorientation as they began to step once more. Below, passing at a leisurely pace of just a few steps per hour, the Long Earth was like the old-fashioned slide-show kit that Joshua had once found among junk in the attic back at the Home. Click once and there was the Virgin Mary, click twice and there was Jesus. You stayed still while worlds went past. Pick the one you want.

That night on the saloon deck's big screen Lobsang showed an old British movie called *The Mouse on the Moon*. In his mobile incarnation, he sat next to Joshua watching it, which would have been weird, Joshua thought, seeing the pair of them through Sally's eyes, had not this voyage long gone past weird and sailed full speed into bizarre. Nevertheless they watched the ancient film, a spoof on the space race of the twentieth century – and Joshua spotted David Kossoff instantly. For what it was worth, Lobsang had got him exactly right.

After the movie had finished, Joshua was certain he saw a mouse run across the deck and disappear. 'The Mouse on Earth Million,' he quipped.

'I will set Shi-mi on it.'

'The cat? I wondered what had happened to that thing. You know, Sally told me how she'd grown up in a family of steppers. Natural steppers, I mean. She wasn't ever alone, out in the stepwise worlds. But her family made her keep quiet about it, as *they* always had.'

'Of course they did. As you have always attempted to, Joshua. It's a natural instinct.'

'Nobody wants to be different, I guess.'

'There is that. With a power like stepping, once you might have got yourself burned as a witch. And even nowadays, since Step Day, there are an increasing number back on Datum Earth who are uncomfortable with the whole idea of stepping, and the Long Earth.'

'Who?'

'You really have no instinct for politics, do you, Joshua? Why, those who can't step at all. *They* resent the Long Earth and those who travel it, and all that this great opening-up has brought. And those who are losing money, in the new order of things. There are *always* plenty of those . . .'

35

S O HERE WAS Officer Monica Jansson, fifteen years after Step Day, her life distorted by the Long Earth phenomenon as much as anybody's had been, trying to make sense of it all as one way or another the world transformed itself around her own ageing carcass – and through it all the police tried to keep the peace. This evening she stared gloomily at a screen which showed Brian Cowley, increasingly notorious figurehead of a poisonous movement called Humanity First, spewing out his manipulative bile, folksy homespun anecdotes hiding some smart, but very divisive and dangerous, politics. Impulsively she turned the sound off. Still the hatred seeped like sweat out of the guy's face.

But then the whole phenomenon of the Long Earth had been laced with hatred and violence from the start.

Only two days after Step Day itself, terrorists had hit both the Pentagon and the British Houses of Parliament. It could have been worse. The boy who stepped into the Pentagon hadn't got his distances and angles right, and his makeshift bomb was triggered in a corridor, the only fatality being its creator. The British terrorist had clearly paid more attention in geometry class, and appeared slap (and instantly) bang in the chamber of the House of Commons – but had failed to finish his homework, so that the last thing *he* ever saw was five Members of Parliament debating a rather insignificant bill about herring fishing. Had he thought to make his appearance in the Commons bar, he would have reaped a greater harvest of souls.

Nevertheless, both of the explosions echoed around the world, and authority panicked. There was concern among private individuals too; it didn't take a genius to figure out that, suddenly, anybody could step into your house while you slept. And where there is panic, profit isn't far behind. Instantly anti-stepper devices were being developed in workshops and private homes everywhere, some of them clever, many of the worst stupid – and quite a few deadly, more often than not to their owner rather than any would-be thief. Attempts to criss-cross the empty spaces of an unoccupied room with anti-stepping hazards ended up trapping children's fingers and maiming pets. The most effective deterrent, as people soon worked out, was simply to cram a room with furniture, Victorian-style, to leave no room for steppers.

In truth, the threat of wholesale burglaries-by-stepping was more about urban fears than reality. Oh, a lot of people jumped worlds to avoid debts, obligations or revenge, and there were plenty of agents who would follow them – and there would always be a few who stole and raped and killed their way across the worlds, until somebody shot them. But in general crime was low, per capita, out in the Long Earth, when the social pressures that sparked so much crime and disorder on the Datum were largely absent.

Of course governments weren't too happy with their tax-payers stepping out of reach. But only Iran, Burma and the United Kingdom had ever actually tried to *ban* stepping. Initially most governments in the free world adopted some equivalent of the US aegis plan, demanding sovereignty of their country's footprint down all the endless worlds. The French, for example, declared that all the French footprints were available for colonization by anybody who wanted to *be* French, and was prepared to accept a carefully put together document which outlined what being French *meant.* It was a brave idea, slightly let down by the fact that despite a nationwide debate it appeared that no two Frenchmen could agree exactly on what being French did mean. Although another school of thought held that arguing about what made you French was *part* of what made you French. In practice, though, whatever regime was imposed, it didn't take you long to step out to a place where the government had no say, simply because the government wasn't there, benevolent or not.

And the people? They just stepped, here, there and everywhere, heading not so much *to* where they wanted to be, as, quite often, *from* where they emphatically didn't want to be any more. Inevitably many went out unprepared and without forethought, and many suffered as a consequence. But gradually people absorbed the lessons learned by folk like the Amish long ago, that what you needed was other people, and preparation.

Fifteen years on, there were successful communities thriving far out across the empty landscapes of the Long Earth. The emigration push was thought to be starting to decline, but it was estimated that fully a fifth of Earth's population had walked away to find a new world – a demographic dislocation comparable to a world war, it was said, or a massive pandemic.

But it was still early days, in Jansson's opinion. In a way, mankind was only slowly beginning to adjust to the idea of infinite plenty. For without scarcity, of land or resources, entirely new ways of living became available. On television the other night Jansson had watched a theoretical anthropologist work her way through a thought experiment. 'Consider this. If the Long Earth really is effectively endless, as it is beginning to look, then *all mankind* could afford to live *for ever* in hunter-gatherer societies, fishing, digging clams, and simply moving right along whenever you run out of clams, or if you just feel like it. Without agriculture Earth could support perhaps a million people in such a way. There are ten billion of us, we need ten thousand Earths – but, suddenly, we have them, and more. We have no need of agriculture, to sustain our mighty numbers. Do we have need of cities, then? Of literacy and numeracy, even?'

But as this vast perturbation of the destiny of mankind

continued, it was becoming increasingly clear that there were an awful lot of folks for whom the ambiguous treasures of the Long Earth were for ever out of reach, and they were increasingly unhappy about it.

And that, fifteen years after Step Day, as she watched Brian Cowley perform with gathering dismay, was what increasingly concerned Monica Jansson.

36

THE AIRSHIP STOPPED again, at a barren world, the air just about breathable when Joshua tried it, but stinking of ash under an overcast sky into which the usual sounding-rockets ascended.

Lobsang said, 'An aftermath world. Possibly an asteroid strike, but my best guess would be a Yellowstone, maybe a century ago. There may be life in the southern hemisphere, but nature's clean-up job will take a long time.'

'It's a wasteland.'

'Of course it is. Earth kills her children over and over again. But the rules are different now. It is a certainty that the volcano under Yellowstone National Park on Datum Earth will become aggressively active in the near future. And what will happen? People will step away. For the first time in human history, such a calamity will be a nuisance rather than a tragedy. Until the sun itself dies there will always be other worlds, and mankind will persist, somewhere in the Long Earth, immune to extinction.'

'I wonder if that's what the Long Earth is *for*.'

'I'm not yet qualified to comment.'

'Why have we stopped, Lobsang?'

'Because I am picking up a signal on an AM frequency. Rather bad reception. The transmitter is very close. Would you like to see who's calling?' Lobsang's face was a perfect simulation of a grin.

The airship's restaurant boasted a pretty good dining table, Joshua had to admit, and certainly better than the makeshift shelf on the observation deck he used when there wasn't any company. The staple of the meal in front of him was a white meat, the flesh rather fine.

And he looked up, into the eyes of Sally.

She had provided the meat. 'It's a kind of wild turkey you see around in the local worlds,' she said now. 'Good eating if you can be bothered, but they are a prey species and can very nearly outrun a wolf. Sometimes I catch a parcel of them and sell them to the pioneers . . .'

For a near-recluse, she did talk a lot, Joshua reflected. But he understood why. Joshua meanwhile just ate, enjoying himself. Maybe he was getting used to the company of women. This woman anyhow.

Lobsang entered, holding a tray. 'Orange sorbet. Oranges aren't native to the New World, but I have brought seeds for planting at suitable locations. Enjoy.' He served, turned away and disappeared through the blue door.

Sally had been reasonably polite upon learning the identity and nature of Lobsang. Well, since she'd stopped laughing. Now she lowered her voice. 'What's with the Jeeves bit?'

'I think he wants to make you welcome. I knew you'd send a signal, you know.'

'How?'

'Because I would have done in your place. Come on, Sally. You came back to us, and we figure that's because there's something you want from us. So let's trade. You know what we need to learn from you. *How did you get out so far?*'

She eyed him. 'I'll give you a clue. I'm not alone. There are more of us out here than you'd think. Every so often, a stepping box *stutters*, you might say. I met a man twenty thousand clicks from the Datum who was certain that he was one jump away from Pasadena, and puzzled by the fact that he couldn't get home. I led him down to a halfway house and left him there.'

'I always wondered why I kept coming across so many bewildered people. I thought they were just dumb.'

'Possibly many of them were.'

The voice of Lobsang floated in the air. 'I am aware of the phenomenon you mention, Sally, and would like to take the opportunity to thank you for giving it a most apposite label. *Stuttering*. But I have been unable to duplicate it.'

Sally glared at the air. 'Have you been listening to everything we have been saying?'

'Of course. My ship, my rules. Perhaps you will be good enough to answer Joshua's question. You've given only a partial response; the mystery still divides us. How did you get out here? Rather more purposefully than stuttering, I would hazard.'

Sally looked out of the window. It was dark outside, but the stars glittered with a vengeance. 'I still don't entirely trust you two. Out in the Long Earth everybody needs an edge, and this is my edge. I'll tell you one thing. If you go much further you will meet trouble coming the other way.'

That throb in Joshua's skull was never far from his awareness. '*What's* coming?'

'Even I don't know. Not yet.'

'It's caused the migration of the trolls and the other humanoids, hasn't it?'

'So you know about that? I guess you could hardly miss it.'

'Lobsang and I think we need to pursue this. Find out what's causing it.'

'What, and save the world?'

Joshua was getting used to her mockery. She was resolutely un-impressed by Lobsang's treasure-ship dirigible, and by his grandiose talk and dreams, as well, it seemed, as by Joshua's own reputation. 'So why have you come back to us? To laugh at us, or to help us? Or because of what we can do for you?'

'Among other things. It will keep.' She stood up. 'Goodnight, Joshua. Have Jeeves make up another stateroom, please. One that is not right next to yours, preferably. Oh, don't look so alarmed, your honour is safe. It's just that I snore, you see . . .'

37

THE SHIP STEPPED all through the night, and, for once, Joshua thought he could feel every step. He sagged into something like sleep just before dawn, and got maybe an hour before Sally hammered on his door.

'Show a leg, sailor boy.'

He groaned. 'What's going on?'

'Last night I gave Lobsang some coordinates to aim for. We've arrived.'

Once decent, Joshua hurried down to the observation deck. The ship was motionless. They weren't far from the Pacific coast in this version of Washington State. And below, far, far into the deep Long Earth, far beyond the consensus on where the colonizing wavefront might yet have reached, was a township, where no township had a right to be. Joshua just stared. It sprawled along the bank of a reasonably sized river, with a clutter of buildings, tracks threading through a thick, damp forest. But there were no fields, as far as he could see, no sign of agriculture. There were people everywhere, doing what people always did when there was an airship overhead, which was to point upwards and chatter excitedly. But without farms, how could they live in such a densely populated community?

Meanwhile, by the river, there were familiar hulking forms . . . Not quite human. Not quite animal.

'Trolls.'

She glanced at him, surprised. 'That's what they're called out here. As you know, evidently.'

'As Lobsang knew before we set off.'

'I suppose I should be impressed. You've met them, have you? Joshua, if you want to understand the trolls, if you want to understand the Long Earth, you need to understand this place. That's why I've brought you here.

'Orientation, Joshua. If this was the Datum we would be hovering over a township called Humptulips, in Grays Harbor County. We're not so far from the Pacific coast. Of course the details of the landscape differ, the track of the river. I hope they've got the clam chowder boiling.'

'Clam chowder? You know this place that well?'

'Of course I do.'

In her way, she could be as irritatingly smug as Lobsang.

The airship came down over a broad dirt square at the heart of the township. The buildings scattered around the square struck Joshua immediately as *old*, of weathered wood, some on eroded-looking stone bases. He had an immediate sense that this township, of maybe a couple of hundred people, had been here long before Step Day. The square itself was dominated by a stout communal wooden building that Sally said was known simply as 'City Hall', and she led the way there. Inside, the building, constructed on a frame of impressive cedar beams, had a high ceiling, polished wooden floors and furniture, glassless windows at eye-level, and large doors at either end. The fire pit in the centre added a decent enough glow.

Lobsang had descended with them, his ambulant unit clothed in saffron robes for the occasion. Despite his 1980s body-builder bulk, he had never looked more Tibetan. And he seemed oddly self-conscious – as well he might, because the hall was full of staring, smiling townsfolk, and *trolls*, mixing with the people as unnoticed as family dogs at a picnic. The air was full of their distinctive, faintly unpleasant musk.

In City Hall there was indeed chowder to be had, boiling up in huge pots, a thoroughly incongruous treat given their remoteness from the Datum.

The mayor greeted them. He was a small, sleek man who had an accent like a middle European with good English. Of course Sally knew him. She handed him a small package as soon as they met, and he led them to a central table.

Sally saw Joshua's glance at this exchange. 'Pepper.'

'You do a lot of bartering, do you?'

'I guess. Don't you? And I stay over. Not just here. If I find settlers who are interesting enough, I stop a while and help them out with their farming, whatever. That's the way to learn a world, Joshua. Whereas you two, rattling along in your great big penis in the sky, are learning nothing.'

'Told you so,' Joshua murmured privately to Lobsang.

'Perhaps,' Lobsang replied quietly. 'But even so, for all our flaws, she came back to us. You're right, Joshua. There is something she wants from us. Among all these distractions we must persist in finding out what that is.'

Sally was saying now, 'This place is pretty unique, among my stopovers, however. I call it Happy Landings.'

Lobsang observed, 'Evidently it has been here a long time.'

'A *very* long time. Folk sort of end up here . . . It seems to be a kind of people magnet. You'll see.'

The only name the mayor gave was Spencer. Over bowls of chowder he was happy to talk about his unique community.

'A "people magnet" – yes, perhaps it is something like that. But over the centuries that people have been coming here they have given it other names, or have cursed it, in a multitude of languages. There is some very old building stock, and we find old bones, some in crude coffins. Centuries, yes. People have been arriving for a long, long time. Thousands of years, even!

'Of course most of the population you see around you were born here – I myself was – but there is always a trickle of new-comers. None of those incoming settlers knows how they got here, and everybody who comes here fresh arrives with the same story: one day you are on Earth, the Datum as they call it now, minding your own business, and suddenly you're here. Sometimes there's stress involved, you're trying to escape something, oftentimes not.' He lowered his voice and added, 'Sometimes there are lone children. Strays. Lost boys and lost girls. Even infants. Often they've never stepped before at all. They are always made welcome, you may be sure of that. Do try the ale, I like to think we are very good at it. Some more chowder, Mr Valienté? Where was I?

'Of course nowadays the scientific types among us are lining up behind the idea that there is some physical singularity, some kind of hole in space, that leads people here. As opposed to the old thinking that this place is at the centre of some kind of mysterious curse – or possibly, in the circumstances, a *blessing*.

'Anyhow here we are, marooned, as it were, although I daresay no shipwrecked mariner ever arrived on a more hospitable shore. We can hardly complain. From what we hear from recent arrivals, our older folk are generally glad they missed out on most aspects of the twentieth century.' Spencer sighed. 'Some get here thinking that they have landed in heaven. Most arrive disorientated and sometimes fearful. But everybody who arrives here is welcomed. From newcomers we can learn about how all the other Earths are going. And we welcome any new information, concepts, ideas and talents; engineers, doctors and scientists are especially welcome. But I am pleased to say that these days we are growing our own culture, as it were.'

'Fascinating,' Lobsang murmured, as he carefully spooned chowder between artificial lips. 'An indigenous human civilization, spontaneously forming in the reaches of the Long Earth.'

'And a new way of travelling,' Joshua said, feeling faintly stunned at this latest conceptual leap. 'A way to cut out the step-by-step plod.' In fact, he thought, thinking of Sally, thinking of the 'stuttering' she had mentioned, *another* way.

'Yes. The Long Earth is evidently even stranger than it seems; we may learn a lot about its connectivity by studying this place. But it remains to be seen how useful this new phenomenon will be.'

'Useful?'

'Less so if it is like a fixed wormhole, a tunnel between two fixed points . . .'

'Like the rabbit hole to Wonderland,' Joshua said.

'We must learn all we can.'

Sally, meanwhile, was watching Lobsang eat, her mouth gaping. 'Joshua . . . it *eats*?'

He grinned. 'Wouldn't it look odder if he didn't, in this company? Nobody else is bothered. We'll discuss it later.'

Spencer leaned back comfortably in his chair. 'We know Sally very well, of course. Now, tell me about yourselves, please, gentlemen. The world is evidently changing, and the change brings your wonderful zeppelin! You first, Lobsang. You'll forgive us our curiosity about your exotic presence particularly . . .'

For the first time in Joshua's experience, here in this crowded, sociable place, and with trolls watching them like an audience at a cabaret, it seemed that Lobsang was flustered. This was one of those moments when Joshua genuinely couldn't tell if Lobsang really was ultimately a human, or just an incredibly smart simulation that was adept at mimicking such subtle human aspects as being embarrassed.

Lobsang cleared his throat. 'To begin with – I am a human soul, though my body is artificial. You are familiar, perhaps, with the concept of prosthetics? The use of artificial limbs, organs to sustain life . . . Consider me as an extreme case.'

Spencer looked totally unfazed. 'Amazing! What a step forward. At my age you do begin to wonder why the universe places intelligence in such fragile receptacles as our human bodies. May I ask if you have any special talents to share with us? That's what we ask all newcomers, so please don't be offended.'

Joshua groaned inwardly, anticipating Lobsang's reaction to that.

'Special talents? It would be easier to list the exceptions. I am not very good at watercolours, as yet . . .' He glanced around curiously.

'Clearly this is an unusual community, with an unusual background of development. What about industry? You have iron, evidently. Steel? Good. Lead? Copper? Tin? Gold? Wireless radio? You have surely passed the telegraph stage. In addition, printing, if you have the paper—'

Spencer nodded. 'Yes, but only handmade, I'm afraid. Since arrivals in Elizabethan times. We made improvements, of course, but we haven't chanced upon an artisan who knows much about paper manufactory for a considerable time. We have to rely on the talents of those who drift here, haphazardly.'

'If you can provide me with ferrous metals, I will fabricate for you a flatbed printing press utilizing waterpower – if you are familiar with waterpower?'

Spencer smiled. 'We've had water mills since the age of the Romans.'

Again Joshua was struck by the depth of time represented here. Sally looked amused at his reaction.

'In that case I can construct a robust alternator. Electrical current. Mayor, I can leave you an encyclopaedia of discoveries in medicine and technology to the present day – although I would advise you to take it a bit at a time. Future shock, you see.'

The crowd around them in the hall, drawn by Lobsang's strangeness, murmured a general approval at this.

But Sally, who had been listening impatiently, said, 'It's very kind of you, Lobsang, but all this Robert Heinlein stuff will have to wait. We are here because of *the problem* – remember?' She looked at Spencer. 'And you know all about that.'

'Ah. The troll migration? Alas, Sally is right. There is clearly cause for concern. It is a slow-burning problem, you might say, but, we believe, it has serious repercussions across the worlds – the Long Earth, as you call it. But even that will wait for tomorrow, Sally. Let us go and enjoy the sunshine.' He led them out of the building. 'You are very welcome here, I can't emphasize that enough. You'll see that we embrace scatterlings from all the families of mankind. Sally is pleased to call this place Happy Landings, which we find amusing. But to us it is just home. There are always spare sleeping places in City Hall, but if you prefer privacy all the family cabins are roomy. You are welcome, welcome . . .'

38

THE VISITORS WALKED through smiling crowds.

Joshua thought the layout of the place was unusual, and the architecture. There seemed to be no plan to the road system; it was a tangle of criss-crossing lanes that wandered off into the forest, as if it had just evolved that way. And the buildings were heaped up on often very ancient-looking foundations. This really did have the feel of a place that had grown slowly but continuously for a very long time, and so was layered with structures one on top of the other, like a tree trunk's rings. But there did seem to be a preponderance of relatively modern buildings overlaying a very ancient core, as if people had arrived in greater numbers in recent times, the last couple of centuries perhaps. Which was just when, he supposed, the population back on Datum Earth had started to grow fast, no doubt sending a larger flood of scatterlings to Happy Landings.

Walking by the river, Joshua began to get a sense of how people lived here. All along the bank there were racks of drying fish – mostly salmon-like fish, big healthy specimens, cleanly filleted – and more hanging inside the dwellings, some smoked. Nobody seemed to be working terribly hard, but he saw weirs in the river, traps, nets, and a few workers mending hooks, lines, harpoons. Though there were in fact a few cultivated fields, he learned, further out from the centre – mostly growing potatoes as an emergency food store, and to power the Steppers of those few visitors who used the boxes – the river provided much of what sustained the people here. During the annual salmon runs, so the friendly locals told him in a variety of bizarre accents, the whole population, human and troll, would come down to the river and harvest migrating fish that swam so thick the river water lapped up over the banks. There were evidently other kinds of fish, and Joshua saw great middens of the shells of clams and oysters. The forest was generous too, as Joshua could tell from baskets of berries, acorns, hazelnuts, as well as haunches of animals he could not identify.

'This is why nobody farms here,' Sally murmured to him. 'Or hardly anybody. Nobody *needs* to, the country is so generous. Back on the Datum, in this area pre-Columbian hunter-gatherer folk built societies every bit as complex as any farmer's, with a fraction of the labour. And none of the backache. So it is here.' She laughed, as rain sprinkled down. 'Maybe that's why Happy Landings turned out to be *here*, one of the most generous places on all the worlds. If only it didn't rain all the time it would be paradise.'

But there were trolls everywhere, and that was something you would *not* have seen in Washington State back in the Datum. The humanoids threaded their way through the human rubberneckers with a care and attention that Joshua would not have expected from creatures that looked like the offspring of a bear and an upright pig. The evidently contented relationship between human and troll here, and the uniform welcome they received, gave the place an air of peace.

Paradoxically, this made Joshua uncomfortable. He had no clear idea why. It was just that with the trolls so firmly embedded in the place, the community seemed *too* calm. Not entirely human . . . Not for the first time in his life he was conflicted and confused; there was much about this place that he had yet to understand.

And then, in the central square, one of the trolls got down on its haunches and sang. Soon the rest joined in. A troll song was always extraordinary; hearing it seemed to nail you to the spot, in a way that Joshua knew he would for ever be unable to explain. It seemed to go on and on, the mighty chords echoing from the distant forest – although when he looked at his watch when it was over, it had lasted only about ten minutes.

Sally tapped him on the shoulder. 'That, young man, is what is called the short call of the troll. The long call can last a month. Heart-warming, isn't it? In a creepy sort of way. Sometimes you will see them in a clearing, hundreds of them, all singing, apparently independently, apparently unaware of each other – until suddenly it ends on one great chord, like Thomas Tallis, you know? Like it's coming at you in four dimensions at once.'

'I know Tallis's entire canon, Sally,' said Lobsang. 'It is an apt comparison.'

Joshua decided he was not going to be left out. 'I've heard of Tallis. Sister Agnes said that if he were alive today he would be riding a Harley. Then again most of her heroes would have ridden Harleys, according to her . . .'

'I detect patterns in the music,' said Lobsang. 'It will take some time to analyse.'

'Good luck with that, mister,' Sally said. 'I have known trolls for years, and I can only guess what they are talking about. But I'm pretty confident that in this case they are discussing us and the airship. And by nightfall, every troll on this continent will be repeating it until they all have it perfect. The songs represent a sort of shared memory – that's what I believe. There's even a sort of checksum in the songs, I think, a self-correction mechanism, so that in time all the trolls get the same information reliably. Eventually it will probably go worlds-wide, depending on troll migration patterns. Sooner or later every troll that can be reached will know that we were here today.'

The others absorbed that in silence. It struck Joshua as an astounding, eerie thought, a song-memory that spanned worlds.

They walked on. It was a calm, warm afternoon, though marked by brief, light showers that everybody seemed to ignore. There were no vehicles, no pack animals, just a few handcarts, and the fish racks everywhere.

Joshua said to Sally, 'Maybe we should cut to the chase. So you know about trolls. In fact you seem very fond of trolls. You know about the humanoid migration. You brought us to this place where there's a strange human–troll community . . . You want something from us, that's obvious. Is it to do with the migration, Sally?'

She said nothing at first. Then: 'Yes. All right. I've had no intention of concealing anything from you. It's just that it's better if you work it out for yourselves. Yes, I'm concerned about the migration. It's a disturbance that's echoing up and down the Long Earth. And, yes, I don't think I can, or should, go investigating the cause alone. But somebody has to, right?'

'Then we have the same goals,' Lobsang said.

Joshua pressed, 'Come on, out with it, Sally. Time for an honest trade. We'll help you but you need to be fully truthful with us. You knew this place was here, and how to find it. How come? And how did you get out so far in the first place?'

Sally looked wary. 'Can I trust you two? I mean *really* trust you?'

'Yes,' said Joshua.

'No,' said Lobsang. 'Anything you tell me that can be used for the betterment of mankind as a whole will be utilized as I see fit. However, I will not do anything to harm you, or your family. Trust me on that. You know something we don't about the connectivity of the Long Earth, don't you?'

A couple walked by, hand in hand; she looked Swedish, he was very nearly midnight black.

Sally took a deep breath. 'My family calls them soft places.'

Joshua asked, 'Soft places?'

'Short cuts. They're usually, but not always, far inland, at the heart of a continent. They are usually near water and they get stronger around twilight. Can't exactly tell you what they *look* like, or how I find them. It's more of a feeling than anything else.'

'I don't think I understand—'

'They are places that allow you fast travel over multiple Earths at a time.'

'Seven-league boots—'

Lobsang murmured, 'I suspect wormholes would be a better metaphor.'

'But they shift,' Sally said. 'They open and close. You have to find the way, and follow it . . . You have to be taught what to look for. But it isn't something you learn, it's like something you remember – something you were told about a long time ago and then when you need it, it pops up. It's not like Stepper stuttering. It's more like, well, a helping hand. It's kind of organic, you know? Like sailors knowing the currents of the sea, the ebb and flow, wind and tide, even the saltiness of the water. And they do drift, they open and close, or reconnect to somewhere new. It's hit and miss at first, but these days I can get to any destination in three or four steps, if the tide's flowing right.'

Joshua tried to imagine this. He visualized the Long Earth as a tube of worlds, a hosepipe, along which he plodded one world at a time. These soft places were like – what? Holes in the pipe walls, enabling you to short-cut vast strings of possible Earths? Or maybe it was like a metro network, invisible beneath a city's roads, connecting point to point, a network with its own topology independent of what went on above ground. And in that network there would be nodes, exchanges . . .

Lobsang asked bluntly, 'How do they work? Your soft places.'

'Well, how would I know? My father had hypotheses, about the structure of the Long Earth. He spoke about solenoids. Chaotic mathematical structures. Don't ask me. If I ever find him—'

'How many people do you know have this talent?'

She shrugged. 'Not even all of my own family. But I know that there are others out there; occasionally I meet people. All I can really say is that I know a soft place when I find one, and then I generally have a good idea of how far it will go and in which direction. My granddad on my mother's side, he was a *real* stepper, he could sense a soft place two miles off. Granddad called them the fairy ways. He was Irish by birth, and he said that if you stepped into a soft place you could *step lively*, as he called it. Mom said that when you stepped lively you were building up a debt which would one day have to be repaid.'

Joshua asked, 'So what about Happy Landings? How come people come unstuck and drift here, like the mayor says? . . . Maybe it's something to do with the network of soft places. People drift and gather, like snowflakes collecting in a hollow, maybe.'

'Yes, perhaps it's something like that,' Lobsang said. 'We know that stability is somehow a key to the Long Earth. Maybe Happy Landings is something like a potential well. And it's clearly been operating long before Step Day, deep into the past.'

'Yeah,' Sally said sceptically. 'Look, all this isn't the point. *The trolls are nervous* – even here; I can tell if you can't. That's what we need to focus on. That's why I'm sticking with you two clowns and your ridiculous aerial barge. Because in your dim way you've seen what I've seen. That all across the Long Earth something is scaring the trolls and the other humanoids. And that scares me. And, like you, I need to figure out what's going on.'

Joshua asked, 'But what concerns you most, Sally? The threat to people, or to the trolls?'

'What do you think?' she snapped back.

At twilight there was evensong, courtesy of the trolls. Troll song *was* the trolls; they lived in a world of constant chatter.

But then so did the people of Happy Landings. Even at dusk they were still out and about, strolling, waving, laughing, generally finding pleasure in one another's company. Fires were lit everywhere; in the Pacific North-west on most worlds there was no shortage of firewood. And, Joshua noticed, as evening drew in more people were pouring in from neighbouring communities, on foot, some drawing small carts bearing children and old folk. The Humptulips core of Happy Landings wasn't isolated, then.

Some, they learned, came from as far away as this world's footprint of Seattle. And that district on this Earth had been called

Seattle since 1954, when a lady called Kitty Hartman, minding her own business on her way home from Pike Place Market, stepped without knowing, and was amazed by the disappearance of the buildings around her. The travellers from the *Mark Twain* were introduced to Mrs Montecute, as she was now known: white-haired, exceptionally spry, very happy to talk.

'Of course, it was rather a shock, you know, and I remember thinking, I don't even know what *state* I'm in! I'm not in Washington any more, that's for sure. I wondered if I should have brought a little dog and a pair of red shoes! And then the first person I met here was François Montecute, who really was kind of cute like his name, who really did turn my head, and who really was an artist between the sheets if you get my drift.' She told them this with the cheerful directness of an elderly lady who is determined to make young people aware that she has had sex, too, and by the sound of it quite a considerable amount.

There was a certain contented aura about Mrs Montecute, and it seemed to Joshua that everyone in Happy Landings shared it, to some extent. It was hard to pin down.

Sally said when he tried to express this, 'I know what you mean. Everybody seems so, well, sensible. I have come here many times and it's always the same. You never get complaints, or competitive-ness. They don't need government, not really. You could say that Mayor Spencer is the first among equals. When there is any big project to be undertaken, they just knuckle down and get on with it.'

Joshua said, 'It all feels a bit Stepford Wives to me.'

Sally laughed. 'It bothers you, does it? A happy human com-munity *bothers* Joshua Valienté, the great loner who's barely human himself. Well, it is – odd. But in a positive way. I am not talking about telepathy or any of that kind of shit.'

Joshua grinned. 'As opposed to the hopping from one world to another at a whim kind of shit?'

Sally said, 'OK, I get your point, but you know what I mean. It's all so *nice*. I've talked to them about it and they say it's the fresh air; no crowding, plenty to eat, no unfair taxes, yada, yada, yada . . .'

'Or maybe it's the trolls,' Joshua said bluntly. 'Trolls and humans, mixed up together.'

'Maybe,' she conceded. 'Sometimes I wonder . . .'

'What do you wonder?'

'I wonder if there's something so big going on here that even Lobsang would have to recalibrate his thinking. Just a hunch, for now. I'm just suspicious. But then a stepper who isn't suspicious is soon a dead stepper.'

39

JOSHUA ROSE EARLY the next morning and explored further, alone. People were friendly and ready to walk, chat and even hand him pottery mugs of lemonade. He overcame his natural inclination to silence, and talked back, and listened.

The area was pretty well homesteaded by now, he learned, with thriving settlements at the coast and along the river valleys. None of them had many more than a couple of hundred inhabitants, though people would get together on festival days – or when interesting visitors showed up, such as Lobsang with his airship. And in response to the greater influx of newcomers in recent decades, the community had had to expand, new settlements seeding across the countryside.

The reason this rapid expansion had been possible, he learned, was the trolls. Trolls were useful, trolls were friendly, companionable – and, crucially, ever ready to lift a heavy load, an exercise they took much delight in. This donation of muscle power had helped the colonists here overcome their lack of manpower, draft animals and machinery.

But in a sense the reason for all the building work, the growth of the new settlements, *was* the trolls. Trolls, he discovered, were allergic to crowds – that is to say, crowds of humans. No matter how many trolls there were, they would get nervous if there were more than one thousand, eight hundred and ninety humans in the immediate vicinity, apparently a number found by careful experimentation in the past. They didn't get mad, they just got going, not coming back, sheepishly, until a few dozen humans had kindly found somewhere else to be, and the numbers dropped down under the limit. But as the goodwill of trolls was immensely valuable, Happy Landings was spreading southwards as a confederacy of small troll-friendly townships. This was hardly inconvenient, since you could always walk to the next township in a matter of minutes, and there was plenty of room in this riverine landscape for more.

Later that morning Joshua learned that this fact, the size of the townships, was of intense interest to a young man called Henry. He had been raised among Amish until one day he stepped into a soft place and landed, as it were, among a different kind of chosen. It seemed to Joshua that Henry had come to terms with this elevation quite happily. He explained to Joshua that back home his people had always reckoned that around a hundred and fifty people was just the right size for a caring community, and so he felt at home here. He also thought, however, that he had died, and that Happy Landings was, if not heaven, at least a staging post for the journey onwards. Being dead didn't seem to bother him very much. He had his place in this little society: he was a good husbandman, gentle around animals and particularly fond of trolls.

And that was why, this morning, when at Lobsang's request Joshua brought Henry up to the airship with a few trolls, Henry believed he had ascended to heaven at last, and was speaking to God. There are some things which you don't put up with when you have been brought up by nuns, even if they are nuns like Sister Agnes. Joshua tried to disabuse Henry of the belief that the impressive saffron-clad personage he met after travelling into the sky was, in fact, God. But given Lobsang's ego and air of omni-competence there was little to dissuade him.

Lobsang, meanwhile, was burning to learn more about the language of the trolls. And that was why now, on the observation deck, there were already a couple of female trolls flanking

Lobsang's ambulant unit, and four or five juveniles having a lot of fun playing with Shi-mi. Henry had been brought along to help calm the trolls – that had actually been Sally's suggestion – but nothing seemed to faze a Happy Landings troll. They had trotted into the elevator quite happily, and once on board seemed to take everything in their great, flat-footed stride, including an artificial man and a robot cat.

Lobsang said, 'Trolls are of course mammals. And mammalian creatures love and cherish their offspring – well, for the most part. Mothers teach their children. And so I am learning like a child, with baby steps, as it were. As I myself play the part of a child, I feel I can with care derive a certain elementary vocabulary: good, bad, up, down. And thus we make progress.'

He was enjoying this, Joshua could tell. 'You're the troll whisperer, Lobsang.'

But Lobsang took no notice of that and walked among his happy band of trolls. 'Please note, I offer a nice shiny ball. Good! Joshua, observe the sounds of appreciation and interest. See the pretty shiny thing! And now, I take it away. Ah, the sounds of sadness and privation, very good. But note that the adult female is alert, emitting sounds of uncertainty, with just a subtle hint that were I to try anything really nasty with her favourite bag of woolliness she would quite likely rip off my arm and beat me to death with the wet end. Splendid! Joshua, see, I give the ball back to the pup; now mother is less apprehensive, and all is sweetness and light once more.'

And it was, thought Joshua. The *Mark Twain*, anchored over Happy Landings, moved gently in a sunlit breeze, with just enough creaking from the woodwork to lull you almost as if you were in a hammock. A pleasant place with happy, happy trolls.

The spell was broken when Lobsang asked, 'Henry, could you provide a dead troll, do you think?'

Henry looked deeply uncomfortable. When he spoke he had an

odd, lilting accent. 'Mister, if one of them dies they scrape out a very deep hole and bury the body, scattering flowers upon it beforehand to ensure the resurrection, I do believe.'

'Ah, then I suppose that a forensic dissection is out of the question? I feared so . . . I beg your pardon,' he added, with what struck Joshua as unusual tact for him. 'I intended no disrespect. But the scientific value would be high. I am confronted with a hitherto unknown species which, despite the lack of what we are pleased to call civilization, and lacking our form of intelligence, has a method of communication of an intricacy and depth unrivalled among humanity until the expansion of the internet. Thanks to this facility I believe that anything interesting and useful that a troll learns very shortly becomes known to every other troll. They *appear* to have expanded frontal lobes, I suspect mostly utilized to store and process memory, both personal and species-wide . . . Oh, for a body to dissect! Well, lacking that, I will do the best I can, which will be the best that there is.'

Henry laughed. 'You don't believe in modesty, do you, Mr Lobsang?'

'Absolutely not, Henry. Modesty is only arrogance by stealth.'

Joshua threw a ball towards a baby troll. 'Neanderthals put flowers on the bodies of their dead too. I'm no expert, I saw it on the Discovery Channel. Are the trolls nearly human, then?' He had the sense to duck as the exuberant return from the pup sailed over his head and splintered the bulkhead.

'The young will experiment,' remarked Lobsang. '"Nearly human" is right, Joshua. Like the dolphins, orang-utans and, if I am being charitable, the rest of the higher apes. It's a tiny gap between us and them. And nobody knows how *Homo sapiens* became, well, sapient. Sally, do the trolls use tools?'

She looked up from her playing. 'Oh, yes. Away from humans I've seen them use sticks and stones as improvised tools. And if you bring a fresh band to Happy Landings, and if they see a guy fixing a weir in the river, a troll might pick up a handsaw and help him, if he's shown what to do. By the end of the evening, every troll in that band will know how to do it.'

Lobsang patted a troll. 'So it's a case of monkey see, monkey do.'

Sally said, 'No, it's a case of troll see, troll sit down, troll think about things and then, if it's appropriate, troll make a half-decent lever or whatever and, by the end of that evening, troll tell other trolls about the usefulness of it. Their long chant is a troll Wikipedia, quite apart from anything else. If you want to find out anything like "Am I going to throw up if I eat this purple elephant?" then another troll will tell you.'

Joshua said, 'Hang on. Are you telling me you've seen a purple elephant?'

'Not exactly,' said Sally. 'But out in one of the Africas there is an elephant which, I swear, has the art of camouflage down to a tee. Somewhere out there in the Long Earth you'll find almost anything you can imagine.'

'"Anything you can imagine",' murmured Lobsang. 'Interesting choice of phrase. Between ourselves, Sally, I can't help feeling that the Long Earth as a whole has something approaching what I can only call a meta-organic component. Or perhaps meta-animistic.'

'Hmph. Maybe,' said Sally, scratching a troll's scalp. 'But the whole set-up irritates me. The Long Earth is too kind to us. It's too pat! Just as we've trashed the Datum, just as we've wiped out most of the life we shared it with and are about to succumb to our own resource wars, shazam, an infinity of Earths opens up. What kind of God sets up a stunt like that?'

'You object to this salvation?' Lobsang asked. 'You really are misanthropic, aren't you, Sally?'

'I've got a lot to be misanthropic about.'

Lobsang stroked his own trolls. 'But perhaps it's nothing to do with any kind of god. Sally, we – I mean humanity – are barely at the beginning of our enquiry into the Long Earth. Newton, you know, spoke of himself as a boy playing on a seashore, distracted

252

by a smoother pebble or a prettier shell, while the ocean of truth lay undiscovered before him. Newton! We understand so little. Why should the universe open itself up to careful and dedicated enquiry at all? And why should it be so generous, so fecund, so nurturing of life, even intelligence? Perhaps in some way the Long Earth is an expression of that nurturing.'

'If so, we don't deserve it.'

'Well, that's a debate for another day . . . You know, my researches *will* be frustrated unless I can obtain the corpse of a troll.'

'Don't even think about it,' said Sally.

Lobsang snapped back, '*Please* don't tell me what to think. I think, therefore I am; it's what I do. May I suggest that you two go and enjoy the pleasures of Happy Landings, and leave me in peace to converse with my friends? Whom I promise not to kill and dissect.'

On the access deck below, the elevator hatch slammed open, a clear enough hint that they should leave.

When they were on the ground again, Sally giggled. 'He can get pretty ratty, don't you think?'

'Maybe.' Joshua was faintly concerned. He'd never heard Lobsang sound quite so unstable.

'Is there *really* a human being in there somewhere?'

'Yes,' said Joshua, flatly. 'And you know there is, because you said *he* sounded ratty. You didn't use the word *it.*'

'Oh, very smart. Come on, let's look around a few more happy homesteads.'

For Sally that evening, it was like greeting one long-lost friend after another. Joshua was happy to follow in her wake, trying to analyse his feelings about Happy Landings.

He *liked* the place. Why? Because it seemed, well, right somehow. Like it was where all mankind belonged, perhaps. Maybe that was because he too had some sense of the soft places, the soft routes all converging here, in Lobsang's well of stability. The *maybes* in his mind annoyed him, however, as he walked alone. And the sense that he disliked Happy Landings as much as he liked it. As if he didn't trust it.

He'd listened to Sally's arguments with Lobsang – she was more voluble on these issues, if not necessarily any better informed – and he tried to make sense of all he was learning. Where *did* man belong? On the Datum, that was for sure, with ancestral fossils all the way down to bedrock. But now the human race was expanding at speed across the Long Earth, no matter what the governments thought, no matter about aegis; nobody could stop it, and certainly nobody could control it, no matter how many god-bothering spittle-flecked homealone tub-thumpers back on the Datum tried. You would run out of people before you ran out of Earths. But what was the point of it all? Sister Agnes used to tell him that the purpose of life was to be all that you could be – with a side helping, of course, of helping others to do the same. And maybe the Long Earth was a place where, as Lobsang might put it, human potentiality could be maximally expressed . . . Was there some sense in which that was what the Long Earth was *for*? To allow mankind to make the most of itself? And in the middle of this cosmic conundrum, here was Happy Landings, where the scatterlings of mankind drifted and sifted. What was *that* all about?

Of course there were no answers.

In the gathering twilight Joshua was careful not to walk into trolls. Trolls seldom walked into people. Indeed the general etiquette of Happy Landings was that everybody should try not to walk into *anybody*. But now, suddenly, Joshua walked into an elephant.

Fortunately, it was neither purple nor camouflaged. It was quite small, about the size of an ox, coated with wiry brown hair, and it had a rider, a stocky, grizzled man, who said cheerfully, 'Another newcomer! And where did you blow in from, sport? My name's

Wally, been here eleven years. Rum go and no mistake, ain't it? Bit of a bugger, good thing I wasn't married! Not for want of opportunity, you understand, before or since.' The self-confessed Wally slid off the back of his miniature elephant, and held out a leathery hand. 'Put it there!'

They shook hands, and Joshua introduced himself. 'I've only been here a couple of days. Flew in. In a flying machine,' he added quickly.

'You did? Great! When are you flying out? Got a spare seat?'

Joshua had wondered at the fact that so few residents of Happy Landings had asked that question; so few wanted out. 'I think the jury is out on that one, Wally. We have a kind of mission to achieve.'

'No worries,' Wally said, apparently unfazed. 'I've been poling down the river, found Jumbo here. Amiable little fella, ain't he? Just the job for the long-haul, and pretty bright. They come up from the plains.' He sighed. 'I like spaces, me, don't like forests, too creepy. I like to feel wind on my face.' As they walked towards City Hall with Jumbo following dutifully behind, he added, 'We've been working on the new road south, clearing the way. Don't mind trees if I can cut them down! But I reckon I have earned my keep here now, so it's time to build a boat and go discover Australia. That's the longest haul of them all, right enough.'

'That's halfway around the world, Wally. And it won't be the Australia you remember.'

'Fair enough. *Any* Australia will do for me. Of course, I can't do it all in one go. But a simple way would be to sail down the coast, staying close to the shore, lots of good eating on the way, and strike out for Hawaii. And you can bet your boots that's one of the first places steppers would want to colonize. And after that, well, we'll have to see, but where there are people there's going to be a pub, and where there's a pub there's sooner or later going to be Wally!'

Joshua shook hands with Wally, wishing him bon voyage.

He found Sally back in City Hall, surrounded by friendly faces, as ever. She broke away when she saw Joshua. 'People are starting to notice. Even here.'

'What?'

'About the trolls. That more and more of them are stepping off East. Wild bands come passing through, and even the local ones, what you might loosely call domesticated, I suspect some of them want to leave too, but they are being kind of polite. The locals are getting disturbed.'

'Hmm. Ripples in the tranquil pool of Happy Landings?'

'Is Lobsang finished playing at Dr Dolittle? It's time we were airborne and heading West again.'

'Let's go see.'

Back on the ship, the observation deck appeared empty save for a pile of trolls, snuggling like puppies. Then the heap moved, and Lobsang poked his head out, beaming.

'Fur is wonderful against the tactile areas, is it not? I feel like one blessed. And they speak! Extremely high-pitched, minimal vocabulary . . . Multiple ways of communicating, apparently; it does seem that communicating is what being a troll is all about. But I suspect the real exchange of information takes place in the songs.

'I believe I now have learned terms for good/bad, approval/refusal, pleasure/pain, night/day, hot/cold, correct/incorrect, and "I wish to suckle now", although I suspect the last will not be of much use to me. I will learn more when we continue our voyage, which by the way we will be doing with alacrity at first light tomorrow. I intend to take these trolls. I hope my new friends do not mind travelling by air. I believe they *like* me!'

Sally's face was a carefully controlled mask. 'Well, that's just peachy, Lobsang. But are you doing any actual work in there?'

'I am coming to tentative conclusions. These are evidently very flexible omnivores. No wonder they're so widespread, across the Long Earth. They're ideal nomads. And the product of a couple of million years' evolution, probably, since the root habiline stock learned to step.'

Joshua asked, 'Habiline?'

'*Homo habilis*. Handy Man. The first toolmakers in the human evolutionary line. You see, I'm speculating that maybe the stepping ability evolved alongside the ability to make tools. One surely needs a similar imaginative capacity: to imagine how a bit of stone might become an axe; to imagine how one world might differ from another, and then to step into it. Or perhaps it is related to the ability to imagine alternative futures depending on one's choices: to go hunting today, or to go back to that rich hazel clump again . . . Either way, once such an ability developed the species would split, between increasingly adept steppers who would drift away, and those less adept or unable to step at all, who would stay at home, and perhaps become actively resistant to the steppers, who would have a competitive advantage.'

'A stay-at-home strand that gave rise to humanity on Datum Earth,' Joshua guessed.

'Possibly. My colleague Nelson's archaeological searches would seem to indicate that. But this *is* just my guess. It may be the stepping ability evolved even earlier, during the age of the pre-human apes. One must describe these creatures as humanoid rather than hominid, until a proper study is concluded, evolutionary relationships established.'

Sally asked, 'Have they told you why they are migrating?'

'I have an idea . . . My conclusion has to be tentative, even though the alpha female is remarkably good at pantomime. Imagine a pressure in your head. Storms in the mind.'

And Joshua was aware of the gathering storm in his own head, that sense of pressure as they headed West, just as if the Datum itself with its billions of souls was up ahead of him. Yes, he thought. Bad weather for the psyche, coming this way. But what's driving it?

Lobsang said no more. Amid the mewings of the troll pups, once again he was submerged in his heap of fur. 'Ah. Tactile surfaces . . .'

And suddenly there was no more Lobsang. The physical presence of the ambulant unit was still here, but some subtle aspect of the ship had dissipated.

Joshua looked at Sally.

Sally said, 'You feel that too? Is it something we can't hear, or see any more? Where's he gone? He can't die, can he? Or – break?'

Joshua didn't know what to say. The ship remained subtly busy, its myriad mechanisms whirring and clicking away as if nothing had happened. But inside this brightly lit complex Joshua could not detect the controlling element, could not detect Lobsang. Something essential was missing. It had been like this when old Sister Regina had died. She had been bed-bound for years, but she liked to see the children, and still, despite everything, had known all their names. They had filed in to see her, nervous of the smell, her papery skin. And then suddenly it had seemed that something that they hadn't known was there . . . wasn't any more.

'I have been thinking he might be ill,' he said, uncertain. 'He hasn't been himself since he got buried under troll cubs.'

The voice of Lobsang came over the loudspeaker: 'Do not be unduly worried.'

Sally was startled, and laughed nervously. 'Should we be *duly* worried?'

'Sally, please bear with us. There has been no malfunction. You are being addressed by an emergency subsystem. Right now Lobsang is recompiling: that is, integrating vast volumes of new information. This will take a few hours. However, we subsystems are fully capable of fulfilling all necessary functions during the period stated. Lobsang needs his time offline; sooner or later every sufficiently sapient creature needs time to take stock, as we are sure you will understand. You are quite safe. Lobsang looks forward to the pleasure of your company around dawn.'

Sally snorted. 'Somehow I was expecting him to add "Have a nice day", but I suppose you can't have everything. How much of *that* was true, do you think?'

Joshua shrugged. 'He is learning a lot, I guess, and very fast, from the trolls.'

'And now he's absorbing their nightmares. So we have a free evening. How about one more trip down to the bar?'

'*Which* bar? . . .'

At the end of a long round of farewell drinks, all of them free, he had to carry her back to the ship. He laid her gently on the bed in her stateroom. She looked younger when she slept. He felt an unreasonable stab of protectiveness, and was glad she wasn't awake to notice it.

There was no sign of Lobsang, no sound of his voice.

And the trolls, it turned out, had left of their own accord. Joshua thought, troll see elevator button. Troll think about button. Troll press button. Goodbye troll . . . Lobsang had wanted to get more out of his contact with the trolls. But evidently the trolls had got all they wanted out of *him*.

Alone, Joshua lay down on his couch on the observation deck, looking at the stars.

At dawn, with all its passengers asleep, the ship rose gently, gaining height until it was above the tops of the highest forest giants, and then stepped, disappearing with a small thunderclap.

40

IN THE MORNING Lobsang was back. Joshua could sense him, sense that a kind of purposefulness had returned to the ship, even before the ambulant unit joined him on the observation deck, as he drank the first coffee of the day. Sally was evidently still asleep.

They were stepping gently, and worlds washed beneath them. As ever the Long Earth was mostly trees and water, silence and monotony. Joshua was glad to be free of the hard-to-pin-down oddness of Happy Landings, but as they headed West once more that gathering pressure in his head had returned. He tried and failed to ignore it.

The two of them sat in silence. There was no mention of Lobsang's departed friends the trolls, or of his offline episode. Joshua couldn't read Lobsang's mood. He wondered vaguely if he was *lonely* without the trolls, disappointed they had chosen to leave, frustrated that his research was evidently unfinished. It was faintly disturbing that Lobsang seemed to be becoming more unstable, more unpredictable. Overloaded by new experiences, perhaps.

After an hour of this Lobsang said, out of nowhere, 'Do you ever think about the future, Joshua? I mean the far future?'

'No. But I bet you do.'

'The diffusion of humanity across the Long Earth will surely cause more than mere political problems. I can foresee a time where mankind is so dispersed across the multiplicity of worlds that there will be significant genetic differences at either end of the human hegemony. Perhaps there will have to be some kind of enforced cross-migration to make certain that mankind remains sufficiently homogeneous to be united . . .'

A burning forest below made the ship dance briefly on turbulent thermals.

'I don't think we need worry about that just yet, Lobsang.'

'Oh, but I do worry, Joshua. And the more I see of the Long Earth, the more its scale impresses itself on me, and the more I fret. Mankind will be trying to run a galactic empire, effectively, on one ever-repeating planet . . .'

The airship shivered to a halt. The world below was shrouded in low cloud.

Sally wandered on to the deck, wrapped in a robe, her hair in a towel. 'Really? Do we have to copy the mistakes of the past? Must there be Roman legions marching into endless new worlds?'

'Good morning, Sally,' Lobsang said. 'I trust you are rested?'

'The best thing about the beer at Happy Landings is its purity, like the very best German brews. No hangover.'

Joshua said, 'Although you did your best to test that theory to destruction.'

She ignored him and looked around. 'Why were we travelling so slowly? And why, in fact, have we stopped?'

Lobsang said, 'We travelled slowly in order that you might sleep late, Sally. But also I took on board your criticism. It pays to inspect the small details, and so I have slowed the flight of our flying penis, as you so amusingly described it. Small details, such as the relic of an advanced civilization just underneath us. Which is why we have stopped.'

Joshua and Sally, electrified, exchanged a glance.

As the ship lost height they peered down through the haze.

'My radar scanner is returning images through the cloud,'

Lobsang said, apparently staring into empty space. 'I see a river valley, evidently long dry. A cultivated flood plain. No recognizable electromagnetic or other high technology. Signs of purposeful construction on the riverside – including a bridge, long ago broken. And rectangles on the ground, my friends, *rectangles* of brick or stone! But no signs of complex life surviving. I have no idea who the builders were. This may be a diversion from our main goal, but I am sure I speak for all of us when I say that we should make an initial survey of this phenomenon. Am I right?'

Again Joshua and Sally glanced at each other.

Sally asked, 'What kind of weapons are we carrying?'

'Weapons?'

'Better safe than sorry.'

Lobsang said, 'If you mean portable weapons we have various knives, lightweight but nevertheless very useful handguns, cross-bows that fire a variety of darts tailored to the metabolism types we might expect to encounter, ranging in power from "ever so sleepy" to "instantly dead", colour-coded, with Braille and pictogram options – I am rather proud of that piece of kit. Aboard the airship there are a number of projectile weapons under my command. If necessary, I can fabricate a small but very sneaky tank.'

Sally snorted. 'We're not going to need a tank. We're dealing with an extinct civilization down there. Although extinct civilizations can leave behind nasty surprises.'

Lobsang was silent for a moment. 'Of course. You are right. One must prepare appropriately. Please hold.'

He stood and went behind his blue door. Joshua and Sally exchanged another glance.

Then, after a couple of minutes, the door opened and the ambulant unit walked back on to the deck, wearing a fedora hat and carrying a holstered revolver and, of course, a bull whip.

Sally stared. 'Well, Lobsang, you have now passed my personal Turing test!'

'Thank you, Sally, I shall cherish that.'

Joshua was astonished. 'You fabricated a bull whip in minutes? Braiding leather takes time. How did you do it?'

'Much as I would like to give you the impression that I am omnipotent, I have to say that there was already a whip in the manifest. A simple and versatile device, requiring little maintenance. Well – shall we go exploring?'

They climbed down into a near desert. Joshua found himself in a broad valley, with a few ragged trees struggling for life on the floor, cliffs on either side honeycombed with caves. There was no sign of animal life, he observed, not so much as a desert mouse. He spotted the remnants of that broken bridge, and the rectangular scrapings on the ground.

But he instantly forgot about all that, because down the valley was a building: one sodding great *big* rectangle, not much from the air maybe, but from down here it looked like the headquarters of some international conglomerate with an aversion for windows.

They set off towards it, led by Lobsang in his hat.

'Generally speaking,' Lobsang pronounced, 'reality having little sense of narrative, ancient sites are *not* heavy with swinging blades that decapitate, or rock panels that fold back to fire darts. It's rather a shame, isn't it? However, I have detected a textbook collection of enigmatic symbols. The valley cliffs appear to be of pale grey limestone, and have been extensively worked by creatures unknown. The symbology seems to have no relation to any known human script. Meanwhile the large building ahead is constructed of black blocks, basalt perhaps, not well dressed as masonry goes. No obvious entrances as seen from this side, but I believe that while we were still airborne I saw on the far side of the building something like a sloping face, a shadow – perhaps a way in.' He added, deadpan, 'Isn't this fun? Any comments?'

Sally said, 'Only that we are almost a mile from the thing and don't have your eyesight, Lobsang. Pity us poor mortals, will you? Why did you land us so far away?'

'I beg your pardon, both of you. I thought it might be sensible to approach cautiously.'

'It is his standard routine, Sally,' Joshua said.

They walked on, with the ship drifting behind them. There were slopes of scree at the base of the canyon walls, and here and there between the sparse trees patches of lichen, moss and scrubby grass had managed to find a footing. But still no animal life; there wasn't even anything like a buzzard in the sky. This was an inhospitable place, a place where nothing had happened for a very long time, and went on not happening now. And it was hot; the sunlight, breaking through the clouds, reflected from the walls, and the arid canyon already felt like a solar furnace. This didn't faze Lobsang, who was striding along as if training for the Olympics. Joshua, though, was hot, dusty, increasingly ill at ease.

They reached the looming building. Sally said, 'Good grief, will you look at that thing? You don't realize how big it is until you get close!'

And Joshua looked up, and up, at the building's sheer face. It wasn't exactly a miracle of architecture – it was unimpressive, in fact, save for its sheer scale. The blocks of black basalt-like rock from which it had been constructed had been roughly worked to fit, but were not of a uniform size. Even from here you could see gaps and imperfections, some of which had here and there been naturally mortared with what looked like bird guano and nests, but even that had evidently been a long time ago.

Sally said, 'Nice architecture. Somebody ordered "big and heavy and last for ever", and got it. OK, let's walk around to the entrance and dodge the rolling rock ball—'

'No,' said Lobsang sharply, standing stock still. 'Change of plan. I have detected a rather more insidious danger. *The whole structure is radioactive.* Short range only, not remotely detectable – I do apologize. I suggest that we ambulate with alacrity back the way we came. No arguments. Please don't waste breath until we are safe . . .'

They didn't exactly run; call it a very determined walk.

Joshua asked, 'So what is this place? Some kind of waste dump?'

'Did you notice a multiplicity of signs that would indicate that entering this building unprepared is going to kill you? No, I didn't either. The technological level appears much too low for this to be some kind of nuclear reactor, or other similar facility. I suspect they didn't know what they were dealing with. I am speculating that this culture stumbled across a rather useful ore with interesting properties, perhaps a natural nuclear pile . . .'

'Like Oklo,' Joshua said.

'In Gabon, yes. A natural concentration of uranium. They found something that made holy glass glow, perhaps . . . That would show the spirits at work, wouldn't it?'

Sally said, 'Spirits that ultimately killed their acolytes.'

Lobsang said, 'We can at least look at some of the more distant caves before we depart. They should be far enough from the temple, or whatever this is, to be safe.'

The first cave they chose to explore was big, wide, cool – and crowded with the dead.

For a moment the three of them stood at the entrance of this house of bones. Joshua felt utterly dismayed at the sight, yet somehow it seemed an appropriate culmination of this lethally disappointing place.

They walked in cautiously, stepping on clear earth where they could find it. The skeletons were fragile, often to the point of crumbling. The bodies must have been dumped in here, Joshua thought, perhaps in a rush, in the final days of the community when there was nobody left to dispose of them properly, however they had managed that disposal. But what were these creatures – or rather, what had they been? At first glance they might have been vaguely human. To Joshua's inexpert eye they looked bipedal, as he could tell from the leg bones, the slim hips. But there was nothing humanoid about their sculpted, helmet-like skulls.

In the heart of the cave the crew of the *Mark Twain* stood there rather helplessly. With a whir, Lobsang's head turned steadily, and for once mechanically, with no human-like artifice, scanning and recording the symbols etched into the walls.

Sally said, 'Have you noticed? These corpses were not scavenged, not by animals. Nothing has disturbed them since they were dumped here.'

Lobsang murmured as he worked, 'I launched the usual drone craft, incidentally. There is no evidence of technology, of high intelligence, anywhere else on this version of Earth. Only here. The mystery deepens.'

Sally grunted. 'Perhaps the poisonous stuff that drew them here inspired them to their greatest cultural peak – before killing them. What an irony. Of course there is another possibility.'

'What's that?' Joshua asked.

'That the nuclear pile under that temple wasn't natural at all. Merely very, very old . . .'

Joshua and Lobsang had no response to that.

'But still,' Sally said, 'a dinosaur civilization? It's a unique find.'

Joshua asked, 'Dinosaurs?'

'Look at those crested skulls.'

'A civilization built by post-dinosaur evolutionary descendants, perhaps,' Lobsang said fussily. 'We must be precise about terms.'

Joshua stared at a bit of bone, what was probably a finger, adorned with a gold ring, massive, set with sapphires. He bent and picked it up. 'Look at this. It can't be anything but decoration. They were so *like* us, dinosaurs or not. They were sapient. They were tool-users. They created buildings – a city, at least this one. And they had art – adornment . . .'

'Yes,' Lobsang said. 'They were like us in one essential regard, and unlike the trolls, say. These creatures, like us, created an environment of culture around themselves. Our artifacts, our cities, are external stores of the wisdom of past ages. The trolls seem to have nothing like it, though perhaps their songs are a step towards it. These creatures had that faculty, evidently.'

Joshua said, 'They even look as if they were upright bipeds, like us. Don't they?'

Lobsang said, 'Perhaps we are seeing universals here – the upright biped is a useful tool-wielding form given a basic four-limbed body plan; and perhaps intelligent incarnate tool-wielding creatures have a natural tendency to aggregate into something like cities. Perhaps even an attraction for bright shiny ornaments is common. Yet it is all gone. They poisoned themselves, and now they are poisoning us.'

Sally looked at Joshua. 'I feel like I just found out I had a still-born twin brother.'

'There's little point our spending much more time here,' said Lobsang. 'This place clearly requires a properly equipped archaeo-logical expedition – with radiation suits. It will keep, after all; we are far from the Datum, and I doubt if there will be tourists any time soon. Come, children. Let's go home. There is nothing for us here.'

As they made their way back to the elevator, Joshua said bitterly, 'It all seems such a waste, doesn't it? All these worlds. What's the point, without mind?'

'It is the way of things,' Lobsang said. 'You are looking at this the wrong way. How likely is it that we might find sapient life on other planets? The astronomers have detected several thousand planets of other stars, but nothing as yet has given us any reason to believe that there is anybody out there. Perhaps it is difficult to evolve tool-making intelligences. And perhaps we should be grateful we came so *close* to meeting these creatures, so close in probability space.'

Sally said, 'But if these creatures were sentient, why did we find them in only one world? We would have picked up evidence of them in the neighbouring worlds, wouldn't we? At least in this location. Couldn't they step, despite their sentience?'

'Perhaps not,' Lobsang said. 'Or perhaps the natural steppers were driven out by those who could not step at all. As seems to be happening on Datum Earth right now. Perhaps this is a glimpse of our own future.'

And Sally and Joshua, two secretive natural steppers, exchanged glances of understanding.

41

'NATURAL STEPPERS. Such a nice phrase, ain't it? I mean, we all step. We all learn to do it when we're weaned off our mammy's milk. "Oh, look, it's baby's first steps."' Brian Cowley, who was nothing if not a showman, took mincing baby paces back and forth across the stage, mike in hand, picked out by the spotlights in the cavernous conference room. The simple stunt won him a few whoops.

Monica Jansson, in plain clothes, glanced around the crowd in this basement room to see who was doing the whooping.

'It's natural. *Walking* is. But what *they* call stepping?' He shook his head. 'Nothing natural about that. You need a gadget to do it, don't you? You don't need no gadget to walk. *Stepping*. That's not what I call it. That's not what my granddaddy would have called it. We plain folk, who don't have the education to know any better, have other words for practices like that. Words like *unnatural*. Words like *abomination*. Words like *unholy*.'

Each term brought louder choruses of whoops. There would come a point, Jansson knew, where she'd have to join in with the whooping to keep her cover.

The room was overcrowded, and dimly lit aside from the stage, the air hot, steamy. Cowley always made a point of appearing in public only underground, in basements, cellars, subterranean venues like this hotel's below-ground-level conference room. Places the stepping folk couldn't get at him, not without digging a hole in the ground first. Jansson was here undercover, along with

269

colleagues from the MPD and Homelands Security (the 's' had been adopted ten years after Step Day) and the FBI and a number of other agencies, who had become alarmed at the wilder noises coming out of fringe elements of Cowley's Humanity First movement.

Jansson had already spotted some familiar faces in the crowd. There was even one on stage, in the row of Cowley's well-heeled backers: Jim Russo, whose grandly named Long Earth Trading Company was still alive, still trading, but who had lost various fortunes as the world had changed beyond his imagination. Since she'd interviewed Russo a few years back over complaints about workforce exploitation, Jansson had made a mental note to keep an eye on him, and how he would react to the next, and inevitable, downturn in his fortunes. Not well, it seemed. Now here he was, aged fifty, bitter after yet another disappointment and perceived betrayal, handing a portion of his remaining wealth to this man, to Brian Cowley, self-appointed voice of the anti-steppers. And Russo wasn't alone in carrying financial bruises from the opening up of the Long Earth; Cowley wasn't short of backers.

Cowley was moving on to the economic arguments that had gained him most traction in the press.

'I pay my taxes. You pay your taxes. It's part of our contract with our government – and it *is* our government, no matter what they might tell you once they get themselves safely installed for life inside the Beltway. But the other side of the contract is this: that they should use *your* tax money to benefit *you*. You and yours, your children and your old folk, to keep you safe in your homes. That's the deal, as I always understood it. But then I'm not inside the Beltway. I'm just an ordinary Joe, like you, like you,' he said, pointing at the crowd. 'And you know what this ordinary Joe has found out they're doing with your taxes? I'll tell you. They pay for *colonists*. They pay for those folk playing at being pioneers, out on some unnatural world where they don't even have regular horses and buzzards and cattle like God made them here. They give them *mail services*. They send up *census takers*. They send up *fancy medicines.* They send *cops*, for when those deranged fools take a fancy to killing their own mothers, or fathering children by their own daughters . . .'

Jansson knew this much, at least, was a pack of lies. In the roomy stepwise worlds, without the pressures of crowding and deprivation, such crimes were comparatively rare.

'And they have a whole system, propped up by your taxes, to ensure that the money those *brave pioneers* leave here, back on the real world, the only true world, is all tied up to keep 'em supplied with all the toys they need – I'm talking about this here Pioneer Support. Some of 'em even have *homes*, standing empty. You know how many people are homeless in America today?

'And it's all for what? What do *you* get out of the deal? And you, and you? There's no *trade* with these other worlds – not beyond Earths 1 and 2 and 3 where you can haul back lumber and stuff. You can't run an oil pipeline from Earth Gazillion to Houston, Texas. You can't even drive a herd of cattle over.

'The federal government has spent years telling you that the expansion into the Long Earth is some kind of analogy of the days of the pioneer trails and the Old West. Well, I might not know much about the ways of the Beltway, but I do know my own country's heritage, and I know the value of a dollar, and I can tell you this is a *lie*. This is a *boondoggle*. Somebody sure as hell is getting rich off this folly, but it ain't you, and it ain't me. Why, we'd be better off going back to the moon. At least it's God's own moon! At least you can bring back moon rocks!

'And I can tell you, when I have my meeting with the President in a few days' time, my central demand is going to be this: cut your support of the Long Earth colonies. If the steppers left assets here, seize 'em. If they're productive out there in the godless worlds, tax 'em until their eyes water. Those guys up there want to be pioneers, fine, let 'em. But not propped up by my tax dollars, and yours . . .'

Growls of approval, disturbingly loud.

Jansson spotted Rod Green, just eighteen years old, his

strawberry-blond mane easily distinguished. Rod was one of a class the cops had labelled the 'homealones', non-stepper kids who had been more or less abandoned by families seduced by the romance of going off to build a new life in the stepwise reaches. A whole class of people injured by the very presence of the Long Earth in ways much deeper than the mere financial. And now here he was, lapping up Cowley's poison.

Cowley was getting to the meat of his peroration. The hardcore stuff, the stuff these disadvantaged people had really come to hear. The reason he banned recordings of his speeches.

'Here's somethin' I came across,' he said, producing a clipping. 'A pronouncement from one of them *pro-fess-ors* in the universities. And this man says, now let me quote, "The stepping ability represents a new dawn for humanity, the arrival of a new cognitive skill on a par with the development of language and multi-component tool-making," and blah, blah, blah.

'Do you understand what this man is saying, ladies and gentlemen? What he's talking about? He's talking about *evolution.*

'Let me tell you a story. Once upon a time there was another sort of human being on this planet. We call them *Neanderthals.* They were like us, you see, they wore clothes of skin and made tools and built fires, why, they even cared for their sick and buried their dead with respect. But they weren't *quite* as smart as us. They were around for hundreds of thousands of years, but in all that time not one of 'em came up with anything as complicated as a bow and arrow, which any seven-year-old American boy could make.

'But there they were, with their tools and their hunting and their fishing. Until one day, along came a new sort of folk. A new sort with flat faces and slim bodies and clever hands and big, bulging brains. And these folk *could* make bows and arrows. Why, I bet there was some Neanderthal *pro-fess-or* who said something like, "The ability to make a bow and arrow represents a new dawn for humanity," and blah, blah, blah. Maybe that Neanderthal prof urged Ug and Mug to give over a tithe of mammoth meat to fund more bow-and-arrow-making, for the benefit of the new folk. And it was all dandy, and everybody got along fine.

'But where are Ug and Mug now? Where are the Neanderthals? I'll tell you. Dead, these thirty thousand years. *Extinct.* Now there's a terrible word if you like. A word beyond death, because extinction means your children are dead too, and your grand-children and their children will *never even be born.*

'You know what I would say to those Neanderthals? You know what they should have done when those bow-and-arrow folk showed up?' He slammed his palm on a table. 'They should have raised their big fists and their ugly old stone tools, and they should have smashed the bulging skulls of those new folk, every last one of them. Because if they had, their grandchildren would be around now.' He kept slamming the palm, punctuating his sentences. 'Now I got federal politicians and university *pro-fess-ors* telling me there's a new sort of human being amongst us, a new evolution going on, a superman among us ordinary Joes. A superman, whose only power is the ability to slip into your child's bedroom at night, without you even knowing it? What kind of superman is that?

'You think I'm a Neanderthal? You think I'm gonna make the mistake they made? Are you gonna let these mutants take over God's good Earth? *Are you gonna submit to extinction?* Are you? Or you? Or you? . . .'

Everybody was on their feet, on the stage too, hollering and clapping. Jansson clapped too, for cover. Around her she glimpsed FBI guys quietly taking photographs of the crowd.

The world was going to change again. That was the buzz. Once the Black Corporation's more or less covert airship developments began to deliver the massive transformations in interworld carry-ing capacity they promised, huge trade flows and massive economic growth could be expected. But it wouldn't come soon enough for the likes of Russo, or Cowley. Jansson fretted about how much harm might be done while everybody waited for the next miracle.

42

THE *MARK TWAIN* was a haven. Once you were airborne and stepping away you left your troubles behind. Now it was a relief to get away from the Rectangles, and head into the new and unknown. Joshua welcomed the escape, despite the increasing, foreboding pressure in his head.

Lobsang was still stepping slowly, inspecting the Earths with relative care, while Joshua and Sally hung out on the observation deck. They were stepping at cloud height – but even so, once, over a dark green world, Joshua thought that he heard the scraping of leaves along the keel, the touch of what must be the titanic trees of some Joker planet.

'Lobsang's worried, isn't he?' said Sally. 'And distressed by what we found at the Rectangles.'

'Well, he *is* a Buddhist. Veneration for all living things and all that. But bones are never feelgood. Elephants are the same, aren't they? Aware of the significance of bones, either as a signature of threat, or of the death of one of their kind . . .' He sensed her attention was elsewhere. 'Sally, is there something wrong?'

'What do you mean by "wrong"?' It sounded like an accusation.

Joshua recoiled from her tone; he didn't feel like a fight. He went up to the galley and started to peel potatoes, a gift from Happy Landings delivered in a woven sack. He gave all his attention to the action of knife on potato. Displacement activity, he knew, but comforting even so, given what he was displacing.

Sally followed him, and stood in the doorway to the lounge beyond. 'You watch me a lot, don't you?'

It wasn't really a question, and so he replied with what wasn't an answer. 'I watch everybody. It's good to know what they are thinking.'

'So what am I thinking now?'

'You are frightened. You're probably as spooked by the Rectangles as me, and Lobsang, and under all that the troll migration has you seriously spooked – you more than either of us, as you know the trolls better than we do.' With the potato chopped, he leaned down and picked another out of the woven bag. He would have to keep the bag; somebody in Happy Landings had probably spent hours making it. 'I'll make chowder. Wouldn't do to leave the clams too long. Another gift from Happy Landings—'

'Stop it, Joshua. Stop with the damn potatoes. Talk to me.'

Joshua cleaned the knife and put it down carefully; you always took care of your tools. Then he turned around.

Sally glared at him. 'What makes you think you know me at all? Do you actually *know* anybody?'

'A few people. One policewoman. My friends at the Home. Even some of the kids I helped on Step Day, who kept in touch later on. And then there are the nuns. It is sensible to know nuns when you live close to them; they can be somewhat mercurial—'

'I'm sick of hearing about your damn nuns,' she snapped.

He kept his calm, and defied his instinct to escape into the cooking again. He had the feeling this was an important moment. 'Look – I know I'm not a people person. And Sister Agnes would leather me for using a phrase like *that*. But there's no substitute for people, I know that.

'Look at the trolls. Yes, the trolls are friendly and helpful, and I would not wish any harm to come to them. They are *happy*, and I could envy that. But they don't build, they do not make, they take the world for what it is. Humans *start* with the world as it is and try to make it different. And that's what makes them interesting. In all these worlds we are rushing over, the most precious thing that we can find is another human being. That's what I think. And if we *are* the only minds like ours in the Long Earth, in the universe – well, that's pretty sad and scary.

'Right now I see another human being. And it's you, and you are not happy, and I would like to help you if I can. You don't have to say anything. Take your time.' He smiled. 'The clam chowder won't be ready for a couple of hours anyhow. Oh, and the movie this evening will be *The Ballad of Cable Hogue*. A bittersweet saga of the last days of the West, starring Jason Robards, according to Lobsang.'

Of all their eccentricities, Sally most ferociously mocked the habit Lobsang and Joshua had developed of watching old movies in the bowels of the *Mark Twain*. (Joshua was glad she hadn't been on board when the two of them had dressed up for *The Blues Brothers*.) This time she didn't react. The silence was punctuated only by the metronomic clicks and whirs of the galley's hidden mechanisms. They were two flawed people, Joshua thought, stranded together.

At last Joshua turned back to his work and finished the chowder, adding bacon and seasoning. He liked cooking. Cooking responded to care; if you did things right, then it went well. It was dependable, and he liked dependable things. But he wished he could have got his hands on some celery.

When he'd finished, Sally was in the lounge, sitting on the couch, grasping her knees, as if trying to make herself small. He said, 'How about a coffee?'

She shrugged. He poured coffee from the pot.

Evening was falling on the worlds below, and the deck lights came on. The lounge was wrapped in a honey glow, a great improvement.

Joshua said hesitantly, 'I find it best to worry about the little things. Things that can be helped by being worried about. Such as the making of clam chowder, and giving you a coffee. The bigger stuff, well, you have to handle that as it faces you.'

Sally smiled thinly. 'You know, Joshua, for an antisocial weirdo you are sometimes almost perceptive. Look – what bugs me above all is that I've had to come to you two for help. Well, to *anybody*. I've been living on my own resources for years. I suspect I can't face this problem on my own, but I hate to admit it. And there's something else, Joshua.' She studied him. 'You're different. Don't deny it. The super-powered stepper. The king of the wild Long Earth. I have a feeling you're somehow central to all this. That's the secret reason I came to *you* specifically.'

That made him deeply uncomfortable, almost betrayed. 'I don't want to be central to anything.'

'Get used to it. And that's my problem, you see. When I was a kid, all the Long Earth used to be my playground, and mine alone. I'm *jealous*. Because all this may be more yours than mine.'

He tried to take all this in. 'Sally, maybe you and I—'

And at that moment, very precisely the *wrong* moment, the door opened and Lobsang sauntered in, smiling. 'Ah! Clam chowder! With bacon, excellent!'

Sally and Joshua shared a glance, parked their conversation, and turned away.

Sally focused on Lobsang. 'So here you are, the android that eats. Gobbling down clam chowder, again?'

Lobsang sat down and, rather artificially, draped one leg over the other. 'Yes, of course, why not? The gel substrate that supports my intelligence needs organic components, and why should those components not be of the finest cuisine?'

Sally looked at Joshua. 'But if he eats, then surely he must eventually . . .'

Lobsang smiled. 'Such minimal waste as I produce is expelled as carefully compacted compost in biodegradable wrapping. Why is this amusing? You did ask, Sally. At least your mockery makes a change from your usual disdain for me. And now we have work to do. I need you to identify these creatures, please.'

Behind him a wall panel lowered, to reveal a screen that flickered into life. Joshua stared at a familiar biped, scrawny, dirty, yellowish in colour. It was holding a stick like a club, and it was staring at its unseen observers with malice aforethought, and possibly afterthought as well. Joshua knew what it was all too well.

'We call them elves,' said Sally.

'I know you do,' said Lobsang.

'I think in some of the colonies they call them Greys, after the old UFO mythology. You see them everywhere in the High Meggers, and sometimes in the lower worlds. They are generally leery of humans, but they will try their luck if you're isolated or wounded. Super-fast, super-strong, highly intelligent hunters who use stepping when they go for their prey.'

'I know,' Joshua said. 'We've met them before.'

'Elves. Not a bad name, when you think about it. Elves weren't always sweet little creatures, were they? Northern European legends portray them as tall and powerful and quite without souls. A nasty name. I can live with that. They need all the bad press we can give them. And in mythology, aren't elves often afraid of iron? No wonder, I guess; iron could be used to trap them, to stop them stepping.'

Joshua went back to the chowder in the galley, and as he worked Lobsang gave Sally a curt account of Joshua's battle with the hog-riding assassins.

When he returned, she looked at Joshua with new respect. 'You did well to survive.'

'Yes. And that was supposed to be my day off. Long story.'

'Fun guys to have around, right?'

'Here's another variant,' Lobsang said. The screen displayed an image of the pregnant, big-brained elf Joshua had tried to save.

'I call this kind lollipops,' Sally said. 'Big-brained, you can see that, but not actually all that bright that I've observed.'

Lobsang nodded. 'It makes sense. The stepping-birth procedure has allowed a dramatic expansion of the physical size of the brain, but perhaps that has yet to be matched by an increase in functional capability. They have the hardware; the software is yet to evolve.'

Sally said, 'In the meantime some of the other elf types farm them. For their brains, I mean. They eat the big brains. I've seen it.'

Silence greeted that pronouncement.

Lobsang sighed. 'Not exactly Rivendell, then, is it, with all these trolls and elves? Tell me, Sally, are there any unicorns in the Long Earth?'

'Chowder's done,' said Joshua. 'Get it while it's hot.'

As they sat down to eat, Sally said, 'Actually there are unicorns. Some not too many steps from Happy Landings. I can show you if you like. Ugly devils, and *not* the kind that hang out with Barbie. Just bloody great slabs of battering ram, and so dumb they get their horns stuck in tree trunks. Often happens in the mating season . . .'

Now the screen showed images of elves feeding on some carcass, squabbling, bloody-mouthed.

Sally asked, 'Why are you showing us all this, Lobsang?'

'Because this is a live feed from what is below us, on our latest Earth. Hadn't you noticed we'd stopped stepping? Eat your chowder; the elves will keep until morning.'

43

THE NEXT DAWN came late, to Joshua's puzzlement. The daylight revealed a wasteland below, a dried-up dustbowl world with, it seemed, precious little water, and therefore precious little else.

Lobsang joined Joshua on the observation deck. 'Not a prepossessing place, is it? But it has its curiosities.'

'Like the sun rising late.'

'Indeed. Also, both trolls and elves are crossing through here, almost all of them heading East, and I am getting good pictures of both species on the belly cameras.'

The deck tilted slightly. Joshua said, 'We're going down?'

'Yes, and I would like Sally to land with us. I would like to apprehend an elf if possible. I wish to try to communicate with one.'

Joshua snorted sceptically.

'I don't expect very much from the encounter, but one never knows. Just in case, I have fabricated helmets and neck armour for you both; anyone trying to strangle you from behind will regret it, stepping or not. I will see you by the elevator in half an hour.'

Sally was fully dressed when Joshua knocked at her door. 'Helmets!' she snapped.

'It was Lobsang's idea, sorry.'

'I've survived in the Long Earth for years without being nannied by the likes of Lobsang. OK, OK, I'm the passenger here, I know. Any idea what he's planning?'

'To catch an elf, I think.'

She blew a raspberry.

Lobsang brought the airship to a halt over a bluff of heavily eroded rock. The landscape was a desert of rust-red dirt. This was a strange Earth, even by the standards of most Jokers. Joshua felt heavy, as if his bones were plated in lead, and his usual pack was a burden. The air was dense, but oddly not satisfying, and his lungs laboured. A wind blew constantly with an empty howl. On the barren plain there was no grass or other vegetation – nothing but a sort of green-purple fuzziness, as if the land hadn't shaved that morning.

And occasionally, Joshua saw, there was a flicker, more sensed than seen. Something stepping, he thought, and stepping away again so fast it had hardly been there . . .

Sally asked, 'What's with this place, Lobsang? It's like a cemetery!'

'Indeed it is,' said Lobsang. 'Though a cemetery empty even of bones.' He stood stock still, like a statue around which the dust swirled. 'Look up at mid-heaven, slightly to your left. What do you see?'

Joshua squinted and gave up. 'I don't know what I'm looking for.'

'Something notable for its absence,' said Lobsang. 'If you were standing at this exact spot on the Datum, right now, you would be looking at a washed-out moon in a daylight sky. *This* Earth has no moon to speak of. Just a few orbiting rocks invisible to the naked eye.'

Lobsang said it was a contingency he had anticipated. The cataclysmic impact which had created the moon of Datum Earth and most of its stepwise sisters had evidently never happened here. The moonless Earth that resulted was more massive than the Datum, which was why extra gravity dragged them down. The tilt of the axis was different, and unstable, and the world rotated more quickly, causing a different day–night cycle, and a wind that endlessly scoured the rocky, lifeless continents. It wasn't a place for life:

the lack of tides caused the ocean waters to stagnate, and there were none of the rich intertidal zones that had done so much on the Datum to promote the evolution of complex life.

'That's the general theory,' Lobsang said. 'On top of that, I suspect this world did not get its share of water during the big soaking towards the end of the creation of the solar system, when comets rained like hailstones. Perhaps this is somehow connected to the big moon-creating impact, or the lack of it. Sadly, this planet is a loser; probably even our Mars got a better deal.'

But there were compensations. When Joshua shielded his eyes from the sun, a band of light was revealed, razor sharp, cutting right across the sky. This Earth was circled by a ring system, like Saturn's. A spectacular sight from space, probably.

Lobsang said, 'Right now I am waiting for a troll. I have been ultrasonic-yelling for help in the troll language for fifteen minutes, and I am extruding troll pheromones – quite easy to duplicate.'

'That explains why my teeth are aching,' said Sally. 'And why I thought somebody hadn't washed today. Do we have to hang around here? This air is crappy, and it stinks.'

She was right about the stench, Joshua thought. This world smelled like the old house at the dirty end of the street that you were told never to go to, the house that had been locked up and nailed shut after the last person in it had died. It offended him, even more so than the quasi-dinosaur world. OK, the Rectangle builders had died out, but at least they had *lived*, they had had a chance.

But maybe, he thought, humans could bring this desolate world alive. Why not? He liked to fix things; this place could absorb a lot of fixing. Now *there* would be something you could tell your grandchildren about. There were still plenty of snowballs out in the Oort cloud, and a fairly small spacecraft on the right trajectory could line itself up to tip one of those and get a bit of water down here. Once you had the water you were home and dry, so to speak . . . But it was all a pipe dream. Mankind had started turning

its back on anything more ambitious than the electronic exploration of space even before the Long Earth was discovered, offering
a myriad habitable worlds within walking distance.

This reverie was broken when Lobsang said, 'Trolls on the way.
That didn't take long. Of course, they step in packs, so expect a
large number. I give you fair warning: I intend to sing to them. Join
me if you wish.' He cleared his throat theatrically.

It wasn't just the ambulant unit that began to sing. The sound of
Lobsang's voice broke in a wave, thundering out of all the speakers
on the airship. '*Keep right on to the end of the road, Keep right on to
the end. Tho' the way be long, let your heart be strong, Keep right on
to the end . . .*' Echoes were thrown up, quite possibly the first time
this dead place had known echoes of a human voice – or nearly
human, Joshua thought. '*Tho' you are tired and weary still journey
on, Till you come to your happy abode, Where all the love you've been
dreaming of, Will be there at the end of the road . . .*'

Sally just stared, astonished. 'Joshua – tell me he hasn't finally
crashed his circuits. What the hell's he singing?'

Quickly and quietly Joshua told her the story of Private Percy
Blakeney and his Russian pals in an unfamiliar France, and she
looked even more astonished.

But the trolls came. By the end of the song Lobsang was
surrounded by trolls, who hooted in harmony with him. 'Good,
aren't they? Group memory with a vengeance! Now – bear with me
while I try to figure out what's bothering them.'

As the trolls clustered around Lobsang, like big hairy children
around a department store Santa, Joshua and Sally backed away,
which was something of a relief. The trolls would do anything
rather than tread on a human, but after a while their musk, while
not really offensive, could simply take control over your sinuses.

But on the other hand this wasn't a good world for taking a
stroll in, while you waited. There was simply *nothing here*. Joshua
knelt down and, at random, levered up a little piece of the green
fuzz. There were a couple of small beetles underneath; they weren't

even interestingly iridescent, just mud brown. He let the piece of fuzz fall back again.

Sally said, 'Do you know, if you took a leak on that patch it would be doing those beetles a favour. Honestly! I won't look. That bit of soil will have more nutrients than it has seen in a long time. Sorry, was that offensive?'

Joshua shook his head absentmindedly. 'No. Just a bit incongruous.'

Sally laughed. 'Incongruous! Lobsang sings Harry Lauder on a desolate planet, and is now surrounded by trolls. Somehow "incongruous" just can't carry the load, don't you think? And now my fillings aren't tingling so much. The trolls are heading out, see?'

Joshua saw. It was as if an invisible hand were picking up pieces on a chessboard, but taking all the queens and pawns first, bishops and rooks next, and knights and kings last of all.

Sally said, 'The mothers go first, because they would punch the living daylights out of anything that threatened their pups. Elders in the middle, and males last, at the rear of the column . . . Elves attack from the rear, you see, so you watch your back.'

And then there were none, leaving nothing more than a slight improvement in the air quality.

Lobsang ambled over to them.

'How does he *do* that?' said Sally. 'Now he's walking like John Travolta!'

'Haven't you heard the fabrication deck working away day and night? He is endlessly bettering himself, endlessly rebuilding. The way you'd go to a gym, maybe?'

'I have never in my life gone into a gym, sir. When you are by yourself in the Long Earth you are either in shape, or you are dead.' She grinned. 'Mind you, I wish I had legs like that.'

'There's nothing wrong with your legs.' And he regretted that sentence as soon as he'd uttered it.

She just laughed. 'Joshua, you are fun to know, and a good companion, reliable and all that, even if you are a little bit weird.

Someday we might be friends,' she said a bit more gently. 'But please don't make comments about my legs. You've seen very little of my legs since most of the time they are inside premium grade thorn-proof battledress. And it's naughty to guess, OK?'

To Joshua's relief Lobsang reached them, smiling. 'I admit I am rather pleased with myself.'

'No change there then,' Sally said.

'We haven't caught an elf,' Joshua pointed out.

'Oh, that's no longer necessary. I have achieved my purpose. At Happy Landings I learned the elements of troll communication. But that sedentary population could tell me little about the forces behind the migration. Now these wild trolls have told me more, much more. Don't you say a word, Sally! I'll answer all your questions. Let's get aboard – we have a long journey still ahead of us, perhaps to the end of the Long Earth itself – and won't that be fun?'

44

SILENCE REIGNED ON the observation deck. Joshua was alone. Once back on board, Lobsang had immediately retreated through the blue door, and Sally to her stateroom.

Suddenly the *Mark Twain* began stepping like a tap dancer on speed. Joshua peered out. Outside, skies strobed by, landscapes morphed, rivers writhed like snakes, and Joker worlds popped like flashbulbs. On the ship, everything that could creak was creaking like an ancient tea clipper going around Cape Horn, and the stepping itself was a juddering deep inside Joshua, a hailstorm. And outside, Joshua estimated, they were crossing many worlds with every second.

Sally came on deck spitting feathers. 'What the hell does he think he's doing?'

Joshua had no answer. But again he fretted about Lobsang's strange instability and impulsiveness.

Lobsang's ambulant unit glided through the blue door. 'My friends, I am distraught if I have alarmed you. I am now eager to progress our mission. I told you I have learned a great deal from the trolls.'

'You know what's disturbing them,' said Sally.

'I do know more, at least. In short, the trolls, and probably the elves and other humanoid types too, are indeed fleeing from something, but not something physical – it is something that gets into their heads, so to speak. And this confirms what we learned from the Happy Landings trolls.

'The feeling is like a plague of pain – like migraine attacks –

sweeping over the worlds from West to East. There have been sui-
cides. Creatures throwing themselves off cliffs rather than suffer
the anguish of it.'

Joshua and Sally looked at one another.

Sally said, 'A migraine monster? What is this, *Star Trek*?'

Lobsang looked puzzled. 'Do you refer to the original series,
or—'

'This really is plain crazy. Joshua, are there any manual controls
on this airship?'

'I don't know. But I do know that Lobsang has very acute
hearing.'

'Joshua is correct in that respect, Sally . . .'

'Do the trolls understand what's coming? Have any of them *seen*
anything?'

'So far as I can tell, no. But they imagine it as enormous,
physically. To them it is a mix of physical and abstract. Like an
approaching forest fire, maybe. A wall of pain.'

The complaints from the fabric of the *Mark Twain* were
beginning to bother Joshua. He had no idea what maximum safe
stepping speed the ship was capable of. And to plummet at such a
rate into entire unknown worlds, and towards an unknown
danger, seemed unwise to him to say the least. The earthometers,
he saw, were whirling up ever closer to the two million mark.

But Lobsang was talking and talking, apparently oblivious to
such concerns. 'This is not the time to share all of my thinking with
the two of you. Suffice it to say that it is clear we are dealing
with some kind of genuine psychic phenomenon.

'Here is the hypothesis. Humans broadcast their humanity in
some way. We sense one another. But we have long evolved to live
on a planet absolutely drenched with human thoughts. We don't
even notice it.'

'Not until it's gone,' Joshua said.

Sally looked at him, curious.

'I suggest that once upon a time some of these creatures, elves and trolls and perhaps other variants, did occasionally step into the Datum, and perhaps occasionally hung around for a spell. Thus giving rise to volumes of myth. But this was in the days of comparatively low human population. Now the planet is knee deep in humans, and for creatures that spend most of their time in the mindless calm of woodlands and prairies, it must be as if all the world's teenage parties are being thrown at once. So these days they stay away from the Datum. However, the stepping species migrating from the West are fleeing from something that is irrevocably pushing them *back* towards the Datum. They are caught between the hammer and the anvil. And sometimes they panic. Joshua and I have seen what happens when they panic – even trolls may be capable of harm when roused, and remember the Church of the Cosmic Confidence Trick, Joshua?'

Joshua glanced at Sally. He would have expected nothing but scepticism from her. But, amazingly, she looked thoughtful. He prompted, 'What are you thinking, Sally?'

'That it's all far-fetched. And yet . . . I mean, I'm like you, I'll go into a city for a purpose, but while I'm in one I'm nervous as a long-tailed cat in a room full of rocking chairs. I can't wait to get out, it *pushes* me out, back out into the empty worlds. Where I feel more comfortable.'

'But you don't run, right? And you don't notice it the rest of the time. The way fish don't notice water.'

Surprisingly, Sally smiled. 'That's very Zen. Almost Lobsang.' She looked at him carefully. 'And what about you?'

She knows, he thought. She knows all about me. And yet still he hesitated before answering.

Then he spoke to them, on this rushing airship, more freely than he ever had to anybody, even to Sister Agnes or Officer Jansson, about his own inner sensations.

He told them about the peculiar pressure in his head he felt every time he went back to the Datum. A reluctance, that eventually turned into a physical revulsion. 'It's something in my head. It's like, you know how as a kid if you *have* to go to some party where everybody else is going to fit in, except you? Like you physically can't take another step, like some magnetic field is pushing you away.'

Sally shrugged. 'I never went to many parties.'

'And you're antisocial, Joshua,' Lobsang said. 'I think we knew that. What's your point?'

'Here's the thing. Whatever it means, whatever causes this, I've been feeling something like it *here*. On the airship. A pressure, making it harder to go on.' He closed his eyes. 'And it's getting worse, the further West we go. I feel it now. Like a repulsion, deep inside. I can stand it when we stay still, but it's harder to bear when we travel, and it worsens.'

Lobsang asked, 'Something out in the far West, pushing you away?'

'Yes.'

Sally asked angrily, 'Why didn't you tell me this before? You let me blab about the soft places, about my family's secrets. I opened up to you,' she said almost with a snarl. 'And all the time you were hiding this?'

He just looked at her. He hadn't told her because you kept your weaknesses to yourself, in the Home, and in most places he'd had to survive in since then. 'I'm telling you now.'

She backed down with an effort. 'All right,' she said. 'I believe you. So this is all real. I admit it now. I am officially scared.'

Lobsang sounded excited. 'Now can you see why I am so eager to bring on this encounter? We are pursuing a mystery, Joshua, Sally! A mystery from the ends of the Long Earth!'

Joshua ignored him and kept his attention on Sally. 'We're both scared. But we're going to face this, right? You won't run away. Animals flee. The trolls have to flee. *We* keep on going, trying to find out what scares us, and deal with it. That's what humans do.'

'Yeah. Until it kills us.'

'There is that.' He stood up. 'Shall I get some coffee?'

*

Later, Joshua realized he should have been paying attention, especially in the final few minutes. The last couple of hundred worlds, worlds where the calm green below was broken up by craters punched like great footprints into the ground. Should have stayed alert, despite the gathering pressure in his head. Should have raised the alarm.

Should have halted the journey, long before the airship fell into the Gap.

45

SUDDENLY JOSHUA WAS falling. He was rising up into the air, off the floor. The observation deck was still around him, its frame, the big windows, but the glistening display panels on the walls were fritzing out one by one. Through the windows he could see the bulk of the airship, its envelope damaged, torn silvery cloth fragments spilling away from the skeletal frame.

Beyond that was only the sun, dazzling bright, against blackness. The sun was just where it had been before, but it was all that was left of the outside world now, as if the rest, the blue sky, the green world, was a stage set that had been ripped away to reveal darkness. But now even the sun was drifting slowly to the right. Maybe the gondola was rolling.

Lobsang was silent, his ambulant unit fixed to the deck but still as a statue, apparently not functioning. The cat was in mid-air, paddling with her limbs, an expression of apparent fear on her small synthetic face. And there was a hand on Joshua's shoulder: Sally, floating in the air, her hair, loose, rising around her head like a space station astronaut's.

The deck creaked. Joshua thought he heard a hiss of escaping air. He couldn't seem to think. His chest ached when he tried to take a breath.

Then the gravity came back, and blue sky unfolded.

They all hit the floor, which was, for the moment, the wall. A kettle full of water spun its way across the deck, much to the apparent terror of Shi-mi the cat, who scrambled to her feet and fled into a compartment. All above and below and around them was a symphony of high technology parting company with itself.

Joshua said, 'We found the Joker of Jokers, didn't we?' And then his stomach convulsed and he threw up. He straightened, embarrassed. 'I've *never* got nauseous after stepping before.'

'I don't think it was the stepping.' Sally rubbed her own stomach. 'It was the weightlessness. And then the sudden return of gravity. It was like falling.'

'Yeah. It really happened, didn't it?'

'I think so,' Sally said. 'We found a gap. A Gap in the Long Earth.'

The gondola slowly righted, but now the deck's lights went out, leaving only the daylight. Joshua could hear the sound of spinning metal things gradually ceasing to spin, worryingly.

Lobsang suddenly came to life: his head, his face, though his body remained inanimate. '*Chak pa!*'

Sally looked at Joshua. 'What did he say?'

'Tibetan swearing, I think. Or possibly Klingon.'

Lobsang sounded oddly cheerful. 'Oh boy, is my face red! So to speak. Well, to err is human. Is anyone hurt?'

Sally said, 'What have you run us into, Lobsang?'

'We have run into *nothing*, Sally, pure nothing. Vacuum. I stepped back in a hurry, but it seems the *Mark Twain* has taken a beating. Some systems are inoperative. Fortunately the gas sacs are intact, but some of my personal systems are compromised. I am checking, but it doesn't look good.'

Sally was furious. 'How did you manage to hit a vacuum *on Earth*?'

Lobsang sighed. 'Sally, we stepped into a place where there is no Earth. A total vacuum, interplanetary space. At some point in time there *was* an Earth there, I suspect, but presumably some catastrophe destroyed it. An impact, probably. A big one, one that would make the dinosaur-killer look like pea-shooter fire bouncing off an elephant. One that would dwarf even the Big Whack, the moon impact.'

'Are you saying you anticipated this?'

'As a theoretical possibility.'

'But you went plummeting into the dark anyhow? Are you crazy?'

Lobsang cleared his throat. He was getting better at that with practice, Joshua noticed absently. 'Yes, I anticipated it. I made a study of likely contingencies based on perturbations of Earth's history, and took sensible precautions. Which included the automatic step-back module that appears to have worked almost perfectly. Regrettably, however, leaving us with a sea of problems.'

'Are we stuck here?'

' "Stuck" in comparative safety, Sally. You are breathing perfectly good air. This world, though right next door to the Gap, is a perfectly healthy one, it seems. However, my ambulant unit is largely inoperable; I cannot access its auto-repair function. I assure you, all is not lost. Back in the Low Earths, the Corporation's airship development programme has continued. The *Mark Trine* should be completed by now and would be able to reach us within a matter of days at full step.'

More lights had come back on now. Joshua started tidying up the debris. From here, apart from the furnishings and some of the crockery everything looked shipshape, but he worried very much about what damage had been done beyond Lobsang's blue doors. 'Of course,' he said, 'the operators of the *Trine*, even assuming it's flightworthy, will not be aware of our predicament. Will they, Lobsang?'

Relatively calmly, Sally said, 'So we *are* stuck here?'

Lobsang asked silkily, 'Are you concerned, Sally? What about all those famous soft places? And what are you thinking, Joshua?'

Joshua hesitated. 'The bigger picture hasn't changed, it seems to me. We must still investigate the migraine monster. You say that the gasbag is OK, yes? Then can you step?'

'Yes. But I cannot steer, geographically I mean, and power is limited. The solar-cell surfaces appear to be intact, but much of the infrastructure— The problem, aside from rupture of gas sacs and pipelines, was the boiling-away of lubricants—'

Joshua nodded. 'Fine. Then *step forward*. Let's go on.'

'Across the Gap?' Sally asked.

'Well, why not? We know the trolls and the elves have been fleeing through this area. Some at least must survive. They must be able to jump the Gap in some way – you know, a two-step. Stepping takes no time at all.' He grinned. 'We will be back in atmosphere long before our eyes explode and dribble down our faces.'

'That's a particularly graphic imagination you have there, mister.'

But Lobsang smiled glassily. 'I'm glad to see you were paying attention during *2001*, Joshua.'

'We've come this far,' Joshua said. 'I vote we continue, even if that means we have to do it eventually on foot.' He took Sally's hand. 'Are you ready?'

'Are you kidding? *Now*?'

'Before we talk ourselves out of it again. Double-step us please, Lobsang.'

Joshua was never able to make much sense of the memory of what came next. Did he really feel the stinging cold of space? Did he really hear the soughing of the wind of oblivion between the galaxies? Nothing seemed real. Not until he found himself gazing out at a clouded-over sky, and heard rain beating at the gondola windows.

They gave themselves a day to recover, to patch up the airship as best they could.

Then the *Mark Twain* stepped on, heading ever Westward, cautiously now, one world at a time every few seconds, maybe half their old cruising speed, and only in daylight.

After twenty or thirty worlds they stopped seeing the crater features that littered the worlds around the Gap, perhaps traces of chance near-misses of the object that had caused the Gap itself in nearby realities. They were somewhere beyond Earth two million by now. The worlds here were bland, uniform. In these deep footprints of America this was still the Pacific coast, and they stuck mostly to the coastal strip, trying to avoid the perils of the deep forest, and indeed of the ocean itself. It seemed a dull band of worlds to Joshua, lacking colourful flowers and insects and birds, and with the vegetation dominated by huge tree-like ferns. But at the sea's edge they sometimes glimpsed spectacular fishing creatures, agile bipedal runners with big sickle-shaped claws on their arms that they dipped into the water to scoop out big fish, one after another, throwing them high up the beach.

Days passed. The character of the worlds began to change further. The forest retreated from the sea, leaving wider coastal bands of scrub and scattered trees. The sea changed too, becoming *greener*, Joshua thought. Stiller, as if the water itself had become glutinous, denser. They didn't speak much. None of the coffee percolators would work, despite their experimental smartness, causing Sally's mood to deteriorate quickly.

And Joshua found it increasingly difficult to endure the stepping.

Sally patted his arm. 'Getting close to that teenage party, are we, Joshua?'

He always resented people seeing any weakness in him. 'Something like that. Don't you feel anything?'

'No. I wish I did. I told you, I'm jealous, Joshua. You have some kind of real talent there.'

That evening, as they relaxed as best they could while the ship stepped cautiously on, Lobsang startled Joshua by talking about access to space.

'I've been thinking. What an opportunity the Gap represents!'

Since the galley was mostly inoperative, Joshua was hammering a grill out of a defunct piece of equipment. 'An opportunity for what?'

'Space travel! You could just put on a pressure suit and step off, into space. None of that messy business of climbing out of Earth's gravity well on rockets. You'd presumably be in solar orbit, just as Earth is. Once you had some kind of infrastructure in place in the Gap itself, you could simply sail off. It would be a great deal more energy-efficient to get to Mars, say . . .

'You know, I was always a space buff. Even back in Tibet. I personally have invested some money in the Kennedy Space Center, where they're not even taking care of the museum-piece rockets any more. Our pathetic handful of microgravity orbital factories gives the illusion that we are still a space-going species, but the dream has gone – gone even before the Long Earth was opened up. As far as we know there is nowhere else in the universe where a human being can exist unprotected. And now, with millions of Earths available to us, who wants to go up into the cold, scorching emptiness in a spacesuit smelling faintly of urine? We could have been *out there*, applying to join the galactic federation, not slashing and burning our way across endless copies of the same old planet.'

Sally said, 'But you're leading the slashing and the burning, Lobsang.'

'Well, I don't see why I can't have both. And, don't you see, if we can develop the Gap, maybe we can find a way to do all that after all. From the Gap the solar system is your oyster Kilpatrick. Don't forget this conversation, Joshua. When you get back to the Datum, stake a claim to the Earths on either side of the Gap before the rush starts, and mankind finds that there *is* such a thing as a free launch. Think what might be out there! Not just the other worlds of our solar system – though surely a universe that has manufactured the Long Earth has manufactured the Long Mars as well? Think about *that.*'

Joshua tried. It made his head spin. He concentrated on finishing his grill. The galley ovens were out, but he planned to barbecue most of what, had it been on Earth, might have been called a deer, the result of some brisk hunting by Sally.

The ship stopped stepping, without warning.

And Joshua *heard* . . .

It wasn't a voice. Something wormed inside his brain, a sensation clear and sharp, and offering no hint of anything other than its existence.

Only that it was calling to him.

He managed to say, 'Lobsang, can you hear anything? On the radio frequencies, I mean?'

'Of course I can. Why do you think I halted the stepping? We're being pinged, with coherent signals at a range of frequencies. It appears to be an attempt at the language of the trolls. I will concentrate on the decoding, if you will excuse me.'

Sally looked from one to the other. 'What's happening? Am I the only one who isn't hearing anything? Is it coming from that thing underneath us?'

'What thing?' Joshua looked out of a galley window at the ocean below.

'*That* thing.'

'Lobsang,' Joshua asked, 'is your port camera working?'

46

JOSHUA AND SALLY rappelled down the panic rope, the only way to the ground now the winches were jammed.

Once down, Joshua clambered on top of a bluff for a look around. Under a sunless, clouded-over sky, a dense green ocean lapped reluctantly at a muddy beach. Inland, a bare landscape stretched away to folded hills, far in the distance. But, just to the south of here, there was a tremendous crater, like Meteor Crater in Arizona. Without warning a huge pterosaur-like creature swept out of the crater, utterly silent, heading over Joshua's head and out into this world's version of the Pacific. Silhouetted against a darkening sky, it was like a nuclear bomber heading for Moscow.

And something moved in this remote version of the Pacific. Something vast, like a living island. Joshua's headache had gone. Cleared utterly. But the sensation he had always called the Silence had never been more profound.

The voice of Lobsang chattered crisply from a small speaker in Joshua's backpack. 'We are back on the Washington State coast of this planet . . . My aerial drones are no longer functional; my view is limited. The object appears to be twenty-three miles long and approximately five miles wide. It's a creature, Joshua. Without a clear analogue on the Datum. I have noticed several appendages along its flank that are changing size and shape – you might think it is a technology park; I see what appear to be antennas, telescopes, but the instruments are morphing one into the other, extraordinary – and a certain amount of movement along the carcass as a whole. I can't estimate threat. I can't imagine that something like this could make a sudden movement, but for all I know right now it might develop wings and fly . . .'

There was a steady rippling along the thing's upper surface. It was slightly white, slightly transparent. Its movements affected Joshua somehow, viscerally, a sensation seeming to arrive in his consciousness by no discernible pathway.

'Sally, have you ever seen anything like this before?'

She snorted. 'What do you think?'

Lobsang said, 'I have just shaken hands with it.'

Sally snapped, 'What the hell are you talking about now?'

'Communications protocols, Sally. We are in contact . . . It is evidently a remarkable intellect; I can tell that immediately from the sheer information-theoretic complexity of its communications. So far I've learned one thing from it. Its name—'

'It has a *name*?'

'Its name is First Person Singular, and before you shout at me about that, Sally, I know that because it has now told me as much in twenty-six different languages of Earth. Including, I'm proud to say, Tibetan. I have been beaming information at it, and it's learning fast; it has already downloaded much of the ship's data store. I believe that it's harmless.'

'What?' Sally growled. 'Something alive and the size of a small reservoir de facto can't possibly be harmless. What's it for? Above all, what does it eat?'

Joshua slipped his packs off his shoulders and dropped them on the beach. There was no noise here, he realized. No animal cries, not even the distant honking of the pterosaur fliers. Only the soft, oily spilling of small waves on the shore. *Nothing but the Silence.* What he had been hearing all his life, in the gaps between people. Huge thoughts, like the echoes from some tremendous brass gong. Now here it was, before him.

More than two million worlds from Earth, he felt oddly as if he had come home.

He walked towards the ocean.

Sally called, 'Joshua. Take it easy. You don't know what you're dealing with . . .'

He kicked off his boots and pulled off his socks. Barefoot, he walked into the water until his ankles were covered. He could smell salt, and the sweetly rotten stink of seaweed. The water was warm, and thick, dense, almost syrupy. And it swarmed with life, tiny creatures, white and blue and green and mobile. Some were like tiny jellyfish, with pulsing sacs and trailing tentacles. But there were things like fish in there too, with huge, strange eyes, and things like crabs with clever-looking claws.

And, a little further out, the thing. Joshua waded out, towards its tremendous edge. The voice of Lobsang chattered in his ear, but he ignored it. The flanks of First Person Singular were translucent, like inferior glass, and if he squinted he could just about see what was inside. And what was inside was . . . everything. Fish. Animals. A *troll*? It was embedded in glutinous fluid, swathed in some kind of frond, like seaweed, eyes closed. It looked asleep rather than dead. At peace.

Walking right up to that misty hull, he touched it with the tip of a finger. There was a slight sensation, nothing painful.

A voice in his head said, 'Hello, Joshua.'

And information poured into his mind, like a sudden awakening.

47

ONCE, LONG AGO, on a world as close as a shadow:
A very different version of North America cradled a huge, landlocked, saline sea. This sea teemed with microbial life. All this life served a single tremendous organism.

And on this world, under a cloudy sky, the entirety of the turbid sea crackled with a single thought.

I . . .

This thought was followed by another.

To what purpose?

48

'THIS IS A HISTORIC moment,' Lobsang babbled. 'First contact! The dream of a million years fulfilled. And I know what this must be. Shalmirane . . . Didn't you read *The City and the Stars*? It's some kind of colony organism.'

Sally said archly, 'Behold the alien! So what now? Are you going to set it mathematical puzzles, like Carl Sagan and those SETI guys?'

Joshua ignored them both. He spoke to First Person Singular. 'I didn't tell you my name.'

'You didn't need to. You are Joshua. I am First Person Singular.' The voice in his head sounded like his own.

Inside the translucent skin, the creatures. He recognized fish, birds, and, he realized after a while, a very definite *elephant*, moving slowly through whatever was in there, half walking, half swimming, eyes closed. And trolls, and elves, and other humanoids.

The tide was coming in. Very carefully, so as not to give offence or cause alarm, Joshua walked backward. 'What is First Person Singular . . . for?'

'First Person Singular is the observer of worlds.'

'You speak good English.' It was a dumb thing to say, but what *was* the right thing to say to a miles-wide slug? Sister Agnes would have known, he thought.

The reply came back immediately. 'First Person Singular does not know what "Sister Agnes" is. I am still learning. Can you define for me a nun?'

On this bleak shore, Joshua's jaw dropped.

First Person Singular said, 'Cross-reference, yes – a nun is a female biped who refrains from procreation to service the needs of others in the species. Comparison with eusocial insects, perhaps? Ants and bees . . . More. Also rides large vehicles propelled ultimately by the remains of ancient trees. More. Is dedicated to the contemplation of the numinous. This is acknowledged as an interim description pending further investigation of relevant details . . . I myself would appear to be a nun, by some definitions. I perceive the world of worlds in their entirety. I believe I understand what is meant by *breathless with adoration* . . . You should move back on to the shore.'

The incoming water was up to Joshua's knees. He backed up across the strand.

Sally was watching in amazement. 'You're *talking* to it?'

'She. Not it. I think so. I hear my own voice asking me questions. She seems to know what I'm thinking – or rather, she knows what I know. I have no idea what she is, but she seems to want to learn.' He sighed. 'I'm kind of overloaded with wonder here, Sally.'

From the backpack the voice of Lobsang called, 'Come back to the airship. Debriefing time, I think.'

As they walked back to the *Mark Twain* more pterosaurs flew over, their silhouettes gaunt against the sky.

Without the winches, the climb back up the rope to the gondola was pretty gruelling, but there were working lights on all decks now, the water heater was functioning, and there was instant coffee, at least.

Of course Sally wanted to talk things over immediately. But she was overruled by both Joshua and Lobsang, for at least the time it took to make the coffee.

Then Joshua tried to relate what he had sensed of First Person Singular's own story. 'She was alone on her world.'

'A survivor,' Sally said.

'No. Not that. She *emerged* alone. She evolved that way. She was always alone . . .'

Lobsang cross-examined him, and gradually they pieced together, if not the truth, then a story.

On the Earth of First Person Singular, Lobsang speculated, as on many Earths, the early ages of life were long aeons of struggle for survival by half-formed creatures that had not yet discovered how to use DNA to store genetic information, and whose control over the proteins from which all living things were constructed was as yet poor. There had been billions upon billions of swarming cells in the shallow oceans, but they were not yet sophisticated enough to be able to *afford* to compete with each other. Instead, they co-operated. Any useful innovation flashed from cell to cell. It was as if everything in this global ocean operated as a single mega-organism.

'With time,' Lobsang said, 'on most worlds, and certainly on Datum Earth, complexity and organization reach a point where individual cells can survive unaided. And then, on most worlds, competition begins. The great kingdoms of life begin to separate, oxygen bleeds into the air as a waste product of creatures that learn how to harness the power of sunlight, and the long slow climb towards multicelled forms begins. The age of global cooperation vanishes, leaving no trace save enigmatic markers in genetic composition.'

Sally said, 'On most worlds, but not on First Person Singular's.'

'No. Actually that world must have been a remarkable Joker. There, the gathering complexity drove a familiar-looking evolutionary story – but the unity of that single global organism *was never lost*. We really have travelled to a very distant branch of the contingency tree. It—'

'She, Lobsang,' Joshua said.

'*She*: yes, the feminine is appropriate, *she* appears to be positively gravid with apparently healthy life forms. She was more like a maturing biosphere than a creature like a human. As complexity increased, knots of control must have formed. To grow further it would have become necessary for the information structure to construct and contain a copy of itself, for the whole to become self-reflective. That is, conscious.'

Sally frowned, trying to take this in. 'But what would such a creature want?'

'I can tell you that much,' Joshua said. 'Company. She was lonely. Although she didn't know it until she encountered the trolls.'

'Ah.'

They would never know how a band of trolls had ended up on that remote world, Joshua realized. They must have come through the Gap; perhaps they were traumatized, some of them injured by exposure to vacuum. 'But she was fascinated,' he said, eyes closed, concentrating, trying to *remember*. 'By the simple fact that there was more than one of them. The way they looked at each other, worked together – each of them recognized the other. They were not alone, as she was. They had each other. She wanted what they had. The one thing in the world she lacked . . .

'A troll came to the water.' He had a vision, like a waking dream, of the troll crouching, innocently scooping crabs from the shallow water – a mound of water rising, embracing him.

'Killing him,' Sally said, when Joshua described this.

'Yes. She didn't intend it, but that was the outcome. The trolls fled. Maybe she caught another one, an infant . . . studied it . . .'

'And learned to step,' Lobsang guessed.

'Yes. It took her a long time. The thing we encountered isn't all of her, all she was; once she filled an ocean. The thing in the sea here is – an expression of her. The essence. A form compact enough to step.'

'So she followed the trolls,' Sally said. 'Heading West down the chain of worlds.'

'Yes,' said Lobsang. 'Slowly but surely heading towards the Datum. And surely she is the reason for the stampede of the trolls, and perhaps other life forms. I am incubating the hypothesis that she has the same effect on pre-sapient species such as the trolls as does a large congregation of humans. Imagine the thunder of her thinking . . .'

'So, behold the migraine monster,' Sally said. 'No wonder the trolls are fleeing.'

'She doesn't mean any harm,' Joshua said. 'She only wants to *know* them. To embrace them.'

'You know, Joshua, you make this thing sound almost human.'

'That's how it felt.'

'But that is only a partial perception,' Lobsang said. 'There is more. The entity you have encountered is only . . . a seed. An emissary of the integrated biosphere from which she originated. Her absorption of local life forms, even of higher mammals like trolls, is only an interim step. Her goal is, *must be*, to transform each Earth's biosphere into a copy of her own. The entirety of it, enslaved. With every resource dedicated to a single purpose. That is to say, her own consciousness. This is not a malevolent phenomenon, or in any way *wrong*. There is no villain here. First Person Singular is simply an expression of another kind of sentience. Another model, if you like. But—'

Sally's face was ashen. 'But for the likes of us she represents a termination. She brings the end of individuality, ultimately, to every Earth she touches.'

'And the end of evolution,' Lobsang said gravely. 'The end of the world, in a sense. The end of world after world as she works her way along the chain of the Long Earth.'

Sally said, 'She is a destroyer of worlds. An eater of souls. If the trolls sensed any of this, no wonder they were terrified.'

Lobsang said, 'Of course there is the question of why she hasn't *already* reached the inhabited worlds. Why she has not already consumed the Earth. Destroyed it, with curiosity and love.'

Joshua frowned. 'The Gap. It can't be a coincidence we found her so close to the Gap.'

'Yes,' Lobsang said. 'She can't cross the Gap. Not yet, at any rate. If not for that she might already have reached the inhabited worlds.'

'We can cross the Gap,' Sally said. 'The trolls can. Surely she'll learn. And then there are the soft places. If she could use them – my God. It's like a plague, consuming the Long Earth world by world.'

'No,' Lobsang said firmly. 'This is no plague, no malignant virus or bacterium. This is a conscious entity. And there, I believe, lies hope. Joshua, how did she speak to you in the first place? You heard your own voice in your head, yes? That doesn't sound like telepathy – a species of communication for which I have yet to find one single reliable piece of evidence. This sounds like something new. It asked you what a nun was! If I may hazard a guess, it accessed the information then currently at the top of your thoughts. Thinking of Sister Agnes, were you? As an engineer I find it all hard to believe. But as a Buddhist, I accept there are more ways to think about the universe than one can imagine.'

'I sincerely hope we are not going to start talking religion,' said Sally sharply.

'Open your mind, Sally. It's only another framework for understanding the universe, just another tool.'

'So what does that make Joshua?' she snapped back. 'The chosen one?'

The two of them looked at Joshua.

'In a way,' he said reluctantly. 'Or at least, she seemed to recognize me. If she hadn't actually been expecting me.'

Sally scowled, evidently jealous. 'Why you?'

Lobsang said gently, 'Perhaps it is because of the circumstances of our hero's miraculous birth, Sally. Your first instants of life, Joshua, when you were entirely alone on another world. Your cries echoed, evidently, across the Long Earth. Or your loneliness, perhaps. And you and First Person Singular, similarly lonely, make up a kind of dipole.'

This bewildered Joshua. Not for the first time he wished Sister Agnes were here so he could talk it over with her. 'Is this why you brought me here, Lobsang? I keep finding you anticipated all we've experienced . . . Did you know *this* would happen?'

'I knew you were special, Joshua. Unique. Yes, I thought that facet of you would be – useful. But I didn't know quite how, I admit that.'

Sally stared at Joshua, stone-faced. 'How does it feel to be so manipulated, Joshua?'

Joshua looked away, hot with anger, at Lobsang, at the universe for singling him out.

Lobsang said now, 'Evidently we need to learn more about First Person Singular.'

Sally said, 'True enough. And we need to find a way to stop her panicking the trolls. Not to mention eating the Datum Earth.'

'Tomorrow we will go and see her again. I suggest we have a decent night's rest, and prepare for another encounter with the ineffable in the morning. But this time, with Joshua having made initial contact, I will lead.'

'Huh! The ineffable meets the intolerable! Oh, I'm going to bed.' Sally stormed off the deck.

'She's got a short fuse,' Joshua said.

'But you understand why she is angry, Joshua,' Lobsang said mildly. 'You were chosen. She was not. She'll probably never forgive you.'

It was a strange night for Joshua. He kept waking, convinced that someone had spoken his name. Somebody desperately lonely, but he didn't know how he knew that. Then he would get a bit more sleep, and the cycle would start all over again. It didn't stop until the morning.

In silence they gathered in the observation deck once more. Sally was bleary-eyed too, and Lobsang, in his soberly dressed and hastily repaired ambulant, was unusually quiet. Joshua wondered how *their* nights had been.

And the first surprise was that First Person Singular was no longer there. She could be seen about half a mile out to sea, moving so slowly there was hardly even a wake. First Person Singular was clearly not one for hurrying, but on the other hand you had to remind yourself that what was doing the not hurrying was twice the size of Manhattan Island.

There was no discussion about whether to follow her. They all took it as a given that they would have to. But the *Mark Twain*, still capable of stepping from world to world, no longer had the means to move across this world.

Joshua said, 'Lobsang, don't you have another marine unit? I know what you are like when it comes to backups. There's hardly any wind, and we've got more ropes than a circus tent. Our big friend over there is hardly racing. Maybe your marine unit could *tow* us?'

It did work, but only just. The *Mark Twain*, aloft, had a great deal of drag to overcome. Sally remarked that it was like the *Titanic* being towed by a motorboat engine – but an engine devised by Lobsang and built by the Black Corporation, which was why the solution worked at all.

Generally the wheelhouse was Lobsang's private domain. But today it was open house, and the three of them watched the barely visible wake of First Person Singular. Most of the traveller was underwater now. 'Only heaven knows what her propulsion system is,' Lobsang said. 'And while it's about it, heaven might like to hazard a guess as to why the seas around her are suddenly teeming with fish.'

It was true, Joshua saw. The water was bright with fins; there were even dolphins somersaulting through the air. First Person Singular was travelling with an honour guard. Joshua was used to seeing rivers vibrantly alive across the worlds; in the absence of humanity the seas everywhere seemed to be as crowded as the old

Grand Banks off Newfoundland, where, it was said, a man could once have walked on the water, so heavy was it with cod. People who'd never left Datum Earth didn't know what they were missing. But probably even the Grand Banks at their zenith couldn't have been as alive with fish as the waters behind the traveller.

'Evidently,' Sally said, 'she has a way of attracting lesser creatures. Maybe it's how she lures them close enough to absorb them.'

Lobsang was in an expansive mood. 'Magnificent, isn't it? Do you see those dolphins? Better than a Busby Berkeley routine!'

Sally asked, 'Who on earth is Busby Berkeley?'

Even Joshua knew the answer to that one.

Sally said, 'If you two are going to start talking old movies again—'

Lobsang cleared his throat. 'Did anyone experience anything *unusual* last night?'

Joshua and Sally shared a glance.

Sally said, 'You raised it, Lobsang. What are you talking about?'

'In my case there was an attempt at what I experienced as hacking. Which is quite a challenge. For the guys in the Black Corporation, trying to hack me was a sport, and most certainly kept me on my toes. Nevertheless, *something* made a spirited attempt last night. I believe, however, that this was done in a beneficent way. Nothing has been taken, nothing was changed, but I believe that some memory stores have been accessed, and copied.'

Sally asked, 'Such as?'

'Information about the trolls. About stepping. It backs up the story you were given, Joshua. But this is a very partial hypothesis. For me it is like trying to recover a memory.'

Sally said, '*Was it a vision, or a waking dream?*' They stared at her, and she blushed, and snapped defiantly, 'What? So I know Keats? Lots of people know Keats, my grandfather often recited Keats. Although he always used to spoil it by saying afterwards that he loved Keats but had never actually seen a keat.'

'I know Keats,' Joshua said reassuringly. 'And so does Sister Georgina. You'll have to meet her. I had a waking dream too. I sensed loneliness again.'

Sally admitted, 'Me too. But in my case it was something wonderful. A kind of welcome.'

Lobsang asked, 'Welcoming enough to make you want to jump into the water and lose your identity? We're closing, by the way. I think she is waiting for us to catch her up, and I very much want to catch up with *her*.'

'Excuse me,' said Sally, 'I have no intention of boarding that floating thing and becoming another souvenir in some internal zoo.'

'Happily, Sally, I intend to be the only one setting foot on First Person Singular. Or at least this ambulant unit will be. I want to communicate with her, much more fully, before she continues her stepping journey, and persuade her to stop.'

Joshua thought that over. 'And if she won't turn back . . . Can she be stopped?'

Lobsang snapped, 'What are you suggesting, Joshua? How would you fight her? Short of destroying each world she can inhabit – working your way back up the line with nuclear bombers—' He sounded contemptuous. 'You think so small, both of you. All you can perceive is threat. Maybe it's something to do with your own biological fragility. Listen to me. She wants to learn from us. But there's so much we can learn from *her*. What does she know, she who can surely perceive on scales of space and time utterly beyond the human?' His artificial voice was flat, yet oddly full of wonder. 'Have you heard of the participatory universe, Joshua?'

'Participatory bullshit.'

'Listen. Consciousness shapes reality. That's the central message of quantum physics. *We* participated in the creation of the Datum, our solitary strand, our Joker world. We've met other minds now, the elves and the trolls, and First Person Singular. Somehow, it seems, *they* participated in the weaving of the Long Earth, a subtle and marvellous ensemble, a multiverse created by a community of minds, which we only now are beginning to join. This is the lesson you must take back to the Datum, Joshua. Never mind variations of geology and geography and collections of exotic animals. *This* is fundamental to our understanding of reality – fundamental to what we are. And if I can communicate with First Person Singular, who surely has an apprehension of the universe beyond anything we are capable of . . . Well, this is what I intend to discuss with our fat friend. That, and to make her aware of the threat she poses, all unconsciously.'

'Wait a minute,' Joshua said, thinking it through. 'You're going down there. You're actually going *into* that thing.'

'Since the creatures embedded in the structure appear to be entirely healthy and mobile, I don't see this as a risk. Bearing in mind that I, and I alone, of the three of us, am dispensable, at least in the form of my ambulant unit. But *I* will be fully downloaded. I, Lobsang, will be fully committed to the joining.'

'You don't intend to come back, do you?'

'No, Joshua. I suspect my joining with the being must be long term, if not one-way, irrevocable. Yet still I must do this.'

Joshua bristled. 'I know you had all kinds of hidden motives for signing me up for this trip. Fine. But *I* signed up to achieve one objective: to bring you home safely. I was your ultimate fall-back, you said.'

'I respect your integrity, Joshua. I release you from your contract. I will lodge an addendum in the ship's files.'

'That's not good enough—'

'It is done.'

'Oh, don't let's have some kind of macho honour fest,' Sally said cynically. 'You have backups all over the place, Lobsang. So you're not really at risk at all, are you?'

'I don't propose to tell you all my little secrets. But should I be incapacitated or lost you will find iterations of my memory in various stores, updated every millisecond. The ultimate "black box", you might say, is in the belly of the ship, armoured in an alloy that I confidently believe makes adamantium look like putty and will, I am sure, remain totally unscathed even in the event of a meteor strike of mass-extinction proportions.'

Sally laughed. 'What would be the point of surviving a collision that scythes all life from a planet? I mean, who would there be to plug you in?'

'There is every likelihood that in the fullness of time sapient life might once again populate the planet, and evolve to the point where it could restore me. I can wait. I've plenty to read.'

It seemed to Joshua that Sally was at her loveliest, if you could use such a term about Sally, when she was blowing her top. And for the very first time, Joshua suspected Lobsang was teasing Sally deliberately. Another Turing test passed, he supposed.

'So,' he said, 'supposing you're successful, and you get her to stop eating worlds. What then, Lobsang?'

'Then, together, we will continue the search for the truth behind the universe.'

'That sounds so inhuman,' said Sally.

'On the contrary, Sally, it is extremely human.'

First Person Singular was looming now. Scoop-shaped objects like fleshy antennas sprouted along her length, and small crabs were hitching a ride – as were a number of seabirds, possibly after the crabs.

'Well,' said Lobsang. 'The rest is up to you. Obviously I need you to get the airship back to Datum. Get in touch with Selena Jones at transEarth. She'll know what to do about the data stores on board, to synch the copy of myself back on the Datum – you see, Joshua, you will be taking me home, after a fashion. Give Selena my regards. I always fancied she saw me as something of a father figure, you know. Even though she is legally my guardian. Well, I am not yet twenty-one years old.'

Sally said, 'Wait – without you the *Mark Twain* has no sentience. How can it take us anywhere?'

'Details, Sally! I'll leave that as an exercise for you. And now, if you will excuse me, I have a mysterious floating collective organism to catch. Oh, one last thing – do please take care of Shi-mi . . .'

And with that he retreated through his blue door, for the last time.

49

WITH LOBSANG DISPATCHED to his strange close encounter, the remaining crew of the *Mark Twain* watched the wake of the traveller until she disappeared from view, long before reaching the horizon. The honour guard of animals, birds and fish flew, dived and undulated away.

The show was over. The carnival had left town. The spell had been broken. And Joshua could feel something had gone from the world.

He stared at Sally, and felt the bewilderment he saw in her face. He said, 'First Person Singular scared me. And there were times when Lobsang scared me, though for different reasons. The thought of the two of them together, and what they might become . . .'

She shrugged. 'We've done our best to save the trolls.'

'And humanity,' he pointed out gently.

'So what do we do now?'

'Have lunch, I'd suggest,' Joshua said, and he headed for the galley.

A few minutes later Sally was grasping a brimming mug of coffee as if it were a lifeline. 'And did you notice? The traveller *steps* underwater. That's a new one.'

Joshua nodded. He thought, that's right, start by asking the little questions – sort out the small problems first, rather than get overwhelmed by the cosmic mysteries. Or even by the problem of how they were going to get home, although he was starting to have an idea about that. 'You know, some of those creatures inside her hull, which must have come from very remote worlds, looked familiar. I mean, one of those floating things looked like a large kangaroo! The cameras have been running. We can check through the footage together. The naturalists will have a field day . . .'

There was a soft sound in the doorway. Joshua looked down to see Shi-mi. She was indeed a most elegant cat, robotic or not.

And she spoke.

'Number of mice and mice-like rodents put into the vivarium for redeployment when we reach the ground: ninety-three. Numbers harmed: zero. It is said that with a stout heart a mouse can lift an elephant but not, I am glad to say, on this ship.' The cat looked expectantly at both of them. Her voice was soft, feminine – human, but somehow suggestive of cat.

'Oh, good grief.'

Joshua murmured, 'Be nice, Sally. Shi-mi – thank you.'

The cat waited patiently for further response.

'I didn't know you could speak,' Joshua ventured.

'There was previously no need. My reports were made to Lobsang through a direct interface. And the rubbish we speak is like froth on the water; actions are drops of gold.'

Sally turned her glance slightly sideways, a warning sign in Joshua's experience. 'Where did that proverb come from?'

'Tibet,' said Shi-mi.

'You're not some avatar of Lobsang, are you? I did hope we'd got rid of him.'

The cat looked up from licking her paw. 'No. Although I too am a gel-based personality. Adapted for light conversation, proverbs, rodent securement and incidental chit-chat with a thirty-one per cent bias towards cynicism. I am of course a prototype, but will shortly be one of a new line of pets available from the Black Corporation. Tell your friends. And now if you will excuse me, my work is as yet incomplete.' The cat walked out.

When she was gone, Joshua said, 'Well, you have to admit it's better than a mousetrap.'

Sally was irritated. 'Just when I think this *Titanic* of yours can't get any more ridiculous . . . Are we still over the ocean?'

Joshua glanced out of the nearest port. 'Yes.'

'We should turn around. Head back to shore.'

'We've already turned,' said Joshua. 'I set the controls after we let down Lobsang. We started back thirty minutes ago.'

'Are you sure that swimming robot thing has the power to get us back over land?' asked Sally, obviously nervous.

'Sally, the *Mark Twain* was designed by Lobsang. The marine unit has enough power to circumnavigate the Earth. He backs up his backups. You know that. Is there something wrong?'

'Since you ask, I'm not any great fan of water. Especially water you can't see to the bottom of. As a rule, let's keep some trees under the keel, OK?'

'You were hanging out on the coast when I first met you.'

'That was the seashore. Shallow water! And this is the Long Earth. You never know what's going to surface underneath you.'

'I imagine you didn't stay long on the one water world Lobsang and I passed through. There was a beast in that ocean that—'

'When I got to that world I stepped from a hillside, fell six feet into seawater, swam to a place I knew I could get back from, and stepped out, all just before a set of jaws closed around me. I never saw what they were attached to. The way I see it, my ancestors put a lot of effort into getting out of the goddamn ocean and I don't think I should throw all of that hard work back in their faces.'

He grinned as he worked on the food.

'Look, Joshua – I'm all for heading back to Happy Landings. What do you say? Suddenly I feel in the mood for other people . . . Oh. But we have to take the *Mark Twain*, don't we? With all that's left of Lobsang. Not to mention the cat. We can find a way to move the *Mark Twain* laterally, if we have to drag it by hand. But how's it going to step without Lobsang?'

'I've got an idea about that,' Joshua said. 'It will keep. More coffee?'

They treated the rest of that day as though it was a Sunday, that is to say what you should expect of a Sunday. You need time for big and complicated new concepts to shake themselves down in your brain slowly, without damaging what is already there. In the end that had even applied to Lobsang, Joshua realized.

Then, the next afternoon, Joshua let Sally guide them to what she sensed as a soft place, a short cut that would take them back to Happy Landings, only a little way in from the shore. They descended to the ground. The *Mark Twain* hovered over the beach where the marine unit had delivered it. The ship was connected to Joshua and Sally by long ropes held in their hands.

And there was a shimmer on the water's edge that even Joshua could see: the soft place Sally had found.

'I feel like a kid with a party balloon,' said Sally, holding her rope.

'I'm certain this will work,' said Joshua.

'What will?'

'Look – when you step you can take over whatever you can carry. Yes? In a way, when he was aboard, Lobsang *was* the airship, so he could step over. Here we are holding the *Mark Twain*, which, though it has a lot of mass, technically doesn't weigh anything at all. Right? So, if we step right now, we'll be carrying it, won't we?'

She stared at him. 'And *this* is your theory?'

'It's the best I can do.'

'If the universe doesn't get your joke, we might get our arms pulled off.'

'Only one way to find out. Are you ready?'

Sally hesitated. 'Would you mind if we step hand in hand? We could get in a mess if we got separated during this stunt.'

'True enough.' He took her hand. 'OK, Sally. Do your stuff.'

She seemed to defocus, as if she was no longer aware of him. She sniffed the air and eyed the light, and made moves oddly like tai chi, graceful, testing, questing – or maybe as if she were dowsing for water.

And they stepped. The stepping itself was sharper than usual, and there was a brief sensation of plummeting as if down a water slide, and it left Joshua *colder*, as if the process somehow absorbed energy. They emerged on another beach, another world – wintry, bleak. The soft places didn't get you all the way at once, then. And *they weren't in the same place*, geographically; Joshua could see that immediately. Stranger and stranger. Again Sally turned this way and that, questing.

It took four steps in all. But at last there was Happy Landings, with the *Mark Twain* overhead.

People were pleased to see them back, if surprised. Everyone was friendly. Genuinely friendly. Because this was Happy Landings, wasn't it? Of course they were friendly. The tracks were still clean, spotlessly swept. The drying salmon still hung from rows of neat racks. Men, women, children and trolls mixed happily.

And Joshua felt oddly uncomfortable, once more. A slight feeling you get when everything is so *right* that it might have gone all the way around the universe and come back metamorphosed into *wrong*. He'd forgotten, in fact, how persistent this feeling was from his last visit. And that was without mentioning the ubiquitous stink of troll.

As a matter of course, the pair of them were offered lodgings in one of the cottages at the heart of the township. But after a shared glance they decided to bunk down on the *Mark Twain*. Inevitably a few troll pups followed them up the cables. Joshua made supper up there, with delicious fresh food; as before, people had been amazingly generous with gifts of food and drink.

Afterwards, poisoning herself with instant coffee once again –

all that was available now on the injured *Mark Twain* – and with trolls lounging around the observation deck, Sally said, 'Come on, out with it, Joshua. I watch people too. I see the look on your face. What's on your mind?'

'The same as on yours, I suspect. That there's something wrong here.'

'No,' Sally said. 'Not wrong. There's something *off*, for sure . . . I've been here many times, but I'm more aware of it with you sulking around the place. Of course what we perceive as *wrong* might be an expression of the significance of the place. But—'

'Go on. There's something you want to tell me, right?'

'Have you seen any blind people here, Joshua?'

'Blind?'

'There are people here with spectacles, old folk with reading glasses. But nobody *blind*. Once I looked at the rolls in City Hall. You see records of people missing a toe or a finger, and you find out that it was the result of a bit of carelessness with a wood-chopping axe. But nobody with any major disability seems to be led to Happy Landings in the first place.'

He thought that over. 'They aren't perfect here. I've seen them get drunk in the bars, for example.'

'Oh yes, they know how to party, certainly. But the interesting thing is that every single one of them knows when to stop partying, and, believe you me, that talent is somewhat rare. And there's nothing like a police force here, have you noticed? According to the City Hall records, there has never been a sexually motivated attack on a woman, man or child. *Never*. Never a dispute over land that hasn't been calmly resolved by negotiation. Have you watched the kids? All the adults act as if all the kids are their own, and all the kids act as if all the adults are their parents. The whole place is so decent, level-headed and *likeable* it can make you scream, and then curse yourself for screaming.' Sally stroked a troll pup, whose purring would have put any cat to shame: pure liquid contentment.

That prompted Joshua to blurt out, 'It's the trolls. It's got to be. We've discussed this before. Humans and trolls living side by side. Here, and nowhere else we know of. So it's like no other human community, anywhere.'

She eyed him. 'Well, now we know that minds shape minds, don't we? We've learned that much. Too many humans, and trolls will flee. But if there are just the right amount of people the trolls will stick around. And for humans, maybe you can't get enough trolls. Happy Landings is a warm bath of comfortable, happy feelings.'

'But nobody disabled. Nobody mixed-up enough to commit a violent crime. Nobody who doesn't fit.'

'Maybe they're kept out, perhaps not even consciously.' She regarded him. '*Sieved*. That's a rather sinister thought, isn't it?'

Joshua thought it was. 'But how? Nobody's standing around with clubs to exclude the unworthy.'

'No.' Sally leaned back and closed her eyes, thinking. 'I don't think it's a case of people being consciously excluded, not by the locals. So how does it happen? I've never seen any signs of anybody *behind* Happy Landings. No designer, no controller. Does Happy Landings *itself* somehow choose who comes here? But how can that happen?'

'And to what end?'

'You can only have an *end* if you have a *mind*, Joshua.'

'There's no mind involved in evolution,' Joshua said, remembering Sister Georgina's brisk homework classes at the Home. 'No end, no intention, no destination. And yet that's a process that shapes living creatures.'

'So is Happy Landings some analogy of an evolutionary process?'

He studied her. 'You tell me. You've been coming here a long time—'

'Since I was a kid, with my parents. It's just that since I met you two, the questions I have always had about it, I guess, have sharpened up. I ought to wear a bracelet. "What would Lobsang think?"'

Joshua barked laughter.

'You know, this place always seemed a regular garden of Eden – but without the serpent, and I wondered where the serpent was. My family got on well with the people here. But I never wanted to stay. I never had the sense I fitted in. I would never dare to call it home, just in case *I* was somehow the serpent.'

Joshua tried to read the expression on Sally's face. 'I'm sorry.'

That seemed to be the wrong thing to say. She looked away. 'I do think this place is important, Joshua. For all of us. All humanity, I mean. It's unique, after all. But what happens when the colonists start getting here? I mean the regular sort, the wavefront, with their spades and picks and bronze guns, and their wife-beaters and fraudsters? How can this place survive? How many trolls will be shot, slaughtered and enslaved?'

'Maybe whoever, whatever is running the experiment will start fighting back.'

She shuddered. 'We *are* starting to think like Lobsang. Joshua, let's get out of here and go somewhere *normal*. I need a holiday . . .'

50

A DAY LATER, ON A distant world, in a warm twilight, Helen Green was gathering mushrooms. She wandered across a scrap of high ground, a couple of miles out of the new township of Reboot.

And there was a kind of sigh, like an exhalation. Helen felt a whisper of breeze on her skin. She turned.

There was a man, standing on the grass, slim, dark. A woman stood at his side, and she looked as if she belonged there. Visitors stepping in weren't an unusual occurrence. They rarely looked quite so confused as these two. Or as grubby. Or with *frost* glistening on their jackets.

And very few appeared with a gigantic airship hovering over their heads. Helen wondered if she should run and fetch somebody.

The man shielded his eyes against the sun. 'Who are you?'

'My name is Helen Green.'

'Oh, the blogger from Madison? I hoped we'd meet you.'

She glared at him. 'Who are *you*? You aren't another tax man, are you? We drove the last one out of town.'

'No, no. My name's Joshua Valienté.'

'*The* Joshua Valienté . . .' To her horror she felt herself blush.

The woman with Joshua said witheringly, 'Give me strength.'

To Joshua, Helen Green looked in her late teens. She wore her strawberry-blonde hair tied sensibly back from her face, and had a basket of some kind of fungi on her arm. She was dressed in shirt and slacks of some soft deer-like leather, and moccasins. She wouldn't have fitted into the crowd on the Datum, but on the other hand she was no colonial-era museum piece. This wasn't some retro re-creation of pioneering days past, Joshua realized. Helen Green was something new in the world, or worlds. Kind of cute, too.

There was no trouble finding a place to stay in Reboot, once they accepted you weren't any kind of criminal or bandit, or worse yet a representative of the Datum federal government which had suddenly turned so hostile to the colonists. In their time here Joshua saw the locals welcome even the hobos, as they called them, a drift of rather vague-looking people wandering through the Long Earth, evidently with no intention of *ever* settling down, and therefore with not much to contribute to Reboot. But out here every new face, with a new story to tell, was welcome, however briefly they stayed, so long as they tilled a field or chopped some wood in return for bed and board.

In the evening, Joshua and Sally sat by the fire, alone together, under the dark hulk of the *Mark Twain*.

'I like these folk,' Joshua said. 'They're good people. Sensible. Doing things right.' He felt like this because of the way he was, he accepted that; he liked it when people did what they had to do, such as build this community, properly and methodically. I could live here, he thought, somewhat to his own surprise.

But Sally snorted. 'No. This is the old way of living, or an imitation of it. We don't *need* to plough the land to feed vast densities of people. We don't just have one Earth now, we have an infinite number and they can feed an infinite number of us. Those hobos have it more right. They are the future, not your starstruck little fan Helen Green. Look, I suggest we stay here for a week, help with the harvest, take our pay in supplies. What do you say? Then we'll head for home.'

Joshua was embarrassed, but he said, 'And then what? We can deliver Lobsang, or what's left of him in the *Mark Twain*, to transEarth. Not to mention his cat. But then – I'm going to want to go back out, Sally. With Lobsang or without. I mean, it's all out there. All these years since Step Day we've hardly scratched the surface of the Long Earth. I thought I knew it all, but I'd never seen a troll before this trip, never heard of Happy Landings . . . Who knows what might be left to find?'

She gave him her sideways look. 'Are you suggesting, young man, that the two of us might travel together again?'

He'd never suggested such a thing to any other human being in his life. Not unless he was trying to save them. He evaded the question. 'Well, there is the Gap. The Long Mars! Who knows? I've been thinking about that. Step far enough *there* and we might find a Mars that's habitable.'

'You're beginning to dribble.'

'Well, I did use to read a lot of science fiction. But, yeah, let's go home first. It feels like it's time. Check out Madison. See how people are. Sally, I would very much like to introduce you to Sister Agnes.'

She smiled. 'And Sister Georgina. We can talk about Keats . . .'

'And then, when Lobsang two point zero launches the *Mark Trine*, I intend to be on board. Even if I have to stow away with the damn cat.'

Sally looked thoughtful. 'You know, my mother had a saying when us kids used to run around like wild things: "It's all fun and games until somebody loses an eye." I can't help thinking that if we keep pushing our luck with this wonderful new toy of a multiverse, sooner or later a big foot will come down on us hard. Though I guess you could look up and see whose foot it was.'

'Even that would be interesting,' said Joshua.

As they prepared to leave they sought out Helen Green, who had been the first to greet them here, more or less civilly, and now they wanted to say goodbye to her.

Helen was in the middle of her working day, a bundle of

much-read books under her arm: calm, competent, cheerful, getting on with her life, a hundred thousand Earths from where she had been born. She seemed a little flustered, as always around Joshua. But she pushed her hair away from her brow, and smiled. 'Sorry to see you go so soon. So where are you heading, back on the Datum?'

'Madison,' Joshua said. 'Where you came from too, right? I remember that from your blog. We still have friends there, family...'

But Helen was frowning. 'Madison? Haven't you heard?'

51

FOR MONICA JANSSON, Madison's bad day had started when
Clichy called, and she had to leave her UW seminar on demographic impacts of the Long Earth. She got glares from her fellow
delegates, save for those who knew she was a cop.

'Jack? What is it? This better be good—'

'Shut up and listen, Spooky. There's a bomb.'

'A bomb?'

'A nuke. In central Madison. Believed to be stashed in Capitol
Square somewhere.'

This convention centre was a long way north-east of downtown.
She was already running, out of the building, heading for her car,
and already panting; there were times when she felt every one of
her forty-plus years.

An outdoor siren started to wail.

'A nuke? How the hell—'

'Some kind of suitcase thing. The warnings are going out. Listen
to me. Here's what you have to do. *Get people indoors.* Understand?
Underground if you can. Tell them it's a tornado if you have to
convince them. If that thing goes off, outside ground zero itself
you can cut your immediate casualties from radiation to a fraction
if— damn it, Jansson, was that your car door slamming?'

'You got me, Chief.'

'Tell me you're heading out of town.'

'Can't tell you that, sir.' Already people were coming out of office
buildings, shops, homes, into the sunlight of a bright fall day,

looking bewildered. On the other hand others were going indoors, reflexively; Wisconsin did get its share of tornado touchdowns, and people knew to listen to warnings. Another couple of minutes and the roads would be jammed by people trying to get out of town, no matter what the official advice was.

She put her foot down while the road was still relatively clear, started up her siren, and roared south-west towards the Capitol.

'Damn it, Lieutenant!'

'Look, sir, you know as well as I do that it's going to be some fringe Humanity First–type group responsible for this. And that's my business. If I can be on the spot, maybe I'll see something. Eyeball one of the usual suspects. Kill this thing.'

'Or get your sorry lesbian ass fried!'

'No, sir.' She patted her waist. 'I got my Stepper . . .'

She heard more sirens wail, over the noise of the car. Inside the vehicle emergency messages started popping up, coming via multiple systems: a reverse-911 call on her civilian phone, emails to her tablet, grave Emergency Alert System messages on the radio. None of it was enough, she realized.

'Listen, Chief. You have to change course on this.'

'What are you talking about?'

'Sounds like everybody's following the standard plays. *We have to get people to step, sir.* Anywhere, East or West, just away from Madison Zero.'

'You know as well as I do that not everybody can step. Aside from the phobics there are the old, kids, bedridden, hospital patients—'

'So people help each other. If you can step, do it. But *take someone with you,* someone who can't step. Carry them in your arms, on your back. Then go back and step again. And again and again . . .'

He was silent a moment. 'You've thought about this, haven't you, Spooky?'

'It's why you gave me the job all those years ago, Jack.'

'You're insane.' A pause. 'I'll do it if you turn your damn car around.'

'Not a chance, sir.'

'You're fired, Spooky.'

'Noted, sir. But I'll stay on the line even so.'

She hit East Washington, and her view of the Capitol opened up, shining white in the sun. People were milling around, coming out of or going into the offices and shops. Some of them tried to wave her down; they looked annoyed, and probably wanted to complain about the noise of the sirens, wailing on and on apparently without reason. The car ahead of her had a prized old Green Bay Packer licence plate. On the walls she saw posters of Brian Cowley, grave, finger-pointing, like a spreading virus.

It was impossible to believe that in only minutes all this was going to be a cloud of radioactive dust. But now, coming over the car radio, she heard hurried instructions to step, interspersed with the standard announcements. *Step and help. Step and help* . . . She smiled. An instant slogan.

Clichy came back with more information. The only warning the police had had was from a kid who had wandered into a district station in Milwaukee, in distress. Fifteen years old. He had run with a crowd of Humanity-Firsters, for the social life, to meet girls. But he was lying to them. He was actually a natural stepper. And when the Firsters found out they had taken him to a doctor, a man on the MPD's watch list, who had opened up his head and inserted an electrode and burned out brain centres believed to be associated with stepping. It had left the boy blind, whether he could still step or not. So he went to the cops and spilled the beans on what his friends were planning to bring down in Madison.

'All the kid knows is that the Firsters got hold of what they called a "suitcase nuke". Now, I'm reading my brief here, the only such device ever to have been acknowledged as manufactured by the US is the W54. A SADM, which stands for Special Atomic Demolition Munition. Yield of around six kilotons, which is about a third of

Hiroshima. Alternatively they could have got hold of a Russian device, such as an RA-115 – get this, Spooky, it's thought the old Soviet Union salted some of these things around the mainland US. Just in case, huh.'

She had reached Capitol Square. Most days this was cluttered with art fairs or farmers' markets, now expanded to feature the exotic produce of a dozen worlds, or else some protest rally or other. Today there was a concentration of cops and Homelands types and FBI officers, some in nuclear-biological-chemical protection suits, as if *that* would make a difference, and their vehicles, including helicopters hovering overhead. The bravest of the brave, she thought, running *towards* the bomb. As she ripped around the square Jansson looked down State Street, that linked the main UW campus with the Square in a straight west–east line. State was still full of bustling restaurants, espresso bars and shops, despite the Long Earth recession and the depopulation, still the city's beating heart. This afternoon it swarmed with students and shoppers. Some were evidently hurrying for shelter, but others sipped their coffees and inspected their phones and laptops. Some were laughing, even though Jansson could clearly hear the echoing voice of a cop loudspeaker urging everybody to get indoors or step away, on top of the sirens' wail.

'People aren't believing it, Chief.'

'Tell me about it.'

She abandoned the car and, flashing her badge at everyone who got in her way, pushed through the lines to the Capitol mound. The racket of the sirens, echoing from the concrete, was deafening, maddening. Down the four big staircases around the Capitol building itself people were spilling out, members of the State legislature, lobbyists, lawyers, in sharp-pressed business suits. And at the foot of one flight of steps a more ragged group of civilians was sitting, watched over by a loose ring of armed cops and Homelands officers. These folk, it turned out, had been in the Square when the warning came, and had been immediately rounded up, their

Steppers confiscated along with their phones and any weapons. Jansson, just outside the perimeter, searched for familiar faces among the resentful, scared crowd of tourists, shoppers, business types. Some of them wore proud-to-be-a-Stepper wrist bands that they brandished at the officers who contained them. *I'm no Humanity-Firster! Look at this!*

And there was Rod Green, sitting a little way from the rest.

She sat down with Rod. He was eighteen years old, she knew, but looked younger. He wore jeans and a dark jacket, his strawberry-blond hair cut short. He looked like any other student. But there were lines around his mouth, his eyes. Frown lines, lines of resentment and hate.

'You did this. Didn't you, Rod?' She had to yell to make herself heard over the sirens. 'Come on, kid, you know me. I've kept an eye on you for years.'

He eyed her. 'You're the one they call Spooky.'

'You got me. Did you do this?'

'I helped.'

'Helped who? Helped how?'

He shrugged. 'I brought it to the square in a big backpack. I delivered it, but I don't know where it's stashed. I also don't know how it was armed. Or how it can be disarmed.'

Shit, shit. 'Is this necessary, Rod? Do all these people have to die just so you can get back at Mommy?'

He sneered. 'Well, *that* bitch is safe.'

That shocked Jansson. Maybe he didn't even know that his mother, Tilda Lang Green, off in a colony on some remote Earth, was dead of a cancer. Now wasn't the time to tell him. 'Do you even think it's going to do any good? I know you people have it in your heads that Madison is some kind of stepping hub. But you can't stop up the Long Earth. Even if you flatten the whole of Wisconsin people will just keep on stepping from wherever—'

'I only know one thing about the bomb.'

She grabbed his shoulders. 'What? Tell me, Rod.'

'I know *when*.' He glanced at his watch. 'Two minutes forty-five seconds. Forty-four. Forty-three . . .'

Jansson stood up and yelled at the cops, 'Did you hear that? Report it in. And get these people out of here. Their Steppers – for God's sake, give them back their Steppers!'

The cops didn't need telling twice, and their captives rose in a mob, panicked by Rod's overheard words. But Jansson stayed by Rod's side.

'It's all up for me,' Rod said. 'I can't step. That's why I came here. It seemed right.'

'Right, hell.' Without warning she grabbed him, picking him up under knees and shoulders like a child, and, straining, lifted him off the ground. He was too heavy for her, and she immediately fell under him, but she switched her Stepper before the two of them hit the ground.

And she landed on her back, on green grass. Blue sky overhead, just like on the Datum today. The sirens had gone away. The scaffolding frame that had been erected here in West 1 to interface with the Capitol loomed over her.

Rod, lying on top of her, convulsed, puked over her, and started to froth at the mouth. A paramedic in an orange jumpsuit pulled Rod aside.

'He's a phobic,' Jansson said. 'He needs—'

'We know, ma'am.' The paramedic took a syringe from her pack and shot him up in the neck.

The convulsions eased. Rod looked Jansson in the eye. He said clearly, 'Two minutes.' Then his eyes rolled up and he was unconscious.

Two minutes. The word went out across Madison Zero, and its nascent twins to East and West, and around a watching world.

And the stepping began.

Parents carried their children, and went back for their own old folk, and their elderly neighbours. In care homes, some bewildered senior citizens had Steppers slapped on them and were sent East or West for the first time in their lives. In the schools, teachers carried over their students, and big kids carried little kids. In the hospitals the staff and the healthier outpatients found ways to lift and step the heaviest, most immobilized patients, even coma victims and babies in incubators, and went back for more, and then waited as surgeons hurried to close up interrupted operations, and carried those patients over too. All across Madison, the majority of humanity who could step aided the minority who couldn't. Even extreme phobics like Rod Green who couldn't tolerate a single step were met by medics who did their best to stabilize them, until they could be hurried away from the danger zone and taken back to the Datum.

In Madison West 1, Monica Jansson watched the results unfold. There were TV cameras all around the area, and eye-in-the-sky images relayed down from drone aircraft. For Jansson, it felt very odd to be *safe* in such a crisis, but the medics had taken away her Stepper, and there was nothing more she could do. So she watched. Somebody even brought her a cup of coffee.

From the air, here in West 1, you could clearly see the lakes, the isthmus, the distinctive geography of the area laid out like a map, a twin of the region on the Datum, a twin that had been entirely uninhabited two decades ago. Madison West 1 had started to make its own mark in this world, with swathes of forest cleared and marsh drained, and some tracks wide and metalled well enough to be called roads, and clusters of buildings, and steam and smoke rising from the mills and forges. But today the inhabitants of West 1 were scrambling to accommodate and help the incoming, fleeing from the Datum.

Here they came. Jansson saw them emerge, one by one or in little groups. There were even some in the lakes, steppers coming over from their boats or their surfboards. Rowboats cut across the bright blue waters to each waving speck.

And, on land, as the steppers crossed, Jansson saw a kind of map of the Datum city emerge on the green carpet of West 1. There were the university students, a multicoloured blur that marked the location of their campus, stretching south from the shore of Mendota. There were the hospitals, St Mary's and Meriter and the UW Hospitals and Clinics, little rectangular huddles of doctors and nurses and patients. There were the schools, teachers with their charges where their classrooms should have been. On the Monona shore the contents of the convention centre appeared, business types, in flocks, like penguins. The area around Capitol Square itself started to fill in, the diamond shape of the square, with the shoppers and diners from State and King lining up along the tracks of the streets leading off to west and east, and the office workers and residents of East and West Washington. It was indeed a map of Madison, she realized, a map made up of the people, with the buildings stripped away. She looked for Allied Drive, where a group of nuns stepped across realities from the Home, with the vulnerable children in their charge.

And in the very last second, she saw, in a view from ground level, that where the high-rise buildings of downtown stood, people started appearing in mid-air. Many were in business suits. They just stepped over from the upper floors because there was no time left to get to the elevator or the stairs, or do anything else. Three-dimensional ghosts of the doomed buildings coalesced, ghosts composed of people who seemed to hang in the air, just for an instant, before falling to the ground.

Somewhere near Jansson, a Geiger counter started clicking.

52

JOSHUA AND SALLY hurried through the last few Madisons, West
10, 9, 8 . . . Joshua wasn't interested in these crowded worlds; all
he wanted now was to get home. 6, 5, 4 . . . In one Low Earth they
had taken the time to cross geographically, from Humptulips to
Madison, flying the airship on the one engine Franklin Tallyman,
boy genius of Reboot, had managed to fix up for them. 3, 2, 1 . . .
There were barriers in the last few worlds, some kind of system of
warning signs; they hurried on—

Zero.

Madison was gone.

Joshua stood in shock, gasping. Sally clutched his arm. They
stood in a plain of rubble. Gaunt shapes, fragments of wall sticking
out of the ground. A few twisted tangles that must be the remains
of reinforced-concrete structures. Dust, dry as hell, choked him
immediately. The battered airship hung blindly over these ruins.

Somebody was standing before them. Some guy in a coverall
suit, no, a woman, Joshua realized, seeing her face through a dusty
visor.

'We're here to meet steppers,' she said, her voice a relay from a
speaker. 'Get out of here. Go straight back.'

Alarmed, shocked, Joshua and Sally stepped hand in hand back
to West 1, taking the airship with them. Here, in the bright sunlight, another young woman in a FEMA uniform approached them
with a clipboard and data pad. She looked up at the airship, shook
her head in disbelief, and said reproachfully, 'You're going to have

to go through decon. We do post warnings in the neighbouring worlds. Hey, you can't catch everybody. Don't worry, you've broken no law. I'll need your names and social security numbers . . .' She started to peck at her pad.

Joshua began to take in the surroundings. This parallel Madison was crowded, compared with the last time he was here. Tent cities, feeding hospitals, feeding stations. A refugee camp.

Sally said bitterly, 'Here we are in the land of plenty, with every-thing anybody could ever want, multiplied a million times over. Nevertheless somebody wants to start a war. What a piece of work is a man.'

'But,' Joshua said, 'you can't start a war if nobody turns up. Listen, I need to get to the Home. Or where the Home would be . . .'

The FEMA official's phone rang, at her waist. She looked at the screen, seemed puzzled, and glanced at Joshua. 'Are you Joshua Valienté?'

'Yes.'

'It's for you.' She handed him the phone. 'Go ahead, Mr Lobsang.'

Acknowledgments

We chose to use Madison, Wisconsin, as a location in this novel partly because as we were developing the book it occurred to us that in July 2011 the second North American Discworld convention was to be held there, and we could get a hell of a lot of research done, as we authors like to say, on the cheap. That convention became in part a kind of mass workshop on the Long Earth. We're grateful to all the contributors to that discussion, who really are far too numerous to list here, but particularly to Dr Christopher Pagel, owner of the Companion Animal Hospital in Madison, and his wife, Juliet Pagel, who gave up an unreasonable amount of their time to show your authors Madison both primeval and modern, from the Arboretum to Willy Street, and on top of that made an incredibly helpful read-through of a draft of this book. Thank you, Madisonians, and we hereby apologize for what we have done to your lovely city. All errors and inaccuracies are of course our sole responsibility. Our thanks also to Charles Manson, the Tibetan Subject Librarian at the Bodleian Library, Oxford, for helping us build Lobsang's world.

T.P.
S.B.
December 2011, Datum Earth

ABOUT THE AUTHORS

TERRY PRATCHETT is one of the world's most popular authors. His acclaimed novels have sold more than 75 million copies worldwide and have been translated into nearly forty languages. In 2009 Queen Elizabeth II knighted Pratchett in recognition of his "services to literature." Sir Terry lives in England.

STEPHEN BAXTER is an acclaimed, multiple award-winning author whose many books include the Xeelee sequence, the Time Odyssey trilogy (written with Arthur C. Clarke), and *The Time Ships*, a sequel to H. G. Wells's classic *The Time Machine*. He lives in England.

Visit www.terrypratchett.co.uk to discover everything you need to know about **Terry Pratchett** and his writing, plus all manner of other things you may find interesting, such as videos, competitions, character profiles and games.

www.facebook.com/pratchett
www.twitter.com/terryandrob
www.youtube.com/terrypratchettbooks

More details of **Stephen Baxter**'s works can be found at www.stephen-baxter.com.